MOON
MAGIC

OTHER BOOKS BY DION FORTUNE

OCCULT STUDY

Machinery of the Mind
The Esoteric Philosophy of Love and Marriage
Psychology of the Servant Problem
The Soya Bean
Esoteric Orders and their Work
The Problem of Purity
Sane Occultism
Training and Work of an Initiate
Mystical Meditations on the Collects
Spiritualism in the Light of Occult Science
Psychic Self-Defense
Glastonbury—Avalon of the Heart
The Mystical Qabalah
Practical Occultism in Daily Life
The Cosmic Doctrine
Through the Gates of Death
Applied Magic
Aspects of Occultism
The Magical Battle of Britain

OCCULT FICTION

The Demon Lover
The Secrets of Dr Taverner
Goat-Foot God
The Winged Bull
The Sea Priestess
Moon Magic

MOON MAGIC

DION FORTUNE

WEISERBOOKS
Boston, MA/York Beach, ME

This edition first published in 2003 by
Red Wheel/Weiser, LLC
York Beach, ME
With offices at:
368 Congress Street
Boston, MA 02210
www.redwheelweiser.com

Cataloging-in-Publication Data is available upon request from the
Library of Congress.

ISBN 1-57863-289-7

Typeset in Sabon by Garrett Brown

Printed in Canada

TCP

10 09 08 07 06 05 04 03
 8 7 6 5 4 3 2 1

I t is because my novels are packed with such things as these (symbolism directed to the subconscious) that I want my students to take them seriously. The 'Mystical Qabalah' gives the theory, but the novels give the practice. Those who read the novels without having the studied the 'Qabalah' will get hints and a stimulus to their subconscious. Those who study the Qabalah without reading the novels will get an interesting intellectual jig-saw puzzle to play with; but those who study the 'Mystical Qabalah' with the help of the novels get the keys of the Temple put into their hands. As Our Lord said: "Know ye not that your body is the temple of the Holy Ghost?"

—Dion Fortune

Dion Fortune's ability as a chronicler of the esoteric can only in the end be equalled by the acknowledged talent of Huysman and Charles Williams.

Details of the 'Work and Aims' of the Society of the Inner Light, founded by Dion Fortune, may be obtained by writing (with postage please) to the Secretariat at 38 Steele's Road, London NW3 4RG, England.

FOREWORD

Dion Fortune, who died in 1946, left the manuscript of this book which is now published.

The Western Esoteric Tradition, to the teaching of which she devoted her life, covers too wide a field to find full expression in the work of any one writer, but Dion Fortune had planned books dealing with other aspects of that teaching than the one covered here. This would have resulted in a balanced presentation in the form of fiction of the main groupings of the teaching.

These main groupings, or 'Paths' as they are sometimes called, refer to the broad divisions of the temperament of the human being in incarnation and the corresponding approach to truth. A full description of them is given in a chapter of the Study Course of the Society founded by Dion Fortune, and an extract is given here:

The Hermetic Path alone is the way of completion. By the Hermetic Path alone is it possible to attain the goal, and those who go by either of the other Paths can make progress in their evolution but will not complete it in that incarnation, but must come back to master the other paths.

The Green Ray or 'Pagan' Path is for the primitive type of soul that has not yet evolved intellectually—the children of nature: equally is it a corrective for those in whom civilisation has deformed the soul and who need to stress the undeveloped in order to bring about a balanced development ... upon the Green Path and upon the Mystic Path will be the pathologies of civilisation (in addition to those to whom the Green Ray or Mystic Path is proper for their evolutionary stage) receiving curative treatment to bring them into equilibrium. In the Hermetic are all three Paths in equilibrium.

The choice of a Path depends upon the soul's development in evolutionary time or upon the abnormal bias given it by the constricting influences of a false sense of civilisation. Some souls are made rebels by 'civilisation' and some are made cripples. The rebels are dealt with in green pastures, the cripples in quiet chapels.

It should be noted that the protagonist of the story—met before in *The Sea Priestess*—is an adept working deliberately: she is an initiate of the Hermetic Path.

FOREWORD
TO THE 2003 EDITION

In Moon Magic, Vivien Le Fay Morgan, Dion Fortune's charismatic "sea priestess" from the novel of that name, reappears to work more of her unique brand of magic. She is now living in London, far from the sea, although not entirely disconnected from the element of water, for her apartment overlooks the River Thames. In keeping with the slightly changed nature of her magical role, she has also taken a change of name, now preferring to be known as Lilith Le Fay Morgan.

Lilith has also chosen a rather different type of man to train as her priest in the magic she has in hand. In place of the small-town real estate agent dominated by his mother and sister, she now finds Dr. Rupert Malcolm, a highly successful medical consultant at the top of his profession, yet married to a demanding invalid. His earthy masculinity combined with a domestic life of sexual and emotional frustration make him an irascible tyrant to patients, nurses, and students alike.

Dion Fortune had a great feeling for the sense of place, as she has demonstrated in her evocations of the western coast of Somerset in *The Sea Priestess*. This sense of place is now extended to London and the river that runs through it. Rupert Malcolm's first awareness of Lilith Le Fay Morgan occurs on the north side of the river, upon the Victoria Embankment. After finding her haunting his dreams, he compulsively follows her along the stretch from Blackfriar's Bridge, past Cleopatra's Needle, to Westminster Bridge over which she turns. She resides on the south bank in an old converted church, whose lighted window can be seen across the river from Rupert Malcolm's own apartments.

In Dion Fortune's day, this location was composed mainly of warehouses. Today, however, it is taken up by the Royal Festival Hall and other leisure facilities extending down to the New Tate Gallery and the Millennium Bridge. Yet the original building that inspired Lilith's house and temple still exists, although it is located north of the river, about a mile distant from Chelsea Bridge in West Halkin Street, Belgravia. Known as the Belfry, it started life as a Presbyterian church in about 1840 but was eventually converted to secular use and for a time acted as the headquarters for a somewhat idiosyncratic spiritualist organization.

In 1936, a wealthy member of the Society of the Inner Light leased it for Dion Fortune's use, and it was here that she staged, to invited audiences, celebrations of her Rite of Isis, extracts from which are featured both in *The Sea Priestess* and in *Moon Magic*. The outbreak of war in 1939 put an end to these activities, but the striking looking building remains and in latter days has operated as a restaurant.

Dion Fortune did not find Moon Magic an easy book to write and made several false starts before she turned to writing it in the first person, in the words of Lilith herself. Then it began to gel. She also had some difficulty in finishing it, probably because of the exigencies of war, which put a great strain upon her energy and organizational abilities. And when shortage of paper had all but crippled the publishing industry, the writing of novels might well have taken a low priority in a busy life. As a consequence, the manuscript was incomplete at the time of her death in 1946.

Because of this, the book falls into three parts. The first part (chapters 1, 2 and 3) may be regarded as the best of her early attempts to start the novel and sets up the action, introducing Dr. Rupert Malcolm and his meeting with Lilith, at first telepathically and then in the flesh. In the second part (chapters 4 through 15) Lilith takes over, explaining much of herself and her intentions, her magical temple, and the work that she intends to do within it with Rupert Malcolm as her priest. The third part (from chapter 16 to the end), which brings the magic to a natural close through the eyes of Rupert Malcolm, was provided by a close associate of Dion Fortune, Anne Fox (later Greig), who attempted to channel the material after the latter's death. How successful she was in this endeavour is for the reader to decide. The completed novel eventually saw publication in 1956, some twenty years after Dion Fortune started it, and ten years after her death.

Dion Fortune claimed that she mostly wrote her fiction by allowing the images to rise, letting the characters have their head and listening to their conversations, not entirely sure what the eventual details of the story would be. This applies to the style of her narrative in part one, as well as the whole of *The Sea Priestess* and her earlier novels. In part two, she pursues much the same method, but writing in the role of the main character herself brings about a much more vivid ambience. We might say it gives a more direct glimpse into the soul of the author than does narrative written in the third person.

As in *The Sea Priestess*, there is a fairly close identification of the author with the character in her mode of dress—the large, floppy-brimmed hats; the long cloak; the furs; and the chunky jewelry. What is more, she goes out of her way to justify this mode of attire, explaining that it is not simply the facile exhibitionism of a poseur, but a way of creating a role in which to focus the magical imagination of those with whom she comes into immediate contact.

Now that she was writing directly from Lilith's point of view, she began to find that the character was also taking on a greater feeling of independence from herself, which led her to wonder, half in jest, if she had created a kind of "dark familiar" for herself, or that the character might well represent her Freudian subconscious. Certainly we are here at the borderline—which is by no means a hard and fast one—between the mental processes of the creative artist and those of the mediating occultist.

She recognised that she had a great deal in common with Lilith Le Fay but that there was also a great deal that they did not have in common. Lilith revealed far deeper knowledge of magical things and taught Dion Fortune a great deal she had not known before. Throughout her life, Dion Fortune was staunchly Christian in principle, if a little unorthodox about it. Lilith Le Fay, on the other hand, as Dion Fortune admits, was purely pagan, a rebel against society, and bent upon its alteration—which she intended to achieve by magical means.

One strange point in common between author and character is the idea of being some kind of changeling. (Oddly enough, a thought that also crosses Wilfred Maxwell's mind with regard to himself in *The Sea Priestess*). The origin of this story came from Dion Fortune's mother, Jenny Firth, who confided to her more intimate friends that the child she bore had died soon after birth, but had revived some hours later with a completely different look in its eyes, as if it were another being. This idea Dion Fortune revealed in a paragraph in *The Occult Review*, a major esoteric magazine of the inter-war years, and it is much the same story that appears in Lilith's introduction of herself in the novel.

The claim to being 120 years old we can perhaps best regard as a symbolic statement, deriving from Rosicrucian or numerological lore, rather than speculate what she might have been doing since 1815 or thereabouts.

An odd sequel to this melding of author with character is that after the publication of the novel in 1956, a certain confusion developed in peoples' minds between Dion Fortune the author and Lilith Le Fay Morgan the character, exacerbated by the paucity of photographs of the real woman that were then available. As a result, an attempt was made a year later to lay the character to rest by creating another sequel called *The Death of Vivien Le Fay Morgan*. This short piece entered the public domain in 1962 as part of a collection of Dion Fortune articles under the umbrella title *Aspects of Occultism* with the annotation: "This fragment which was mediumistically received after Dion Fortune's death, is an epilogue to *Moon Magic*." The medium concerned was Margaret Lumley Brown, some of whose remarkable work I have edited, along with her story, in *Pythoness* (Sun Chalice Books, Oceanside, CA, 2000).

In this fragment, Vivien, or Lilith, prepares for her death and, after taking leave of her friends, is ritually assisted by a fellow senior initiate to voluntarily pass out of her physical body and into the dissolution processes of the post mortem state, described under the ancient Egyptian symbolism of the Judgment Hall of Osiris.

It is interesting to note the ancient Egyptian ambience of this fragment as compared to the largely ancient Greek basis for Dion Fortune's Rite of Isis. But as Bernard Bromage, a London University academic who befriended Dion Fortune and attended a performance of the Rite of Isis notes, the costumes she used were more Egyptian than Greek. On being asked about this, Dion Fortune confided that it was the ancient Egyptian overtones to the Greek symbolism that had always attracted her.

In any case, Bromage came away impressed by what he witnessed, writing afterward that it was "one of the best attempts I have ever witnessed to stimulate the subconscious by means of 'pantomime' drawn from the more ancient records of the hierophant's art." While one might question his choice of the word "pantomime" in relation to ritual magic, there is no doubt a certain connection between ceremonial magic and the performing arts. One principal difference is that ceremonial magic is performed for the benefit of the participants rather than the spectators, in addition to whatever objective results, via the inner planes or the collective unconscious, might be deemed to accrue therefrom.

Objective results were certainly sought by Lilith Le Fay Morgan as (in chapter 15) she tries to explain to Rupert the existence and nature of etheric magnetism, which is given out in any form of human interchange but more so when the emotions are aroused and focused upon a single person. What Lilith is trying to get across to Rupert is that the process of magic requires the two of them to form an imaginative—not physical—relationship, with one another. An important point being that magic of this type, although dependent upon the polarity of gender, is not preliminary or accompaniment to erotic games. A physical relationship, should it occur, would simply be the operation of a safety valve if the forces—via the instincts and emotions—ran out of control and would consequently spell failure in magical terms.

As she explains:

> The physical is simply the end result, and we never let it get there. When you and I work together in ritual, you are the archetypal man and I am the archetypal woman. . . . What I do to you, I do to all men; and what you receive from me, you receive from Great Isis Herself, for I am Her priestess and you represent the people. . . . Telepathy is the active factor but it is more than that. We are telepathing the group mind of our race, but we are transmitting cosmic forces…This was what was practised in the temples of the Great Goddess in ancient times. It is practiced to this day in India, and they call it Tantra.

At the time Dion Fortune was working upon her novel and practicing the Rite of Isis at the Belfry, she was also in close contact with Bernard Bromage, a specialist upon Eastern religions at the University of London. His research at that time included texts on Hindu tantra and some of this material he put at her disposal. She began to draw her own conclusions from this in a series of articles published in the *Inner Light Magazine* from February 1939 to August 1940, under the title *The Circuit of Force* (subsequently published in volume form by Thoth Publications, Loughborough, in 1998), in which she examined what, in her view, constituted "the lost secrets of western occultism."

It is of some interest that her immediate successors in the running of her Fraternity did not share her enthusiasm for this line of work, and probably not without reason. It is a type of magical relationship that is easily misunderstood, even by sympathetic colleagues, and that as Lilith had warned can easily run out of control. But if sex creeps in through the door, so magic flies out of the window—to say nothing of whatever personal and social consequences may result if those concerned have obligations outside their charmed esoteric circle. As Dion Fortune had pointed out years before in *Sane Occultism* and *Practical Occultism in Daily Life*, this is an area of esotericism that is fraught with hypocrisy, involving specious claims of reincarnationary links, twin souls, and linked destinies that at root are no more than mutual self-deception.

Its most positive manifestation outside of the esoteric world is probably best seen in the function of the poetic or artistic muse—where the artist is stimulated by some desirable member of the opposite sex without necessarily entering into a physical relationship. Examples have abound ever since the troubadours of Languedoc spun enchanting lyrics inspired by inaccessible, twelfth-century ladies and perhaps saw its apogee when the young Beatrice transported the imagination of Dante into writing one of the greatest works of western literature.

Lilith reveals at the same time something of her high magical intentions and the difficulty of retaining the necessary impersonality of the adept at the end of part two (and incidentally in the last words of fiction written by Dion Fortune herself):

> As I thought of him as he lay sleeping in the room below with my cloak thrown over him, there came to me a wave of such intense tenderness that it alarmed me. I must not feel like this towards my priest, I thought, or I shall spoil the magic; and then it came to me that only thus could I do magic with him—the magic that was to be done through one man for all men in order to lift burdens grievous to be borne in a world that has forgotten the holiness of the Great Horned One.

By this somewhat unusual title, she refers to the goddess Isis, whose headdress is the horned moon, rather than to the god of the witches, "Old Horny." For that side of things she had already written The Goat-Foot God with its Rite of Pan.

By the "burdens grievous to be borne" she has in mind the rigid sexual and social mores of the 1930s. This was a time when, for instance, the heir to the throne of England, who would have been Edward VIII, had just been forced to abdicate for insisting on marrying a divorcée. At the same time, a play by Charles Morgan, *The Flashing Stream*, caused something of a sensation, provoking the playwright to justify himself by publishing an explanatory book. Dion Fortune was moved to call it "one of the great plays of all time." It certainly was not that, but its theme—"the face of the whole world would be changed if the experience of sex were considered to be innocent unless its circumstances made it guilty"—was close to her heart. Such an idea would be regarded as commonplace today but it was highly controversial in 1938.

The subsequent liberation of sexual mores in the succeeding decades would have been much in line with what Lilith Le Fay Morgan was trying to aid with her magical rites. As she later says to Rupert: "We have done what we set out to do. Something is present in the world that was not there before, and it will work itself out in its own way." Perhaps it began to do so in the liberating decade of the 1960s. However, for the inner side of the magical experience we must turn to part three, which reverts to third person narrative, although expressed largely from the point of view of Rupert. In the magical climax of the novel he finds himself passing through a number of stages of consciousness, as memories of incarnations of the distant past come welling up from the depths of the instinctual and emotional levels. These his rationalizing mind tries to cope with, explain or justify as best it may. Then passing through the levels of consciousness of the personality in the world, he finds himself at a level of higher awareness that transcends all previous doubts and justifications and rationalizations.

He feels the beginnings of the gathering of power as the magic starts to work. He feels a tide rising within him along the hollow rod of the spinal column until with a flash the spiritual and physical levels coalesce beyond the bounds of physiology and even of psychology. He finds himself floating among the stars with Lilith as Isis before him. The two have passed beyond personality. They are no longer two circles bounded by their peripheries, but are two centers of radiation whose contact and interchange is like a lightning bolt as the cosmic forces run down through the lower levels, blowing clear all obstructions and blockages. After this virtual initiation, he feels as a man utterly reborn or re-made.

He has, in other words, passed through "the Door Without a Key." This is the subtitle of the concluding part of the novel and it has been previously defined by Lilith, as "the Door of Dreams. It is the door by which the sensitives escape into insanity when life is too hard for them and the window in a watchtower used by artists. Psychologists call it a psychological mechanism, magicians call it magic, and the man in the street calls it illusion or charlatanry, according to taste. It does not matter to me what it is called, for it is effectual."

Here speaks the voice of the pragmatic magician that was Dion Fortune and in this, the last of her novels, she demonstrates how, and in what way, it can be effectual. The tools of her trade may be the magical temple with its symbols and mirrors and lights, but within that construct is the power of the trained mind and imagination honed into diamond sharpness by an unreserved dedication to the forces of light, as she understands them.

—Gareth Knight

INTRODUCTION

I t has been said that when a novelist imagines a situation he brings it to pass. Be that as it may, when I imagined the character of Vivien Le Fay Morgan, or Lilith Le Fay, as she variously called herself, I brought into being a personality, and in the second book in which she figures— the present volume—she is very far from being a puppet in my hands, but takes charge of the situation.

Any fiction writer knows that characters can "come alive," and that if they fail to do this, the resultant novel is a pasteboard affair. Any reader with experience of the writer's craft knows the difference between dialogue that is "reported" and dialogue that is merely written. The truly creative writer records the dialogue he hears his characters using; but I have gone one better than this in the case of Lilith Le Fay—I have let her speak for herself. After the conclusion of *The Sea Priestess* she would not lie quiet in her grave, but her ghost persisted in walking. It walked to such good purpose that it forced upon me the writing of this book.

I had no clear idea of the plot. Six times I started the book, and six times I scrapped the result, till finally the rejected chapters reached the dimensions of an average novel. Then finally I decided to tell the story in the first person, and Lilith Le Fay took charge.

I had not the haziest idea of the plot, and had to write the book in order to find out. Nor was I in the least expecting it to end as it did. Some people, perhaps, would call it a piece of automatic writing; I do not know that I should dignify it by that name; I should say rather that I carried out the intentions of the principal character; but in any case I accept no responsibility for either the plot or the characters—they created themselves.

It is exceedingly difficult for me to judge of its merits in the circumstances. I have not a very high opinion of it as literature, but it is certainly a psychological curio. It contains, moreover, an amount of very odd lore, much of which I did not know anything about until I read it in these pages.

The viewpoint of Lilith Le Fay is purely pagan, and she is a rebel against society, bent upon its alteration. She may, of course, represent my Freudian subconsciousness, and there is admittedly a great deal of me in

Lilith Le Fay, but there is a great deal more that is not me. At least I am not a hundred and twenty years of age—not yet, anyway.

Malcolm comes from many sources. I have never been guilty of the bad taste of pillorying my friends. I have known a great many Malcolms in my time, and shall probably know a great many more before, like Lilith Le Fay, I decompose into my component particles, the power that supports me being withdrawn.

The house, however, is an actuality. Its doors have been shut in my face, and I go there no more, but it is nevertheless a dedicated place.

Those who read this story for the sake of entertainment will, I am afraid, not find it very entertaining. It was not written for its entertainment value. I wrote it, in fact, to find out what it was about. I have put a great deal into it, and there is a great deal more in it than I ever put in. One might even say that the writing of it was a magical act. If it be true that what is created in the imagination lives in the inner world, then what have I created in Lilith Le Fay? Malcolm can take care of himself in this world and the next, but who and what is Lilith, and why did she live on after the book about her was finished, and insist on appearing again? Have I furnished myself with a dark familiar?

Lilith considers herself a priestess of the great goddess Nature, and as such can claim divine right in the face of all man-made laws. This is a matter in which I cannot judge, for I do not know. I can only know that Lilith lives after a curious manner of her own; she lives for others as well as for me; and it may well be that to some of those who read these pages she will come as a shadowy figure half-seen in the twilight of the mind.

For to how many have the laws and conventions done a cruel and unnecessary wrong, as to Malcolm? And may there not be for them a way of escape out onto the hills of dream even as Lilith led her lover? These are questions that all must answer for themselves, for as Lilith sang to a weary man: "Forgotten are the ways of sleep and night", we may well echo the ending prayer of that hymn of invocation:

Open the door, the door that hath no key -
The door of dreams whereby men come to thee.
Shepherd of goats, O answer thou me!

—Dion Fortune

PART I

A STUDY IN TELEPATHY

Come back to me, stay by me, lull me with a touch of forgotten
  caresses,
    One warm dream clad about with a fire as of life that endures;
The delight of thy face, and the sound of thy feet, and the wind of
    thy   tresses,
    And all of a man that regrets, and all of a maid that allures.

For thy bosom is warm to my face, and profound as a manifold
  flower,
    Thy silence as music, thy voice as an odour that dies in a flame;
Not a dream, not a dream is the kiss of thy mouth and the bountiful
  hour
    That makes me forget what was sin, and would make me forget
    were it shame.

Thine eyes that are quiet, thine hands that are tender, thy lips that
      are loving,
    Comfort and cool me as dew in the dawn of a moon like a dream;
And my heart yearns baffled and blind , moved vainly towards thee,
    and   moving
As the refluent seaweed moves in the languid exuberant stream.

—Swinburne

CHAPTER ONE

The fine hall of the medical school was crowded for the prize giving. On the dais, under the famous memorial window that commemorated the charity of the founder, sat a long semicircle of scarlet-clad figures brilliant against the dark panelled oak of the background, the hoods of the different universities, crimson, cerise, magenta and various shades of blue, rendering the colour-scheme even more startling. Above the bands of the hoods appeared a row of faces, bovine, vulturine, vulpine; and in their centre, looking comparatively normal among the striking selection of headpieces that housed so many first-class brains, sat the titled chairman who had just presented the prizes. Down in the body of the hall the dark mass of students and their friends and families stared up at this collection of birds of paradise.

"He oughtn't to wear that coloured hood with that coloured hair," said a little old lady, obviously up from the country, to the clumsy young colt at her side who sat nursing a diploma which entitled him to do his worst to his fellow men.

"He's got no choice. It's his university hood."

"Then a man with that coloured hair oughtn't to go to that university." The mixture of magenta and scarlet certainly was an unfortunate combination for a red-haired man, but the granite-hard, granite-grey face under the brushed-back red hair that was beginning to recede slightly on the temples, stared out into space oblivious and indifferent.

"He looks a proper butcher," said the little old lady.

"You're wrong, he's one of the physicians."

"I shouldn't like him to physic me."

"I don't suppose he could; there's not much physic given in his department."

"What does he give?"

"Doesn't give anything. Nothing much you can give. Sometimes the surgeons can operate, and sometimes they can't. He tells them whether they can or they can't. Only chap they take orders from. If he says go in, they go in; and if he says leave it alone, they leave it alone."

"I only hope he leaves me alone," said the little old lady.

"I hope so, too, mother," said her ribald son with a chuckle, and

1

made a mental note of the joke for the students' common room. Then the singing of "God save the Queen" brought the proceedings to an end and the object of their interest took advantage of his position on the extreme wing of the semicircle to slip quietly off the platform ahead of the crush of his colleagues.

His end of the platform, however, was the end remote from the robing-room, and he found himself in the passage leading to the refectory still clad in his gaudy plumage and engulfed in a sea of humanity surging in search of refreshments. Pressed up against him by the crowd was a little old lady who stared at him with the same absorbed, impersonal interest that is bestowed on the Horse Guards on duty in Whitehall.

He, not being accustomed to this kind of attention concluded she must be an old patient.

"Good afternoon, how are you keeping?" he asked with a curt nod.

"I'm very well, thank you," she replied in a meek, rather startled voice, obviously not expecting to be spoken to.

"My mother, sir," said the youth beside her.

"Huh," said the older man ungraciously, and suddenly, to the astonishment of all present, peeled off his gorgeous robes, appearing in his shirt-sleeves. Twisting the magnificent garments into a bundle, he thrust them into the hands of the startled student.

"Put these in the senior common room, will you?" he said, and went shouldering off through the press, using his elbows mercilessly to clear a way for himself.

"What a funny man!" said the little old lady.

"You can afford to be funny when you've got a reputation like his," said her son.

"I don't think I like him," she said.

"Nobody likes him," said her son, "but we jolly well trust him."

Meanwhile the object of her disapproval raced up a flight of stone stairs three at a time, entered an empty laboratory, got an old tweed jacket from a peg, and thus incongruously clad and hatless, let himself out by a side door into a dark quadrangle. He crossed it, treading heavily on the gravel, causing a nurse to glance out of a ward window and add another item to the legend of the famous Dr. Malcolm's eccentricities, and went on his way regardless, through back streets to the Underground station. Arrived there, he swore—his pocket-book, with his note-case and season ticket, was in the breast pocket of the jacket left behind in the robing-room, and the miscellaneous collection in his trouser pockets yielded exactly three halfpence in coppers.

2

He was too impatient by temperament to return to the hospital; the weather was exceptionally mild for the time of year, and he determined to walk back along the Embankment to his rooms in Grosvenor Road, no great distance for a man as active and energetic as he was.

He made his way over cobblestones past warehouses, till climbing up steps by the abutment of a bridge, he came on to the Embankment.

It had been raining, and the usual quota that gather on the Embankment seats at dusk had taken refuge in casual wards and the shelters of voluntary charity; there were few pedestrians at that hour, and he had the wide riverside pavement practically to himself.

He strode along at his usual rapid gait, enjoying the freshness of the rain-washed air after the stuffy steam-heat of the great hall in which he had spent a boring afternoon. He watched the shimmer of the lamps on the water and the riding-lights of the hulks moored here and there; a tug toiled upstream with its barges, and a launch of the river police went chugging down-stream; all the familiar life of the river went on as the man watched it, forgetful for a time of the great city and the great hospital and the daily grind of his routine that alternated between Wimpole Street and the slums.

With the abruptness that characterised all his movements he halted so suddenly that another pedestrian following just behind had to *chassée* sideways to avoid a collision. Leaning his elbows on the granite coping, he followed in his imagination the ebbing tide going down past the docks and shipping, and thought of himself as he would have been if he had followed his first choice of a career and gone to sea. He would be a ship's officer now, keeping watch—a poorly-paid, hard, comfortless life. His present life was hard because he was a merciless taskmaster to himself, but it was not poorly paid, and as comfortable as he had the wit to make it.

But that was not saying a great deal. He was not a man who knew how, to make things comfortable either for himself or others. His wife, an invalid since the birth of their child in the first year of their marriage, made her home at a seaside resort where he visited her at fairly frequent weekends. She dreaded these visits, and he hated them, but he was a man with an inflexible sense of duty, so they went on year after year till his fiery red hair began to be dulled by grey and to recede on the temples and his temperament likewise cooled down a little, and he congratulated himself on the achievement of self-mastery.

The years of semi-celibacy had not been easy ones; endowed by Nature with a fierce integrity and uprightness, the idea of an illicit liaison was abhorrent to him. Moreover there was in him a pride in his own imperious will that made him take a perverse delight in wrestling with wild beasts at Ephesus, and the more Nature tried to force the door of his moral code, the tighter it jammed. The result was admirable from the ethical point of view, but it had not sweetened his temper or made him a pleasanter colleague or more agreeable companion. Red hair does not take well to repression, and a restless irritability of temper was the reward of virtue. Moreover, he was an uncertain sleeper, which did not improve matters, and only his tremendous vitality and rugged physique took him through a terms work.

His students hated him because he bullied and drove them mercilessly, yet he could have a sanguinary row with a fellow examiner over an unfair viva; the nurses disliked him because he was exacting, yet he would move heaven and earth to get sick-leave for them when he thought they needed it; patients were terrified at his brusque, harsh manner, yet he never spared either himself or the hospital in their service; in addition to which a large portion of his work consisted in weeding out the hysterics from the genuine organic cases, and it did not add to his already scanty popularity when his duty obliged him to tell the professional paralytic to take up his bed and walk.

He camped out year after year in furnished rooms; books, papers, and specimens in various states of preservation accumulating around him; letting his landlady feed him how she liked and his tailor dress him how he would. It was less than half a life but the half that was lived, though singularly barren for himself, was fruitful for others. The blind, the halt, the dumb, the epileptic, the lunatic, were freed from their bondage and returned to normal life when this man who never touched a knife himself, stood at the elbow of the surgeon and directed him to the precise spot in the brain where lay the root of the trouble that expressed itself in so many grotesque and bizarre guises. What he did not know about the machinery of the mind was not worth knowing, but what he knew about the mind itself was precious little.

He resumed his walk, striding along beside the darkly-running water, and wondered why it had never occurred to him to use this route before instead of the crowded Underground. He had not bothered with a car of his own of recent years, preferring to rely on taxis, a car being an intolerable nuisance in the City area, and parking space at the hospital congested by the magnificent vehicles of the junior staff, who could ill afford them but had to have them for the sake of prestige; he, who had all the prestige that any man could need, turned up at a consultation in a taxi.

He liked walking; whenever he went down to see his wife he always spent the day in a long tramp over the downs, returning in the evening tired out by the fresh air and unaccustomed exercise and falling asleep in an armchair over the fire, the irony of it all never occurring to him. He had often thought of taking a tramping holiday, but somehow he never managed to take a holiday at all, doing three men's work all through August when the hospital was short-handed, to the consternation of old chronics accustomed to more urbane methods. He had no interests outside his profession and no relaxation save reading the international literature of his own speciality.

It was a grim, joyless, hard-driven existence. Most of his work was diagnostic, little treatment being possible in his speciality. There had been a time when, improbable as it might appear to his colleagues, he worried over his cases; but of recent years he had begun to accept the acts of God with some degree of philosophy, barking out a diagnosis and a prognosis and dismissing the matter from his mind—save in the cases of children. Sometimes he thought of refusing to take children, but it was not feasible in his hospital work, where he had to take all comers. Children worried him. He would detect the first slight sign of trouble in some hitherto bonny youngster, and the future would rise before his eyes and haunt him for days. In consequence his manner of dealing with children was even more unfortunate than that of dealing with adults— the yelling child, the indignant mother and the disgusted students forming a singularly unpleasing picture, especially as it was believed that from his judgment there was no appeal to God or man—if he said a child would grow up a cripple, grow up a cripple it would. It seemed sometimes as if he were passing sentence rather than giving an opinion.

He was a man who habitually walked fast, going charging down hospital corridors and letting trolleys and stretcher-bearers do the dodging, and he was covering the ground on the Embankment in his usual manner, overtaking and leaving behind all other pedestrians going in the same direction as himself, when he noticed that one shadowy figure on ahead was not being overtaken, but keeping its distance steadily. He must have noticed it subconsciously for some time, for when he noticed it consciously, he was aware that he had been following it for a considerable distance, and with the dawning awareness his imagination was intrigued, for it so closely resembled a recurring dream that had come to him on and off for years whenever he was more than usually overworked.

On such occasions his normally insufficient sleep became unsatisfactory in quality as well as in quantity, and he would lie in a curious half-dreaming state between sleeping and waking, not sufficiently asleep to be immersed in his dream, and not sufficiently awake to know that it was a dream. He would spend the night sliding backwards and forwards over the borderline of sleep, sometimes actually in the kingdom of dream, sometimes looking into it more or less consciously and watching its shadow-show like a cinematograph picture.

These dreams were invariably of landscapes and sea-scapes—very often of land and sea-scape combined, which he attributed to his walks over the downs when visiting his wife, and in these scenes there were never any figures, with one exception—occasionally there appeared a cloaked figure in a wide-brimmed hat, which he attributed to an advertisement of Sandeman's port in coloured lights that flickered up and down on a building he had occasion to pass when travelling between his consulting rooms in Wimpole Street and his lodgings in Pimlico. It was quite simple, quite obvious; and though psychology was merely a side-line with him, and only for differential diagnosis, he had a sufficient working knowledge of its theories to trace one set of symbols to the bungalow-sprinkled downs behind the seaside town, and the other to the frequently seen advertisement. He attributed the one to sex-repression, a safe guess in the case of most respectable citizens, and a particularly safe one in the case of a professional man placed as he was; the other symbol he attributed to his subconscious desire for the stimulant thus picturesquely advertised—a very understandable desire in an over-worked man given to worrying. Both desires being repressed without any shadow of compromise, even Dr. Rupert Annersley Malcolm, neurologist and endocrinologist, could see that they might turn round on him and escape into his dreams. That they might do more than that never entered his head.

It intrigued his imagination to see this cloaked figure of dream moving ahead of him in the dusk over the wet London pavement as it had so often done through the landscapes of sleep. True, he knew it was only a woman in a mackintosh cape, but nevertheless it thrilled him to meet his subconscious fantasy thus exteriorised.

The figure moved some twenty yards ahead and kept its distance. Dr. Malcolm put on a spurt in order to come up with it and inspect it more closely, but as he invariably moved as fast as he could, his spurt did not greatly increase his speed or perceptibly reduce the distance between himself and the figure he was now pursuing—for the failure to achieve his intention had, for his cross-grained temperament, turned a passing interest into a determined pursuit.

His first impulse was to break into a run, but he knew that such conduct might not escape the notice of the guardians of law and order, and he had no wish to figure in a police court on a charge of insulting behaviour, where his explanation that he was merely analysing one of his own dreams was hardly likely to be accepted.

He therefore pressed on determinedly, heel and toe, confident that he could, given time, walk any female down. He was a man who had no use whatever for women, and for whom women, so far as he knew, had likewise no use. This woman, however, continued to keep ahead, and though he was slowly lessening the distance between them, it was clear that, even if the traffic lights favoured him, he was unlikely to come up with her unless her walk was very prolonged. Dr. Malcolm found that he was getting the last ounce out of himself that could be done without attracting the attention of the police; as it was, he observed a police-woman, looking exactly like Mrs Noah in her unbecoming uniform, eyeing him with suspicion.

Then the thing he greatly feared came upon him—the traffic lights gave the object of his pursuit free passage, changed before he could come up with them, the released traffic poured over the bridge in a solid mass, and the cloaked figure disappeared in the shadows of the London dusk, leaving him with an inexpressible sense of loss, frustration and emptiness. Another five minutes at a slightly easier pace took him to his lodgings in Grosvenor Road, chosen for cheapness when he was struggling for a footing in his profession and retained from habit, indifference and lack of incentive to move. In their slovenly comfort he stripped and had a rub-down, for he had been sweating profusely from his exertions in the mild mugginess of the evening. Then, and only then, did it occur to him to marvel at the pace at which the woman had moved.

In bed, later in the evening, he wondered whether the extra fatigue of the long walk home would be sufficient to cause the cloaked figure to appear in the landscape of dream where he had been wandering almost nightly for the last fortnight. But that night he passed swiftly into more normal sleep than he had known for many a long day. It was as if all the pent-up ennui of his joyless existence had discharged itself into his fantastic interest in the figure of an unknown woman half seen in the dusk.

The term being over, he went down the following day to spend the weekend with his wife; but she, poor soul, having one of her bad turns, definitely did not desire his company, so he was free to take his usual walk over the downs and to prolong it beyond its usual range. He came back to the red-brick villa as dusk was falling, tired out, for the walk had been unduly prolonged by the unexpected boon of freedom from an evening meal with his wife and her companion. Sandwiches and a bottle of milk had been left for him beside a banked-up fire in his bedroom, but the sandwiches were dry and curling at the edges, so he drank the milk and left them alone. Then he fell into an uneasy doze in the wicker armchair drawn up beside the fire.

It was not a particularly comfortable chair, moreover it creaked with his breathing and disturbed him; but in spite of everything, he realised that the dream that had eluded him all the week was about to come, and resisting all temptations to move and so rouse himself, he lay watching the shifting pictures on the threshold of sleep forming and dissolving and forming again into more and more definite shapes.

At first they concerned themselves with scraps of everyday life. His landlady; the laboratory cleaner at the hospital; his wife's companion; the elderly maid who was half nurse, half housekeeper. He waited patiently, knowing that it was the usual trick of his mind to disburden itself of surface impressions before opening the deeper strata. Some lingering remnant of his conscious mind, disciplined by his scientific training, observed that he was seeing a procession of elderly, plain and "itless" women. Then there appeared the policewoman he had seen on the Embankment, and his hopes rose; but she merely took her place in the procession.

Movements on the landing roused him momentarily, and he heard his wife's voice, faintly querulous, coming through her open bedroom door. They were evidently having a bad night. His first instinct was to go in and do what he could, but he knew from past experience that this would merely fuss and upset her. Her own local doctor was competent; he would hear from him what was amiss, and through him could do whatever could be done for the unhappy woman who alternated between her bed, her couch, and her wheeled chair since her unsuccessful attempt to bring his child into the world.

The slight disturbance had been sufficient to rouse him temporarily, from the torpor induced by the long day in the open. He lit a cigarette, and stared into the fire; his mind went back to the night twenty years ago that had changed the vivacious, petite, childlike girl he had married, into a neurotic, obese, semi-paralysed invalid. He did not rail against fate, he was long past that, he merely sat with his cigarette smouldering between his tobacco-stained fingers and thought about it.

In fact he did not blame fate. In an obscure way he blamed himself, as if he had made some gross error of judgment over a diagnosis. It was true that they had both eagerly desired the child that had wrought all the havoc, but that did not seem to make any difference. In the end the

8

responsibility was his; if it had not been for him there would have been no child—the logic of that was inescapable. But it did not do to dwell on what might have been. That was an expensive luxury which exacted its price in days of depression. Only by a rigorous control of mind and imagination could the Ephesian wild beasts be managed. He had discovered that trick for himself years ago, and it was always a surprise to him that it had never occurred to his colleagues in the psychiatric department.

To turn his mind away from the dangerous subject, he called up before his imagination the picture of the Thames Embankment on a mild wet winter night, the last of the fallen plane-tree leaves making patterns on the pavement and the river running down swift and dark and full of eddies. He lived that incident over again in vivid imagination, going back further and further towards its inception as its savour took hold on him. He could see the scene at the prize-giving—the students coming up for their diplomas, coltish and shambling, immature boys entrusted with responsibilities too great to be fairly borne by any human being liable to err. He considered their faces, and wondered how many of them he would trust to set a mousetrap, let alone to hold the issues of life and death—it was a miscalculation on the part of his own professor of obstetrics that had resulted in the wreck in the next room.

He pulled his mind back again, and thought of the puzzled face of the little old lady when he had mistaken her for a patient, and the grinning countenance of her son, well aware of certain of the implications of his speciality that called for routine exclusion; and remembered how, his nerve completely gone, the professor of obstetrics had hinted in self-excuse at some such predisposing cause for the disaster his own lack of discretion had precipitated, and he thought with bitterness of the ideals and self-discipline of his youth and young manhood that had served to spare him nothing of either humiliation or self-reproach.

Once again he dragged his mind back under control and pictured the river and the Embankment and the shadowy, swiftly moving form which, after some tag from a forgotten school poetry-book, he named the beckoning fair one, though, God knows she hadn't beckoned, and he would have been most indignant if she had. Moreover it was highly problematical if she were even passably good-looking.

He imagined himself walking behind her as he had on that evening; but this time there was no sense of haste and failure, but only the swift effortless flight of dream. The Embankment and its lights faded, and he was out once more in the wide landscape of sleep, colourless as shadowed silver in the light that never was on land or sea.

But there was no vision. She had vanished. Holding himself desperately, on the threshold of sleep, he tried consciously to press on into the shadowy landscape, but it eluded him and threatened to turn to nightmare. Then the spell was broken by the voice of his wife's companion trying to make herself heard on the telephone in the hall, and he was wide awake again.

He waited; he heard a car on the drive, steps on the stairs, a murmur of voices in the next bedroom, but he did not stir. Only when he heard the bedroom door open once more, and a heavy tread on the landing, did he rise, and moving quietly as a cat, open his own door and silently beckon his fellow doctor to enter. Then, in the dull glow of the dying fire, the two men faced each other, for it never occurred to Malcolm to turn on the light.

The other, however, had known his patient's husband on and off for years, and was quite used to the many minor eccentricities of which he was so unconsciously guilty. He could just see the pale outline of the square, hard-set face in the dimness, with the high line of the swept-back hair and the glitter of the keen pale eyes that he used to think were just like those of a snake getting ready to strike. The perpetual alertness of the man always seemed to be his outstanding quality, and now, at 2 a.m. in a darkened room when he had obviously been dozing, he was as alert as ever.

"Well?" said Malcolm, untroubled by the necessity for any of the normal small change of social intercourse.

But Dr. Jenkins was used to that. "Nothing serious," he replied. "Nerves mainly, but of course that upheaves the other condition. If you don't mind my saying so frankly, I think it was the prospect of your visit that upset her. As a matter of fact, it happens every time you come, only it generally doesn't come to a head till after you have gone. If I were you, I should restrict your visits to the bare necessities, Christmas, her birthday, and so on, don't you know."

"I see," said the other curtly. "Very good, I'll do as you say."

They took leave of each other, and Dr. Malcolm returned to his chair by the dying fire, wondering why this solution of his monthly purgatory had never been suggested before.

Next morning Mrs Malcolm was still in a drugged sleep when the time came for him to leave. He had a few words with her companion, his explanations being received with such an air of devout thankfulness that he experienced a sharp pang of conscience as to whether he had always done all in his power to make his visits acceptable.

Staring out of the window of the train on his journey back to town, he asked himself what he could have done that he had left undone, for he honestly did not think he had done anything in the course of all the long years with which to reproach himself. Finally he gave up the problem as insoluble and travelled on to the hospital, where the students scattered before him like frightened poultry and a clinical clerk kept dropping his pencil and muddling his papers out of sheer nervousness. The patients fared a little better, but not much, and after an exhausting morning for all concerned, he snatched a cup of coffee and a sandwich from the buffet at the Underground station, and went on to his rooms in Wimpole Street, where, with variations, the routine of the morning was repeated. Some doctors boast that their hospital patients get exactly the same treatment as their private patients, but Dr. Rupert Malcolm, without ever thinking about it, treated the patients in his private practice in exactly the same way as his out-patients. He could not possibly do more for either class than he already did, but it was characteristic of the man that he did it in precisely the same way. The prince had to scramble in and out of his clothes with the same precipitancy as the pauper, and he extracted the same reluctant admissions from the princess as from the charwoman, and by the same unmitigated methods.

CHAPTER
TWO

Such social relaxation as Rupert Malcolm permitted himself consisted in listening to or reading papers before learned societies upon his own speciality or its allied subjects, and as he invariably cleared out when the learned part of the proceedings was over and the social part began, the relaxation thus obtained was minimal; his brusque, forbidding manner and hard expressionless face made it improbable, however, that he would have got much more even if he had stopped on.

The long day following his return from the seaside was rounded off by one of these evenings of mutual edification among the learned. Leaving as early as he decently could, he took a taxi back to his rooms and climbed wearily up the hundred-odd steps to the top of the house. His present landlady was the niece of his original one, but things went on unchanged. Occasionally she threatened to have his rooms done up, but retreated intimidated before his scowl and contented herself with painting them piecemeal during his absences at the seaside villa.

Into this dingy abode with its old-fashioned furnishings he entered without a glance, threw his hat and despatch-case on the table and his overcoat after them, dropped into the worn leather armchair beside the hearth, kicked the banked-up fire into activity with the toe of his shoe and sat staring at it. It was the first moment since he had quitted the train, taking his unsolved problem with him, that he had had any time for thought.

He had been amazed to find that his release from what he had always considered a duty sternly to be discharged had cut the very ground from under his feet. All through the long years of the marriage that was not a marriage he had been supported by the belief that his wife needed his care, and now he found that that belief was without foundation. He ought, he knew, to have felt relief, but instead he felt like a lost dog. The man who had spoken the few common-sense words in the fire-lit room had not the faintest realisation of the effect they had on the man who heard them. Not a tone of the voice, not a quiver of the face had betrayed anything; it was the same granite-hard countenance it had always been. Nevertheless, one life had ended, and some means had to be found of enabling another to begin. Rupert Malcolm felt rudderless, anchorless, at the mercy of every wind that blew. His own code of honour still imposed the same inflexible fidelity upon him, but he knew now that all the invalid in the seaside town required of him were the comforts his income so easily provided, and that from the man himself she wanted nothing save to be let alone. Her little dog, her budgerigars and her faithful companion filled all her emotional needs. When the dog, or an occasional budgerigar died, it was replaced, and life, after a brief tearful interlude, went on as usual in the pleasant, sunny house overlooking the sea. The sole disturbing influence—himself—had now been removed, and he could picture the two women singing as the evening hymn they always had: "Now thank we all our God."

The uncurtained window irritated him, and he crossed the room and jerked dusty green serge across it. His hand on the second curtain, he paused and looked out onto the arc-lit night and the sullen river. Immediately opposite his quarters, across the dark water, a cul-de-sac debouched onto the further embankment, and at its end he could see a thing he had never noticed before—the lit-up facade of a small church. He could see the circular outline of the west window, but whether it held the coloured glass of a fanciful religion or the plain glass of a plain one, distance prevented him from discerning. He stood staring at it, the curtain in his hand, wondering what faith it was that conducted its devotions at that hour of the night. Catholic, he supposed; Protestants attended to their religious duties during an eight-hour day. Staring at the lighted facade behind which folk might be presumed to be adoring their Creator, he marvelled that anyone could see anything in religion. He supposed they must get something out of it or they wouldn't stick to it, but what that might be was beyond his comprehension. Then, as he watched, the light went out in the distant facade, and he took the hint and went to bed himself. There, once again, he wandered in the silver-grey country between sleeping and waking, but there was no companion.

☾

The fact that he now had all his weekends at his own disposal gave Malcolm a vague sense of freedom and relief. Missing his walks on the downs, he thought of going off for country weekends, but somehow never got started. He did not know where to go, or what to do, or how to make a beginning, so he just relapsed back into an orbit that was narrower than ever. He made an abortive attempt to improve his mind with a modern novel, but soon found it best to let sleeping dogs lie. He went to the National Gallery, but found himself studying the endocrine balance of the nudes. So on the whole he decided that he would have to go on as he had always gone, accept life as he found it, and think about it as little as possible. He was still dreaming of landscapes, despite the fact that the medical school was closed for the holidays and his work consequently considerably lightened. This worried him a little, for if he were like this now, what would he be like when the new term got going in good earnest?

It suddenly occurred to him that the additional fatigue of the teaching and lecturing might serve to bring back the cloaked figure in his dreams, and he found himself looking forward to the beginning of the term with a strange eagerness. He found himself counting the days and realised how much the idea of the woman whose face he had never seen had taken hold on his imagination. It had even begun to console him for the fact that he had cast such poor pearls as he possessed before one who had no conceivable use for them.

He discovered that the surest way to put himself to sleep was to set off in imagination for that walk on the Embankment with the cloaked woman on ahead. He never tried to catch up with her and see her face—dreaded to do so, in fact, feeling certain of disillusion; but he felt that in the shadowy cloaked figure he had found a kind of spirit-guide through the bewilderments of life, for he was at heart a simple soul, despite his brains.

More and more did the fantasy of the cloaked figure grow on him as night after night, with unfailing regularity, he took the same path into the kingdom of sleep—the path along the Thames Embankment with the leafless plane-trees on one hand and the darkly glittering, hurrying water on the other, and always, sooner or later, the cloaked figure on ahead would appear and he would follow it with a sense of intense relief into the land of sleep.

Presently he noticed a curious fact. Last thing before getting into bed he always drew back the curtains from the window to let in the air, and as he looked out across the river he saw that sometimes the facade of the Surrey-side church was lit up, and sometimes it was not. There seemed to be no rhyme or reason in the hours kept by that denomination. Frequently it would be in action till one or two in the morning, and upon these occasions he noticed he could never get to sleep till the light across the river was put out. Sometimes when sleep defied him, he would raise himself in his bed until he could see it out of the window. He would watch it and wait, and as soon as the light went out, would settle down on his pillow in expectation, and then in twenty minutes or so he would pick up the trail of the figure ahead and pass into sleep; and sleep thus

15

obtained, he discovered, was particularly restful, and sometimes he came back from it with a strange sense of happiness—a sensation to which he had long been a stranger.

More and more, as the days went by, did he become obsessed by this quest of the cloaked woman. He never desired to catch up with her, but if a night passed and he had not glimpsed her shadowy figure, he was agitated and miserable all next day; not until once again the fantasy had ushered in his sleep was he restored to peace of mind. But it was more than fantasy. He could picture to himself the Embankment in the dusk, with its plane-trees and swirling river, but the picture of the shadowy cloaked figure meant nothing; only when it appeared spontaneously in his fantasy did it afford him any satisfaction. Then, for just so long as he could maintain himself on the threshold of sleep, neither rousing into full wakefulness nor sliding off into unconsciousness did he experience the joy, rising as time went on into ecstasy, of keeping her in sight. At the hospital after such nights they found him rather absent-minded, but much easier to work with.

Finally the holidays came to an end; term started again and he flung himself into his work with a kind of frenzied energy, intent on wearing himself down to the point when the vision should appear in his dreams in good earnest. Then, when he was already doing the work of three average men, a colleague went sick and he took over his private practice for him.

The days were lengthening, but the extra work kept him so late at the hospital that he never seemed to come home by daylight. He had promised himself that as soon as he was a little less busy he would walk home every night and so replace he walks on the downs to which he had been accustomed. But somehow he never seemed to have the energy after being on his feet in the wards or the lecture room for hours on end, and so the spring advanced and he never heeded it.

Then, one day, he came out into the hospital quadrangle and saw the evening star, great Venus, low in the western sky in the last of the sunset, and a sudden resolution determined him, fatigued though he was, to walk home by the Embankment. Someone caught him and delayed him however; papers had to be signed in the almoner's office; and by the time he climbed up the steps by the bridge that brought him on to the Embankment, Venus had disappeared in the evening mist and the dusk was drawing in.

He walked as if in a dream. He had pictured that walk so often that he hardly knew whether this particular evening was fantasy or reality.

Staring ahead into the gathering dusk, he looked for the shadowy cloaked figure, but she failed to appear, and finally, footsore and disappointed he turned into his lodgings, dropped into his old armchair more dead than alive, and then, in the very act of kicking off his shoes, moved by what impulse he knew not, heaved himself wearily out of the frowzy cushions, crossed the room, drew back the curtains, and looked out to see if the facade of the church across the water were lit up. Sure enough, it was. That settled it. She never came while they were holding a service, and somehow reassured, he knew not why, he went to bed without bothering about supper, and to sleep without bothering about cloaked women. Towards midnight he woke up, however, and raising himself in bed, looked out to see if the church window were still illuminated. It was, but even as he watched, the light went out, and in a short time he saw ahead of him the cloaked figure and entered once more the land of dreams in her company.

Next day, well pleased with his walk on the Embankment, he repeated it at an earlier hour, and went home with the glory of the sunset over Westminster in his face; and from then on the walk home beside the river was an unvarying routine, and his health benefited in consequence. He was more serene in his mind also, but he realised how dependent he was upon this nightly vision.

Once, for a whole week, she failed to appear, and he went nearly demented. Nothing would have induced him to consult a colleague, and nothing would have induced him to take sedative drugs of his own prescribing, so he began to be in a bad way. Then, when he was almost at the end of his tether, there came the dream, the genuine dream of the cloaked figure in the grey landscape—the actual dream that hitherto, despite his efforts to exhaust himself, had never come. So desperate was he in his eagerness that for the first time he pursued that cloaked figure with determination to catch up with it. Over the grey dream landscape he toiled in a kind of nightmare, his feet held at every step as if in a bog, his heart beating as if it would burst. Then, as he was almost upon the figure and was just putting out his hand to catch the floating cloak, he woke, bathed in sweat, with the sound of a woman's scream ringing in his ears. He sprang out of bed, flung up the window and put his head out, and even as he did so, saw the light go on in the church over the water. All was quiet in the moonlit roadway, however, and all was quiet in the stuffy house when he leant over the well of the staircase and listened. Little Miss Humphreys, his landlady, he knew would come rushing up to him if anything were wrong—scared of him as she was at normal times; but all was quiet, and he went back to bed again, concluding that the screamer was either dead, delivered, or a phantom of his imagination.

Next day he was kept late at the hospital, and though tired after his broken night, his mind was at rest, and so things went better with him. Late as it was, he determined to walk home. It had become a kind of ritual with him, part of his worship, and for no amount of fatigue would he miss it. It was just about the same degree of dusk that it had been upon the occasion of his first Embankment walk, and his pilgrimage of faith seemed that evening to have a peculiar kind of reality about it. As he walked, he wondered what sort of a husband he would have made if his marriage had run a normal course. He would have been a difficult one; exacting, tempestuous, jealous; but he knew that he could have given an intensity of love that the light-hearted little thing he had married would have had no idea what to do with. He realised for the first time that even if catastrophe had not descended on his marriage, it was unlikely to have been an outstanding success, and the realisation gave him an extraordinary sense of relief and release. Then in the very moment of the burden rolling from his shoulders, he saw some thirty yards ahead of him the cloaked figure of a woman, not in fantasy, but in actuality.

For a moment he swayed as if drunk, and then pulled himself together. The reality possessed nothing like the same fascination as the fantasy. Mackintosh capes were common among women, and it was highly improbable that this was the original cape-wearer who had started him off on his dreams.

He continued his walk, watching with a faintly cynical amusement the cloaked figure on ahead. The reality was in every way inferior to the dream. There was nothing that he could see to make a fuss about over a woman in a mackintosh. Then suddenly he realised the pace at which he, and consequently she, were walking, and knew that it must indeed be the original cape-wearer, for few women could hit that gait and keep it up. By a sprint that was almost a run he shortened the distance between them and was able to observe the manner in which she moved. Accustomed to diagnosing by pit and stance, he learnt much. He saw that she moved all in one piece, gliding over the ground with a movement that ran like a ripple from the ball of the foot to the hip, swinging the folds of the cape from the square-held shoulders as rhythmically as a pendulum. He had never seen a human body more perfectly balanced and poised, and forgetting his romance for the moment, he watched that walk with professional interest, assessing the perfect co-ordination of every muscle in the rhythmically moving body. Her figure and build he could not judge, for the folds of the cloak hid all, but that gait he would never forget as long as he lived. A mad idea entered his head of hastening after the woman and accosting her, but was instantly dismissed; apart from the inadvisability of such a proceeding for a professional man of standing, he was, and always had been, as shy as a schoolboy behind his brusque exterior. So he strode on till the traffic lights again played him a scurvy trick and he lost her once more.

He raced up the stairs to his room, flung back the curtains, stared across the river, and even as he did so, the lights went on in the dark facade of the church over the water. Some time, he told himself, when he was less busy, he would cross by the neighbouring bridge, have a look at that church, and see what denomination worshiped so capriciously.

But it was some time before he was less busy; he was so busy, in fact, that he had temporarily and reluctantly to abandon his Embankment walks, but his vision still served the purpose of putting him off to sleep each night with unfailing regularity. He did not have to visualise her now, for as soon as he put his head on the pillow she came of her own accord.

☾

There had been a meeting of the governors of the hospital, of which he was one, and it had been not altogether peaceful. A complaint had been made in influential quarters about his manners and methods, and the matter had been raised—as tactfully as possible, it is true, but still it had been raised—and just as when his wife's doctor had bidden him remove his unwanted presence, so now he was startled, bewildered and humiliated to find he had been upsetting people and making himself generally detested. The council, who had been dreading the ordeal of belling their formidable cat, were amazed to find him begging to be told what he had done wrong. This so took the wind out of their sails that they ended by assuring him that he had done nothing wrong, and generally smoothing him down and soothing him, and then sat back and stared at each other in amazement after he had taken his usual precipitate departure.

It was foggy when he came out into the hospital quadrangle in the dusk, but that did not alter his decision to walk home. Nothing, he felt, could soothe and console him so effectually as the imagined presence of his fair one. When a man has given of his best for a quarter of a century, and is suddenly told that his best is not good enough, he is apt to feel as if the world were falling about his ears.

What did he do that upset people? It is true that he had never cultivated the social side of hospital life, but he had genuinely done his job to the best of his ability. He tried to console himself with the memory of his outstanding successes, and they were many—patients rescued from a living death whom everyone else had abandoned as hopeless; surely that counted for something? But apparently not. Hurt, bewildered, his self-confidence shaken to its foundations, he walked more slowly than was his wont, and as he walked he saw as if in a dream the cloaked woman overtake and pass him.

For a moment his heart seemed to stop, and then it began to hammer at his ribs. She was only a dozen feet ahead instead of the usual twenty or thirty yards, and even in the thickening fog could not escape him. He followed her, drawing as close as he dared, and at the first check at the traffic lights he was at her elbow. A heavy fur round her shoulders and a wide-brimmed slouch hat prevented him from seeing her face, but he had a thrilling sense of being in her atmosphere and felt himself beginning to tremble. He crossed the road almost at her side, and then judged it advisable to drop back a little lest she became aware of his presence and resented it.

So they went, one behind the other, past the Savoy and Temple and Westminster, and then, at the old stone bridge, she turned to cross the river.

For a moment the man hesitated. Even in the fog there had been enough walkers on the Embankment pavement to make his presence in-conspicuous, but it was unlikely that, even in the fog, he could follow her over Lambeth Bridge without her becoming aware of it. However, he was determined to risk it; there was nothing in his conduct she could complain of, even if she realised he had followed her from Blackfriars Bridge; his shoes had rubber heels, he could move quietly for all his stocky build, and determined to chance his luck.

The fog grew thicker and thicker as they got out into the centre of the river, and with a sudden pang he realised that he was acting like a cad. He would frighten the life out of the woman if she detected his presence. Here was he, doing the very thing for which they had blamed him at the hospital, and to the last person in the world he wished to alarm.

But she kept on her way without turning, and the centre of the river was already overpassed. In a few minutes he heard the sound of her footsteps change as she left the hollow pavement of the bridge for the Surrey-side embankment, and realised how close he had drawn to her in the fog when almost simultaneously he felt the roadway under his own feet.

The fog was thicker here, much thicker, and he had to follow her closely, but there were more people about, and his presence passed apparently unnoticed. At any rate, she never looked round.

She crossed the road, the man dropping back a little for safety's sake, and then, after an anguished moment when he thought he had lost her, getting close on her heels again, closer than he had dared to get before. Then throwing him into complete confusion, she stopped so abruptly that he nearly trod on her heels, and saw that she was about to enter a church. She paused for a moment fumbling at the latch in the darkness; then the door yielded. Hardly knowing what he did, he snatched his opportunity. If she were attending a service, why shouldn't he? He laid his arm on the door as she turned to close it, and passed through, shutting it behind him, to find pitch darkness and perfect silence. The church, if it were a church, was empty!

The man stood thunderstruck, realising his predicament; realising only too clearly how his behaviour must appear to the woman he had been following. Struggling in vain to find words to reassure her, for she must be scared to death by his behaviour—struggling in vain to find words to explain himself, for if she turned him over to the police, as she had every right to do, he was going to find himself in an exceedingly unpleasant position, with his reputation lost beyond redemption, it seemed to him that professional ruin stared him in the face. He felt cold all down his spine at the enormity of his offense. Stepping back, he groped for the door by which he had entered, but his hand ran along panelling. Swinging round, he stood awaiting developments, involuntarily clenching a fist. Then, leaving him in doubt no longer, the beam of an electric torch shone on his face.

"What is it you want?" asked a calm, level voice.

The man gave a gasp of relief.

"I—er—I thought it was a church and I came in for the service", he stammered.

"It is not a church any longer, it is a private house," came the calm voice. "The door is behind you if you care to go." He turned, and she shone the beam of her torch onto the knob of a yale lock. Thankfully he grasped it, and the door swung open. Then, on the very threshold of deliverance, he again turned and paused, unable to resist the attraction she had for him. But the light shone full on his face, blinding him. She would know him again, but he had not had a single glimpse of her. He hesitated a moment, but she kept the beam of her torch steadily in his eyes, and knowing that all the cards were stacked against him, and that explanations were as undesirable as they were impossible, he hastily clapped his hat on his head and stumbled out into fog that seemed to have suddenly thickened into an impenetrable mass of flocculent murk.

By some fluke of luck he heard a taxi discharging its load a few doors down the street, and hurrying towards it, he bade its driver get him home as best he might. Eventually it did get him home, but the route was a circuitous one, and took time. Long before he arrived at his own door Dr. Malcolm had had ample opportunity to realise the kind of hot water he was liable to get himself into if he went on like this; and what with the telling-off he had had at the hospital, and the realisation of the kind of fool, and also the kind of cad, he had made of himself, his stock stood very low in his own estimation when he let himself into his dreary rooms and found little enough there to put heart into him.

A friendless and unsociable man, without hobbies or any interest outside his work, if anything succeeded in penetrating the tough epidermis with which he had encased himself, it got him very badly on the raw, for there was nothing to mitigate it; no friend with whom he could talk things over, nothing with which he could distract his mind; moreover, a man of his deadly earnestness and cast-iron sense of duty was incapable of laughing at his own foibles. The sole consolation life held for him was his dream-woman—who had just shone an electric torch in his eyes till she blinded him and given him a very broad hint that if he did not take himself off he would be handed over to the police. He knew only too well the motive of the kind of elderly satyr that pesters decent women, and probably so did she, if she were any sort of woman of the world, as her calmness in an unpleasant situation indicated; how was he to explain to her that he wasn't that kind of brute? He couldn't explain anything to her—all he could do was to leave her alone. He must sacrifice his dream along with all the other sacrifices that life had demanded of him, and stick rigidly to the one thing he knew, the one thing he could do, his professional work. The minute he left that narrow path, he was in trouble.

He walked over to the window and put back the curtain. In some way he associated the cloaked woman with the lighted church—why, he had never been able to imagine, save that he could only find her when the light was extinguished in the church across the water. He stared out into the blackness of the foggy night, but even the slight consolation of seeing the familiar light was denied him. The fog smothered everything and only a faint glow from the nearer lamps was visible.

Then suddenly an idea leapt to his mind. The woman he had followed had crossed the river and entered a church on the Surrey side. She had said that it was no longer used as a church, but had become a private house. Was it by any chance possible that the lit-up facade he had so often gazed at was her actual dwelling-place? Allowing for the curve of the river, and the way they had turned after crossing the bridge, it appeared quite possible. The capricious hours of the lighting and darkening of the window would then be explained.

Dr. Malcolm leant his elbows on the ledge of the window and tried to penetrate the impenetrable blackness by sheer concentration. He was a man accustomed to intense concentration. When at work it could easily have happened to him as to Isaac Newton, that his papers had caught fire without his noticing it. He was also a man with a vivid pictorial imagination, who could draw without reference to books or specimens any ramification of the nervous system and its anatomical background. Despite the fog, he could see the lit-up facade of the church across the water as clearly as if he stood in front of it. He could see its door, the pointed, iron-studded door of conventional modern Gothic; he could feel the cold, fog-dewed iron of the heavy latch under his hand; could feel the warm air in his face as he entered on the heels of the cloaked woman—but instead of the painful debacle of actuality, he found himself, not in a church, but in a lofty and beautiful room with a large open fireplace where a fire of logs was burning. For one second he perceived it as if he actually saw it with his physical eyes, and then it vanished.

He turned away from the window, letting the curtain fall back against the gloom outside. He knew it was merely a trick of the imagination, a curious, involuntary feat of fantasy, in which his rational mind had no part; but it had wiped out the unpleasant taste left behind by his sordid adventure, and left him not merely at peace, but curiously uplifted.

He knew perfectly well that, according to all the accepted canons of psychiatry he was playing dangerous tricks with his mind; nevertheless each contact left him calmer and happier than he had been for many a long day.

He dropped into the worn leather armchair beside the fire and tried to consider the situation as objectively as he could. He had obviously built up a fantasy around the figure of a woman seen two or three times in the dusk. There was nothing out of the way in that. Plenty of imaginative men did that sort of thing. He had done it himself as a young fellow, before his marriage. Once he had become engaged to Eva, he had rigidly cut it out, or rather had limited his imaginations to her face and form, and then only within the strictest limits of propriety. He did not think he had, even in imagination, ever let himself go where women were concerned. He had made up for it, however, by some magnificent scientific battles, and was not averse to personal rumpusses with anyone

23

who was disposed to show fight.

He saw, however, that he was within measurable distance of breaking his own rule, for although his feeling was idealised to the verge of tenuity, it was nevertheless a surprisingly strong feeling, and not one that ought to be harboured by a married man; and when it led him into following a flesh and blood woman for miles through the London streets, forcing his way into her house, and generally making an unmitigated nuisance of himself, even if no stronger term were applicable, it was decidedly not a feeling that a professional man with any regard for his career was wise to give way to. The dream must be cut out, and that was that. He had nipped complications in the bud before, and they had died stillborn and given no trouble. There had been a nurse once at the hospital, a woman medical student at one of the clinics, and—the thing of which he was most ashamed—one of Miss Humphreys' little maids. The two former had never, he was certain, had any suspicion of the feelings they had aroused in him; the third, the little wretch, had deliberately set herself to arouse those feelings, and, to his eternal shame and amazement, had succeeded with the greatest ease. But the moment he realised what was happening he had stalked down to Miss Humphreys in her underground den and said straight out: "That girl goes, or I do, and she goes *now.*" and handed the startled and indignant landlady the necessary month's wages.

But cutting out his new obsession was going to be an entirely different matter. He had enjoyed her companionship for several months, had, in fact, sedulously cultivated her. Fantasy though she was, she had wrapped herself round the very roots of his being. But he had trained himself, like Napoleon, to close the drawers of his mind on their pigeon-holed subjects, and he slammed this one shut resolutely, rang for his supper, got out the papers relevant to an address he was preparing, and when his supper arrived, ate it with one hand and wrote his notes with the other, thus allowing no scope for wild beasts from Ephesus.

He worked late, but when he went to throw open the window before getting into bed, he saw through the clearing fog that the church across the water was still lit up. He turned away, trying to put the whole business out of his head by recalling certain points in his paper, but even as he switched off the bedside lamp he knew that he had as much chance of getting to sleep as he had of flying to the moon. He had a heavy day ahead of him, and a presidential address to give in the evening, and the prospect was not pleasant.

He lay flat on his back, his arms across his face, trying to get his mind under control. But it was no use, the Ephesian beasts were out of their cages.

He got out of bed and went across in his thin pyjama suit to the wide open window, where the last of the fog was blowing clammily into the room. Involuntarily he looked across the river. The light was out in the church on the Surrey side—if he yielded to the temptation he could get his lady any time he wanted her. He turned back to the bed again and sat down on its edge, elbows on knees, head in hands, and groaned aloud. Surely she was better than the beasts of Ephesus? But that was nonsense, just sophistry. It was only a matter of time before she ended at Ephesus. He had got enough sense to know that. The only thing to do was to cut the whole thing out—cut it out—cut it out.

Then suddenly, through the fingers that pressed against his eye-balls, he saw the cloaked woman face to face. She stood in the room before him. She spoke.

"Do not be disturbed. All is well."

He lifted his head from his hands, giddy, sweating, shaken, but she was no longer there. She had gone as she had come.

He was trembling all over like a frightened horse. He could feel the sweat trickling down his chest and his thin pyjama jacket was sticking to his back. He had too much sense of risk pneumonia, and rolled into bed and lay there panting. Then there came to him, as he grew warm between the blankets, the most extraordinary sense of peace and relaxation. Muscle by muscle, the overwrought man slacked off. He turned over onto his side, almost asleep as he did so, and it seemed to him, from some configuration of the pillow, that his head lay on a woman's shoulder.

CHAPTER
THREE

Next morning the fog had cleared away and Spring was in the air. At the hospital they found their formidable physician singularly vernal, which surprised no one more than himself, for no one knew better than he did the kind of wreckage left behind by such storms as that of the preceding night. He felt well disposed towards the whole world. He was glad to give the students a helping hand—explaining to them instead of cursing them for not knowing what they had come there to learn. He even achieved a kind of grim geniality towards the patients.

"Old boy's fallen in love," was the perspicacious comment of the students. Little did they know how far from falling in love was Dr. Rupert Malcolm—that the lady in the case had turned him out of her house like a stray dog, and that he had resolved to cut her out of his life and thoughts for ever.

Nevertheless she was there—she was there like a kind of running accompaniment to all he did. He had not seen her face, so his imagination had free rein. Being himself a fair-skinned man, he naturally idealised her as a brunette. Not a lissome young girl—he could see even through the veiling cloak that she was not that, and in any case he, a hard-bitten man of forty-five, had nothing in common with young girls—but a woman in the maturity of her beauty, which is quite a different thing from girlish charm. He tried to call to mind pictures that might have resembled her, resuscitating the memories of his abortive visit to the National Gallery and determining to go there again and see if he could find a picture that would represent her to him, for he felt that only among the work of the Old Masters would he find her. She was too dynamic and natural for a Society beauty; too sophisticated and cultured for a professional of the studios.

But even as the ideas rose in rapid succession to his mind, her image came clear of its own accord, and he saw her face as a rather long, pale oval framed in blackness. Her eyes were dark and almond-shaped; her nose slightly aquiline; her mouth scarlet-lipped after the modern fashion. Her eyes gazed at him steadily, velvety brown, gentle and inscrutable. He could not tell what she was thinking; he could not, fantasy how he would, picture the personality behind those eyes. She remained aloof, with her inner life concealed, and yet there was about her a kindness that was infinitely comforting to the lonely man.

He had, though his colleagues would never have believed it, an odd taste for martyrdom hidden deep in his heart. He could never feel justified to his own conscience unless he were over-driving himself—denying himself minor luxuries—doing acts of impersonal service for which he neither expected nor received any thanks. As a young man his choice had fallen on a helpless, clinging little bit of prettiness whom he could cherish and protect; now that he was an older man, and beginning to get a little weary, a change had come over the spirit of his dream; he still wanted to make a martyr of himself, but he no longer desired to go pricking across the plain looking for dragons; he no longer wanted a clinging maiden in distress to minister to the ideal of manhood he was trying to realise. He wanted to be martyred after another manner; he wanted to find himself in the hands of a possessive woman who would make demands on him. He was tired of martyring himself; the satisfaction this afforded had begun to pall since he had been disillusioned with regard to his wife's need of him. He shrank from the pain of presenting any more unacceptable sacrifices; he wanted to know exactly what was required in the way of burnt offerings before he laid himself on the altar again.

And because of this, the sense of latent and aloof strength in his dream-woman appealed to him. If such a woman as that made demands on him, he would pour out his life like wine for her. Most men would hate her for being an ever-unconquerable fortress, but she delighted him.

Viewed from this angle, he decided that there was no reason why he should not day-dream about her as much as he liked; there was no disloyalty to his marriage vows in such a spirit of service. He must cut out the woman in the cape and Embankment walks, that was quite certain; but the dream was another matter. That harmed nobody, and helped him beyond all reason or belief. In his feeling for her there was nothing of sex or sensuality. She was just a dream-woman, an ideal that in some inexplicable way calmed him and soothed him and met his emotional need of a woman, not his physical one. It seemed to him, provided this aspect was kept out of it and never allowed to debase either of them, that there was no harm in enjoying imagined companionship.

It was the first concession he had ever made to any human weakness in himself in all his hard-driven life, and once made, he found himself revelling in it. He was in no mood to contend with the Underground at the end of his day's work, and made them phone for a taxi.

The traffic hold-ups in the narrow streets of the City area did not exasperate him, for *she* was beside him, occupying the other seat in the darkness of the cab's unlit interior. He could feel the warmth of her atmosphere enwrapping him in a kind of glow. He thought he could smell some aromatic kind of scent.

He turned to her.

"I am very happy to be with you here," he said. "I think it a great privilege. I appreciate it."

The sound of his own voice broke the spell, and he knew that the seat next to him was unoccupied. There was no one there—even to the eyes of his imagination; yet, despite the disillusion the sense of happiness remained with him. He waited quite contentedly in the darkness, with the sound of car-engines in the traffic block all round him, and the fumes of exhausts coming in at the window, and as he waited, he felt his dream-woman gradually building up at his side again.

He knew better this time than to break the magic, and made no attempt to turn his head and see her, for he knew she wasn't there. Yet all the same she was there, but in another dimension. She *was* there to the eyes of the imagination, and he could feel an emotional response. He was happy with her—that was all that mattered. She was real to him.

☾

During the boring remarks of the chairman before he read his paper he called her up before him, and she came. She did not come with the same vividness that she possessed when she appeared spontaneously, but nevertheless she came. On his way back in the taxi through the empty streets she came again, spontaneously, and he found her beside him before he realised her presence. She was tremendously real. He could almost hear the sound of her breathing in the dark. He could definitely smell the aromatic scent she used, and it went to his head like alcohol and set all his pulses throbbing. He hesitated for a moment—after all, lots of fellows carried on like anything in taxis, and he did not propose to do anything desperate—he leant over and put his head where the shoulder of the imaginary woman should have been—and in doing so broke the spell. He sat up and cursed savagely, feeling as if he had been thoroughly well snubbed, and stared fiercely out of the window for the rest of the journey.

As he turned away after paying the taxi-driver he glanced back into the cab, with sudden compunction, at his abandoned companion, feeling that he had been a brute and possibly hurt her feelings, and as he did so, a face rose before him like moonlight in the darkness, and he saw an oval contour, dark, steady eyes, and a crimson-lipped, close-held mouth. It was so clear that for a moment he almost thought he saw it with his physical eyes, and only the knowledge that such a sight was impossible in the darkness prevented him from looking for the actual woman.

Up in his sitting-room, he stood with his elbow on the mantelpiece beside the dying fire and called her again—and she came again. He saw nothing, but he felt her presence and knew the particular spot in the room where she stood.

As he turned over in bed after putting out the light he punched up the pillow into the configuration it had had the night before, and lay tense and still, waiting—would she let him—or would she not? But nothing happened and he felt himself gradually sliding off into sleep along the normal channels. And then, as he began to pass over the threshold, he felt the softness of a woman's breast beneath his cheek and the rise and fall of her breathing. His first instinct was to put out his hand and touch her, but he had learnt his lesson and knew better than to break the illusion by trying to reduce it to actuality. He could only enjoy so long as he never tried to possess.

He lay still, tense, hardly daring to breathe, so sweet and real was the illusion. He wondered whether in his imagination he dared turn and kiss her, but decided not to risk it, the experience was too precious as it was. Then deep sleep took him, and he slept without stirring till morning and awoke alert and alive and happy as a lad.

He had a sudden twinge of conscience concerning his responsibilities at the seaside villa, but dismissed it as quixotic. What he was doing was harming no one, and the blessing and peace of it all was so great a boon. He had tried cutting it off drastically once, and the result had been an explosion of emotion he had no mind to precipitate again. What earthly need was there to give up his dream-woman who harmed nobody and helped him so tremendously?

He stood for a moment looking out of the window in the direction of the church across the water, veiled from his eyes at that hour by the morning mists; and suddenly, beyond all control, a cry burst from him:

"My God! you can't want to take that from me—even *that* from me?"

The reaction of this sudden uprush of emotion was so great that he found himself clutching the window-sash, holding on by it, setting it shaking and rattling as if in a gale.

Lurching across the room, he dropped into his chair and buried his face in the frowzy cushion.

"No", he muttered, "that is too much. I won't agree to it!"

He had thought that he had long since outgrown the superstition of religion, but the hybrid form of jealous-Jehovah-gentle-Jesus that had been impressed upon him in his childhood rose before his eyes, half idol, half angel. He hated the idol, but the angel aspect pulled at him painfully. He found himself on the verge of tears, horribly childish.

That broke the spell. Raging at himself as he had never raged at the most stupid student, he wrenched off his collar and tie; plunged his face in a basin of cold water; towelled his head till it looked like a quickset hedge; then forced the collar back on to its studs, swearing like a trooper; tied his tie as if garotting the object of a life-long vendetta; tore at his hair with a comb; caught up his despatch case without examining its contents, and arrived, for the first time in hospital history, late for his lecture. His lecture, and the following clinic, were just plain hell for all concerned.

He got through his private cases that afternoon in his Wimpole Street rooms in much the same manner as his clinic, but as patients were always warned what to expect by the doctors sending them, nothing very untoward occurred; one lady collapsed in hysterics, and two children howled dismally, but except for these minor *contretemps*, to all outward appearance business was as usual. Dr. Malcolm had one of those faces that could be hit with an axe without making much impression on it, and his receptionist, a superannuated hospital Sister, certainly suspected nothing beyond an unusually irritable temper.

Finally, towards seven o'clock, the last patient on his list having been dispatched into outer darkness looking rather like a lost soul fleeing from the wrath of the Lord, Dr. Malcolm tied his stethoscope in a knot, flung it into his despatch case, and pitched his delicate ophthalmoscope in after it. But before he could get the lid shut, the door opened, revealing the shrivelled face of Sister.

"Well, what is it?" he snarled looking as if about to hurl the entire case at her head.

"There is another patient in the waiting-room, sir. A lady who rang up during the afternoon and made an appointment."

"My God!" exclaimed the disgusted man, seeing his release deferred, and already bone-weary and sick at heart. "All right, send her in."

He released the lid of his despatch case, but before he could get out his instruments again, the stethoscope uncurled itself and came writhing out like a snake and escaped to the floor. He stooped to grope for it, the effort seeming to add the last straw to his weariness and irritability, and as he

31

straightened himself, he saw coming in through the door the woman in the cape.

He stood and looked at her.

"This is an hallucination!" was his first thought.

There she was, just as he had pictured her, wearing her flowing black cloak and wide black hat, like Sandeman's port. There was her pale oval face, her aquiline nose, her scarlet lips, and above all, her velvety brown eyes with the kindness in them; for one second, as he saw the kindness in the eyes, a lump came in Malcolm's throat as it had come that morning, and immediately, as before, his mood turned to fury—a livid, concentrated fury which he would not have believed himself capable of towards a woman. She must have identified his face, seen in the light of her electric torch, from some photo or other in the papers, and had hunted him out, intending to blackmail him! Or was she seeking adventure? He had never thought of such a thing before in connection with himself, and to his horror he felt the unregenerate man within him thrill with faint furtive triumph, and his temper, if that were possible, worsened accordingly.

"Good afternoon," he snapped in his harsh, strident voice. "I have not the pleasure of knowing your name, nor who sent you to me."

"My name is Morgan, Miss Le Fay Morgan. My dentist told me of you, but he did not send me to you. I came of my own accord because I thought you might be able to explain to me certain things I want to know."

"That is a very unusual method of approaching a consultant," said Dr. Malcolm, glaring at her hostilely, and yet with a dreadful kind of numb aching inside him, as if she resembled some one dead who was dear to him.

"Mine is a very unusual case," replied his visitor, quite unperturbed by his unconcealed resentment of her presence. "May I tell you about it?—and then perhaps you will know whether you can help me or not."

"Er—yes, certainly. Won't you sit down?" said the man, pulling himself together; his ingrained rough chivalry refused to allow him to do anything worse than snarl at a woman. She seated herself in the patient's chair with a swirl of her flowing cloak and he, feeling more dead than alive, dropped into his own seat and tried to concentrate on the consultation.

"What is it you complain of." he asked.

The brown eyes calm and veiled, gazed back into his own grey-green ones; there was no kindness in them now; they were like a duellist's in the motionless moment preceding the commencement of a bout. He liked her better for that, and relaxed slightly in relief. It was the kindness in her eyes he could not stand because it made him feel his own weakness.

"I have—" she paused, picking her words carefully, "sensations—impressions—that cannot be accounted for by any ordinary explanation. I am anxious to know whether they are hallucinations, or whether they have a genuine cause."

"What is it you experience? Tactile, visual, auditory sensations?"

"Visual—frequently, but that is nothing new to me, for I have a vivid imagination. But several times recently I have had tactile sensations, and finally, this morning, an auditory one, which was what caused me to come to you. The others I should have ignored, putting them down as subconscious fantasies, but this—this morning—went beyond what I am prepared to ignore."

"It sounds to me as if your case were one for a psychologist, madam, not for me, who am a neurologist."

"I want to know whether there is any physical basis for my sensations," said the woman, never taking her eyes from his.

"No, I should say there isn't."

"Can you tell that for certain without examining me?"

He winced at this home-thrust.

"Do you want me to examine you now?"

"I should like your considered opinion, Dr. Malcolm."

"Very well. We will take the tactile sensations first.
What is it you actually feel?"

"I have, on several occasions, been wakened from sleep by a sense of pressure on my shoulder or chest, and on two occasions by a sensation like a pair of powerful hands gripping my upper arms."

"You ought to—have your heart examined," Malcolm managed to say, clinging to his medical science like a drowning man to a straw and refusing to allow his mind to swerve from its concentration on the central nervous system of the patient before him, though his own heart was pounding like a trip-hammer and threatening to suffocate him.

"Do you think it is necessary?" asked the woman in front of him, watching him with her unfaltering gaze.

Malcolm could not speak: he could only sit and look at her.

"Have you ever made any investigations in psychic research?"

He shook his head.

"You ought to read this book," she said, and taking a substantial volume from under her cloak, she pushed it towards him across the desk. For the first time since the interview had started her eyes released his, and he bent his head and read the title: "Phantasms of the Living," by Gurney and Podmore.

The man sat with his head bowed over the book so long that his visitor began to think that, little as she wished to, she would have to break the silence. Suddenly he lifted his head and gazed straight at her.

"I can only say—I am sorry. I had never dreamt—such a thing was possible."

He bowed his head over the book again, bending so low that she could no longer see his face at all, but only his thick greying red hair.

"It shall never happen again—you have my word for that," he said in a voice she could hardly hear.

Then suddenly he sat bolt upright and looked at her, and if ever murder looked out of man's eyes, it looked out of his, for it seemed to him that the mangled body of his dream lady lay dead between this woman's hands. Then, as he saw her likeness to his beloved, he weakened; it was as if she reminded him of the dead—he could not hate this woman who was so like the one he loved. He wavered for a moment, fighting for his self control, and then put his elbows on the desk and covered his face with his hands.

"I'd be glad if you go," he said, almost inaudibly.

"He heard her rise, and her footsteps on the parquet, and thought she was quitting the room, but instead he felt a hand laid on his shoulder. He shuddered, and drove his finger-nails into the skin of his forehead, but except for that he gave no sign.

She stood quietly beside him for a few moments, and the blood began to pound in his temples till he thought his eye-balls would burst as he pressed his hands savagely against them, trying to shut out thought as well as sight. He was numb, as men become numb in a heavy bombardment, and at the same time he was one bare nerve of agony. He could not move; he knew his self-control would break down if he tried to speak; he could only sit still, and endure, and wait for her to go.

He heard her voice speaking to him—a rich, low contralto, velvety, like her eyes, and it moved him as great music had never moved him. It was like bells tolling, tolling for the dead. He could feel his self-control beginning to slip; if she played on his emotions any more he would cry out as men cried out on the examination couch when they came to the end of their fortitude.

"You said that—it should never happen again," he heard her say. He nodded his head slightly.

"I am going to ask you to do something harder than that," came the low quiet voice. "I am going to ask you deliberately to experiment with me along these lines."

He shook his head.

"Yes, you can do it if I help you," the voice went on. She paused for a moment; then her hand pressed his shoulder. "My friend, what will you do if you don't go on? There will be nothing left of you."

He knew she spoke the truth, and his head sank yet lower over his desk as he felt the resistance ebbing out of him.

"Yes, we will see this thing through together, for good and not for evil. Do not be afraid of it. Believe me, it is not evil. Will you work with me, Rupert Malcolm?"

For a long minute he sat motionless, then he nodded.

"I felt you would," she said. Her hand shifted from his left shoulder to his right, and she drew him to her. Suddenly relaxing, he let his whole body go limp as he leant against her, feeling her brace herself to take his weight. But he didn't care, he let his full weight go onto her—the dead weight of the upper part of his body, limp and inert; only a strong woman could have held him, and he liked that strength. More than anything else about her—more even than her kindness—he liked that strength. And in him, shaken as he was, rose a strange joy like the morning stars singing together, for she had penetrated his day-dream to its very core; she had martyred him—flaying him alive, and then she had been tender to him; yet she was still an unconquerable fortress, he could never possess her. He did not want to possess her—not in that way—it would spoil everything; yet he was not unfulfilled, for he was possessed by her. He might not possess her yet he was absorbed into her. His being was lost in hers and he was utterly satisfied.

He turned his head slightly, and his face was in the folds of her cloak. She stood patiently supporting his heavy bulk, waiting for him to pass through his crisis and come back to his self-control.

The clock in the hall struck eight, and he raised his head. She looked down at the face in the crook of her arm. All the lines had gone out of it, and he had the faintly bewildered look of a small child awakening from sleep in a strange place. All the tensions were gone, and in their place was an utter serenity and trust like a child's. The tears suddenly pricked behind her own eyes as she looked down into that face from which twenty years of over-strain had suddenly been wiped away.

Dr. Malcolm rose unsteadily to his feet.

"I—I suppose I ought to apologise," he said.

The woman smiled.

"I don't believe you have any intention of apologising," she replied.

"No," he said, "I haven't," and looked up with a quick smile and down again, shy as a school-girl with her, but intensely happy.

"I am going to drive you home," she said. "I have got my car here. Where do you live?"

"Oh no, don't bother. I'll get a taxi." He started to cram his instruments ruthlessly back into the already over-crowded dispatch case, and forced the lid down on them. Something went crack inside, but he snapped the locks home regardless. Then, forgetful of his refusal of her invitation, he followed her meekly into a smart black coupé standing outside the door, oblivious of the indignant glances of Sister, who had been kept an hour over her time, and being of unsullied virginity herself, did not approve of his driving home with pretty ladies.

PART II

THE MOON MISTRESS

Oh Thou, that didst with Pitfall and with Gin
Beset the road I was to wander in,
Thou wilt not with Predestination round
Enmesh me, and impute my fall to sin?

—Omar Khayyam

CHAPTER
FOUR

I am not absolutely sure how old I am, but I think I am about 120. At any rate, I have lived long enough to see the things for which I worked come about. It is for this reason I think I shall go soon.

There was a time when I was regarded as the priestess of all evil. A certain wise man said that every step forward in morality must always be immoral to start with. Anyway that time is long past, and the crimes of Martaban are chaste in Clapham nowadays. I expect in due course I shall be identified with the principle I exemplified and worshiped as a goddess, for who am I to expect to escape the universal fate of the Light-bearers? At any rate, the world I live in today is as free from nervous disease as the world in which I did my work was free in its civilised parts from typhus and plague and cholera, improved mental hygiene like improved physical hygiene, clearing up the dirt diseases. It was recognised, even in my day, that if a man lived in insanitary conditions he could not expect to be healthy, and still less could he expect to rear normal children, but we little realised the insanitary conditions in which the vast majority of people led their emotional lives. To read of them today is like reading an account of working class conditions in the Hungry Forties. We ask how such things could be endured; but people will accept as inevitable anything they are used to, never dreaming that it is due to ignorance and bad management.

I was born at a time when a repressive morality was in full force and still serving its purpose. In those days women were divided into two classes, the sheltered, protected women, who suffered from the vapours and the unsheltered, unprotected women, who suffered many things, some of which are unprintable. I was born into the sheltered class but poverty forced me into the other, and I suffered. Such was the first stage of my apprenticeship.

My father, as the family name of Le Fay indicates, was of Gallic extraction, with Breton blood in his veins; my mother was of that strange pre-Keltic strain that lingers on in the remote valleys of the central mountain mass of Mid-Wales. Some say these people were Phoenicians, but that is incorrect; they were older than the Phoenicians being Atlanteans, drawn to these metal bearing islands by trade and surviving when the parent country was cut off by catastrophe. They are a strange folk, set apart even to this day by a remoteness of soul, for they do not, I think, fully belong to this world. The Bretons, too, are an other-world people, and the faith of Carnac lives on in their hearts to a much greater extent than is suspected. These two strains, crossed, produced me. They were normal enough until they were crossed, and then they produced me. To add to the complications, I was supposed to have died when a baby. I was declared dead, and lay dead many hours on my mother's lap, for she could not be persuaded to lay me down; and then, at dawn, I revived, but the eyes that looked up at my mother, she told me many years afterwards when I asked her the cause of my strangeness, were not the eyes of a child, and she knew with the unerring instinct of a mother that I was not the same one.

I was never young, even in those days; I had the same mind that I have now, but with the emotional outlook of a child; with such a mind I could never be a child with children, and the adults of that day were a hostile race. Moreover we were gentle-people who had become poor and we saw at its worst the workings of the class system of the time; so although I was a friendly child, eager for play and companionship, I was forced back on myself and compelled to solitude. This I believe to be the pre-requisite for that which was to follow, for it is only by turning within that we can find the Inner Path, and those whose fate destines them for that path are prevented from turning outward and finding their place in life, just as the feet of the Chinese child are bound. It is a painful process at the time, but the result is a personality that can be used for the purpose for which it is designed, being free from attachments and inured to solitude. Such, I believe, is the law of the Higher Path, for I have many times watched it at work. To those who are accustomed to find happiness in their attachments and can conceive of no other kind, it may appear a melancholy lot; but once the fact of detachment has been accepted, life opens up in the most marvellous manner, only one must be very careful never to form ties, for they invariably have to be broken. Yet, by a strange paradox, one has an extraordinary richness of experience, for one may enjoy anything as long as one does not become dependent on it. It is an old saying that an initiate possesses nothing but has the use of everything.

Wilfred Maxwell has told the story of my beginnings, and how I found the Inner Path, so there is no need for me to tell it again. * He has also told of the experiment we worked together; but what he has not told, for he could not know, was the way in which that experiment

* See *The Sea Priestess*

40

appeared to me.

That I will now tell as briefly as may be, for it is the prelude to what is to follow.

I had travelled some distance down the Inner Path, and had developed my psychism to the point where it was as reliable as psychism is ever likely to be—that is to say I could trust it in matters in which I had no personal concern. I was also well acquainted with the theory and philosophy of the Secret Teaching as it has come down to us by tradition. But there is a big difference between the psychic and the adept; for the psychic is a psychic and nothing more, but the adept, to be worthy of the name, must be not only a psychic but a magician—that is to say, he must be able to wield the powers of the spirit objectively as well as subjectively. When I met Wilfred Maxwell I was what is called an Adeptus Minor, and I had not made that transition.

I used Wilfred's faith in me to establish my own confidence in my magical powers; for if one believes in them, one can use them; and if one does not believe in them, one cannot use them, and a sceptical, rational person like myself does not find it easy to believe in such things until they have been put to the test and found to work; and, paradoxically, they will not work unless one believes in them, for one is all the time receiving negative suggestion from one's own incredulity, and by the same token, breaking up the astral forms as fast as one makes them. But when I made Wilfred, who had faith, see an astral form by means of suggestion, his faith held it steady for me to see. This is a subtle but useful point in the practical workings, and I offer it to those who can appreciate it. There are not many people who know these things, or, if they know them, will tell them.

I made Wilfred see me as I wanted to be, and by this means I built up my magical personality. A magical personality is a strange thing. It is more like a familiar than anything else, and one transfers one's consciousness to it as one does to an astral projection, until finally one identifies oneself with it and becomes that which one has built.

Then having used Wilfred, I left him, but not until I had put him in touch with the cosmic forces.

I remember coming into London at the peak hour of the traffic. I came in by an unfamiliar route and lost my way in the great tangled boroughs of the Surrey side, where all the streets look alike but are pushed askew by the windings of the river, and one loses all sense of direction. The only landmark I had was the great chimney of Doulton's factory, which I knew would guide me to the bridge I wanted; but the twisted streets would not run as I wished, for that part of the world is a mass of *culs-de-sac* owing to the railway. Suddenly I saw ahead of me at the end of a street the leaden-grey surface of the river. Thinking that this would be the Albert Embankment, and known country, I made for it only to find myself in the oddest little forgotten village in the world, looking across the water at the ragged sky-line of the mean streets of Pimlico.

It was not a slum but, in fact, intensely respectable. Every little house had a little front garden, and without exception they all had lace curtains to their windows. A number of the gates bore brass plates to the effect that sweeps, undertakers, midwives, and suchlike folk lived there. It proved to be another *cul-de-sac*, however, and I had to turn perilously on a tumble-down wharf at its end, and retrace my route to the right-angled turn. In that angle stood a small and dismal church, black as a London cat with accumulated grime, its upper windows protected from stone-throwing by closely woven wire screens; its lower ones by heavy, wrought-iron grilles; its door a massive oak affair studded with great nails. It looked, in fact, like a miniature private fortress disguised under the cloak of religion. I have never seen a more forbidding façade; it might have been a prison of the Inquisition.

To complete the picture of neglected gloom, a To Let board drooped in front of it. This surprised me, for I had believed that once a church, always a church, and that ecclesiastical property could not be sequestrated. But this church had apparently been too much even for the ecclesiastical authorities and they wished to be rid of it. It looked to me as if it might be very badly haunted.

I got across the river at last, and found myself in civilised parts once more.

I was glad to be back, and my little home in the hayloft looked very welcoming, with its huge fire and deep divans piled with innumerable cushions, and all the soft, rich, dark colours that I love.

The flat seemed strangely alien although I had only been absent a few months. I could tell that my life had already withdrawn from it and that I should not be pulling up any roots when I left there. But that did not make me any happier, but rather the contrary, for I felt alien and alone and homeless, and atmospheres have always meant a great deal to me; they have meant, perhaps, more than persons, owing to the law of aloneness under which I live.

I was glad, on the whole, that the atmosphere of the flat was dead, for I had been dreading the parting, fearing that I would feel as if I were abandoning some humble friend by whose help I had climbed, for this was the first settled home I had ever known. But it does not do to be sentimental over either places or persons upon the Path. The days of my training were finished, and I was changing over from the Lesser to the Greater Mysteries. What I had learnt I now had to put into practice.

The Law by which I live is so strange that unless I tell something of it, no one will understand what follows. Many tales have been woven round the theme of the black-cloaked adept with mysterious powers, appearing from nowhere in response to some call for help, and disappearing equally mysteriously after help has been given; but no one, not even Bulwer Lytton, who could have done so, has told the story from the adepts point of view, showing why he came and why he went and what he really did.

This, then, is what manner of person an adept is. There are those who are concerned with the inner governance of the world; not its politics and wire-pullings, but with the secret spiritual influences that rule the minds of men. Behind them are those greater than they, who are concerned with elemental forces and the influences that rule the æon. These are to those others as the tides are to the breaking waves. Then, upon the physical plane, are those who are sent through into incarnation to co-operate with them. They are sometimes spoken of as initiates, and they are that, but also something more than that. They must, of course, be initiated into the Tradition otherwise they would not have the keys to the contacts and would not command co-operation. There are, of course, also initiates who become adepts, but I am speaking now of what are called the cosmic adepts, and they come in for a purpose, and all their time until maturity is given to preparing the personality as an instrument for that purpose; it would be a cruel training if there were not within one an inner awareness which knows whence one comes, and why—as I had known, even as a child, that I was a stranger and a sojourner and did not belong; therefore things do not hurt as they would hurt others. But one is always alone, for there are very few with whom to find companionship, and because one is strange, one is hated.

Then there comes the time when the transition must be made from one mode of consciousness to the other, when we learn to use the instrument we have wrought for the purpose for which it has been designed—and that instrument is our own human personality. It is a strange thing to stand back from one's personality and use it, and not easy to do.

Those of us who come in thus have been trained and made in a previous life, and I have always been a priestess of the Great Mother. Such male incarnations as I have had, have been negligible, and mostly violent and unhappy. But a priestess I have been, and a great one, right down from the days of Atlantis, for the higher the grade, the earlier the initiation, and I was one of those who served in the courts of the great Sun temple of the City of the Golden Gates in the island of Ruta.

It was I who was sent away before the end, when they were taking out the Seed-bearers for the next epoch, and I saw from the sea great Atlantis go down in the last final catastrophe that ended all. Then my soul became affiliated to the group-soul of Egypt and I came in and out through the doors of the royal house down through all the Egyptian Dynasties. I was never of those that sat upon the throne, but I was a mysterious figure that came and went in the background of the temples.

I was of the cult of the Black Isis, which is very different from that of the green-robed Goddess of Nature to whom the women prayed for children. They represent Her with a human face, or horned like a cow; but the Black Isis is the Veiled Isis, upon whose face none may look and live, and because I represent Her, I too went veiled and cloaked, and I have never lost the habit to this day; I do not like people to look upon my face in bright light, and if I must show it, I show it masked in laughter and animation. Very few have ever seen my face in repose, for repose is a transparent mask.

Some equate the Black Isis with Kali, and say that She is evil; but I do not think She is, unless one counts elemental force as evil, which I do not. She is indeed the Breaker in Pieces, but then She sets free. She is also most ancient Life, and people fear the primordial as they fear nothing else. Freud knew that. She is a reservoir of tremendous and dynamic force, and when dynamic force comes welling up, that is She.

I broke Wilfred, and he rose like a phœnix, reborn from the ashes of his dead life, and knew Great Isis. I slew him and I gave him birth. That is not evil, unless you reckon pain as evil, and I do not; for pain brings power, and destruction is freedom.

I do not think there is any such thing as innate evil; what men call evil is simply misplaced force. Some define good as that which preserves, and evil as that which destroys; but destruction can be cleansing and purifying, for there is such a thing in both men and races as spiritual constipation, which comes from too much preservation of the *status quo*.

So I came back to the world yet once again as the priestess of the Great Goddess, bringing with me the memory of forgotten arts, one of which is the art of being a woman. I came because I was sent. There was that needed which I had to give. They did not send in a priestess of the Bright Isis, but of the Dark and Veiled One, because that was the need; and They said to me: "You will have tiger teeth, for you will be a Breaker in Pieces. Men will call you the Priestess of All Evil, but you know better."

So I came in at the dawn of a new æon. There were those who had gone before me who watched over the break-up of the old world. They had been armed and mailed—great sworded Ones, but I was unarmed save for the weapons of a woman.

I had only my woman's personality with which to work, and I had to create and build it as if it were a work of art, and I worked on myself like a sculptress. It was an odd sensation to feel the two aspects of myself merging, and finally uniting. In the earlier stages I would be either in one consciousness or the other. I would slip into the wider consciousness, returning on waking, but able to bring through no more than faint shadowy memories of dreams. Twice, in crises that might have destroyed the physical personality I was so laboriously building, I united my two selves momentarily, but the child-mind could not stand more than a brief uniting—life was difficult enough as it was.

With adolescence everything closed down—for no mind could stand the double strain; then, when I stabilised with maturity, it began to open again and I was conscious of an overshadowing, for by this time the focus of my being had been fully transferred to the physical body. Familiar with the language of spiritualism, I thought of this overshadowing as a spirit-control, but gradually I became aware that it was simply my own higher self, and still more gradually I learnt to rely on it. My two selves have never been permanently in me, for no human physique would stand that; nor can I invoke my higher self at will, but I know how to make the conditions that cause it to come in. Unfortunately that is a thing in which I always need to have help: I cannot do it single-handed; some one has to see the Goddess in me, and then She manifests. I am not the Goddess, but I am the priestess of the Goddess, and She manifests through me, for all women are Isis. Not many can see the Goddess manifest, and of those that can see, not all can bear it, and then they hate me because they fear Her. I have been much hated in my life, and I have, likewise, had more than my fair share of love.

As I have already said, Wilfred gave me the help I needed in formulating myself to myself. My weapons were now ready, and the next phase of my career lay with the world. I had already passed the age when a woman can hope to charm by her looks, but the forces that came through me had miraculously re-created me, and I lived with a strange inner vitality that was ageless and deathless and timeless. I was neither young nor old; neither a young girl nor a mature woman. People knew I was not young, and yet they could not think of me as old. I was simply alive with a vitality that prevented people from seeing me as I really was; that glamoured them into seeing me as the ageless and deathless priestess of Great Isis. I knew, moreover, how to set myself against an appropriate background, and when I chose I could wrap my aura about me and pass unseen as a shadow. People sneered at my backgrounds as theatrical and called me a poseuse; but I knew that my backgrounds were psychological and my pose an auto-suggestion.

It was my task to bring certain new concepts to the mind of the race; not to its conscious mind, but to its subconscious mind, and this is done by living them. One who had knowledge once said that an adept must not merely tread the Path, he must be the Path, and this is true. It was not my task to lecture or write or appear in the public eye as is done by those who speak to the conscious mind of the race, but for the carrying out of my work I required a certain amount of cooperation. Like King Solomon, I required men and materials. The necessary money had been placed in my hands, and I could always invoke for more if I wanted it; but that in itself was not enough. Mere wealth would not create of its own accord, and the kind of background I needed was not one that could be entrusted to a professional designer.

Moreover, I needed cooperation, and that was even less easy to procure. I needed people with gifts, but they must also have a sense of dedication. I needed people with minds, but pure intellect would not do, they must also have something of the artist in them. I needed above everything, people with that curious gift of magnetism whom I could use; and I needed, lastly, people on whom I could experiment. But it is not easy to get people to let themselves be used. Little do they know how Isis pays, and I might not tell them. For this is one of the tests of the Path—that they shall not bargain. You will remember that a certain man gave all he had to buy the pearl of great price. They give to Isis and she gives to them; but they give as men, and she gives as a Goddess. Onlookers see the sacrifice that is laid on the altar in open temple, but they do not see the initiation that takes place behind the veil. They see the candidate go down into the grave; they do not see the resurrection on the third day. All they ever know of what occurs is what they learn from those whose courage fails and who turn back, and are they the best judges?

I knew that all I needed would be provided, and that I could draw it through into manifestation just in proportion as I had faith. Those who were behind me knew what was necessary for the work, and had made provision for it on the Inner Planes, but I and I alone could draw it through into manifestation on the earth plane. In proportion as I could realise the powers at my disposal, I could use them. It was said by them of old time that the treasures of earth were in the keeping of the gnomes, the earth elementals, and that there were spells and words of power that could compel the spirits of elemental earth to surrender their treasures; and this is true, though not after the manner that the ignorant believe. There is a life of the earth-soul, and gold is the blood in its veins and equates with that which on the subtle planes we call vital force. It is indeed the social equivalent of energy, and we exchange for it our energy of mind, body and estate and use it as the dominator thereof. It is possible to come to terms with the guardians of mineral life, and they will permit access to the unseen fountains of wealth in the earth-soul; but this power is possessed only by high initiates to whom money, as money, means nothing, for in magic we can only work with power when free from desire; desire defeats its own ends, for it is the parent of fear. So I, to whom poverty and wealth were all one, had resources placed at my disposal, and I used them to build my magical personality in the eyes of men and to make them see me as I wished to be seen.

For the once-born cannot look into the heart, and only a few of them can interpret the subtle workings of the mind; but one can suggest to them through the eyes what one wishes them to believe. This is better than suggestion given by the spoken word, for they discount that so heavily, being versed in that art themselves.

I, for my part, knew how little the true adept needs for his magic, but I had to work upon men's imaginations, and for that I needed a stage setting. I had to make them see me as an adept or I should never have been an adept in their eyes; and to this end I had to have about me that which should suggest the great days of the past when the cult to which I belonged was at the height of its power, so that their thoughts being turned thereto, memories might be awakened and they might come on to my wave-length.

And so, little by little, I had collected ancient things from the old temples; and these had to be kept in a dim light so that their magnetism might not be dispersed, but gather about them and pervade the atmosphere as incense pervades it.

I also used colours for my background, knowing their power over the mind—over my mind as well as over the minds of those who came to visit me. There is a science of colours, and we classify them in magic under the ten stations of the heavens which are the seven planets and space, the zodiac and the earth. There are also the four elemental kingdoms, but these are another matter.

For my purpose I used the opalescent moon-colours on a base of silver; the purple that is a plum-colour and the reds that are magenta or maroon, and the blues of sea-water and the sky at night; never the strong primaries such as a man uses when he is a magus. Always the shadowy, blended colours are mine, for I am the shadow in the background.

As for my body I had made that to be the instrument of my personality, training it, suppling it, learning its arts and its powers. Nature had not been unkind, but she had not been lavish, and I had to make of myself something that I could use for the purpose I had in hand. Being dedicated, I had the right to ask for what I needed, and I, naturally, asked for that beauty which should enable me to hold men's eyes and attention; but instead I was given insight and imagination, and with the knowledge that came from these I created my own kind of beauty.

It was said of another: "She had the face that suits a woman for her soul's screen," and this was true of me. My face was pure Egyptian, slightly high in the cheekbones, which makes my eyes look almond-shaped; slightly aquiline as to the nose, for there was Assyrian blood in the royal caste of Egypt. My eyes are very deep-set, which makes them look darker than they really are. Seen in a good light, they are almost green—to match my tiger teeth, it has been said. I am supposed to be like Cleopatra—or perhaps Cleopatra was like me. I have an immense amount of hair of that very dark brown that is just not quite black; it is perfectly straight and sometimes I wear it in a knot on the nape of my neck; sometimes I twist it round my head in a coronet; sometimes in hot weather I let it hang in two plaits down over my breasts. Always I wear it parted in two smooth crow-wings upon my forehead as the Indian women wear theirs. For this reason people have talked of coloured blood, though my skin should give the lie to that, for it is the white of ivory, or of the great magnolia blooms that have no touch of pink in them. I am bold, even rash, in the matter of lipsticks, and I love long ear-rings. It would require Huysmans to do justice to the ear-rings I have possessed—jade, amber, coral, lapis, malachite for day; and for the night I have great jewels—square-cut emeralds; long, pale, drop-shaped pearls; and all the fires of the different opals, which I adore.

I am a little taller than middle height, and but for my length of limb could walk straight out of the shop in whatever model gown I might try on. But I never wear model gowns. I wear my own fashions, and they come from the "soft furnishings" as often as not, for there is a richness in the great breadths of the draperies that one does not find in the dress materials, and who shall say me nay if I choose to wear what was meant for the windows of a Venetian palace? I like my gowns to hang full and straight and lie upon the ground around my feet, and I wear soft sandals of silver and gold and iridescent colours.

Then I love furs, for I am a cold-blooded creature—it is my one physical weakness; I wear furs even in the house, and I have my houses hot. I love the whole skin with the great wicked head, and I love it to be a noble one, not the little mean mask of a fox. I have the pale skin of a timber wolf, and a blue wolf verging on black; of the great cats I have a spotted jungle leopard and a lovely pale leopard of the snows from the Himalayas that the Tibetans say are the ghosts of bad lamas who die in sin.

I like rings, too, so big that I can hardly get my gloves on over them; and bracelets like fetters on my wrists. My hands are supple with ritual, and I am as bold in my nail lacquers as in my lipsticks. I have used silver and gold lacquers, and reds so dark that they are almost black; and iridescent lacquers that make my nails look like opals, and I wear my nails long to match my tiger teeth.

I like my shoes to be very soft and light and supple, like gloves rather than shoes, so that I can move in them without sound. I was trained as a dancer in the days of my youth, and I know the meaning of movement—how it should flow like water. I know too how the body should swing and balance from the waist, and that this is worth more in beauty than a slender line.

I am not, and never have been, a fashionable woman. Not that I decry the fashions; they are for some, but they are not for me. Some say that fashions are artificial, the work of the trade, but that is untrue. Fashions change because novelty attracts and stimulates. But I who am the eternal woman, the archetypal feminine—I do not speak to the surface of consciousness, the sophisticated mind that the novelties catch, but to the archaic and primordial that is in the soul of every man, and I will pit my charm against that of any fashionable woman. They may have lovers, but I have been loved.

And I will pit my silences against their speech. Yet there is much in a voice, and the tones of a voice; they should be singing ones, even when speaking; sweet and soft on the lips, yet with reverberation behind them, for in that reverberation there is power, a strange power that beats upon the soul. I know it well, for I have used it. I shall tell presently how I use it.

49

For I use colour and movement and sound and light as other women use fashions, but more important than all these is scent. I value scents highly, and attach great importance to them, for there is a whole psychology and theology of scents. The scents I employ are spicy and aromatic; the flower odours are not for me—no one has ever likened *me* to a flower though I have been told I am as beautiful as a leopard. Sandal and cedar and Russian leather—these are my favourites. I love also the after odour of burnt musk and the way it clings. Camphor, I like too, for its cleanliness. Of the essential oils, I use geranium, jasmine, and attar, none other. These are the psychology of scents, but of the theology there are two I esteem most highly—galbanum and frankincense—the harsh, musky, hyrcinian sweetness of galbanum that is earth of earth, and the sharp stimulus of frankincense, which is as if all the trees of Paradise were burning. I have also a taste which I have never found anyone yet to share with me—the smell of iodoform gives me pleasure.

So much for my personality, or as much of it as I can convey in words. The rest must be told by what I do.

As to my mundane background—my little home in the hayloft I made when I was poor, and I made it to suit myself; but, as I have said, for what lay ahead I must have a background that would make people see me as I wanted to be seen, and yet, at the same time, I did not want to be burdened with elaboration. It was in my mind that a studio flat would serve my purpose, for the studio would give me space for what I had to do, and an artist's exiguous quarters would be enough for my simple needs, provided I spent money on the bathroom, for I like a nice bathroom—a legacy, perhaps, of my Roman days. I did not easily find what I wanted. After sharp words with the house agent I decided to advertise—and learnt at a cost of much petrol the unbelievable optimism of people who have something to dispose of. It seemed strange that the work I had before me should be held up for so simple a thing as suitable premises, especially as I was not narrowly limited as to money. Upon each previous occasion when I had had to find a place for my work, it had come straight to my hand—my hayloft, my fort, had both come like that, as if I had held a wishing-stone when picturing what I wanted; yet now, with the real work just beginning, I was as badly off as Noah's raven.

I went over again in my mind what I needed. I must have quiet, that was a *sine qua non*, for the work of the higher magic can be shattered by noise just as a photographic plate can be spoilt by light.

50

I must have a place that was readily accessible, and yet a little off the beaten track so that the people who visited me should not be in any danger of running across their acquaintances. It must possess one large and lofty room in which I could entertain, and another room suitable for use as my private temple, and then such living accommodation as a single woman of simple needs might require— excepting of course, the bathroom, which I knew I should have to be prepared to instal myself, for I have yet to meet the artist who shares my views on bathrooms. All this seemed simple enough to find, and yet I could not find it.

Then suddenly there came to my mind the memory of that dingy little church that had had such a depressing effect on me as I came into London at the end of my dreadful drive. I had never seen a property I liked less, but was it possible that this was the destined place, that had been waiting for me all those years while its To Let board gathered grime, and that the other eligible residences, knowing this, had fled at my approach in order to leave it a clear field? I only hoped this was as impossible as it sounded, but a sense of duty compelled me to give it its chance.

It was certainly very suitable so far as position went, in its quiet *cul-de-sac* beside the river; it was well off the beaten track, for, to the people I sought, the Surrey side was as remote as the mountains of the moon, yet it was easily accessible, for one only had to cross the neighbouring bridge and one was back in civilised parts.

So I took my little car and impelled, as I have said, by a strong sense of duty, went down to have a look at it. I went with the streaming traffic over Vauxhall Bridge and found myself in the mysterious land where Wandsworth abuts on Battersea. I had for my landmark the great chimney, standing up like a beacon with its pale plume of smoke, and yet could I find that spot where I took the wrong turning? I could not. The curse was still on me, and the little church, offended perhaps by my lack of discernment, hid its face.

No one, neither the policemen, nor the postmen, nor the street sweepers, could tell me anything about it, and indeed it was just as well I had consulted the police early in my search or I am sure I should have been arrested as a suspicious character long before the day was out, so thoroughly did I comb that dingy district. When at length I gave it up as hopeless and made for Vauxhall Bridge, it was once again the peak hour of the evening's traffic; so, having got across the bridge, I turned along Grosvenor Road intending to slip down a by-street to avoid the congestion of the main roads. And then I saw it! The setting sun was sending low, level beams across the river, and on the far bank the stained glass of its west window lit up like a jewel.

I turned my car so sharply that I nearly ran over a man who was crossing the road, and who, being a cross-grained individual, did not accept my apologies with at all a good grace, but told me what he thought of me, in which he was probably quite correct, for I had very nearly dispatched him to eternity. Then I told him what I thought of him, and he lifted his hat and said: "I beg your pardon, madam," and I saw that allowances must be made for him as he had red hair. I had thought for a moment, too, that he was a doctor, and I have a liking for doctors, for a faint waft of iodoform came into the car as he stood staring at me angrily, but the old-fashioned, double-fronted house he entered bore no brass plate. If he had been a doctor, I think I should have pursued the acquaintance then and there, for there was something about that man that was rather striking, a sense of power and dynamic drive, and it was such as he that I had in mind to help me in my work. Moreover a doctor, with his special knowledge, is often very useful in occultism. But perhaps it was just as well I had no designs on this individual, for not only was he in a very bad temper from having been half run over and wholly scared, but he must have been a dour type at the best of times, and encased in the plate armour of middle class convention and professional prestige. A professional man I judged him to be from his be-damned-to-you air when angry, which is not developed by those who serve either God or Mammon.

CHAPTER
FIVE

I had no difficulty in finding my church after that, and a very few moments' driving brought me to it. But how different it looked now. Then it had seemed sinister. It had rather lovely lines, as if some one had cut down a cathedral, and with its pantiled roof rising to a lantern it looked like a little bit of Italy. The London grime that lay thick upon it had caused the soft stone of its facing to weather rapidly, giving it an air of antiquity to which it was not entitled, being, if the truth were known, a bit of Victorian Gothic toned down by dirt.

The To Let board stated that a caretaker was within, so I beat upon the door with an enormous knocker, raising such a din that I thought I should bring the whole district to its doors; but nothing happened; not even a fold of the Nottingham lace curtains all down the road was stirred by an inquisitive hand. I did not repeat the fusillade—if the caretaker were within he would have come rushing out—and was making a note of the address of the agents, when there issued from a little house tucked away under the wing of the church which looked like a gate-keeper's lodge on a country estate, a man in a bowler hat. The To Let board had not been strictly accurate; the caretaker was alongside, not within.

There is something about bowler hats that always rouses my prejudices, they are so offensively unexceptionable. No man whom I have called friend has ever worn one. Slouch hats; pork pies; Trilbies; Homburgs: cloth caps; even, under certain circumstances, billycocks, but *never* a bowler among them. But this was not an ordinary bowler—it had been tarred! This went a long way towards removing my prejudices, for I had never before known a man who tarred his hats. There was a vaguely horsey air about this individual, and I guessed, and subsequently found I was right, that he was a retired cabby.

"D'ye want to see the plice, lidy?" he enquired.

I said I did, and he produced from his hip-pocket a key so huge that it would certainly have prevented him from sitting down if he had carried it in the more accessible trouser pocket. The heavy door creaked on hinges so corroded that it was evident he thought that the light of his countenance on its exterior was all the caretaking the property needed.

However, although it was close and un-aired, the place did not smell damp.

We entered a broad lobby that ran the length of the façade and was partitioned off from the main hall by panelling of yellow varnished pitch-pine. We went on through double doors, and I found myself in a typical chapel interior, save that at the east end there was a sanctuary, complete with saints in niches and a lofty stained glass window representing a most horrible scene from the Last Judgment. At the other end was a rose-window over the gallery which appeared to consist of two concentric circles of devils. Whatever sect had owned this tabernacle must have held some pretty lurid views.

Whoever had built that place had evidently employed a good architect, for the proportions were lovely. It looked, however, as if it had been abandoned before it was quite finished, for there were no pews or pulpit, and no marks on the stone-flagged floor to indicate that there ever had been any.

I walked slowly across its broad expanse and mounted the three steps into what appeared to be an Anglican chancel intended for ritualistic uses, for it was large in proportion to the nave, and if that was what one should call it in an obvious conventicle, and discovered to my amazement that what I had taken for an out-size in altars was actually a small stone tank like a miniature swimming bath.

"What in the world is this?" I asked the caretaker.

"That's the font," he answered, surveying it with obvious pride, grimy and unprepossessing as it was.

"Was this a Baptist chapel?" I enquired thinking that its ornate architecture was not quite the usual style of that austere set.

"Well, it was, and it wasn't. 'E baptised 'em, but 'e also 'ad a service. 'E was 'alf way, you might say, between the Baptists and the Cath'lics."

This horrible hybrid left me dumb. How could it conceivably work? One would imagine that the two halves of his soul, whoever "he" might be, would spend all their time cursing and excommunicating each other.

"What religion did he belong to?" I asked when I had recovered my poise.

"E didn't belong to no religion, lidy, 'e run 'is own. Called 'emselves the Resurrectionists, they did."

Remembering the other connotation of the word, I could not repress a smile, which he saw and answered.

"No, mum, not body-snatchers. They reckoned they'd rise again, all on 'em, just as they was, so they dressed accordingly, and 'e give 'em baptism all over every Sunday—ducked 'em right under, so's they'd rise nice an' clean."

"Did he have many followers?" I asked, thinking of all the Sundays in Trinity, and wondering how many could be found to put up with such drastic salvation, for there appeared to be no way of heating the tank.

"A tidy few," said he.

"And what was the end of it all? I enquired.

"Well, yer see, mum, 'e believed in total 'mershun, like the Baptists; but then 'e also believed in infant baptism, like the Catholics, and 'e 'mershed an infant and it died and 'e up and 'anged 'isself. Never even stopped to tike up the collection, 'e didn't, and so the plice was never paid for, and the builders went bust an' the agents collared it, and there it is, just as it allus was, these forty years."

"There must be a curse on it," I said.

"Oh, I dunno, it's suited me very nicely," said he with a wink. "If you was to take it, mum, would you be wantin' a caretaker?"

"No," I said, "I should not, but I could find plenty of work for a handy man, and might be able to give your wife some cleaning."

"My wife was took orf to the 'sylum this mornin', lidy, but I could do anythink you wanted in the way of cleanin'. I'm real 'andy, I am. Yer see, of recent years she got that religious she wouldn't do a 'and's-turn, and I 'ad to do everythink. Cookin'. Cleanin'. Make the beds. I'm reel 'andy, lidy."

"I'm very sorry to hear that," I said, hoping he would know I was referring to his wife, not to his cooking.

"Well lidy, perhaps it's orl for the best. I could do fer ye fine, mum, if you'd give a chanst."

"I don't know that I'm coming here yet," I said. "Everyone connected with the place seems to go either bankrupt or mad."

"Not me, lidy, I ain't bust an' I ain't bats."

"But your wife?"

"Bats but not bust, lidy. She'd a nice bit o' cleanin' if she'd only 'a done it. But she got that religious, yer see, she couldn't put 'er mind to it. They said to 'er: "Mrs Meatyard, you'll 'ave to go if you can't do better'n this.""

"Oh, says she, the Lord's comin'.""

"Well. 'E ain't 'ere yet. Won't yer get on with your work while you're waitin'?' they sez to 'er."

"But she wouldn't. It weren't no use. Couldn't give 'er mind to it, yer see. Then she took off 'er clothes an' tried to baptise 'erself in the kitchen copper an' they sent 'er 'ome."

"Good heavens!" I said. "Was the kitchen copper alight when she did it?"

"Oh no, mum. Their ole prophet didn't believe in no comforts. I 'ad 'er 'ome for a bit, but it weren't no use. She kep' yellin' the Lord was after 'er. Seemed to get 'im mixed up with the Devil towards the end an' couldn't tell 'em apart, so I 'ad to 'ave 'er fetched away, and now she's gorn. An' if yer want to know the truth, lidy, I was 'avin' one with meself to cheer meself up when I 'eard you knockin'."

"You must be feeling very lonely," I said, though he looked exceedingly cheerful.

"So-so. It's lonely, but it's peaceful. There weren't no peace for nobody while she was savin' 'er soul. I tell yer straight, lidy, I wouldn't 'ave saved it if it 'ad been mine. I'd 'ave chucked it away if I couldn't 'ave give it away. It wasn't worth savin', it was such a worry to 'er."

I thought I had better stop this flood of psychology.

"Are the agents near here?" I asked.

"Yus, lidy, just round the bend. But if you'll wait till ter-morrer before you see 'em, I'll chuck a few buckets of water abart the floor and tell 'em the roof's leakin' an' then they'll let it go cheap. I'd like yer to 'ave it, fer I think you an' me 'ud suit each other fine, though I won't deceive yer mum as to me 'avin' bin in quod."

In the face of such frankness, what could I do save tell him that if I took the place the job was his? As a matter of fact, he would probably suit me much better than a woman, for he would be less likely to take fright at my doings.

Well, I bought the place, though not without many qualms, for I am sensitive to atmospheres, and I wondered what sort of atmosphere would be left behind by the homicidal prophet and his suicidal congregation. I could picture so clearly the kind of crack-brained fanatic it must have been who had gathered together the "tidy few" followers for his crazy views and produced the architectural hybrid I proposed to inhabit. Then there were the religious opinions of this nonconformist with a liking for ritual. The Baptist and the Catholic sides of his nature would both hate me equally, but as they would hate me for different reasons, it was possible they might cancel each other out. The moment I had obtained possession I did a thorough exorcism with the Banishing Ritual of the Greater Pentagram. I wondered what Meatyard would think when he smelt the incense, but all he said was:

"You needn't worry about the drines, lidy, for there ain't none,' and this I found to be true, which explained the price at which I got the place. It was just as well that this was low, for I was put to a pretty penny of expense before I was through with it. There is an old saying that whatever is wanted for magical purposes must be bought without haggling, but there is a limit to that sort of thing—I did not haggle over the bathroom however. It was of a very pale pink quartz-like marble as to the walls, and the floor was black marble, warm to the foot because the heating was under it. My bath was black and looked like a tomb, but inside it was of the same pale fawnish pink as the walls. It was square, too, and had to be specially made for me, which was an extravagance, but baths are one of my weaknesses. I got the idea from the prophets dreadful font, though I would never admit it; but Mr Meatyard guessed as much, and said to me with a wink:

"I see you believes in total 'mershun, mum."

"I believe in having what I like," I said.

"Most folk does that, if ye comes ter think of it, only when they gets it, they finds they doesn't like it.

My bedroom I had of the curious blue-green of shagreen, which is also the green of the sea on a rocky coast. It held no furniture save my bed and my dressing-table and a cabinet beside my bed; all else was fitments. Such of the wall as was not mirrors was worked in bas-relief in the semblance of breaking waves. It faced east, as a bedroom should, though I nearly had to tear the place to pieces to get it so, for the non-ecclesiastical accommodation was exiguous. It was only the fact that the prophet had been obliged to provide dressing accommodation for his drowned rats after baptism, that had made the place a practical proposition for me. His vestry was my kitchen, and the places where he separated the sheep from the goats were respectively my bedroom and bathroom. He must have expected mass conversions, for they were of by no means inconsiderable dimensions. For the rest, I lived and moved and had my being in the great hall.

This, as I re-planned it, began to take on a strange and unique beauty. The pitch-pine panelling was replaced with old oak, and dark parquetry covered the cold grey flags. I made no attempt to clean the stonework, which rose in groins to a central boss, the plaster in between, mellowed to the colour of old parchment, still bearing the tarnished shadows of golden stars. All this I left as I found it; but I smashed those dreadful stained-glass windows to pieces and out of their multi-coloured fragments had them re-made into a bewildering mosaic like a Rococo jewel. Into the pointed arches of the chancel I put leaded windows of clear glass through which I could see out into what had been a dingy and cat-haunted dungeon but was now like a corner of an Italian courtyard. I think the architect must have had some Italian church in his mind, for the place responded instantly to figs in great earthenware jars and a vine trained over a trellis.

In the summer I intended to focus my existence in the chancel where the sun came through the leaves of a great plane tree, graceful as a willow because it had never known the pruning-saw; and in the winter I would retire to the panelled ingle-nook surrounding the vast fireplace I had built.

Resisting all blandishments of the builder to buy a ready-made one, I had stood over the masons while they laid a hearth bigger than most folks' dining tables and sloped the back to my liking; and this, with a great copper canopy, was all the grate I had. On it, three-foot logs and a bank of peat blazed in the winter and smouldered in the summer, for the great hall was cool even in the hottest weather. There were deep divans, and great chairs, and low tabourets and poufs, and cabinets to hold my beautiful things and display them; and I had as many cushions as Gabriele d'Annunzio. In the gallery, where the casual visitor could not get at them, were my books.

Not that I had many casual visitors, however, for I had work to do and no time to waste on them, being there for a purpose. Callers were not encouraged, and Mr Meatyard's way of discouraging callers was devastating. Such people as I saw, I saw for a reason, and they knew it.

Mr. Meatyard himself was wonderful, once the problem of his hat was solved. He was bald as the proverbial egg, and explained, most reasonably, that draughts blew on his pate in the winter and the flies walked about on it in summer and he had to have some sort of shelter; so we compromised on a black velvet skull-cap that made him look like a gnome, with his bat-ears and pug-nose, and the effect was very fine indeed, seen against a background of old oak; he was, in fact, the ideal retainer for such a person as myself, with a reputation for vampiricism to maintain, and no one could tell from the looks of him that he had been a cab-driver. He also developed, under my tuition, into a most admirable cook.

It was a strange ménage. There was I, with my cab-driver and my cooking, tucked away in an abandoned chapel in a Surrey-side alley, yet even priestesses of strange cults have to live while they are in incarnation, and there are stranger cults than mine.

My establishment sounds simple, and so it was in its fastidious way;

but it took time to equip, for I would not go to the big stores and order this and that, but picked up my things as I found them from queer small shops in side-streets of mean parts, for there one finds strange and beautiful things if one knows where and how to look, and what to look for. Heavy Victorian mahogany covered with knobs and curly-cues is one thing, and the same piece, denuded of its trimmings and lacquered and dusted with gold, is another. Little by little I got my new home together, while living in my old one, but it was late summer before I moved in.

That moving-in was something of an ordeal. I am, as I have already said, very sensitive to atmospheres. I had performed an efficacious banishing and the place was inoffensive, but it was as devoid of personality as outer space. I had had many picnic meals in it while the workmen were still in possession, but that is not the same as entering in and living there, as I was very soon to learn.

Mr Meatyard remained in his cottage, so I had the whole building to myself, and it was like being sealed up in a vacuum jar. I have never known anything so strange. I think one would feel like that when flying a single-seater plane across the Atlantic—I must have done a very effectual banishing. Luckily for me, it was a lovely day of sun and breeze when I left my hayloft for the last time and drove my new car, a smart black coupé, across the bridge to take up my transpontine existence. If it had been wet and cold I do not think I could have borne it.

As it was, although Mr Meatyard made me a marvelous meal such as only a man accustomed to cooking on a shovel over a bucket of coke could have prepared, and although, despite the warmth of the day, peat and cedar were softly flickering on my hearth, I fled forth from that place as dusk drew on as if pursued by furies, and took refuge on the wharf to watch the the last of the sunset.

The sun was already below the roofs of Pimlico across the river, for here the bend of the stream took it north and south and there was a sky-line against the sunset that reminded me of the Andes. The river to mid-stream already lay in the shadow of the dusk, indigo-blue; but under the Surrey bank it flamed in every shade of orange and the ripples caught the light like tumbled jewels. A barge coming down with the tide, black against the gold, contrived, with its high deck cargo, to look like a gigantic gondola. I sat down on a great balk of timber, the water lapping beneath my feet under the rotten planking, and watched the glory fade and the night come on.

In that deceptive light the sordidness was gone from the mean streets of Pimlico; their irregular roofs and twisted chimneys stood out against the paling sky in jagged silhouette, modernist, startling; then, with the waning of the light and the coming of the mist, they slowly blurred till their serrated skyline became soft folded uplands fading into hills. The lamps in Grosvenor Road grew brighter as the dusk came on, and threw long glittering lines of light across the darkening water; but they never grew very bright, for their part of the world was neither busily commercial nor smartly fashionable. The houses facing the river were old and high, and the light of the street did not reach above their first floors; but presently the dark irregular line of their cliff-like façade began to be picked out here and there with squares of yellow light as rooms were lit up, their occupants not troubling to curtain the windows that looked river-wards.

Then I noticed that across one pair of windows on a top floor, that had been among the last to light up, something moved as regularly as a pendulum. I wondered what manner of manufacture was being pursued up there at that hour, but suddenly the rhythm was broken as the square of one window was blocked, and I saw the outline of a man's head and shoulders against the light, and I guessed that an individual who had been pacing his room was now leaning his elbows on the window-sill and contemplating the river. That it was a man, I was certain, for no woman paces a room like that, and I wondered whether it was my red-headed, tempestuous friend, whom I had so nearly run over. It was about the situation of his house and that restless pacing was just the sort of thing he would do.

My mind went back to the man as I had seen him. His image was very clearly printed on my memory, as it is apt to be in such circumstances, for it had been a near thing, very near indeed, and only the fact that he was as active as a cat in spite of his thickset build had prevented it from being a very nasty accident, and I was not surprised that he had lost his temper with me, for I must have scared him very thoroughly.

He was a middle-aged man, with the pallid face of an indoor worker; the red hair on his bull-dog head was greying slightly and receding at the temples; his face was much lined, with the two upright lines between the eyebrows that indicate nervous tension, and the deeply-scored lines from the angle of the nostril to the corner of the jaw that indicate irritability, yet his deep-set eyes, startled wide open under their heavy brows, were candid and bright as a child's, and he did not look an ill-natured man. He impressed me rather as an over-strained, embittered man than a bad-tempered one, though I have no doubt he would be none the pleasanter to live with on that account. His clothes were good, but old and carelessly worn, and though he carried the brown leather despatch case of a professional man, his double-breasted blue reefer suit did not point to the professions, nor did his slouch hat. Yet when he lifted it there appeared a forehead as broad and high as most folks' top hats, and the hand with which he grasped my door to recover his balance was a most beautiful and beautifully tended hand, broad and square, even as he was, yet with a sensitive suppleness in its muscularity that one sees in the hands of great pianists, which, contrary to popular belief are never slender and long-fingered.

That angry, bull-dog face with its marvellous brow was vaguely familiar to me, and I should not be surprised if I had seen it, and should see it again, in the illustrated papers, for a man with a head and hands like that could not be a nonentity and might quite well be a somebody for all his careless dress and unfashionable abode.

I sat on in the warm dusk, watching him pace his room, perfectly certain in my own mind that the restlessly pacing man and the one I had nearly run over were one and the same person, and wondering what experience of life it was that had graved those lines on his face and turned him into a restless tiger. For a woman with my experience of men it was not difficult to guess—that man had a sex problem, and a bad one. The untended clothes; the two rooms on the top floor of an obvious lodging-house, where he was probably a permanency; the rigid line of the close-held mouth, all told the same story. I suddenly saw him as a man living apart from his wife from no fault of his and making no compromise with his conscience. That poverty was not his problem was obvious from the fact that his clothes were good, though carelessly worn; he had, moreover, an air of being sure of himself that does not go with failure. That the situation was due to no fault of his I deduced from the rigid mouth and steady eyes—there was a man with a terrific sense of duty. Perhaps he had overdone the duty—women are strange things and do not always esteem a man for his virtues—yet I judged that a man with hands like that would not be impervious to feeling—on the contrary, he would be highly sensitive. Add that, then, to the vitality indicated by his quick, alert movements and the driving force obviously caged up in that rugged, stocky physique, and one had the explanation of the lined face and angry, unhappy eyes.

And this brought me back to my own problem, not a personal one, for I have no personal ones, but the problem presented to me by my work—I had, through my own life experience, to find the solution for just such

61

tangles as were represented by that man. Straight, I felt sure of that, but frustrated by the circumstances of his life from all natural and decent human outlet, and frustrated because he was straight. What could one say to such a man? Tell him to run crooked? It probably wouldn't solve his problem if he did, and he was quite likely so placed that he daren't. It was a tragic problem, and one towards the solution of which, a religion that preaches the gospel of love offers no useful suggestions, unless we count counsels of perfection as useful suggestions.

Yet what suggestions had I, who am a pagan, to offer, that would be any more useful? For the man had to live in a Christian country and face the consequences of the wrath of the meek if he were caught transgressing, and Mr. Gladstone said, I believe it was in '84, that there is nothing more dreadful than being chased by a mad sheep; and he ought to know, for he was the great apostle of middle-class evangelical righteousness.

Between the Scylla of chastity and the Charybdis of promiscuity our much-suffering modem Ulysseses have to steer their way. A noted authority on the subject once gave a lecture on the limits of promiscuity. Personally I should have thought there were no limits when you once start that game. Equally, apparently, there are no limits to chastity, when once you start that game, either. For myself, I have always been of the opinion that the real secret of life lies in knowing when to stop, whether you are inclining to the right hand or to the left.

Yet supposing I were to come forward as priestess of nature and point out that it was possible to have too much of a good thing, what sort of a hearing would I get? Would I not simply defeat my own ends? How wise had been Those who sent me when They said: "Do not preach the Law but exemplify it."

A cold breeze had sprung up with the dusk, and there seemed little point in sitting any longer on the bollard. I had got to face my new abode some time, and the sooner it was done, the sooner it would be over. There seemed little point in watching the man across the water any longer, either; he was still at his tiger pacing and seemed to have settled down to make a night of it. It was fortunate for me that the full moon had by now come clear of the housetops, for the wharf was unlit, and its rotting timbers were no place for my thin slippers.

I walked slowly down the length of the little street. Warm as the evening was, every window was decorously curtained. Behind one of them somebody was laboriously practising a hymn-tune on a harmonium. I wondered what kinds of lives were led there amid the aspidistras, and whether they harboured human beings who chafed against the restrictions of their circumstances and longed for a life that was denied them. There is always a generation's difference between a country's intelligentsia and its average, and another generation between the great centres of population and the provinces; and yet another between the provinces and the remote parts; so there is always close on a century of social conditions being lived out in the land at one and the same time; so it might well be that the general run of the folk behind those close-shut windows were smugly content, thanking God they were not as other men whose doings were chronicled in the Sunday papers; but it was probable, on the law of averages, that out of the twenty-odd houses even in that short street there was one whose curtains shrouded a little private hell.

As I turned to close the heavy door behind me, I looked down the length of the street and out across the water, and it seemed to me that even through the thickening river-mist I could still see the light in an upper window being passed and repassed by a restless shadow. Then I shot the heavy bolts and turned away and entered the great hall.

I paused with a flange of the double doors in either hand and looked within. Through the high, uncurtained eastern window the full moon was shining. The stained glass of the upper window glowed dimly with a shadowy glittering like the light in a black opal; through the clear glass of the line of windows that now filled the lower arches the moonlight came clearly and threw the sharp shadows of their leaded panes on to the piled cushions of the wide window-seats. A pale Persian rug lay on the dark polished floor, and in its centre stood a Moorish inlaid table on which was a broad and shallow glass bowl wherein water-lilies were floating. The moonlight fell full on this, and a spot of bright light focussed in the curve of the glass. The lilies lay colourless on the silver surface of the water, but underneath there were strange gleams of golden fire. I stood watching this softly-glimmering bowl across the wide hall, and being raised by the altar steps, it was on a level with my eyes. And as I watched, it seemed to me that mist was rising from the surface of the water and floating upwards like smoke in still air, and that within the mist there was a Light. Then I knew that all was well, for the power had come down; Isis was indwelling the temple I had prepared for Her, and in the language of the initiates, I was on my contacts.

CHAPTER
SIX

It is a strange thing this question of contacts. I have told how my dwelling was as empty as outer space, and my soul as desolate as if I were astray between the stars. I went out, and all unthinking, went towards water, and returning, all unthinking, gazed at water, and lo! I was onto my contacts and power was pouring in, for these things always come through living channels and never by themselves. It was the change in me that made Isis come in, and not any change in Isis; yet Isis reached me through the water.

I left the windows uncurtained to the moon, but went over and stirred the smouldering fire into flame, for I was cold from the river mists, and there is little doubt that one has to supply the basis for all manifestations that come to one, and it depletes. I was cold and tired, and very glad that coffee in a copper pan stood among the embers. I drank it, and lighting a cigarette, lay back among the cushions of a deep chair, resting and watching the fire.

Now the moon and water are after the nature of women, but fire is after the nature of man, and as I gazed into the fire I thought of the man across the water. Then I pulled myself together. This will not do, I thought; I shall pick that man up telepathically if I go on like this. So resolutely dismissing him from my mind with a banishing gesture, I turned my thoughts onto my work and settled down to meditation.

I had got my place of working, and had got it contacted, and now my problem was to find the people who should work with me. I who had hitherto always had to rely on myself had now got to rely on other people, and this galled me. I was so accustomed to knowing that I had only to make the right conditions in myself and everything would follow, that it gave me a most unnerving sense of insecurity to realise that I was dependent upon other people's discernment, dedication, courage, or the lack of these, and in operative occultism nerve is everything. The factor of free will came in with the introduction of other actors in the drama, and the fact that I had made my own soul ready was not enough.

The thing I have always feared most in occult work is loss of nerve in the people I am working with. Treachery is quickly dealt with; inexperience does not matter if there is dedication; but loss of nerve is a thing that no one can cope with, and one that is not always easy to foresee. Those who promise most, often perform least when it comes to the point; one is used to that. The "brittle intellectuals who snap beneath a strain" are the ordinary stock-in-trade of "advanced" circles; one is used to them. But what is one to do with a person who appears to be free from inhibitions and then suddenly wings back to his childhood's faith? Back he goes to his mother's knee, and the age of reason is over for that incarnation. "Give me a child till he is seven," said Ignatius of Loyola, "and anyone who likes can have him afterwards." That grim saint seemed proud of the fact, but in my opinion it is nothing to boast about any more than that you have pulled the wings off a fly. For, after all, if a middle-aged person takes a child of seven and forces his own views on him, what chance has that child got of adapting to the changing conditions of life as the years go by? He starts life a generation behind the times, and by the time he is mature he is two generations behind the times. It is a grim business, this righteousness, and if we were not so used to it we would soon see the sort of Moloch we had got. I would carve over the door of every church and chapel in the land the words of Cromwell, himself a deeply religious man: "I beseech you, in the bowels of Christ, conceive it possible you may be mistaken", but I do not believe there is a church or a chapel in all the length and breadth of the land that would let me do so.

Probably the man walking the floor across the water was wrestling with inhibitions rammed into him before he was seven. For, after all, if his own wife wouldn't live with him, why shouldn't he live with somebody else's wife whose husband wouldn't live with her, and have a new deal all round and make everybody happy and comfortable? It would all be so simple if it were uncomplicated by the property value we attach to sex and the magical value we attach to virginity, both of which are irrational taboos judged by any standard except the sentimental ones. People break them, and as long as they do not get found out, nothing happens, any more than it happens when the savage, driven by hunger, eats a fish in which is the soul of his ancestor. Yet his tribe, if they learn of it, will drive him out into the wilderness to die; or his own conscience may hound him to his doom. We can see the mote in the eye of our Polynesian brother, but the beam in our own is the pillar of the temple.

There was nothing for me to do but watch and wait. I could not go and find the people I wanted; I had to wait for them to find me. This I knew they would do because I was sounding the call of Isis, vibrating it on the Inner Planes as a wireless operator sounds his key-call. Those who were on my wave-length would soon be picking it up, and then curious combinations of circumstances would do the rest. They would come from the ends of the earth like homing pigeons, picking up the call subconsciously and not knowing what it was that drew them. Then I should be faced by the problem of explaining myself to their conscious minds, for the conscious mind is often widely at variance with the subconscious mind. This was not going to be easy, for that which I had set out to do was so alien from ordinary concepts as to appear incomprehensible or even insane at first sight, and people fear what they do not understand. I have been greatly feared in my time, and it is only one remove from being hated. Some explanation, therefore, I must give if what follows is to be comprehensible.

I have made no secret of the fact that I am a pagan and worship Isis, which is but another name for Nature; in saying this, I do not deny the One God, the source of all being, for Nature is God made manifest; but I think there is a time for spiritual things and a time for natural ones, and we make a mistake when we overdo the spiritual. People observe this precept in practice, though they are afraid to say so; but I am not afraid to say so.

I place my trust in Nature and regard it as holy, and I represent it to myself under the glyph of Great Isis whose symbol is the moon. The cult of Great Isis I believe I have served down through the ages, and my task today is to stand for Nature against those who blaspheme Her and so wrong themselves.

But the herd-mind is ignorant and ruthless and powerful, and we who would return to Great Nature, the All-Mother, are driven down into the catacombs for our worship; and it seemed to me that, at the time of which I speak, my special task was to show the hidden way down into the catacombs—the way of the inward-looking eye, the psychic way through onto the inner planes where the worship could be conducted in safety and the worshippers escape the wrath of the mob. This we call the Door Without a Key, which is also the Door of Dreams; Freud found it, and he used it for the coming forth by day; but we who are initiates use it for going forth by night. I regret that I must speak in riddles concerning these things, but not otherwise can they be spoken of, and this book is full of riddles, anyway, so one more or less will not make much difference.

But to return to practical matters—I wished to work magic, and for this I had to have help, for the magical organisation is a pyramidal structure—at the apex the godhead on the inner planes, and on the physical earth, two to bring through the power—Shakta and Shakti, as the Hindus call them, and Shakti, be it remembered, equates with Isis. They understand these things in the East, but in the West the knowledge had been lost with the break-up of the Mysteries; but I knew these things, for I remembered the Mysteries.

I, who represented the Goddess, had to meet one who would be Her priest; then the work could begin and all else would follow. This was the first step, and the most difficult, for I could do nothing in the matter save make ready the place and wait. Isis would choose Her own priest.

So the days went by. Summer had passed into autumn, and autumn was sliding into a delayed winter, for it was marvellously mild for the time of year. I had come to love my new home but its furnishing was now finished and I no longer had occasion to rake the byways for lovely old oddments, so time began to hang heavily on my hands. I had not yet been able to bring myself to proceed with the preparation of my secret temple, where the really important part of my work would be done. The inspiration would not come; so knowing that it is useless to force these things, I set it aside and waited. The thrones, the cubical altar, the couch for trance and the great mirror for the mirror-working I already possessed, and I had some of the magical instruments, too, but nothing was consecrated.

I was doing a great deal of study, but the solitary working was wearisome and I was becoming unpolarised. No magician can work long alone. My chief amusement was watching the floods, for the river, when in flood, was a magnificent elemental being. I missed the open spaces and solitude to which I was accustomed and which were so necessary to me, and I disliked having people always about me and never being able to get away from them. I began to take my walks at night, and in fogs and bad weather, for then I often had the Embankment almost to myself. I would cross by Lambeth bridge, and walk to Blackfriars and back. Policemen used to shake their heads over me when I loomed up in my black mackintosh cape, and warn me of the awful fate in store for me if I persisted in perambulating at such unfashionable hours and in such inauspicious circumstances, but I have no nerves in such matters. I possess no valuables in the burglar's sense of the word, and walk faster than most, so I offer no temptation to the prowling bag-snatcher and very little to the prowling satyr, who is usually a person with a poor wind. Prowling satyrs, in my opinion, are vastly overrated as a source of danger to sensible women. No man risks a snub if he is sober, and if he is not, he can run neither far, fast nor straight.

However, before the light summer evenings arrived, I was to have an experience that looked as if it were going to make me review my opinions in these matters, for I began to be aware, in that intuitive subconscious way in which one is aware of such things, that I was being followed from time to time. There is a sensitive spot on the nape of the neck, as every psychic knows, and if any one stares hard at it, one feels it. I had been vaguely uneasy on several occasions, but had not paid much attention, going on the principle that a cat may look at a king, and that as long as the individual concerned did not make himself an active nuisance, he had as good a right to the City of London as I had. I knew better than to look over my shoulder, but contented myself with giving my pursuer a run for his money, and if he arrived home as hot as I did, it must have done him a lot of good.

Nevertheless, the repetition of the incident had more effect on me than I was willing to admit. Moreover, the prolonged inactivity and solitude were telling on me. I could not understand why my work should be held up thus when everything was ready on the physical plane; my self-confidence began to be shaken, and in magic self-confidence is everything. I caught myself wondering whether I was self-deluded, and though I destroyed the thought as soon as it arose, it was not a good sign that it should have arisen. I found I was becoming over-sensitised by the abnormal conditions of my life, and the individual who had annoyed me by following me on the Embankment had got woven into the fabric of my dreams. I was dreaming more frequently, too, than was my wont, and though my dreams were of scenery, and perfectly innocuous, I was not pleased to find that the feeling of being followed persisted in them, even though I had no fear of my uninvited companion, whether in the flesh or in the imagination. Nevertheless I felt that something must be done in the matter. It did not do to let one's mind get out of hand like this, especially in such work as I was doing, so I determined to make a start on the task that I had hitherto postponed, and get my secret temple into working order.

As I have said before, it was necessary for me to have a place for magical working that should be kept for that purpose and nothing else, and into which no one not concerned in that working should set foot. There was a good-sized cellar under the building in which the heating apparatus had been installed; it was much larger than was needed for this purpose, so I decided to get it partitioned off and use the inner part for my magical temple.

I sent for the builder to come and look at it and give me an estimate, and Mr. Meatyard, stoking the boiler, leant on his shovel and listened to what was going on, for he regarded himself as absolutely one of the family, as in fact he was, for that little man knew a lot more in his intuitive way than any one would have given him credit for. After the builder had put up his note-book and departed, my gentleman char approached me in a mysterious manner, as if he were inviting me to participate in a crime, and whispered huskily:

"As it ever occurred to you, mum, that there's a lot o' waste space in this place?"

"No," I said, "it had not struck me."

"It's square outside, ain't it? Well, it ain't square inside." And then I remembered that the hall itself was considerably higher than the chancel, as high again, to be precise; consequently there must be, over the chancel, a room of approximately the same size. This was indeed a gift from the gods if we could locate the entrance to it, but I was not minded to go burrowing about the building at random, like the explorers of the Great Pyramid, for my abode had not been built by the Pharaohs, and I doubted if it would stand such treatment. However Mr. Meatyard had his views on that point also, and directed me to the cupboard in the corner of my bedroom, which had once been the women's dressing room, and we found, as he had long suspected, that it had a false back.

Mr. Meatyard fetched the chopper with which he split the kindling and smashed the flimsy matchboarding to splinters and revealed a dusty stair going up into darkness. We went up it, and came, as expected, into a room over the chancel, a perfectly inhabitable place, with a fireplace and cobwebbed window, scantily (though no doubt adequately) furnished with an old double bed and a quantity of bottles.

"I allus reckoned," said Mr. Meatyard, "that nobody could 'ave bin as good as 'e looked."

But this was not all. In the corner was another cupboard. Mr. Meatyard tapped its back.

"Same as before," he said. "Shall we 'av it out?"

Out it came, and again there was a stair winding up into darkness.

"Didn't trust nobody, 'e didn't," said my retainer, and led the way up. We found ourselves in what was obviously the space beneath the lantern, but whereas it should have contained no more than the pitch of the roof, there were ten-foot walls before the pitch started. It was windowless, and floor, walls, beams and everything were all painted jet black.

"Well, I dunno wot 'e thought 'e was playin' at," said Mr Meatyard, surveying this spot in perplexity. I knew, however—he was playing at the same thing I was playing at.

We descended from this not particularly well-omened retreat, and I for one was glad to get back to the normal light of day. There was something about the prophets antics that had left a bad smell behind. The difference between his paganism and my paganism was the difference between Priapus and Pan.

I had Mr. Meatyard sweep the place out, and burn the bed, and then I did an exorcism and a thorough one. The room over the chancel would do to hold magical equipment, which is bulky, and would also serve as a robing-room, and the octagonal apartment under the lantern would be the temple. I had a good deal of gear already, brought over from my flat and stored in the gallery, and Mr. Meatyard and I got it up those narrow stairs between us, for I did not desire the intrusion of any strangers in this matter.

"Cor, mum, yer' strong!" he murmured, mopping his streaming brow after we had lifted the big mirror into position.

So we got everything into position. The black walls needed nothing but varnishing to give them a lustre. Upon the black floor I put a heavy black carpet to deaden sound in the room below. From the central boss hung the bronze lamp of a mosque, bearing the Perpetual Light, and under it stood the cubical altar that represents the universe. At the angle opposite the door I placed the great mirror for the mirror-working, and between it and the altar was my long, narrow black couch like a bier for the trance work and meditation, flanked on either side by the Pillars of Equilibrium, the black and the silver pillars. Round the seven sides were the symbols of the seven planets; the eighth side, where was the door, represents the Element of Earth and is without a symbol, for we leave earth behind when we enter into the cosmic temple. That was all, save for the two thrones on low platforms that faced each other across the breadth of the room with the altar between them, and which are used for working in polarity. On the altar were the Elemental Weapons governing Earth, Air, Fire and Water, and in front of the mirror hung the symbol of the Goddess—a lunar crescent with the horns upwards. It was all very simple—no magical names or numbers, and save for the planetary symbols, no colours save black and silver—just the essentials of ceremonial magic minus all the trappings that are needed to impress the imagination of those who do not know what magical working really is. Then I sent for a friend to come and help me with the consecration.

She came, and was greatly intrigued and frankly envious, openly lamenting that the exigencies of family life prevented her from discovering derelict churches and derelict cabmen and dedicating her life to the pursuit of occultism.

I am always greatly amused at the manner in which outsiders expect the mysterious adept of the occult Orders to live their lives. They seem to think the bow is always bent. If it is, they may take it from me that it is a fake—a theatrical property, such as little Cupid's twang in a pantomime. A good bow has a forty pound pull, even in archery, and the tension on the whole being that launches the magical arrow is very much more than the psychic equivalent of forty pounds. Is any one going to pose with *that* bow bent for all his days and nights? It cannot be done. Something would snap. So I go in for cooking as a fine art and make my own clothes, for it has always been a tradition for the initiates to be craftsmen, a tradition that lives on even amid the Lost Secrets of modern Masonry.

It is a great temptation to use the facile short cuts of technical terms, but if I said that my friend and I started work on the building of the astral temple, it would convey nothing. Let me therefore explain what we did and why we did it. I cannot answer for what other occultists do, especially in fiction; nor do I always know why they do it, and I sometimes doubt if they do either; I can only answer for myself and those of my own Tradition.

First of all, the place of magical working is a place set apart and concealed, for no one must know where it is because it is vulnerable to thought. Secondly, it has to be equipped with the symbols used in the working and nothing else, because it is a place where the mind has to concentrate. Thirdly, it has to have the astral temple built over it, and that is the really important part; and this is how we do it—we sit down and imagine it—nothing more—*but*—it is the imagination of a trained mind!

So we sat down, my friend and I, in that dark octagonal room up in the pitch of the roof, and we pictured the temple of Isis as we had known it near the Valley of the Kings in the great days of the cult. We pictured it in its broad outline, and then we pictured it in all its detail, describing what we saw till we made each other see it more and more clearly. We pictured the approach through the avenue of ram-headed sphinxes; the great pylon gate in the temenos wall; the court with its lotus pool; shadowed colonnades, and the great hall with its pillars. All these we pictured just as they have been in every temple of the Goddess from time immemorial. And as we did this, alternately watching and describing—the fantasied scenes began to take on the semblance of objective reality and we found ourselves in them—no longer looking at them with the mind's eye, but walking about in them. After that there was no more effort of concentration for the astral vision took charge. We had gone up the avenue of sphinxes, and under the great pylon, and across the court of the lotus pool in our imagination, but we passed through the bronze doors into the great hall in actuality.

Overhead hung the lamp of perpetual light that is in every temple of the Mysteries. Underfoot was the circle of the Zodiac inset in the marble. At the far ends of the long hall the high seats of the priests gleamed faintly, opposite us the heavy folds of a curtain concealed the holy of holies; beside it, hidden in the recess of the arch, was a sloping passage-way that led underground from this temple to another—a temple in the distant hills, cut out like a tomb from the living rock, and down this passage the water for the lotus pool ran in a conduit, for there was a spring in that underground temple. It was a temple of a more ancient faith than ours, being pre-dynastic. It must, I think, have belonged to the black Hamitic people who preceded the red Egyptian stock, for its Goddess was of black basalt and Her features were negroid. Before Her great knees was a table altar, and there was a channel in it to take the blood, which showed that it had been used for sacrifice, and as it was of the size of a man, we knew what sacrifices it had been used for. This temple had fallen into desuetude in my day, and though there was a tradition of its existence, its entrance was lost beneath the sand and no way in remained save the underground passage known only to the senior priesthood, who knew, too, that it was back in these dark and crude beginnings that the roots of our cult drew their sustenance. It was in this temple that the higher priests were made, but still fewer knew that.

The great floor of the hall stood empty, but we of the temple knew that it was not empty, for here the astral form of the mummified Isis lay as in a sarcophagus. We took our places on the thrones, my friend and I, she down at the far end on the left, and I on the high dais to the right, as befitted my status, and sitting there in the darkness, we watched, in a vision within a vision, the mummified form of Great Isis become visible.

Then, that part of the work finished, I said to my friend: "Shall we go to the Black Temple?"

She nodded her acquiescence, and I came down from the dais and joined her before the low entrance to the underground passage. But even as I put out my hand to raise the curtain, we realised simultaneously that we were not alone.

I said to my friend:

"Do you see anything?"

"Yes," she said. "One of the priests is here."

"Can you see who it is?" said I, for she was a better psychic than I was.

"I think it is the sacrificial priest," she said.

Now the sacrificial priest would have been entitled to come with us to the Black Temple, for that was where his work lay; but he was a grim and sinister figure, and we did not particularly want him. The sacrificial priests were always priests who had committed some serious crime and who were given the chance of expiating it thus. They were shunned by the other priests, though by virtue of their office they stood high in the hierarchy; so though we did not want the company of the sacrificial priest, we could not refuse him, for he had as good a right to go to the Black Temple as we had, who were high priestesses.

But as soon as we began to descend the stairs we knew there was something wrong.

"That isn't the sacrificial priest," said my friend. "It is someone's astral projection. You haven't got this place properly sealed."

Now I pride myself on my sealings. What I exorcise is exorcised, and stays exorcised, and I was a little inclined to be annoyed at this, for I could have sworn the seals were on. Privately I thought that she had been guilty of mind-wandering, and had thought of someone, and so called him up. She apparently thought the same of me, for she said:

"Did you get any break in your concentration?"

"I did not," I said curtly, for this was impudence, I being very much her senior.

"Well, he has to do with you not me," she said. "Have you given anyone leave to come into the temple?"

"No one," I replied.

"Do you think it is someone you intend to work with? For if you had been thinking about inviting him, even if you had not actually done it, if he is a good psychic, he might have sensed it and been able to come in. As a matter of fact," she went on, "I got the impression that there was someone already here when we came into the Hall of the Sphinxes. I thought I saw someone kneeling and worshipping in front of the Holy of Holies."

"That is unlikely," I answered; for although the populace would kneel like that, a priest wouldn't, and no one but a priest could do the astral projection. My friend admitted the improbability, and we left the mystery unsolved and went down to the supper Mr. Meatyard had left for us in the great hall.

That night I dreamed, and dreamed with extraordinary vividness, that I was walking over rolling grey hills with the sea away below cliffs on my right. I was alone at first, and was enjoying my dream, when it suddenly occurred to me that I might dream of my unknown pursuer, and even as the thought passed through my mind—a dream within a dream— I thought I heard footsteps behind me, and for the first time I knew fear. I quickened my pace, and soon found myself flying over the ground in a nightmarish effort to escape, but I could hear my pursuer coming up behind, drawing nearer and nearer. I completely lost my head, but even in my panic I knew that my pursuer was not evil, and yet I fled in fear and would not let myself be overtaken. For a moment it seemed to me that the dream was beginning to turn into vision and I was about to learn something very important, when my pursuer put forth a sudden effort and caught up with me, and I felt his hand take hold of a fold of my cloak.

I woke, bathed in perspiration, with the sound of my own scream in my ears.

To rid myself of the horrible atmosphere left behind by this incubus I got out of bed and went into the great hall where the remains of our supper still lay on the table, drank what was left of the milk and ate a sandwich, for there is nothing like food to close the psychic centres. The nightmarish feeling wore off. It was a warm night, and I went and sat in the window, watching the moon.

I was very perplexed. All was not well with my work, I knew that. First the long delay, which showed I was off my contacts, and then the repeated penetrating of my sphere of sensation by an intruder. That it was no subconscious fantasy was shown by the fact that my friend had also perceived the presence of an intruder. I made up my mind that I would go away for a holiday, and go away at once.

But next day, when I tried to put my resolution into practice, there was a most curious subconscious blocking and resistance within myself, so I abandoned it. There was more in the situation than I realised, I saw that; but there was nothing I could do save wait for it to clarify.

I had been over a year now in my place of working, and had somehow settled down to accept my vigil as a matter of course. The police too had accepted my nocturnal habits as a matter of course, and for some time past, though I still dreamt of him at intervals, I had seen nothing of my pursuer. Then, one night of fog, I knew he was behind me again. I hastened, but could not throw him off, for there was no traffic to delay him at the crossings. Once, in fact, I felt him almost at my elbows as I paused on an island for a gap in the traffic; this was more than he had ever dared to do before, and if I had seen one of my policemen friends I should have stopped and spoken to him. My pursuer, however, evidently thought also that he had gone too far, and dropped behind, though I was certain he was still there, and when I came to cross Lambeth Bridge, I knew he was there, for I could distinctly hear his footsteps behind me. It was not too pleasant, being followed like that across the foot-bridge in thick fog, for both banks were invisible, and there was nothing to be seen save the swirling leaden water on either hand and the great chains disappearing into darkness overhead. My pursuer's footsteps rang close behind me, drawing steadily closer, and there was not another sound in all the fog-blanketed darkness.

It is very easy to open the higher consciousness in a fog for one is cut off from the world and alone with the elemental powers, and it seemed to me as I went through the darkness with the water beside me, that I was really going down the long underground passage that led to the temple of the Black Isis, and that behind me followed the sacrificial priest. Yet I did not think that he would force me down onto the grim altar he served, but rather that he desired me.

This, of course, may have been that I knew what manner of urge it is that sets men to following women through the streets, even if they mean them no harm; and it seemed to me, in the strange exalted condition which was coming upon me as I fled through the darkness ahead of those pursuing footsteps, that I knew what was in the mind of the man who was following me, and that he would do me no injury, nor were the imaginings of his heart crudely evil. Perhaps I was to him a creature of dream, and he hardly realised there was a woman of flesh and blood under the cloak, to be alarmed by his pursuit.

However, I arrived unmurdered on the Surrey side, and made all speed for home. My way now led through populous streets, and I could not tell whether my pursuer were still on my heels or not, but thought not. I had my latch-key all ready to get the door open quickly, and slipped through into the warm, scented darkness of my home with a sigh of relief. But even as I did so, I felt the door thrust open behind me, and knew that my pursuer had crossed the threshold and was there inside with me, alone in the darkness. I was really badly alarmed then, for I knew that unless I kept my head I was in for an unpleasant, possibly a dangerous, experience. However, I had myself well in hand, and threw my visitor into a complete panic by turning my electric torch full on his face. Imagine my amazement, not to say disgust, when I found that he was none other than the man I had nearly run over that day in Grosvenor Road and who had played so great a part in my imaginings ever since!

I realised immediately, however, that I had been right in my belief that he was not dangerous. I have never seen a man so utterly taken aback and ashamed of himself. I bid him go, and he went like a flash.

I switched on the lights and entered the great hall, feeling rather shaken. It was the fog, I think, that had made the experience so alarming. I was, in fact, much more upset than I had any reason to be, for after all, the man had not been at all formidable at close quarters. Determined to get the taste of the business out of my mouth, I went up the long flights of narrow stairs to my temple up under the lantern. The lamp burnt dimly; I renewed the wick and lay down on the couch to meditate. The astral temple built up vividly and without any effort on my part; there was more power about than I had ever known before, and I saw, clearly as if it were a physical presence, the sacrificial priest lying face downwards on the floor with outspread arms in front of the curtain that shrouded the Holy of Holies.

He had a right to be there, and no banishing of mine could dislodge him, even if I had chosen to do one. I was not pleased by his presence, for that night in particular I wanted the temple to myself, but I had to put up with it. I went up to the throne and took my seat without saluting him, and he too ignored my presence, even if he were aware of it.

I did my best to gather my thoughts together, for I was profoundly disturbed—most unreasonably so, I thought, and the presence of the sacrificial priest was a distraction. I wanted to be rid of him, but there came to me a very strong feeling that I must take no steps to banish him, for he was definitely part of what was afoot. This pleased me even less, for I had the instinctive aversion of the regular priesthood for the sacrificial priests, who are sacerdotal outcasts, belonging to an epoch that has passed away, and only the very advanced members of the priesthood knew their real rôle and significance.

So I accepted the silent presence of the outcast man, and between us there presently began to be established a rapport, a feeling of comradeship, and I disliked his presence less. Then suddenly he rose and came across the temple towards me, and kneeling down at my feet, put his head on my knee in an attitude of utter submission and abandonment. He seemed like a man who was surrendering his self-respect. I laid my hand on the sensitive spot on the nape of the neck and blessed him, and as I did so, I saw that he had greying red hair and was none other than the man I had just turned from my door!

But I had hardly touched him before he was on his feet again and had disappeared like a flash down the stairway leading to the Black Temple. I followed him instantly for I saw that he was insecure in his psychic projection, and what would happen to him if he got into the Temple of the Black Isis and failed to keep his concentration did not bear thinking about. We went down the long gallery beside the water, far too fast, and I found myself in the Black Temple. The man was already there, clasping the great knees of Black Isis in an agony of prayer. At all costs he must be got back into his body again. This would never do; the Black Isis is a terrific force, and how did he come to know his way into Her Temple? I hesitated to make the banishing pentagrams that would break the vision and force him back off the astral plane. Had he the right to be there since he was able to pass the seals I had set on my place of working and come and go apparently at will, or was the fault with me? Had that lurking stranger so shaken my nerve that my own mind-wandering caused his image to be mingled with my vision? I did not know; the vision was out of control, and there was nothing to do but break it.

I sat up on the black couch, badly shaken. It seemed to me that my psychism had become inextricably tangled with my sub-conscious content. I had come up here, to this sealed and consecrated place, for the express purpose of putting the stranger out of my mind, and here he was, part of the vision. I did not like it at all.

I got off the couch, did the circumambulations and banishings again, got the incense going afresh till its clouds filled the whole room to suffocation, and lay down once more on the couch, determined to spend a night of meditation and vigil till I got the whole problem clear and cleared up.

Great Isis built up, the terrible Black Isis, the source of all power, who seldom comes, and only at the great moments. I am used to Her power and received it fearlessly, knowing that in a few seconds She would change into Her beautiful aspect, which is so much more beautiful than anything that can be built under the symbolism of the White Isis, who is always liable to change over into the Black Isis if much power is brought through Her. Therefore we who have knowledge work with the Black Isis and transmute Her.

This I knew, was the big thing, the thing for which I had waited; though why it had delayed so long, and why it had come now, I did not know. Then it suddenly occurred to me that there was a kind of pattern running through my slowly formulating work which I had not observed before. It is well known to those who deal with the hidden side of things that such patterns exist, they are, in fact, caused by the invisible forces with which we work, and when these have been got in hand and are being directed by a planning will, the pattern appears. I knew, therefore, that if I could discern the plan of the pattern, all would be clear. There is a central thread that runs through all these things; find that, and you have the clue.

I know how to look for this thread—one seeks that which recurs and keeps on recurring. In the present instance there was one recurring factor, and one only—the man with the red hair. Like it or not, I had to accept it. I had sought my place of working in vain until I met him face to face—and very nearly offered him up as a sacrifice—and then, after one glance from his angry green-grey eyes, I had gone straight to it. Then I had entered my home and found myself unable to settle down, and had gone out beside the river, and the same man, if it were the same man, had rested his hands on his window-sill and stared at me across the water. It might have been that I was visible to him, for I was wearing a white linen dress against a dark background and the last light was on me; anyway, from that moment I entered into peaceful possession of my new home and the power began to build up. Then, walking behind me on the Embankment, he managed to enter into my dream; but I would not look over my shoulder at this intrusive stranger, and so nothing came through to the physical plane, for it seemed as if that could only happen when eye met eye, and I remembered how all those who work with the unseen forces attach great importance to the glance of the eye.

Finally, in that night of fog he drew close to me, entered my house, met me face to face—and I turned him away like a stray dog.

I remembered vividly the way in which he went—bewildered, confused, ashamed. No, that man knew nothing—nothing consciously, at any rate. But there are more levels of the mind than the conscious one, and I knew that there was both knowledge and power lying latent in him. This was no ordinary man, even so far as the mundane plane was concerned. That fine head and those beautiful hands told me that. Who he was, what he was, I did not know, but that he was "somebody" I knew for certain. This pleased me, for I like achievement.

I wondered, too, how far he knew that there was something afoot. Was I mingling with his dreams even as he was with mine? Did he identify me with the woman who had so nearly run him down and made a casualty of him? If so, his first impressions must have been just as unfavourable as my own. He had thought me a fool, that was obvious; in fact he had said as much; moreover I judged he was one of those men who disapprove of make-up, and I had that day been using coral lipstick and cardinal nail lacquer; my right hand was ungloved, for I was wearing a garnet marquise ring on my forefinger over which no glove would go, and he had had a good view of it, resting on the steering-wheel, as he had laid hold of the door of my car and given me a piece of his mind. Yes, I certainly must have startled the gentleman on every plane of his being!

Then there was the last scene of all—and I wondered whether it was indeed the end of this strange eventful history—the scene within my doorway in the dark, when I flashed my torch in his face and drove him forth, ashamed and disgraced. It would certainly be the last scene of all, and end of the play, unless there were indeed an underlying bond to bind us one to the other, for no man would risk the renewal of such an experience. There would be no more shadowing on the Embankment, I was perfectly certain; in fact the man would run a mile at the sight of me. How, in view of all this, could I make any sort of contact with him, or enter into any sort of rational relationship, let alone explain to him what was afoot and induct him into the part he had to play?

There was only one way I could do it, I knew that; only one way that was safe and right—the true way of the Tradition—I must pick him up psychically on the astral, and let matters work out in their own way on the physical plane. Then I should know that I was on the right track and had made no mistake in my chosen priest. I must sit still and wait—a year—five years—it did not matter; in the end, if he were the chosen man, he would come. The call had to come through to him from the inner planes; it had to work through from his inner consciousness to his outer consciousness and could not be forced; he had to realise it for himself, and God only knew against what resistances of prejudice, convention, preconceived opinions, and even downright fear it would have to prevail, for people are often afraid of Isis.

Very well, I thought, we will pursue the age-old policy—on the outer plane, passivity: on the inner plane—Come!

So I called my priest to me on the inner planes, and on the inner planes he came. He was the sacrificial priest beyond any question. I wondered what history lay behind him and what expiation lay ahead. He came, and he was simply all to pieces. I felt very sorry for that man. He had reached the point when he was at the end of his tether. He was certainly not a man to thank anybody for sympathy, but he was at the end of his tether this man, and he knew it, and I knew it. Unless something were done for him, he would break up completely. Men of his type are like that if their shell is once penetrated.

So I projected by means of the astral projection which takes out so much of the etheric that it is visible even to the non-psychic. It is a dangerous thing to do, especially over water, for water absorbs astral emanations. I projected my mind, clothed in the body of light, to that room across the river I had once seen lit up and crossed and re-crossed by a restless shadow.

Yes, I had not been misled. There was my man right enough; nor had I been mistaken as to his condition.

"This must be coped with," I said to myself, "or I shall not only lose my priest, but hurt and injure this man very badly."

So I set to work, with my knowledge and with my power, I, the priestess of Isis. For my own sake I would not have done it; nor do I think I would even have done it for his sake, for in those days he was nothing to me; but I did it for the sake of Isis because She needed him for Her work.

CHAPTER
SEVEN

I will tell what I did, putting my cards on the table, for it shows how we use the Door Without a Key to escape the Lord of This World, who is Moloch, and take refuge in the Secret Kingdom, which is the dark side of the Moon, the side She turns away from earth.

The Door Without a Key is the Door of Dreams; it is the door by which the sensitive escape into insanity when life is too hard for them, and artists use it as a window in a watch-tower. Psychologists call it a psychological mechanism; magicians call it magic, and the man in the street calls it illusion or charlatanry according to taste. It does not matter to me what it is called, for it is effectual.

I made the astral projection by the usual method; that is to say, I pictured myself as standing six feet in front of myself and then transferred my consciousness to the simulacrum thus created by my imagination and looked at the room through its eyes. Then I visualised the face of the man with the greying red hair, and imagined myself speaking to him. The magic worked. I had the sensation of the descent of a swift lift, which always characterises the change of level of consciousness; all awareness of my physical surroundings faded, and I seemed to be in a strange room; a shabby, untidy, badly lit and ill-tended room, crammed with books and papers in utter disorder. A fire of cheap dull coal smouldered in an old-fashioned grate from which no one had swept the cinders for the last twelve hours. Above it, in the centre of the cluttered mantelpiece, was the photograph of a girl in the fashions of twenty years ago. A girl with a pretty face, foolish eyes and stubborn mouth. If that were the wife, one could understand why the man lived apart from her. The pretty face had caught him; and though she had not had the intelligence to understand life, she had had sufficient strength of will to give effect to her misunderstandings.

The only thing to do with such a woman was to desert her.

Among the débris of a meal a man was working at his papers, concentrating on them. Under such conditions telepathy is impossible. I could read him, however, and knew why he was concentrating with such determined intensity. I knew, too, that despite his efforts, my image kept rising over the horizon of his consciousness, for I kept on feeling my own sense of the reality of the vision suddenly intensify for a second.

"He cannot keep this up for very long," I said to myself. "Between sleeping and waking I will be able to come through to him."

But neither could I keep up the astral projection for very long, and I had to withdraw my consciousness into my physical body and rest for a while before undertaking once more the risky astral journey over water.

Late at night I made the attempt again. As I expected, the man's will-power was failing him. One cannot drive oneself as he was trying to drive himself, by sheer brute force, clean against nature. It cannot be done; and nature, as was to be expected, had risen and rent him in return for so much mishandling.

What was I to do with this man? I hate domination. It is not only all wrong, but quite useless, the inevitable reaction destroying all that has been built. But this was an emergency operation. Something had to be done, and done quickly, for there is a point beyond which the will cannot drive the temperament without damaging it irreparably.

There was but one thing I could do—dominate his will as a hypnotist dominates it and make him see things as I saw them. The risk and responsibility appalled me, but it had to be done if he were not to go under. So I did it—out of compassion and for no other reason.

I made him see me. I impressed my image upon his whirling mind till, torn by emotion as he was, he saw me—and I had the happiness of seeing him gradually grow calm and steady where before he had been threshing himself to pieces. Then, his resistance being lowered on the threshold of sleep, I did what vampires do, and it may be said I am a vampire to do it— I drew off from that man his seething, tormenting vitality till the pressure dropped lower and lower, down to the threshold of depletion. Then I left him asleep, sleeping himself back to normal. He had had a visit from a succubus; whether his imagination presented me to him as fair or foul, I did not know; it would be according to what was really in his heart, apart from all built-up inhibitions.

I returned across the water to my temple; that dangerous journey across running water which absorbs and carries away magnetism and may break up the projection. In my temple, from which the astral forms we build with so much care are never banished, I laid my two hands on the altar and faced the Moon-symbol that hung upon the mirror that is a door-way to another plane, and in the mirror I saw my own reflection with the image of the Great One behind me, and to that shadowy form, built up by the mind, I surrendered the vital force that I had drawn into myself.

I saw Her build up and grow bright, and Her outlines become clear and tangible—the astral form was taking on etheric substance—soon one would have a materialisation.

But that was not what was wanted. Presently, having surrendered to Her my vitality, I felt a return flow begin—Isis was giving of Her magnetism to me now, and I felt myself grow vital, and young, and dynamic, and knew that in me was Her image reflected; knew too, with a painfully clear realisation, that in dealing thus with the man across the water, I had made a link with him that would not easily be broken, and that to him from henceforth I should be Isis. That was a responsibility I had to take and dare not refuse. I knew, too, that I must now take the bold step of seeking him on the physical plane, and turned over in my mind how it could be done.

To cross the bridge and ring his door-bell was not feasible, but that did not trouble me unduly; when there is a link established on the inner planes, it works upon the outer with the minimum of human enterprise. All one has to do is to grasp opportunity as it goes by on the wind. Sometimes it is so tenuous that it can hardly be seen, but it suffices.

I closed down my temple and went to bed. In the dreams that came on the threshold of sleep I saw again the scene at my door when I turned a man away into the fog. It seemed to me that I went after him, trying to find him, entirely forgetful of the fact that he should not follow women in the streets.

I was intensely sorry for him. I knew how ashamed he was, and I wanted to find him and tell him that I had the understanding to know what had happened, and did not place the ordinary interpretation on the incident, and that, despite the unconventional manner of our acquaintance, a bond of sympathy had been forged between us.

It seemed to me that I was in psychic touch with him, and that he, on his side, was visualising me, though under what form of wish fulfilment he represented me to himself I did not know; but I could feel that "virtue had gone out from me" and that there was a psychic flow between us. Of this I was glad, for I had a strong urge to help that man if it were in my power, for I felt I understood him and his twisted nature.

In the morning he was still "on the line," and I had an intuitive feeling that he was a happier and calmer man than he had been for a long time; and then, suddenly, almost with the physical ear, I heard his voice crying out as if he had touched hot iron.

It startled and shook me like a blow on the head. As best I could I concentrated on him and coped with him till I felt him quiet down; but the experience left me shaken and upset, and all through the morning and the rest of the afternoon I kept a psychic hand on him for fear of what would happen next.

That afternoon I had occasion to visit my dentist for the annual overhaul by which even such strange mortals as I render unto Caesar the things that are Caesar's. Turning over the ancient illustrated papers in his waiting-room I suddenly saw, looking out at me from among the society beauties and sporting loungers, a face of a very different type.

He had obviously had his hair cut for the occasion of the photograph, but except for that, he was the same, even to his reefer jacket and soft-collared shirt, as he had been when I flashed my electric torch in his eyes and turned him from my door, and in the letterpress I read his history.

He had involved himself in a controversy with some anti-vivisectionists—he looked a controversial individual—and they had all ended up in the law-courts for libelling each other. The decision had gone in his favour, for both the claim and the counter-claim, but the judge had bidden him mend his manners.

As I had thought, he was a very eminent person, a doctor with an international reputation. He looked rather a brute, I thought, but I remember seeing another expression in his eyes when startled out of his self-possession. He had looked more like a lost and wandering soul then than a famous scientist; but perhaps the two are not incompatible, nor so far apart as we are led to believe by their pontifical utterances.

I considered the sidelight thrown on his temperament by the fact that a man in his position had turned aside to quarrel vituperatively with people who were not worth powder and shot, and guessed that repressions were being worked off at their expense. The damages he had received for being libelled he had given to his hospital; as a matter of fact, he had in all probability not suffered the slightest damage, but his opponents, being humanitarians, had been particularly ruthless in their onslaughts, and an exasperated jury had made them pay for their lapse from good sense and good manners. The whole business was an abuse of the process of the courts in any case, and the judge had said as much.

So that, I thought, looking at the bull-dog head that glowered back at me from the glossy page—so that is the man to whom I have got to represent Isis!

There was more biography than dentistry done when my turn came to occupy the chair. I mentioned to my dentist that I had recognised, in one of his illustrated papers, the portrait of a man I had nearly run over

86

in the Grosvenor Road, and the floodgates of reminiscence were opened. It was even as I had thought.

Dr. Rupert Annesley Malcolm, M.D., DSc., F.R.C.P., to give him his principal distinctions—he had many others, foreign and honourary—was a man of enormous scientific prestige and complete social non-existence. His irritable temper, his brusque manners, his mean lodgings—were traditional among generations of medical students. His extreme generosity, his absolute integrity and selflessness, his enormous capacity for work and his courage in tackling abuses and pricking bubble reputations had a smaller audience among men of his own calibre—my dentist spoke of him with respect but without enthusiasm. Of his private history he knew nothing save that he was the son of a Presbyterian minister; that his wife was an invalid residing at the seaside; that he was reputed to make a colossal income and spend it all on research—he certainly did not spend it on himself. My informant doubted the colossal income, although Dr. Malcolm had had some very eminent patients, for he was notoriously indifferent to money, and money is not made by those who are indifferent to it. Anyway it was probable that he had an income more than adequate to his solitary way of life.

Such were the bulletins to date. After the session was concluded I supplemented them from the Medical Directory and found how very eminent Dr. Malcolm really was, and wondered still more what the crazy idiot was doing, chasing me along the Embankment. It was the very last sort of adventure in which a man in his position ought to have involved himself. If he must, he should, for his own sake, do it a trifle more discreetly—and then, from the very indiscretion of his doings I realised that he was not in the habit of doing that sort of thing.

I rang up the telephone number given in the directory and made an appointment for 6.30 that afternoon. I insisted that it was urgent, for it seemed to me that if my psychic perceptions were correct, the sooner Malcolm and I met and had things out, the better. His secretary was reluctant, but I showed her no mercy, and a few minutes before 6.30 that evening I found myself in the typical waiting-room that one sees in one of those houses in the doctors' district that are let out in penny numbers to a crowd of consultants—the furniture heavy, handsome, without individuality and inadequately dusted; the inevitable centre table strewn with dog-eared illustrations—just such another room down to the last detail as I had sat in a couple of hours earlier.

There was another patient ahead of me when I arrived—Dr. Malcolm was evidently running late—a miserable, misshapen little boy, his legs in irons, accompanied by an over-anxious mother, far more nervous than he was. We began to talk. I gathered that she abominated the great Dr. Malcolm, but for some unknown reason her small son didn't seem to mind him. I counted this as a point in favour of the man I was about to confront; a child's instinct in these things is very sure and penetrating, and if the boy were not frightened of his rough mannerisms, they were probably no more than mannerisms. Presently my companions were summoned, and the boy slipped off his chair and stumbled towards the door with his uneven gait quite eagerly—the great Dr. Malcolm had no terrors for him.

I waited, and I waited. My companions had been far from prosperous-looking, and big fees were unlikely to be forthcoming from them, but they were not stinted for time. The dusk was gathering in that gloomy room, so I could no longer distract my mind with the papers, and the atmosphere of the place began to get hold of me. It seemed as if it were thickly populated by apprehensive ghosts. I began to get quite nervous myself, and when at last my turn came I had to take hold of my courage with both hands.

I knew that I must, from the very outset, dominate the interview or it would be a great deal worse than useless; ground once lost could never be recovered in such a matter. I had to lay hold of Malcolm's imagination and touch the very springs of his being. It sounds like charlatanry, but actually it was psychic surgery. If I had done such things to gratify my own vanity or serve any selfish ends, it would have been abominable; but I did it because there was nothing else that could effectually help this man, just as, without any sense of the conventions I would have thrown my arms round him if I had seen him stepping backward into danger.

The attendant nurse opened a heavy mahogany door and showed me into a large and handsome room, scantily and impersonally furnished. At a flat-topped desk under the glaring centre light stood my red-haired friend, looking very tired and very cross. He stared at me, thunderstruck, and I saw at once that he recognised me. I took my courage in both hands, invoked Isis, and advanced to the attack.

My reception was far from encouraging. The man was both angry and agitated, but I had to get past that, and ignoring his conscious reactions, I spoke to his subconscious, evoking what I knew must be there; and as I knew there would be, there was a response. He resisted it and fought it, but I was too sure of my ground, too experienced in handling human beings, to be put off my stroke; I got my fingers on to the vital spots in that man's soul and I put on the pressure. It was like a surgeon breaking down a stiff joint, and there are no anæsthetics in psychology. Such things do not bear talking about. It is a terrible thing to see a man's soul naked.

When the reaction was over, I took Malcolm home with me. I do not know what would have happened to him if I hadn't. I think he would have got himself run over at the first crossing, so completely had he gone to pieces.

CHAPTER
EIGHT

It was an odd drive across London with the man who had so often pursued me on the Embankment sitting quietly beside me, his slouch hat pulled over his eyes, and his hands folded over the instrument case that rested on his knees. Not a word passed his lips for the entire trip. He just sat there looking like an Epstein sculpture. I was not sorry to turn off the bridge approach into the quiet streets, for the concentration necessary for driving in traffic was not easy in the circumstances.

I wondered with what mixed emotions he would approach my door. As I held it open for him to follow me our eyes met for the first time.

"I have been here before, you know," he said curtly.

I admired him for that. It could not have been easy to say.

"I know," I said. "I wish I had recognised you."

"Recognised me?" he checked on the threshold, like a jibbing horse. "Who are you mistaking me for?"

"Nobody," I said. "Won't you come inside? There is a great deal to tell of my side of the story."

That brought him in. Curiosity is not an exclusively feminine prerogative. For a moment I had thought he had been going to take refuge in flight.

He deposited his hat on the nearest chair, but, I suppose from habit, retained possession of his instrument case. He stared round my big room wonderingly. There was at times, when caught off his guard, something oddly childlike about him; apart from that, he impressed one as a man who had never had any youth.

Then he met my eyes again, and coloured to the roots of his hair.

"You have been here before also," I said, thinking these things had better be voiced.

He bowed his head. "Yes," he said. "I have."

I judged from that that he was quite a good psychic, better than I had realised—perhaps better than he had realised also. It must be a startling experience suddenly to discover that one's secret dream-life is an actuality.

I put him into my big chair, and he dropped into it like a very weary man. I offered him a sherry, which he declined. I suggested a cup of tea, which he accepted gratefully. After he had had it, he looked much more reconciled to life.

"Why aren't you a surgeon?" I said to him, more for something to say than for anything else.

He smiled, if it could be called a smile, that slight, grim curl of the lip.

"I ought to have been a surgeon," he said, "I should have liked it."

"Then—why aren't you?"

He sat silent for a moment. "I have a horror of blood," he said at length. "No good going in for surgery with a trait like that."

"How did you manage to become a doctor at all?"

"Put up with it. But it wouldn't have done to risk operating."

Silence fell again. I refilled his cup. The silence continued so long that when he finally broke it I could not think for a moment what he was referring to.

"You are the first person to whom I have ever told that," he said.

Then silence fell once more, and I let it rest unbroken, feeling that, in his queer way, he was travelling far and fast.

Again he broke it. "What made you ask me why I wasn't a surgeon?" he asked.

"Your hands," said I.

He inspected them; examining the finger-tips one by one; viewing with evident distaste the tobacco-stains that marred the otherwise well-kept nails. I rose, and took from the wall a small engraving of Durer's "Praying Hands" and gave it to him to look at.

"Hands are wonderful things," I said.

"Yes—I know," he said "I depend on mine a lot. More than on my eyes, really."

He considered the picture carefully.

"I like that picture," he said. "Could I get one like it?"

It was on the tip of my tongue to tell him he could have it; instead I told him he could get a copy at any picture shop.

He rose abruptly.

"I've taken up enough of your time," he said. "I must be going."

He seemed to have forgotten the promised revelations that had tempted him in; or perhaps he wished to avoid them. I knew better than to press him to stop.

"Would you like me to drive you back?" I asked.

"No, I'll walk."

"Then I'll show you the short cut," I said .

We went down the little street on to the wharf.

"Not far, if you could fly," I said.

"Is that my place opposite?" he exclaimed, coming to an abrupt halt. "Good God!"

I wondered why the occasion called for such strong language. I thought I would find out.

"Do you ever walk up and down your room at night?" said I.

"Yes," said he, then—"Do you ever wear white dresses?"

He gave me a curious, side-long look, like a nervous horse, and without waiting for my reply, walked to the edge of the unfenced wharf and stood looking down at the water.

I joined him.

Without looking up, he spoke.

"If I hadn't been a swimmer, there are times when I should have gone in there. I shan't do it now, though," he added.

Then he turned to me with the abruptness which I had begun to see was habitual.

"Well, are you going to show me the way home?"

"Yes," I said. "I'll show you the way home—if you have the nerve to take it."

"What d'you mean?" he asked sharply.

"You'll know one of these days," said I.

I walked ahead, and he followed me—he couldn't very well do anything else—and I led him down a narrow alley between walls to a flight of worn steps that led up to the bridge approach.

"I don't call that so very terrible," he said, as I bid him farewell, under the flickering gas-lamp.

"I wasn't referring to that," said I.

He stood hesitating, as if disinclined to move off.

"Shall I see you again?" he asked curtly.

"That is as you wish," said I. "You will always be welcome."

"Thanks," said he, and raising his hat, turned on his heel and went off.

I started to make my way back down the dingy alley. I had not gone very far when I heard footsteps rapidly overtaking me. My first impulse was to quicken my pace and reach the road, for it was not a place in which to risk an encounter with unpleasantness.

"Miss Morgan, I want to ask you something," said a voice behind me, rather breathless, rather more breathless, I thought, than should have been occasioned by a walking-pace over so short a distance.

I turned. Unmistakable, even in the gloom, were those square-set shoulders and that bull-dog neck.

"My friend," said I, "what is it you want with me?" I spoke as gently as I could, for I knew he was nerving himself for an ordeal.

"Look here, do you mind—my day-dreaming? I can't altogether help it, you know. But if you say so, I will try."

"I thought you couldn't help it," said I.

"Of course I can if I make up my mind."

"At what price?"

He was silent.

"I do not mind in the least," said I. "It hurts no one, and I think it helps you."

"I don't like doing it, now I know you," he said.

"These things come from something much deeper than the surface," said I. Don't inhibit the visions. Watch them, and see what they do. You understand the theory of psychoanalysis?"

"Yes, of course."

"Then never mind if the symbolism has organised around me, I shall understand perfectly."

"The—Freudian transference?" said he.

"Yes," said I, thinking that that was the best thing I could say. Reassured, he turned on his heel and took himself off.

I walked slowly back to the wharf and stood there till I saw the light go on in the window across the water. Then a shadow blocked the lighted square, and I knew that Malcolm was leaning out of his window. I was glad I had on my black mackintosh cape. I waited a little, to let him tire of his vigil and draw the blind, for I thought it possible he might be able to see me as I walked down the short, well-lit street, and I did not particularly want him to know that I had kept watch on the wharf. But he showed an inexhaustible patience, and in the end he wore me down. I went back and let myself in to the warm, scented room in which I lived and moved and had my being. Then, and not till then, did it occur to me that Malcolm had been waiting to see the lights go on in my big window.

I wondered what thoughts had occupied his whirling mind. That it was whirling, I was perfectly certain. I judged from his whole demeanour that he was a man who had nothing whatever to do with women save as patients, not that, grim granite image though he was, he would have been unattractive to women, for the curious sense of dynamism about the man would have been very attractive to many of them; but he was altogether too brusque and forbidding for anything in the way of an affair ever to have got a start.

94

I wondered whether he would consider his relationship with me in the light of an "affair," and make up his mind to shun it, as I felt sure he would if he saw it in that light. I had done my best to give it the air of a psychological experiment, as it really was; but of course that was only the half of it. I had had no chance to tell him anything of the other half, and he might not unjustifiably conclude that it was an "affair" and take fright.

However, there was nothing that I could do. He was in the hands of the Great One, and so, for the matter of that, was I. I only hoped that he would be all right; that he would not get himself tangled up with the conventions, but would follow his inner urge and steer a straight course. I had practically given him a "dare" when I had told him I would show him the way if he had the nerve to take it, and that might put him on his mettle; or it might make him shy off still further; or, from sheer social ineptitude he might have entirely missed the point. I could only wait and see.

For about a month nothing happened, and I began to wonder whether Malcolm had judged that I was too dangerous to know and had imposed on himself a self-denying ordinance or whether, having met me, he found that the reality did not come up to expectations and had gone off to pastures new. I was puzzled to know what to do. That he was the sacrificial priest and the man chosen for the work I had not the slightest doubt; that in his higher self he knew this I was perfectly certain. But should I be justified in putting any traction on his subconscious mind in order to draw him to me?

Some people would have said: Yes—you have the knowledge, you should use it. But such use involves a responsibility I was little inclined to incur, for if I drew Malcolm to me by an act of will, as I very well could, whatever came after would lie at my door. I have a deep-rooted horror of any form of spiritual coercion, so subtle, yet so potent. How can one be sure that one is right in judging for another when it is so difficult to be right even in judging for oneself? Yet if I were right in my judgment of the situation, what I proposed to do would not only serve the Great Goddess, and through Her, my race, but would incidentally confer an inestimable benefit upon that troubled soul across the water.

> It's a dangerous business, playing with souls,
>
> And trouble enough to save one's own—

said Browning, who I have always esteemed a very wise man. He goes on, moreover, to say:

> But there was my friend with the burning coals
>
> He played with for bits of stone!

This too was true of Malcolm, for the man was mishandling himself

95

abominably. Here was he, concerning himself with the central nervous system, which is the place where mind and body meet, and in spite of his nodding acquaintance with Freudianism, he knew as much about the mind as he knew about Polar exploration. He had been a student, I suppose, in a day that knew nothing of the modern developments of psychology, which are bringing it so near to the Secret Teaching. His inner life was receiving the same kind of nutriment as fell to the lot of children of the poor during the Industrial Revolution, and with, if I were not very much mistaken, the same kind of results. That man's soul was warped all out of shape and sick unto death. And the cause? Sheer ignorance and unhygienic ethics. It was to such as he that Isis should come down in silver light.

"When in doubt, do nothing," is a sound maxim in magic; for the consequences of action on the inner planes are so far-reaching that one dare not risk a mis-step. Moreover, time does not count, and I, being an initiate, could afford to wait.

So I waited. I waited so long that I began to wonder whether Isis really had any use for Malcolm. Then suddenly it was like a dam bursting, and I knew that, even as I had thought, Malcolm had judged me too dangerous to know; had reckoned that I would deflect him from his duty, and had determined to break off relations with me. I could not but admire the cast-iron integrity of that decision at the same time that I deplored its needlessness and folly.

It was a curious study in telepathy, and I will record it exactly as it happened.

I was much alone in those days; I am always alone a great deal, and with this strange business on hand I was avoiding all other entanglements and commitments till I should see how it was going to work out. I put aside my studies, even, in order that my mind might be tranquil and receptive, and was sitting quietly one evening beside my fire in the great hall. It was falling dusk, and I had put on the reading-lamp at my elbow, not troubling to cross to the door to turn on the concealed lighting that filled the great room with a soft tawny haze. The high windows stood uncurtained and dark, for though it was the night of the full moon, she had not yet risen. The ceiling was invisible in the gloom, and the far corners of the room were in shadow. Just around me, where I sat, the glow from the fire lit up the floor, but in my lap lay a pool of concentrated light from the shaded lamp, and in this my hands moved, working at one of my iridescent robes, sewing on the gold thread that lent brilliance to the soft lustre of the silk. I had, I remember, a black diamond on one hand and a black pearl on the other, and as my hands moved, the savage black flash answered to the soft lustre, like Isis and Nepthys. Then suddenly, not a yard from me, I saw the face of Malcolm. I have never seen anything so clear, short of a materialisation.

How did I know it was not my imagination? I will tell you how I knew—the eyes were alive and the soul of the man looked out of them. If I had called up his face in my imagination the soul would not have been behind those eyes. Therefore I knew that I had not called up the image of Malcolm, but that he had come to me in an astral projection, and I wondered what it was that had brought him to the point where he had let his mind escape him.

Did he know what he was doing? I thought so, for I had left my book with him, and if he had read it, he would have known exactly what he was doing. Then why was he doing it? That was a mystery I could not solve. I could only see that face, with its strange light eyes looking at me with concentrated attention. There was no attempt at speech and no expression on the face save of strained attention; but there it was, poised in the air before me. Whether the man were asleep and dreaming, or whether he were gazing at me with psychic vision, I had no means of knowing. There were the watching eyes, however, and there they stayed.

From that time onwards I enjoyed the almost constant companionship of Dr. Rupert Malcolm. Sitting quietly in my chair—going down the crowded street to do my shopping—it made no difference, Malcolm would appear, looking at me with those intent, expressionless eyes.

One night I had gone to bed at my usual time in that great bed of mine which Mr. Meatyard used to shake his head over as giving him unnecessary labour, I being a single lady. I was doing the usual meditation with which an initiate passes over into sleep, going down the long avenue of cypresses to my temple, when I found I had a companion. I had no need to look over my shoulder to see who it was, though hitherto our excursions into dream had always been over downland beside the sea.

I turned, and looked my companion in the face; then, taking his hand in mine, I drew him level with me, and side by side we entered the Temple of Isis, priest and priestess. I took the precaution, however, of drawing close the curtain across the Holy of Holies.

We stood beneath the hanging lamp where burns the Perpetual Light; we stood in the centre of the mosaic Zodiac which symbolises the universe and all that in it is; we stood facing the black curtain that is drawn across the Holy of Holies, and we worshiped as it is permitted to all men to worship; but to him it was not permitted to pass that curtain.

Clearly, and repeating it again and again lest his psychism was not equal to bringing it through, I told my companion that he had the right of entry into the Temple of Isis and was free to come in to the worship. Then I left him, and myself went on through the black curtain. Concerning the Holy of Holies I may never speak, not even after this long time to explain my story. I may only say that the room is empty. Let who can pass that curtain and gain the priesthood: I may not draw it.

I returned, and my priest was still there, kneeling where I had left him. I took his hand in mine again, and led him back, out through the lotus court and down the long avenue; at its end we parted—he to cross the river and return to earth-life, and I to the House of the Virgins for the night.

Thenceforth I seldom had the Temple of Isis to myself. Those who worked with me at times were also aware of his presence. Some resented it, and some, with more insight, knew he belonged.

Then, on Christmas Eve, the culmination came. I was well used to the presence of my priest by now, and it had ceased to trouble me, either waking or sleeping. I had made the usual journey in meditation to the temple, and the meditation had passed over into dream, as it should, and I was standing facing my priest under the Perpetual Light, when my sleep was disturbed. The friend with whom I was in the habit of working was spending Christmas with me, and I thought I heard her come into my room. I was annoyed, for my dream was interesting, and I did not wish to be aroused. I knew she was a nervous person, and thought she had probably come in to tell me of some foolish psychic experience. I lay still, though awake, hoping that if she saw me thus, and the matter were of no real importance, she would go away again. But instead I felt a firm grip on my upper arms. She had evidently no intention of being put off. I could not very well be an inhospitable hostess, so with an effort I roused myself—to discover that there was no one there! I knew then, with an absolute inner certainty, who had been there, and had materialised sufficiently to leave black bruises on my arms.

I sat up in bed. This, I thought, is a serious matter, for that which came was a complete materialisation, and it had been projected over water. But there was nothing I could do about it, save wait and see.

I had to wait some time before I saw anything more. Next morning there was dead silence, a complete vacuum. Malcolm had evidently succeeded in scaring himself as well as me.

I missed my priest. The magnetic flow between us, which is the basis of the moon magic, had already begun, and I felt its deprivation. It made me feel flat, aimless, unsure of myself and my mission. But I was used to these psychic reactions and took them in my stride. They were unpleasant while they lasted, but they did not last long. I had a suspicion that although I had warned him not to speak of these things to any living person, Malcolm had taken counsel with someone who was helping him to resist my influence. I had no intention of forcing his will against his better judgment, but I had no such compunction with regard to that other person. We were, however, getting into the broken water that heralds the Vernal Equinox, and I was reluctant to try any psychic work under such circumstances. At the Equinoxes, the Vernal and the Autumnal, all contacts break automatically as the astral tides change, and it remained to be seen whether I should pick Malcolm up again or not on the new tide. I might not; if he were recalcitrant, Isis might drop him; but if I *did* pick him up again, I should know that the work was going through.

And sure enough, as the swirling astral conditions came slowly to calm water after the vernal moon, there was the astral form of Malcolm again, but it was only a pale shadow of his former self. Someone had intervened. Now what was I going to do? I had the power, should I use it? I hated the idea of using it arbitrarily, for a soul is a sacred thing to me. Yet some other person had used power arbitrarily. I made up my mind that, although I would bring no pressure to bear on Malcolm, I would thrust that person aside.

As the new moon gathered power I went up to my temple, which had already been re-sealed and re-dedicated on the new tide. I will tell what I did, for it is interesting. First I put on the Pentacles, the great signs drawn in astral fire at the four cardinal points. I was already robed in the straight black robe and silver head-dress of a moon-priestess; now I assumed the astral robes, imagining myself clad as befitted my grade. I felt the weight of the Uraeus serpent arch itself over my brow; I felt the pressure of the silver kestos on my hips. In my hand was the astral ankh as well as the terrestrial one. With this I drew the moon-signs and invoked with the greater Names of Power. The power came down. Every piece of ritual furniture, every symbol on the walls, was edged with light. The room was getting quite bright, though nothing save the lamp before the Goddess and the Perpetual Light overhead were burning in all its shadowed darkness.

I laid the ankh back on the altar and took up the fire-wand. I traced the symbol of Fire upon the air, and little flames followed it. The smoke that was rolling off the incense in clouds became red-tinged. Then I called upon the Goddess Sekhmet, the Lion-headed One, and over my head I felt the head of a lioness formulate.

I laid the fire-wand back on the altar and took up again the ankh, the crux ansata, the sign of life, and with it I drew the magic circle and the triangle of art. Then I called upon my priest, and called him till he came. He formulated in the triangle of art. Then, round him and myself, he in the triangle and I in the circle, I drew with the fire-wand the circle of fire. The flames rose higher and higher till they were higher than our heads; a glowing heat came off them. With my eyes I held the eyes of the form I had evoked, and saw that the soul of the man was behind them.

"Oh beloved of Isis!" I said. "You and I are alone in the circle of fire where none can intervene. You will do your own will and no one else's."

Then I slowly relaxed the power. The flames died down. The man's figure faded, and I did the banishing that released the psychic tensions and restored all to normal. The room was intensely hot. I think something would have gone on fire if I had prolonged the experiment much longer. I was dripping with sweat and completely exhausted. The whole experiment, including the preliminary meditation, had occupied less than half an hour, but I was two days getting over it.

So much did I do for Rupert Malcolm, and I had my doubts as to whether he would thank me for it. If I had known for certain that I was never to set eyes on him again, I would have looked for replacements without missing a heart-beat. But as it was, there was an insistent urge behind me which said: "This is the man for the work; he must, if possible, be got to do it. Never mind his feelings. Never mind yours. Personal feelings do not count in this matter. He will suffer and you will run risks, but the work must be put through. It is important."

Then came the confirmation that is never lacking when big things are afoot, for Those on the Other Side never expect one to trust blindly—my friend came to me and said:

"I have had a strange dream. I dreamt that I was with you in the temple; and the Priest of the Moon* came to me and told me I was to tell you that you must give the message. Do you know what that means?"

"Yes," I said, "I do."

"Will you give it?"

"Yes, I will."

"How?"

"In my own way," said I. "Rest assured it will reach the person for whom it is intended; but whether he will act upon it or not is another matter."

* See *The Sea Priestess*.

CHAPTER
NINE

It was a stormy evening. The river was in flood, sand-bags were piled all along the Grosvenor Road and Mr. Meatyard had got out the heavy boards that fitted into slots across the lower part of my front door. I had put on a sou'-wester instead of my usual wide-brimmed felt hat and had gone down to the wharf to watch the flood water going past. It was a fine sight. I was absorbed in watching it oblivious of all else, when I felt a touch on my elbow.

Taken completely by surprise, I started, my foot slipped on the wet timber, and I all but went over the edge of the wharf. I felt myself gripped from behind by a pair of hands like a gorilla's and lifted into safety. I turned round to see the face of Dr. Malcolm, white as a sheet.

"My God," he said, "you nearly went in the river! I'm frightfully sorry. I'm afraid I startled you. I didn't mean to. I spoke to you, but you didn't hear."

"How did you know I was out on the wharf?" I asked.

He coloured slightly. "I don't know how I knew. I just knew, that was all. I couldn't make any one hear at your house, so I came on here."

We turned and walked slowly back down the short street. Dr. Malcolm walked with his eyes on the ground, never looking at me and never speaking a word.

"I am glad you have come," I said, for the silence needed breaking. "I should have been sorry if I had never seen you again."

"I have been pretty hard driven at the hospital," he replied. "They are short-handed. My junior has been ill."

I accepted this excuse, though I did not believe it; and presently he too thought better of it.

"As a matter of fact, I suppose I could have come if I had really meant to; but I couldn't get things clear. I couldn't adjust the relationship between you and the woman I had dreamt about."

"Aren't we the same person?" said I.

"Not altogether," said he. "I can't imagine you doing the things I have imagined her doing."

I thought it best not to query this.

We came to the big door. I inserted my key and got it open, but it was heavy, and inclined to swing shut of its own weight, and the knee-high flood-boards made entry difficult.

"Will you give me a hand?" said I, and put mine out to him. He did so, but kept his eyes cast down, whether to avoid mine, or whether to gaze at my ankles, of which he received a good view, I do not know. So we arrived back in the house.

"What does this place always smell of?" he asked as he came through the inner doors into the great hall.

"Different things," said I. "Tonight it smells of frankincense."

"Why do you use that sort of thing?" said he.

"For its psychological effect," said I.

He walked over to the fire, turned his back to it, and with his hands in his trouser pockets and his reefer jacket rucking over them like the feathers of an angry fowl, he stood staring into space, an extinct cigarette between his lips. It only needed a peaked cap cocked at an angle to make him look exactly like a ship's officer keeping watch. Presently he discovered that his cigarette was extinct, and pitched it into the fire.

"I'm sick of the central nervous system," he said.

Who would have believed that this was the world-famous authority on the subject!

He fished a crumpled packet of Player's out of his pocket, and lit up without asking my permission.

"There's been a hell of a row at the hospital."

"What about?"

"Me, as usual. Tell me, Miss Morgan, do you think my manners are so very bad?"

They were, of course, simply vile, but I hadn't the heart to tell him so.

"I think you are very absent-minded," I said, "and that probably makes you give offense without meaning to."

"Why can't the fools see I don't mean to?"

"Probably because they are fools."

"Yes, they probably are. But I'm a fool outside my own line, and my God, don't I know it!"

"That is the beginning of wisdom."

"So I have discovered. I hadn't meant to come and see you again, you know, until I'd got things straight in my own mind."

"And have you?"

"No, I haven't. They wouldn't come straight. That's why I'm here this evening."

I felt that this was a momentous confession, coming from him.

"You called me," he said, stating a fact.

"Yes," said I.

"Why did you do that?"

"Because I wanted you."

"What do you want me for?"

"That," I said, "is a long story. You could, if you chose, be useful to me."

He digested this for the length of a cigarette. Finally he spoke. "I'll tell you how I'm placed." I noticed that he never asked me what use I wanted to make of him. "I'm a married man. My wife's an invalid. She's down at the seaside. I used to go down and see her every other weekend or so, but her doctor told me to clear out, I was a nuisance, I only upset her. I'm on at the London and several places, but I could pack 'em up if necessary. I fancy they'd be rather glad if I did, from what I've heard today. I've got to earn a certain amount in order to keep my wife going, but I could always do that. I don't need much myself. Beyond that, I am at your disposal."

This sudden and complete capitulation took me utterly aback. It was the point at which I had known we should eventually arrive, but I only expected it to come by gradual stages, and how to handle my formidable recruit I did not know. My mind was a blank except for Hilaire Belloc's lines that kept repeating in it—

I had an aunt in Yucatan
Who bought a python from a man
And kept it as a pet.
She died, because she never knew
Some simple little rules and few—
The snake is living yet!

I spoke, though my voice did not seem like my own, and he looked round at the sound of it.

"That is an extraordinarily generous offer. Too generous for me to take you at your word straight away. You must get to know me better, and learn what I am doing. Then if you care to repeat your offer, I shall be very glad to accept it."

"Very good. Fix things any way you like. I haven't the faintest idea what you want, but I'll do what I can."

"Then sit down," I said, "and I'll make you tea, and after that I'll talk to you."

Obediently he seated himself in my own especial chair, I drew the hot peat embers forward on the wide hearth, laid them on an iron griddle, and made scones peasant-fashion. He watched me, absorbed, growing even more absorbed when the smell of the baking began to waft into the room. Finally he ate such quantities that I feared for his health.

I put the tea things on the trolley and pushed them into the kitchen that had been a vestry, for Mr. Meatyard to cope with at his leisure. My domestic methods are very simple, but perfectly efficacious. Then I slipped into my bedroom and changed into one of the loose, iridescent robes I wear in the house. This, I thought, would be good for Dr. Malcolm.

It was; but beyond a startled look and a slight uneasy movement of the hand that held his cigarette, he gave no sign.

I lit one of my own cigarettes, for it never occurred to my companion to offer me one of his—the hospital were quite right to tick him off for his manners. Nevertheless, he had offered me himself, asking nothing in return, and a man in his position had a good deal to offer. A four-figure income and, beyond any income, an enormous prestige. He was one of the Royal Physicians.

"Tell me," I said, "why are you sick of the central nervous system?"

"It doesn't get you anywhere."

"If you drop that, what will you take up?"

"Endocrinology."

"Not psychology?"

"Grrr!"

"Then you do not think that mind influences matter."

"I never found it did. But I'm damn sure that matter influences mind. I beg your pardon. I shouldn't use such language to you, but I keep on forgetting you're not a man. You're so dashed like a man."

This was rather surprising in view of his reaction to my iridescent draperies.

"I don't mean your mind's like a man's. I mean you look at life like a man."

"How do you know how I look at life?"

"I know how you've handled me. No woman with an ordinary woman's outlook would have taken me the way you've done. They'd have been scared of me, wondering what they'd let themselves in for if they took me on."

"How do you know I'm not scared of you?"

"You aren't, are you?"

"Not in the least, but I wondered how you knew."

"I'd hate you to be scared of me. You've absolutely no need to be. All this time I've wanted to apologise for the way I've behaved to you—before I knew you, I mean. You must have thought me mad, or a most horrible cad. Really, I'm neither. Of course I never dreamt there was anything in telepathy beyond music hall fakes—I've been reading your book, by the by. I suppose I ought to have kept my thoughts to myself, and not begun to imagine things about you, but I never dreamt you'd get on to it. I suppose the sin's in the intention, and if so, I'm a guilty sinner. I can't make out what your attitude in the matter is though, Miss Morgan."

"If I told you my attitude, Dr. Malcolm, you wouldn't understand it in the very least. Not at present, anyway. You may, later. But I wish you wouldn't call me Miss Morgan."

He turned pink, whether from pleasure at being asked to call me by my Christian name, or panic at being expected to, I did not know. However, I soon disillusioned him.

"Morgan is not my own name, you know. I had to take it in order to benefit under a will, but I have never liked it. It just isn't "me." My own name is Le Fay, and if we are to be friends I would sooner you used that. The other name jars me. Vivien Le Fay—that is my real name."

"Vivien doesn't suit you either. Too like something out of Tennyson."

"You are quite right, it doesn't. I was called after the young witch in the Arthurian legend who beguiled Merlin to his doom; but I don't think I'm in the least like her. The first name my father chose for me was the right one, only the clergyman wouldn't let him use it."

"What was it?"

"Lilith."

"Lilian?"

"No, Lilith."

"Who's she?"

"She was a friend of Adam's before he knew Eve, his wife. Some say she was a fallen angel, and some say she was a soulless spirit of earth; I believe the psychologists say she is the archetypal woman of man's collective unconscious. Anyway, she was a kind of demon, or so the churchmen said, though the Qabalists did not; they said she taught Adam wisdom. But even after God, who did not approve of her, had replaced her with the mate He thought meet, Adam could not forget her. Some say it was really she, and not the Serpent, who was responsible for the Fall."

"Hm. I see," said Malcolm. "The archetypal woman of man's

105

collective unconscious. Perhaps that accounts for it."

"For what?"

"For my dreaming of you."

"Do you really think so?"

He was silent for a minute, then:

"No, not really. My wife's name's Eve," he added. "I wish you'd tell me what you mean to do with me," he concluded irrelevantly.

"Do you know anything of magic?"

"Conjuring?"

"No, magic. Would you believe me if I told you I practiced it?"

"Yes, I should. You're so utterly unlike anything I've ever known, I'd believe pretty nearly anything you chose to tell me about yourself. But you aren't serious, are you?"

"I am perfectly serious. Would you believe me if I told you that you also practice magic?"

"I see what you're getting at now. You mean this queer sort of telepathic business that's been going on between us, that you wanted me to experiment with? But I thought that was spiritualism and not magic."

"Isn't spiritualism magic?"

"Is it?"

"You take it from me, it is."

"I'll do anything you like, Miss—Miss Le Fay. You want to do thought transference with me? What sort do you want to do?"

"The same that you have been doing."

"My God, no, you can't mean that! You don't know what I've been doing."

"Don't I?"

"Miss Le Fay, you do not!"

"Rupert Malcolm, I do."

He sprang out of his chair.

"How much do you know?"

"A good deal. But of course I don't know how much there is to know."

"You know I'm in love with you?"

"Yes."

He stood rigid and immobile for a long minute; then, in a perfectly controlled voice, he said:

"What are we going to do about it?"

"Transmute it into power."

"I don't know what you mean."

"That is the difficulty. I know exactly what I mean, but you don't. I shall have to tell you, and show you, and you will have to trust me until you see your way clear. Won't you sit down and let me talk to you? Won't you sit down, Rupert?"

I heard him catch his breath, but he dropped down into the chair and lay back in it.

"You know how I'm placed," he said, "for I told you straight away."

"I know exactly how you are placed," I said, "and I shall never put you in any position that will embarrass you."

"I don't see how you can help putting me in a position that will make things pretty difficult for me."

"Too difficult?"

"Yes, I'm afraid so."

"More difficult than they will be if you break with me?"

He put his hands over his face.

"Oh, my God, I don't know!"

I did not want to push this reserved man to the point when he would lose his self-control, so I spoke calmly and impersonally, as if we were consulting over someone else's case.

"There are three things we can do. We can break with each other completely. We can disregard the conventions and go the whole way____"

"You aren't proposing to do that are you?" said Malcolm sharply, looking up. "I couldn't do that."

"I am not proposing anything," I said. "I am simply analysing the situation at the moment."

He coloured and looked down.

I continued.

"We can break with each other completely; we can go the whole way; or we can use the power that flows between us for magical purposes."

"That, of course, is a matter beyond my comprehension," said Malcolm. "But I know this, that although we might postpone the decision by working magic or whatever it is, we shall have to come to it in the end. I know my own nature, so I give you fair warning. I have managed to keep straight so far by avoiding temptation. I am not by nature a pure-minded man. I have to wrestle with wild beasts at Ephesus. If I see much of you, feeling as I do about you, I shall have a very difficult problem on hand, and if you give me an inch I shall probably take an ell, and we shall both be sorry afterwards."

"If we work magic together," I said, "it will drain off that force and make life much more manageable for you."

"As to that, I cannot express an opinion. I have never had any experience of magic—nor ever expected to," he added with a faint smile, which told me that the worst of the emotional crisis was now in hand.

"Will you take my word for it that it is as I say?"

He hesitated.

"I have no doubt that you speak in good faith, Miss Le Fay, but I am afraid I doubt your knowledge of a man's nature."

"I have a very great deal of knowledge of men's natures Dr. Malcolm—all sorts of men."

He stiffened.

"That, of course, is nobody's business but yours," he said.

"You have been frank with me, and I will be frank with you," I said. "How old do you think I am?"

He looked at me under down-drawn brows.

"In the latter half of the thirties, probably, though you do not look it."

"I am much older than that. Never mind how old, it would be a shock to you if I told you. Did you ever read Rider Haggard's "She"?

"Yes, when I was a boy."

"I am just such another as She."

He sat silent for a while. Then he spoke.

"That book made a great impression on me when I read it."

"You believe me, then, when I tell you that? You do not think I am just romancing?"

"Yes, I believe you. God knows why, but I do."

"Then—will you work magic with me?"

"Yes, if you wish it—but you realise what you are up against, don't you? I can't absolutely guarantee my good behaviour. I've behaved rottenly to you already—following you, and all that. But I expect you'll always be able to pull me up if you handle me firmly. But—Miss Le Fay—I'll never forgive you if you don't pull me up."

"My friend," I said, "I don't want trouble any more than you do. Rest assured of that."

And with that he had to be content.

I knew by now his habit of long silences, when he seemed to sink deep into himself and commune with his subconscious. Oblivious of his surroundings, he would sit staring into space for minutes on end. There was at such times an absorbed, worried intensity in his face that made him look angry with life in general. On this occasion his silence lasted much longer than usual, and on his face was an even fiercer look of irritable perplexity. It was a forbidding countenance, and if I had not had glimpses of other expressions in those queer, light eyes of his, I should have been put off by it. But I was beginning to like Malcolm as well as respect him.

Finally he spoke.

"I wish you would tell me, Miss Le Fay, what your attitude is in the matter?"

"Do you think you would understand it if I told you?"

"Yes. I'll understand it all right if you'll have patience with me and let me question you. It's my business to understand things. If you don't mind being put through my sieve, I'll soon get you sorted out. Now then, give me a brief outline of the position as you see it."

"My dear Dr. Malcolm, you are asking a most difficult thing of me. I don't know where to begin."

"Begin anywhere. I'll get you sorted out. I'm used to dealing with illiterates."

Luckily he was too intent on gazing into space to observe my countenance. No wonder he got into hot water with the pomposities at the hospital!

So I began on this labour of Hercules.

"Do you believe in life after death Dr. Malcolm?"

"No."

I wondered whether my task was that of Sisyphus, not Hercules.

"Do you believe in an invisible reality behind appearances?"

"Certainly. Bound to be. We've traced it a long way; we'll trace it further yet."

"What do you conceive its nature to be?"

"Electrical."

I sighed, and put my shoulder to the boulder again.

"Do you believe in the existence of an ancient, secret, traditional wisdom, handed down from one initiate to another through the ages?"

"I see no reason to; but then I have never studied along those lines, so I am not in a position to form an opinion."

"Would you believe it if I told you so?"

"Yes, I would."

"Very well, then, take it from me, there is."

"Very good."

"I am one of the recipients of this knowledge."

"I have no difficulty in believing that."

"I have, because of this knowledge, certain powers that are—unusual, perhaps is the best word."

"I can vouch for that from personal experience."

"You also have them."

"Have I?"

"Haven't you realised it?"

"I have certainly had some unusual experiences since I came across you but I put those down to you, not to myself."

"It takes two to have those experiences, Dr. Malcolm, I could not induce them in you if you had no capacity for response. And don't you realise that you were having these experiences independently of me—before I even knew of your existence?"

"I never had them till I came across you, Miss Le Fay. You may have had no conscious part in them, but you acted as a catalyst."

"That is because the power in me stimulated the power in you. I will tell you another thing, Dr. Malcolm; you act as a catalyst to me."

He turned round and looked at me.

"I had hunted in vain for a place to start my work; I simply could not find it. It was much more than the usual difficulty of house-hunting, for I only wanted a studio with living quarters—a very ordinary form of accommodation. Then I remembered having seen this church when I had once taken a wrong turning; but do you think I could find it again? I could not. I spent hours looking for it. I know now that I must have passed the end of the road half a dozen times, and turned down every other road except this one. Then, in despair, I was going home, when I nearly ran over you, and straight away the sun caught the west window and lit it up, and I saw where my church was."

"Good God, was that you?"

"Yes, it was me. I am afraid I gave you a turn. I ought to have apologised before this."

"I certainly had a turn, but not from the dunt in the back you gave me. Do you know, you were like someone in a nightmare I used to get during my student days—I used to dream I got locked in the dissecting room after every one had gone, and there was a woman with long black hair lying on a slab in the moonlight, and I had to dissect her. We hadn't heard of Freud in those days, and I took my recurring dream as a warning, and got as nervous as a cat over it."

"Why did it make you so nervous? Surely you were used to dissections?"

"Oh, perfecly—eat my lunch with one hand and do a post mortem with the other. But this was different. I hadn't so much got to dissect her as gut her like you clean poultry, and for the job I was provided with nothing but a couple of button-hooks; no scalpel, no forceps, no nothing. And when it was over I knew they'd come and find me, and chase me down the street and kill me. Apparently I was allowed to pull the lady to pieces with button-hooks at my leisure, but as soon as I'd finished, I was to be killed."

"And I was the lady?"

He moved uneasily.

"Yes, I am afraid you were. But I didn't ever connect her with the woman on the Embankment in the black cloak."

I rose and went over to my bookshelves and returned with Elliot Smith's book on mummies in my hand.

"Does that strike a familiar note?" I asked, pointing him to a certain page.

"My God, it does!"

"How do you explain it?"

He went into one of his silences, and I knew I must wait. Finally he spoke.

"You asked me if I believed in life after death, and I told you no. I suppose I was rash, I ought to have said I was not in a position to form an opinion. I believe there is evidence, but I have never been sufficiently interested to investigate it. I will tell you what I do believe in, though. I believe in lives before this one—always have believed in them, ever since I can remember. Nobody told me, I just knew it. I can't prove it. I simply believe it, that's all. Only act of faith I ever performed. It never occurred to me to associate my dissecting room nightmare with anything to do with another life, but this book—well, it might not be proof to anyone else, but it's good enough for me, for all my ideas have always turned round Egyptian things. I never could get on with religion, though I am a son of the manse; but I always felt that the Egyptians had a religion worth having, and I could have got on with that."

"What sort of thoughts about your past lives did you have?"

"Nothing edifying. On the contrary. Pretty gloomy, in fact. Quite the last sort of ideas you'd expect a lad to have. It seemed to me I was an outcast and a bad lot. Partly I resented the injustice of it, and partly I knew I deserved it. It played the dickens with my psychology as a child. I never got religion, but, my God, I got conviction of sin! But, Miss Le Fay, when I had a bit of psychoanalysis done recently, the content that dream yielded was just the usual Freudian muck."

"Did you have the psychoanalysis done in order to get rid of me?"

"Well, yes, I'm afraid I did. I tried to look at myself impartially, and judged by the rules of psychology as I know them, it seemed to me I

111

was getting pathological. So I had a second opinion, and it confirmed mine."

"Did the analysis help you?"

"Not in the least. But apparently it wasn't expected to, under three years. It was purely diagnostic. The fellow tried suggestion, but I wasn't suggestible; so he sent me on to a woman who went in for New Thought. Grrr! I could have wrung her neck. Bilge! Talked to me—to *me*, mind you—about the power of the mind over the body. I told her to try a cerebral tumour and learn the power of the body over the mind. She didn't like me. I didn't like her. She smiled all the time like a Cheshire cat because it was in accordance with her principles to be amiable, but all the same she didn't like me. I don't smile like a Cheshire cat. If I don't like people, they know it, and I don't mind their knowing it."

I pitied that poor woman. My present labour of Hercules was as nothing to what she had undertaken in trying to convince her formidable patient that All is Love. I thought it much more likely that Malcolm had disillusioned her than that she had made any impression on him.

"There is one thing I deeply regret, though, Miss Le Fay—I talked to her about you. God knows why I did it. God knows how I could have been such a fool. But anyway, I did, and I'm frightfully sorry about it."

"What did you tell her about me?

"I told her how you attracted me, and how I'd let my imagination play the fool till it got out of hand."

"And what advice did she give you?"

Told me to cut it out, naturally. She knew I was a married man."

"I thought of the usefulness of that advice. It was because Malcolm couldn't cut it out that he had come to her at all.

"Tell me, Dr. Malcolm, what made you disregard her advice?"

"Oh—you called me! The minute I knew you wanted me, I had to come. I'd do anything in the world for you, you know that, don't you?"

"Yes, I know it. That was why I called you."

"But you don't feel about me as I feel about you. I've got no illusions on that score."

"No, I don't. That's true. It's just as well, too, don't you think? We couldn't work together if I did."

"No, of course we couldn't. I quite agree. And that brings us back to the point we started from. You were going to tell me about what your attitude is in this matter. So I understood, at any rate—but damn it all, madam, you've been psychoanalysing *me*! And with button-hooks, too!"

112

"I'll do my best to tell you, Dr. Malcolm, but I cannot guarantee you will understand."

"Oh, go on. I'll understand all right. I'm not altogether a fool, though you might think it from the way I'm behaving."

"Very well. Listen. I told you you had magical power, and now it has been pointed out to you, I think you see it for yourself. It is that power I want to make use of. It is rare, in the degree you have it, at any rate. You are psychic, but psychics are common enough. But you also have, along with your psychism—and that combination is far from common—a degree of dynamism, of vital force, or energy and drive, that in my experience is unique. Some of it goes into your work, of course, and that is why you have arrived where you have in your profession, but what becomes of the rest of it, Dr. Malcolm?"

"Goes to my head, I'm afraid, and I get following folk along the Embankment and making a fool of myself generally, as you ought to know."

"Are you in the habit of doing that sort of thing?"

"No!—please, Miss Le Fay—no never. Never before. Never in my life. I give you my word of honour!"

"I thought you weren't. I couldn't understand why you said that."

"I was just speaking generically, you know. Didn't want to be too personal."

"You can see for yourself, can't you, Dr. Malcolm, how the tremendous driving-force you put behind your fantasying made it come over as telepathy?"

"Yes, I've realised that, and I'm very sorry about it. Unpleasant for you."

"Not in the least."

"You're beyond my comprehension. I should have thought a woman either liked that sort of thing or disliked it, and no half measures about it."

"Have you ever studied the ancient religions at all? The Hindu, the Egyptian?"

"No, never. The Higher Thought woman talked about Yoga. I'm inclined to think there's something in Yoga. Not as she put it, though. Love! Spirit! Grrr!"

"Never mind the Higher Thought woman. A maiden lady?"

"She wore a wedding ring. But, oh yes, she was a maiden lady all right. I know what you mean."

"Well, if you had studied the ancient religions, you would have seen that their outlook is quite different from ours. They worship the creative force, whereas we try to suppress it."

"The creative force?"

"Isn't the reproductive force creative?"

"I'm afraid I don't quite get you."

"Dr. Malcolm, I am going to ask you a question which you need not answer unless you want to. Does your marriage meet your need?"

He sat silent.

"My wife became an invalid after the birth of our child," he said at length. "I owe her a heavy debt."

"And the child?"

"They couldn't save both."

"They made you choose?"

"Yes."

"Any other children?"

"No, out of the question."

"Does your marriage meet your need, Dr. Malcolm?"

He sat silent. At length:

"No, of course it doesn't."

"What becomes of all that side of your nature that should have gone into your marriage?"

"God knows. I don't. Churns around, I suppose, and works itself off in one way or another. Makes me bad-tempered, I expect."

"Sleep badly?"

"Rottenly."

"Have I got my diagnosis?"

"I expect so."

"Do you dream a lot?"

"You ought to know."

"And after you have dreamt, are you happier?"

"Oh, my dear, indeed I am."

"Do you see how the tremendous life force that is in you overflows into your dreams and passes telepathically to me? And because I know how to receive it, and take it in and absorb it, you are at peace? If I threw it back at you, it would be a sickening experience for you."

"Is such a thing possible?"

"You have dreamt, and you have been at peace, isn't that so?"

"How can I say it to you—? Yes—yes. Indeed I have. You know. You understand."

"And you have tried cutting yourself off from me. How have you

114

been then?"

"All to pieces—all to pieces. I couldn't stand it."

"Do you see how the force comes over?"

"It comes over on the imagination. But you meet me half-way. It would be different if you didn't. And yet you don't care for me?"

"That is the secret of it. I meet you half-way. I take that force from you and I use it in my magic. And that, Dr. Malcolm, is why you are at peace."

"But is it right? Is it fair to you?"

"Does it injure anybody?"

"No, I can't see that it does."

"Does it help you?"

"Immeasurably."

"Have I, who would be considered a pagan, helped you more than the New Thought woman, who would be considered very spiritual?"

"Oh—don't talk about her!"

"Then—my friend, will you trust me to experiment with you?"

"You know I will, surely I needn't tell you that. But—will you tell me this—what end have you in view?"

"Not exactly research; I have done all that and know what I am about. But—I hardly know how to express it—"

"Is it a working model you want me for?"

"Not quite that either. And yet in a way it is. If you knew anything of magic you would understand, but you don't. Let me put it this way—you and I are part of our race, aren't we? and therefore our race is part of us. What is the British nation made up of? Norse and Kelt, mainly. I am a black-haired Keltic woman, you are a fair-skinned Nordic man; we are the two extreme types of our race.

"We certainly are. Anything more contrary in type, character, outlook, than you and I, I should imagine you would go a long way before you would find. You've got one kind of skull and I've got another, to begin with."

"And it's in the diversity that the attraction lies."

"No, it lies deeper than that. It's not just your looks that attract me."

"Never mind personalities for the moment. Let me take my next point. We hold, we initiates, that you can bring a thing through from the Inner Planes into manifestation by acting it out symbolically. That is why ritual is used. Now if you and I were to work out together the particular problem I want to solve, it would be solved for the race because we are part of the race, and whatever is realised in our minds becomes part of the group mind and spreads like a ferment."

"Is that a fact?"

"It is indeed a fact, Dr. Malcolm, and the knowledge of it is part of the Secret Tradition."

"I get you. You want to make a culture from me."

"Precisely."

"Now what exactly is that going to involve? Is there any risk attached? I am not asking that because I shirk it, but because I want to know how to regulate my affairs. I must provide for my wife. I mustn't let the hospital down unexpectedly. Beyond that I am, as I have already told you, entirely at your service. I don't know a thing about it. You'll have to teach me everything, but I'll learn, if you'll have patience with me."

All this from one of the greatest scientific intellects of the day! I was amazed at the utter simplicity and modesty of the man. Perhaps it was in that that the secret of his greatness lay, for he had probably said the same to Nature as he had to me.

"I find it difficult to know how to thank you for that," I said.

"Thank me? Don't be silly. You've got nothing to thank me for. Aren't I lucky beyond anything I had any reason to hope or expect? I am very honoured, Miss Le Fay, honoured far beyond my deserts. It is a case for gratitude on my side, not thanks on yours." He paused. "Do you realise what this means to me? Now tell me what you want with me. Let's get down to practical business. How much of my time do you want, to begin with?"

"A fair amount at the start, till you learn the technique. After that one night a week with occasional runs of work. It will always be in the evenings. I am a creature of the moon; I do not function till after sundown."

"I'm a night worker myself, so that will suit me nicely. When do we start?"

"Now, if you like."

"Certainly, so far as I am concerned; but ought I not to see my affairs in order first?"

"My dear Dr. Malcolm, do you think I mean to murder you?"

"How do I know? I gather there is a not unappreciable degree of risk."

"But not to life or limb. The risk, the only risk *you* run, is of a rather unpleasant emotional upheaval; it might possibly go to the length of a nervous breakdown, but I think you have too much stamina for that. But it would not do you any permanent damage."

"Supposing the worst occurred, for how long would it put me out of action? I am simply asking that so I can arrange accordingly—I don't want to let folks down. Someone's got to do my work if I can't."

"If the worst came to the worst, you would be upheaved for a sun-tide, that is, till the next Equinox; but I do not think you would be out of action and unable to do your work for more than a moon-tide, which is till the next new moon."

"I'm used to being upheaved. I don't suppose I shall notice any difference. But if the only risk to *me* is a nerve storm, who is going to take the *real* risk in the affair? For risk I am convinced there is, although you are so matter of fact about it."

"I take that, Dr. Malcolm, but it isn't so very terrible. I know what I am about, and am thoroughly used to it. The only real risk is loss of nerve. I am unlikely to lose mine, I am too habituated. The thing I really fear is loss of nerve on your part because you have never had any experience of this sort of thing before, and you and I cannot help working at a high voltage."

"My dear child, it is my business to have a nerve. What do you take me for? Old lady doing tatting?"

"When I said loss of nerve I did not mean failure of courage; I am quite satisfied that would never occur in your case. What I fear with you is a sudden attack of conscience. As you truly said just now, you and I have very different outlooks on life, and we shall be working with and on life. I am in the habit of taking all my corners on one wheel—it is the only way corners like mine can be taken. It looks dangerous, but it isn't, not for me, at any rate. You might suddenly get an idea I was leading you into sin. We shall sail pretty near the wind, I admit it. But any damage we do, we shall do to ourselves. There will be no injury to any one else."

"I am glad to hear you say that. I wouldn't be willing to do anything that would hurt my wife."

"I should never ask you to."

"Very good, go ahead. We will take the risks as read. I don't know why you have got the idea I am so strait-laced. I don't want to get put off the register, but short of that, I'm your man,"

"You have got certain inflexible principles, have you not? Supposing we came up against one of those?"

"Then I'd just cut my loss and take myself off."

"Then in that case you would spend a sun-tide getting over it. But if, instead of that, you would trust me to steer you through, even if I had to drive a coach and six through your principles, I should simply blow the safety fuse we always have in magic, and there would be no loss to cut beyond that of the experiment."

"Who would take the brunt?"

"I should take the brunt, but I know how to take it. It wouldn't hurt me."

"How would you take it, Miss Le Fay?"

"Like a lightning-conductor. Give the force free passage through me to earth. It ends the experiment, for the time being, at any rate, but does no damage."

"I think I understand. It's like boat-sailing. Never belay the sheet. If a squall came, you'd let the gear carry away to save capsizing, is that it?"

"Exactly."

"I understand. But I don't see why you think I would necessarily carry away along with the gear."

"You won't, if you know when to let go."

"And you think my principles are so rigid that I'll go overboard with the mast before I'll surrender them?"

"That is precisely what I fear."

"But surely you carry an axe to cut the gear adrift?"

"Do you think I'd cut you adrift, Dr. Malcolm, if you went overboard?"

"No point in my dragging you under if my principles are likely to drown me."

"I am the captain of this ship, if it goes down, I go down with it."

"Why must you?"

"Point of honour, my friend. My principles are as rigid as yours, though after another manner."

Malcolm ruffled his red hair.

"I don't see any occasion for such rigidity," he said.

"That is because we are discussing my principles and not yours. If we were discussing yours and not mine, I should feel just the same as you do—no occasion for such rigidity."

"It seems to me a suicidal sort of expedition. When do we start?"

"When you like."

"No time like the present. I suppose you feel about me like I feel about the animals I vivisect—do the best you can for the poor brute and get on with the job. The job's worth more than he is."

CHAPTER
TEN

I took Malcolm up to the robing-room. In order to get there, we had to pass through my bedroom. Malcolm gave one startled look round and cast down his eyes. Beyond that, he did not flinch, though I think he breathed more freely on the stairs, steep as they were.

I left him in the robing-room, and taking from the cupboard the black velvet vestment and silver head-dress of a moon priestess, went up to the temple to robe, for it was not fitting to appear in the presence of the Goddess in mundane garments. Having robed, I invoked, and remained in meditation before the moon-symbol for a few minutes. Then I went to fetch Malcolm.

Framed in the dark arch of the stairs, I must have looked an amazing figure in my robes, for Malcolm threw back his head like a frightened horse. Neither of us spoke for a moment; then:

"Come," I said.

I held aside the heavy curtain for him to pass into the temple. Silently he crossed the threshold of Isis. I came and stood beside him.

"This is my temple," I said.

"What do you do here? said he.

"Contact the moon," I said.

"I understand," said he, though I don't suppose he did.

He stared about him. Never in his wildest dreams had Rupert Malcolm, F.R.C.P., seen anything like it, and they see a good many queer things before they get the F.R.C.P.

"This is a diagram of the universe," said I. "Those symbols round the seven sides represent the seven planets and indicate where their influence comes in. The side by which we entered represents the way back to earth. The four sides of the cubical altar represent the four elements—those are their symbols, those triangles. Go up to the altar. How high is it on you?"

"Waist high to me, and I am five foot seven."

"It is the height of the navel of a six foot man, and it is a double cube, meaning "As above, so below." It is the cubical altar of the universe. Double the cubes again, and it is the height of a man. That other table-altar, or couch according to which way you look at it, which forms a T with the cubical altar, is the altar of sacrifice. That big mirror is the doorway to the higher planes. We hang on it the symbol of whatever force we are working with, and shift the other symbols round accordingly. That light hanging overhead is the spirit-light. It represents the Creator. The floating wick in the lotus-shaped vase on the altar represents the power of the Creator brought through into the universe—God made manifest in Nature. That light in the opalescent bowl in front of the mirror represents the Moon-power. There are coloured bowls with floating wicks under all the symbols of the planets, but only the Moon-bowl is lit tonight because it is only the Moon-power with which we are working. Those two pillars, black and silver, represent positive and negative force, and they stand on either side of the sacrificial altar at present because that is the focus of power in the work we are going to do. The two lights on their tops bring the number of lights in the temple up to five, which is the number of man. Four of those get reflected in the mirror, but not the fifth, the spirit-light up in the roof; that brings the number of lights up to nine, the number of the Moon."

Malcolm's eyes followed my pointing hand.

"I understand," he said, and I think he did, for his mind was diamond clear and diamond keen, a delight to work with.

"But there is more than that," I said. "That is only the physical temple; there is also the astral temple which we build in the imagination, and what we build in the imagination is real on its own plane. I shall take you through into that astral temple tonight if all goes well."

"How do we go through into the astral temple?"

"Through the mirror."

"I see. So that's what that big mirror is for, is it?"

"Yes, this is what we call the mirror-working. It is much easier to see psychically in a mirror than in the actual room, and one can build the astral images in the mirror and the crystalline structure of the glass will hold the magnetism. Look in the mirror. Do you see my face appearing just over your shoulder?"

I drew close behind him, and the light from the floating wick on the altar fell on my face. Light shining upwards brings out the modelling of a face in an unaccustomed manner and makes it look quite different. Even I, seeing my own face in the glass over Malcolm's shoulder, hardly knew it. Our eyes met in the mirror.

"Who is that? said I.

"The woman of the dissecting-room," said he, and I felt him shudder.

This was not the answer I either expected or wanted.

"Look again," said I, "and tell me who she is. Tell me frankly."

"Well—you know," said he.

"Yes, I know," I said, "but I want to know if you know."

"As far as I know, at any rate as far as I could make out from my dream, she was a priestess of one of those old temples where I was a priest, and I desecrated her dead body, and got into trouble over it."

"Did you desecrate her for the sake of magic?"

"No," said Malcolm, and I felt the man's mind close down like a shutter: he would tell me no more, I knew that, however much I pressed him. But that did not matter. He knew, and that sufficed. For my part, I could make a fairly good guess, knowing the ways of the ancient Egyptians.

"You say you got into trouble. Do you know what your punishment was?"

"Stoned to death, of course."

There was no "of course" about it. I had seen Malcolm working out another punishment, and I wondered why, since he knew so much, he did not know it.

"Did you ever belong to a cult that performed blood sacrifices?" I asked. I felt Malcolm shudder again. It was a strange thing to see that hard-boiled, stocky, case-hardened man shiver like that.

"I think I must have," he said quietly, "and that's probably at the bottom of my horror of blood."

"I think you must have, too," I said. "But it was not a blood cult, you know. It was part of the innermost worship of Isis, the most ancient worship, predynastic, where at long intervals they killed a man in Her honour. The priests who were made to do that were high up in the cult and did it as an expiation for some wrong-doing. I expect that was your punishment for desecrating the body of the priestess."

"No, it wasn't," said Malcolm quickly, "or at least that wasn't the story as I imagined it. My idea was that I got into the priesthood under false pretences. I believe I really came from one of the outcast classes who disposed of the dead, and they wouldn't have had me at any price if they had known. I had been exchanged as a child for a child that had died in order to safeguard an inheritance. I knew the secret of my birth, though no one else did, and I ought not to have tried for the priesthood, but I couldn't resist it; and they found me out, and made me do the blood sacrifices and kind of outcasted me, though they couldn't turn me out of the priesthood because I knew too much. Then, to make matters worse, I got fond of one of the priestesses. Then there was all sorts of trouble. They didn't give me a second chance after that, but put an end to me, and quite rightly. At any rate that's the story I used to put myself to sleep with as a child."

"What a story for a child!"

"Oh, I was that sort of child. Brought up by my father's housekeeper—my mother died when I was born. Odd, isn't it, how these obstetric calamities seem to haunt me? That was the end of the priestess, too."

"Did you fantasy that too as a child?"

"Yes, the whole story, just as I've told it to you. Of course I had the death of my own mother to put it into my head. Still, it was a queer thing for a lad to imagine. I wasn't so frightfully young, though, about thirteen."

I could see how the stirrings of puberty had brought through the memory.

"Was the girl you married of the same type as the priestess?" I asked.

"No, the exact opposite in every way—and I knew even at the time that I ought to wait for my priestess."

His hands gripped the edge of the altar and the lamp-flame quivered. "But my nature was too strong for me. That always has been my problem. Then her people pressed the marriage, too. She didn't really want it. She was scared of me, and I don't blame her. But I was too headstrong to pay any attention to that. So you can see why I feel I owe her a debt, can't you? She was offered up as a sacrifice, if anyone ever was. It's the old story over again. Still sacrificing and still outcast." The altar shook under his convulsive grip, making the flame flicker till the shadows danced all over the walls and I feared we should have an extinguished lamp.

What could one say? Malcolm, staring into the mirror, was finding out the nature of the mirror-working for himself.

"Do you know why I went in for medicine? Reparation. Work off my sense of sin, don't you know. Hang it all, I was to have been a medical missionary!"

I began to wonder what I was going to do with Malcolm, for he seemed to have taken root at the cubical altar, with his two hands laid thereon. I wanted him at the other altar, however, the sacrificial one. I knew what I had to do—I had to sacrifice this man, even as he had sacrificed others—not his physical life or his physical blood, but his magnetic vitality and everything that makes up life for a man. I had to do this, and I had to chance his coming through to the rebirth. He had divined rightly when he had compared himself to a vivisected animal.

"I want you to lie down on this couch," I said. "Will you?"

"Certainly." He walked round the altar—widdershins, God help

122

him—and stretched himself on the long, low couch that is tomb and altar in one. I fetched a stool and placed it behind his head and sat down there. Our eyes met in the mirror. I bent over him, and the long ends of my silver head-dress fell to his shoulders, framing his face. I took his head in my hands. He stiffened and drew away, but I kept my hold on him.

"Aren't you in the habit of handling patients when you treat them?"

"Sorry," said he, and relaxed.

"Look in the mirror," said I.

Our eyes met again. I began the temple-building.

"Don't think of me. Never mind the human woman. Think of the priestess in the mirror. You are going to use me as the channel of the force you want to contact. My personality plays no part in it. It will fade right out as soon as the force begins to come through. All women are Isis and Isis is all women. Watch the mirror."

"Now I am going to take you on a journey. We are in Egypt, beside the Nile. It is moonlight, the full moon. There is a mist rising from the water, and it is cold. The cold river-mist. The cold moon-mist. The cold astral mist. Now we are out on the astral."

Malcolm shivered. He had felt the astral cold.

"There is a great pylon gate in front of us. Its shadow lies black upon the sand. We enter its shadow." Malcolm shuddered and the couch shook under him.

"We pass under the dark arch of the pylon and are in the Court of the Lotus-pool. The moonlight falls on the water where the lotuses float sleeping. We pass beside it, up some steps across a wide terrace and in at a door—a great door that stands open. Now we are in a dark and lofty hall, lit only by a hanging lamp. It is the Hall of the Sphinxes."

Malcolm started.

"Facing us is a dark curtain veiling the Holy of Holies."

Malcolm drew a shuddering breath and his hands came and caught hold of my wrists. He was seeing it all in the mirror.

"The curtain parts. The Goddess appears! Worship Her. Pray to Her. Ask Her for what you need."

Malcolm rose to a sitting position, dragging my arms after him. I had to place one knee on the couch to save myself from overbalancing. Now I was kneeling on the couch behind him, my elbows on his shoulders, my hands crushed against his breast. I could feel it heaving, and the pounding of his heart. His nails were cutting my skin. I thought I should be lucky if no bones were broken. Rigid, motionless, under intense strain, we both looked in the mirror. There was the man's haggard face, the eyes almost mad; and above it a woman's face, perfectly calm, floating apparently in space, for my black robe was invisible in the darkness. The silver head-dress caught the light. The black pools of the eyes held no expression. It did not seem like my face even to me.

Then behind me, there began to be a warmth and a power. Isis was formulating. Above my head I saw Hers. I was no longer conscious of the agony in my hands or the strain on my body. All I felt was the power flowing through me in electric heat. I no longer tensed my hands to protect them against Malcolm's crushing grip; I let them go limp and felt the bones slide one over the other as the hands crumpled. But they were numb now, I felt nothing, for the power was coming through.

Over the man and myself there formed a cloud, a silvery cloud of palest moon-mist, slowly glowing to gold and growing warm as it glowed. It was the aura of Isis emanating from us, from our united magnetism. It is the thing that is behind marriage. It held for a while, and then it slowly dissolved. Magnetism had gone off from both of us, and Isis had absorbed it. Malcolm dropped back against my breast, and I thought he had fainted till I heard him give a prolonged sigh. I laid him back on the pillows, but he still kept hold of my hands. I could feel his hands sweating. Mine were cold as ice, so I knew which way the power had flowed. He rolled over onto his elbows, seizing again my hands, and staring up into my face.

"But *you* are Isis!" he said. "You are Isis!"

Then he pressed his face into my hands and lay still.

How long he lay like that I do not know—a considerable length of time, little short of an hour, I should think. Finally he roused, sat up, swung his legs off the couch and turned and looked at me. He lifted my hand to his lips.

"Thank you very much," he said.

He looked sharply at the hand he held. The nails were blue; the fingers swollen.

"What's the matter with your hand?" he exclaimed. "My God, did I do that?"

Questing, impersonal fingers, so gentle they caused no pain to the bruises, went over every sinew and bone and joint. Then he laid that aside and took up the other. Malcolm, the man, might have his problems over women, but Malcolm the doctor had none—the hands that tested mine were utterly clean. Then he took up the first hand again, and compared the two.

"I'll reduce that œdema for you," he said. "Sit down."

I sat beside him on the couch. This was an utterly different man from the one who, partly from shyness, partly from principle, shrank from any near contact with me. Resting my hand on his knee, he began to work with it as if he were putting on a glove. From nail-tip to knuckle, and down the channels between the bones, his fingers felt gently, so gently, again and again and again. I watched his face. He was not looking at what he was doing. His eyes were gazing into space with a blank, intent expression. It was as if he were listening to my hand. I remembered his saying that he depended on his fingers more than on his eyes. Then the first hand was laid aside as if it were an inanimate object, and the other was taken up and the process repeated. The relief was enormous; the hands felt almost normal. He compared them again. Save for some scarlet abrasions on the ice-cold pallor of the skin, there was nothing to tell of the rough treatment they had received, and I had certainly thought there was a dislocation in one hand.

"I'll massage them again for you tomorrow," he said.

"They feel cold. Are you cold?"

"Not really," I said. "It is the psychic cold. Power has gone out of me."

"Where to?"

"Difficult to say. Has power gone out of you, too?"

"Yes, definitely. It has dropped my blood pressure, I think. I feel strangely at peace."

"Then it has gone into the Goddess. Did you feel Her formulate."

He looked up and met my eyes.

"I saw you as the Goddess," he said in a low voice.

"I am Her priestess."

"What is the difference?"

"You do not see me as the Goddess now, do you?"

"I see you as I have always seen you."

"And how is that?"

He bent over my hands till I could not see his face.

"As the Goddess, my dear, as the Goddess!"

I sat rigid. Too taken aback to make any reply. Who was this man and what secrets had he penetrated?

"Have you been through the curtain?" said I.

"What curtain?"

"In the House of the Net."

"I am afraid I don't know what you mean."

"Dr. Malcolm, how much *do* you know?"

"I don't know a thing, I've told you that already."

"You don't know these things as you know anatomy or physiology.

You know them in dream and day-dream and imagination. They are the representations of the invisible reality."

Malcolm sat rigid for a moment.

"My God, what a reality! Do you really mean, Miss Le Fay, that my—imaginings—have some sort of correspondence in an invisible reality?"

"That is so."

"Well—God help us, that is all I can say."

"Can you tell me what they are?"

"Is it necessary? You won't like them."

"Never mind that. I can deal with you as impersonally as a surgeon." He sat silent for some minutes. At length he spoke.

"I did not take you altogether seriously when you stressed the difficulties of this work. I do now. I wonder, however, if you realise exactly where you are taking me? Or perhaps it would be truer to say where I am taking you if you push me down this path."

"Yes, I realise it."

"Very well, I will take you at your word. You are acquainted, I take it, with the language of psychoanalysis?"

"I am."

"I had my dissecting-room dream psychoanalysed when I went for that consultation recently; it was supposed to have a sadistic basis. I do not consider that to be correct, for, believe it or not, Miss Le Fay, sadistic tendencies are exactly what I haven't got. I make a martyr of myself—that's my tendency. I grant you my temper is vile, but that is because I am so beastly irritable. I've got no malice in me."

"There was another dream, however, that has occurred at intervals throughout my life. That one has not been analysed; I have never told it to a living soul. It always comes before some important event in my life. I don't mean that it is prophetic. No such nonsense. But it comes when I am under stress—the night before an examination, for instance. It is this—I knife a man in a garden by moonlight. Any quantity of blood, as you can imagine. I enter a temple by a side door—it is an Egyptian scene, I may tell you—and I impersonate the man I knifed, who was the priest of the temple. A woman comes in at the main door—the place is empty and lit by a hanging lamp like this place—she comes up to me and gives a start when she finds I am not the man she expected. I take her by the hand and pull her through the curtains—by God, you asked me if I had been through the curtain—is that the curtain you mean?"

"It is."

Malcolm sat petrified.

"You enter the Holy of Holies," prompted I. "What do you find there?"

"Nothing. An empty room."

"You install the priestess as the goddess."

"I do not."

"You do."

"I don't."

"You do."

"I understand," said Malcolm after a moment. "But that cannot be in this life, you know."

"I know that. That epoch has passed away. Evolution has moved on. We are in the airy sign of Aquarius today. The workings are astral. That is why you get the ideal of celibacy in religious life instead of the old ideal of fecundity. The priestess is installed on the astral, Dr. Malcolm."

"I get you. But does that work?"

"You ought to know."

He thought a minute.

"Yes, it does. I've proved it. I don't know how it works, though."

"All magic works in the imagination."

"But the—vital force doesn't transmit in the imagination."

"It does."

"Can't see it."

"What is a sacrament?"

"The outward and visible sign of an inward and spiritual grace."

"Is marriage a sacrament?"

"Supposed to be, I believe."

"And what is the nature of its inward and spiritual grace?"

"Love, I suppose."

"Something more tangible than that—magnetism. You remember telling me that the invisible reality behind all physical manifestation was of the nature of electricity? Well—there it is—in function—more tangible than emotion; less tangible than protoplasm."

Malcolm sat lost in thought as he took in the implications of what I had said.

"Does the protoplasm emanate the magnetism, or does the magnetism emanate the protoplasm?" he asked at last.

"Both," said I, "but the magnetism came first in evolutionary time, and comes first in all manifestations of life. You can't have protoplasm without magnetism."

"Can you have magnetism without protoplasm?"

"Yes, and that is one of the secret occult keys. Over and above the outward and visible sign there is the inward and spiritual grace."

"And the outward and visible sign is—protoplasm? Yes, of course. Protoplasm—the basic substance—pure albumen—yes, it would work like that. Have you ever considered the miracle of the chick developing out of white of egg, which is also pure albumen?"

"Have you ever considered the miracle of the universe developing out of space?"

"My dear child, if you consider anything long enough you find it is a miracle. I have worked on the central nervous system all my life, and I am supposed to know something about it, but I haven't the haziest notion how sensation transmutes into movement. The talk of afferent and efferent impulses is the talk of a fool—it means nothing—it's just baby noises on a higher arc. Goo—goo—ga! That's what the half of scientific terminology is. The fools can't see that description isn't the same thing as explanation. I can describe the central nervous system, no one better, but I'm damned if I can explain it. Child, do you know that the principal service I do for the patients that come to me is to stop other folk mucking them about? It's a red-letter day for me when I get a case I can treat. Diagnose? Yes, I'll stick the label on all right; and prophesy their latter end if that's any comfort to them, but it generally isn't. That's why I get sick of the central nervous system—there's so little you can do about it. Mind you, I like the fine-drawn accuracy of neurology, and I've contributed my share to that; but when I look at the patients lined up at my clinics, I feel like an old hen sitting on a clutch of china eggs. I can't do anything for ninety per cent of the poor devils. All these fancy treatments are no earthly use—cause a lot of pain and cost a lot of money and do no good. Salvarsan and morphia are the only drugs that are any real use to me, and I tell you, I get fed up with them."

I rose. "Shall we finish here and go downstairs and have some coffee?"

He rose, too.

"Keep those hands up as much as you can," he said.

He took the left hand, which was the worse of the two, and laid it in the bosom of my robe, and taking a safety-pin from his own tie, improvised a sling. He unfastened the brooch that held the crossed-over folds and readjusted it to help take the strain. It was just like dressing a child. Malcolm never let his mind come near the woman he was handling.

I was simply the patient, and his gentleness was extraordinary. It was not that he handled me gingerly. Far from it. The hands were firm, the movements definite, as he bent the arm to bring it into the position he wanted it to be in; but it was so smooth, so exact, the pressure came on so gradually, the angle was so perfectly calculated, that he gave the wrenched and bruised hands no pain. I would not have believed one could have handled battered flesh to soothe it till I saw it done. Nor would I believe that Malcolm, who was generally simmering like a kettle on the perpetual point of boiling over, could suddenly become remote and quiet and abstract. It was as if he were a long distance off. But as he fastened the catch of the brooch his eyes met mine, and suddenly Malcolm, the man, came back again. He went rigid, the folds of my dress still in his hands. It was as if he had touched a live rail and was held by the current. I smiled at him and gently disengaged my frock from his grasp.

"Thank you, my friend," I said. "I do not give the name of friend lightly," I added.

"I'm so very sorry I hurt your hands," he said in a low voice, turning his head away.

"Do not be sorry. It is well. There always has to be a sacrifice in these matters. We would have done something like that deliberately if it had not happened incidentally. But it is much better as it is. When the magic works of itself, spontaneously, it shows that the cosmic forces are behind it. That is a very different matter to human will power, you know."

"I won't have to twist your wrists again, will I? I don't think I could do it in cold blood, you know."

"Oh, no, there isn't anything like that. It isn't done deliberately. But magic is a terrific strain, we may as well face the fact. A physical strain as well as a mental strain."

"When I stood at your altar it was next door to tetanus, is that what you mean?"

"Yes, that is what I mean. You dare not move, because if you do, it breaks the contacts, and the muscular tension becomes simply terrific, especially when invoking or projecting power with the arms outheld."

"I have noticed the development of your neck muscles and shoulder girdle. You have the same kind of neck as the women who carry heavy weights on their heads. Am I going to see all these performances in due time?"

"You are."

"Hmm. It will be very interesting."

It will be more than interesting, thought I, knowing what I meant to do with Malcolm.

He watched me while I did the salutations that cut the contacts, for we do not banish in a sealed place of working. Then he followed me down the narrow stairs back to the normal world again—if, of course, any spot where I was could be called really normal.

Malcolm came with me to the kitchen, and made tea under my direction, for my hands were not to be trusted with boiling kettles at the moment. He was an utterly helpless creature in a kitchen, without an idea on the subject, and all thumbs with the teapot despite his exquisite manipulative skill. He got quite as much tea into the turn-ups of his trousers as we subsequently drank. I wanted to get him back to normal again before he left me, but he was so utterly changed that I wondered what normal for him might be. He lay back in my big chair in a day-dream, and I thought he was going to sleep. However, the tea roused him, and he blinked at me as if surprised to see me there. "

"So that is the sort of thing we are going to do, is it?" said he.

"It is the beginning of it," said I.

"Satisfactory?"

"Quite, so far as it goes."

"More to follow?"

"Yes, but the worst is over. The beginning is always the biggest strain. It gets easier as it goes on. Usually we can ease in the power a little more gradually than this, but it came with a rush because you had already got so much lying latent in you, and it roused at a touch."

"Not particularly latent, Miss Le Fay. I had all this well up on the surface when I was a lad. Naturally it faded a good deal of recent years, but it has never been very deeply buried; it never took much to rouse it. A magazine story I read on a railway journey did it once."

"Was it illustrated?"

"It was. In colour, too. It was a Christmas number."

That explains it. Colour is all-important."

"Why?"

"Because colour equates with force; and so, for the matter of that, do musical pitch and rhythm."

"You are opening a completely new world to me, Miss Le Fay, and yet I think I knew it existed. I knew the exact delimitations of science; I knew where the proven ended and the speculative began, and I have always been very careful of the distinction, particularly in my own line of work, where we always have to be on the look-out for the hysterias, and suggestion plays so big a part. Miss Le Fay, I have seen things happen to the mind through the body, and to the body through the mind that—well—you might believe, but nobody else would. You asked me whether I believed in the power of the mind over the body, and I poured scorn on you. I was thinking of those New Thought tinkerings with organic disease. Of course they can't do anything except administer placebos, though placebos are well worth having to the poor devil that's got the disease. But genuine mind-healing of a genuine disease—well, I have yet to see a case.

"You should see me do mind-healing, Miss Le Fay. Funniest thing you ever saw. A large part of my work is distinguishing between organic and functional nervous disorders. The functional cases, of course, are the hysterics. In comes the paralytic on his stretcher, and we get to work. Some folks use a mallet; I don't, I use my fingers.

"So you can't use your arm, my poor man?"—"No sir, I can't— What's your trade?"—He tells me.—"Foreman bully you?"—Then comes a tale of insult and oppression and general injury to his *amour-propre*. I get my fingers on his elbow"—Malcolm leant over towards me. "No, I won't do it to you, it will hurt your bruises." He laid a hand on my knee. "So you've been paralysed from the waist downward, have you, madam, since your motor accident?" "Yes, doctor."

Malcolm's fingers suddenly pressed. I kicked out sharply and involuntarily. He chuckled.

He repeated the pressure, and up came that ridiculous foot once more.

"You do that again," said I, "and I'll kick you in good earnest."

"I did get kicked in good earnest once by an alleged paralytic," said he, "and it very nearly cost me my front teeth. If I drew a commission on all the money I've saved insurance companies, I'd be a millionaire. But the patients aren't all frauds, you know, by any manner of means. Lots of them genuinely think they are ill. So they are, but not physically. And that's the sort that get healed at these big religious meetings at the Albert Hall. I've known my own cases come up there, Miss Le Fay, and some damn fool of a G.P. gives 'em a certificate to say they're genuine physical healings. It's not my business to spoke their wheels, but you can see what I've come to think of these things, can't you?"

"Not that I blame G.P.s for making mistakes over the central nervous system. I know what gets sent up to me from our our own Out Patients. What I blame them for is putting their names to a thing they haven't checked up on. It seems to me that when people go in for these mystical things they take leave of their wits, Miss Le Fay. What happens to them?"

"Auto-hypnosis and deliberately induced dissociation of personality are part of the method of the Mysteries. Some people know what they are about, and some do not. Those that do not, get dissociated and stay dissociated."

"I see. Artificially induced and localised insanity. Hyper-suggestible to start with, and then cultivate it. That was suggestion you were giving me this evening, Miss Le Fay."

"I know it was, Dr. Malcolm. But there was something more to it than that. It started as suggestion, but it ended as something much more. Or rather, it would have ended as something much more if I had let it go on, but I pulled it up in the early stages, as it was our first attempt at working together, and I did not want to put too much strain on you."

"So you were just trying my paces, were you?"

"Yes, trying your paces; picking up the starting point and getting you used to the feel of the forces."

"And the next stage?"

"We have got our starting point in your recurring dream. That gives us all we need. Now I will be teaching you the technique we use, and you will be gradually getting used to the force and we will be able to increase the voltage."

"What does my recurring dream give you, Miss Le Fay?"

"It gives us, both you and me, access to the higher levels of your consciousness, the levels that lie beyond the subconscious to which ordinary, fleeting dreams give access."

He looked at his watch.

"Good Lord, look at the time! I have made you a visitation. Lucky tomorrow is Sunday. May I come in and fix your hand? It will want doing."

"You may. You will be very welcome. But tell me this before you go, and tell me frankly, as you would if you were one of your own patients— what effect has your experience this evening had upon you?"

He smoothed his greying red hair, pushing it back from that wonderful forehead with both hands, a very characteristic gesture of his.

"To begin with, I was half glamoured and half sceptical. Now I am not nearly so glamoured nor nearly so sceptical. I can see that this business has a psychological aspect that comes within the range of reason, just as I could see that yoga has a physiological basis in the central nervous system. I can see that you understand that basis, which is more than the New Thought woman did; and I can see that you are a sensible woman, which is also more than she was. I shall thoroughly enjoy experimenting with you, especially if you will allow me to keep systematic records of what we do and the results we obtain. I am turning over in my mind the question as to whether you are an exceedingly clever hypnotist with a knowledge of psychology which you use in combination with the imaginative powers of a first-class novelist, or whether there is something more in it all than that, as I see you believe. I don't know. I am keeping an open mind. I haven't seen anything—so far—that couldn't be explained psychologically, but it is early days yet, and you may have a few cards up your sleeve that I haven't seen. I have not yet discovered where the risk lies which you take so seriously. You might capsize the arty-arty type of youth, but I should not think there was very much you could do to a tough old bird like me. However, I'm quite willing you should have a free hand to do your damnedest. I'm with you, Miss Le Fay. It is exceedingly interesting."

"Will you write up the records?"

"I will," said he.

"Will you tell me one thing before you go. Have I brought you peace?"

"Yes, certainly you have. I feel very comfortable and rather sleepy."

He rose. I accompanied him to the door. He paused, hesitating on the threshold. I drew my fur about me and strolled slowly down the road with him. He did not speak till we came to a standstill on the wharf. Then he said:

"How did you know I wanted you to walk down the road with me?"

"It is my business to know things."

"Can you read my thoughts?"

"More or less. If you put any force behind them in my direction, I expect I should know it."

"Do you know when I lie to you?"

"Yes."

He stood staring across the now ebbing river towards his own rooms.

"Yes, Miss Le Fay, you have given me peace, the peace that passeth all understanding, and I thank you for it."

He lifted his hat and turned on his heel and left me.

CHAPTER
ELEVEN

Next morning my hands were so swollen and stiff that I could neither dress nor do my hair, but sat in front of the fire in a white velvet dressing-gown, toasting my toes in their scarlet mules and drinking chocolate and wondering when Malcolm would turn up to give me the massage he had promised. It was on an occasion like this that I found the disadvantage of having a gentleman char instead of the more usual char-lady. I thought Malcolm would survive the sight of me in a dressing-gown, for it differed but little save in voluminousness from the loose robes I habitually wore in the house; but I did not wish him to see me with my hair streaming over my shoulders.

I called my domestic, who was busied about his duties.

"Mr. Meatyard," I said, "have you ever plaited a horse's tail?"

"Lor bless yer, mum, I taken prizes at the van-'oss parades."

I thought it was more likely his charge had taken them than he had, but did not wish to hurt his feelings by pointing out the inaccuracy.

"Do you think you could plait my hair for me? I don't want any straws in it, or anything fancy like that."

"Course I can. Do yer fine!"

He set to work with my silver-backed brushes with great gusto, and had got my mass of hair disentangled and spread out like a cape when there came a bang on the knocker. Brush in hand, he went to the door, and I heard him greeting a friend.

"Blimey, guv'nor! Is it you?"

"Yes, it's me," came Malcolm's voice. "What are you doing with that brush, stealing it?"

"Naow. Given all that up since I 'ad this job. I'm doin' 'er 'air."

He opened the door and ushered in Malcolm.

"Tike a seat, guv'nor. I'll soon 'ave 'er finished."

"Would you like a cup of chocolate?" said I, thinking it best to take everything as a matter of course.

"Thanks very much," said Malcolm, helping himself from the earthenware pot keeping warm in the embers.

Mr. Meatyard laid down my brush and started on a plait, backing away from me as the plait lengthened, Malcolm watching him.

" 'ang onto that for 'alf a mo', will yer, sir?" he said, handing Malcolm the tip to hold while he got to work on the other plait. Then, filling his mouth with a handful of hairpins, he twisted both plaits round my head in a very creditable imitation of my usual coiffure.

"There now, wodjer think o' that, sir?" said my gentleman char, surveying me with pardonable pride.

Malcolm's eyes met mine for a brief second which was all that either of us dared risk.

"Fine," said he. "I couldn't have done it better myself."

"An' that's praise from a expert," said Meatyard, preening himself. "I seen you do some fine jobs while I was goin' to the clinic."

"Not so bad," said Malcolm. "Each to his trade. How's the leg serving you?"

"Does me orl right. Mightn't suit a beauty chorus, but then I ain't thinkin' of joinin' one."

He gathered up my toilette articles and took himself off.

"Like me to powder your nose for you?" said Malcolm." I will, if you say the word."

"You wretch!" said I, completely taken aback at such a remark from Malcolm, for I should never have believed he had it in him.

"There's your report," said he, dropping a sheaf of papers into my lap. "you can read it while I do your hands."

I turned over the pages as best I could. On the first was a beautifully drawn diagram of my temple, complete in every detail, duly annotated with all the information I had given him.

Next, in neat, formal handwriting, came a practically verbatim account of the astral journey I had taken him. Finally came an account of his subjective experiences.

"From the beginning of the whole transaction I have had the sensation of being sucked down by a whirlpool. The sensation has been extremely painful when I resisted it; extremely pleasurable when I yielded to it.

When Miss L.F. proposed to make a start on the work, I felt great anticipatory nervousness. Respiration hurried and shallow. Heart rapid and irregular. Mouth dry. Unpleasant sensations in epigastrium. Sweating. This continued till she left me alone when she went to dress, when I succeeded in getting myself in hand and calmed down a little.

"I got myself in hand by telling myself that there was nothing in the whole business. That she was self-deluded, and that I was merely amusing myself.

But when I saw her come down the stairs in her robes, I knew it was real. My nervousness, however, left me. Or, to be more precise, my agitation changed into a keyed-up feeling which was not unpleasurable. I knew, as soon as I saw her in her silver head-dress, where I had seen her before. She was the woman I had always seen in my temple dreams.

"I knew now that Miss L.F., the woman in the temple, the body in the dissecting-room dream, and the cloaked woman were all one and the same person, and I recognised that this fact must have significance.

"I had a very curious sensation when Miss L.F. held up the curtain for me to get through the doorway. I felt as if more than a physical curtain was being drawn back—as if a curtain were being drawn back in my mind.

"The room was absolutely familiar, though smaller than I had expected. It seemed perfectly natural for me to walk up to the altar and stand there with my hands on it. My hands tingled all the time they were on it as if an electric current were coming through them.

"The mirror had a very curious effect on me. I kept on seeing things in it. I had thought for a moment it was an archway leading into another, and more elaborately equipped room. Then I saw in it the temple I have always seen, where I met the woman.

"Then Miss L.F. made me lie down on the couch and began to describe things to me. These I saw in the mirror as she described them. Finally I had the sensation of being on the other side of the mirror.

"I omitted to say that it upset me for a moment when she put her hands on either side of my head. I got the whirlpool sensation again. When however I gave myself up to the pleasure of it, I passed straight through the mirror and found myself in the temple on the other side in her company. I then re-lived with great vividness, much pleasure and much agitation, my usual dream. In this instance, however, I had a peculiar sensation that instead of impersonating the priest, I was myself the genuine priest, and that in doing what I did, I was playing my proper part in a regular ritual. In consequence, instead of the dream concluding in shame, terror and self-loathing, I had a profound sense of satisfaction and fulfilment, as if my life had in some way opened up, like the opening of a door that led me through into wide spaces. So great was the sense of relief and gratitude that I with difficulty restrained my tears. Although entirely restored to normal consciousness myself, Miss L.F. continued to appear to me as I had seen her in my vision."

I gathered the papers together as best I could.

"Thank you," I said. "If there is one thing I respect more than another, it is the courage to be honest with oneself."

"I have never found it difficult to be honest with myself," said Malcolm, starting on the second hand. "My nature has never left me in the slightest doubt as to what was there and what it was like. I find it very difficult to be honest with you, however. I know, theoretically, that I can speak to you as man to man, and that you will understand, but I find it extraordinarily difficult to deal with a woman like that in actual practice. Do you know the kind of dream in which you are climbing about among girders or on a precipice, but are sufficiently awake to know that you are dreaming, and that you can throw yourself down with impunity?

"And then, as you are just about to throw yourself down, comes an awful feeling that it mayn't be a dream after all, but a kind of risky reality? That's how I feel when I start to let myself go with you. I know it's all right. I know you know what you're about. And then there comes the awful feeling—my God, supposing it isn't anything out of the ordinary, and we're just making a mess of things! I tell you, I simply go cold all over."

During all this recital Malcolm, with a perfectly calm face and perfectly steady hands, was massaging my fingers.

"You will lose that fear as you get habituated to the forces," said I.

"Well, I hope I shall," said Malcolm, "for it is very unpleasant. As a matter of fact," he added, "I think I have cleared a lot of it in telling you about it. That was why I did it, in fact. I hope you don't mind these goal deliveries. You are, I take it, a woman with a pretty wide experience of life. There was a time when I resented that, but now I am thankful for it. Bend those hands at the wrist and move them about. They are suppling nicely."

"What do you generally do on Sundays?" said I, for Malcolm appeared to be hanging around at a loose end, rather like a stray dog, and I did not want him on my hands all day till the evening, when I would be ready to work with him again.

"I always used to go down to my wife one week-end and catch up with arrears of work the next. Nowadays—I don't know. I go for a walk in the Park if it's fine and if it's wet, go to a concert—I don't care for the pictures. I don't care for concerts much, either, for that matter. I suppose I generally end by working, same as week-days."

It was not difficult to guess at the dreary emptiness of life for that man. He had nothing but his work and his duty to his wife, and now that last had been reduced to the bare minimum of supporting her.

I had not the heart to turn him away completely, so sent him out to take his walk while I got dressed and attended to such few things as required my attention.

In due course Malcolm reappeared, and ate his lunch with such gusto that I wondered what his landlady fed him on, or if, in fact, she fed him at all. Then I put him into my big chair with a selection of Sunday papers, and he went peacefully to sleep and slept till tea-time. Malcolm as a visitor was really no trouble at all.

"I thought you said you suffered from insomnia," said I when he was finally roused by Mr. Meatyard bumping him with the tea-trolley.

"So I do, as a rule," said he, "but not when you're around. I always go straight off to sleep then."

"Do I take that as a compliment?" said I.

"You would," said he, "if you knew what a luxury it is for me to feel relaxed.

We made a Yorkshire high-tea of it, as I knew it would be late before we got another meal. Malcolm enjoyed it all like a schoolboy home for the holidays. I discovered that I was developing a soft spot in my heart for him, and liked giving him pleasure. Magic makes a curious bond of sympathy between the people who practice it together; and conversely, if things go amiss with the magic, the personal ructions are correspondingly vigorous.

After tea I tried to entertain Malcolm with comments on the contents of the Sunday papers, but he brushed me aside. Desultory conversation was a thing he had no use for.

"I am going to ask you a question," he said, "which you may say I have no business to ask. Of course you need not answer it if you don't choose, and I shall make no attempt to draw conclusions. In fact, with a person like yourself, so far out of the ordinary run, one couldn't draw conclusions that would be likely to be anywhere near the mark. You made a remark to me once that you had had a pretty wide experience of men—what exactly did you mean by that remark?"

"What you really want to know is exactly how far I go," said I.

Malcolm reddened. "Well, yes, I suppose so. But not with any personal reference, mind you. I think you know me well enough to know that. I suppose it is a thing every man wants to know about any woman who interests him. I want to know it, partly so that I may understand you, and partly so that I may be sure that you understand me, for if you do not, I could be damn dangerous to you."

"I will give you excerpts from my emotional history," I said. "Not the whole of it for that would bore you, being too long and too repetitive.

As a girl I was plain, severe, serious-minded, critical and sharp-tongued. I was strictly virtuous, both by inclination and necessity, having, as you will understand from that catalogue of qualities, no opportunity to be otherwise. Later in life, after I touched the invisible side of things, I changed considerably, both in outlook and appearance."

"You certainly must have, if you were a plain girl," said Malcolm. The invisible side of things, thought I, was evidently not without effect on Malcolm, either.

"When I came to study comparative religion I found that there were many different kinds of morality in the world, both ancient and modern; some worked well, and some did not, if one judged them by the happiness or otherwise of the societies they ruled. Ours, I soon came to the conclusion, was one of those that did not work well. I wondered, therefore, whether it was necessary to accord it more than the politeness it is always well to give to such an influential person as Mrs Grundy, and concluded that it was not, for I saw its rules scrupulously observed, and yet result in misery and destruction."

Malcolm stirred uneasily in his chair.

"I saw them systematically defeat their own ends. I also saw them disregarded, not only with impunity, but with, in many cases, excellent results. I concluded, therefore, that although a code of some sort there had to be if human beings were to associate together, it need not necessarily be the code we had got; for that appeared to be most lamentable in its workings. I therefore dropped Mrs Grundy a curtsy whenever I saw her looking my way, for no individual is strong enough to defy openly the social code under which he lives, and set to work to formulate a code of my own that should really be effectual for the purposes it was intended to serve.

"It seemed to me that the trouble lay in the fact that sex was a dual-purpose contrivance—so many dual-purpose gadgets give trouble, don't they?—it had to provide for the continuation of the race and at the same time for the happiness of individuals, and the two purposes were mutually antagonistic—what one gained on the swings, one lost on the roundabouts—and the real problem was to balance the rival claims."

"And how did you strike an adjustment?" asked Malcolm.

"Like the Hindus do, my friend, by allocating the rival claims to different ages. Why should I reproduce my race before or after my prime? Why should I, in fact, reproduce it at all in a densely populated country if I have other contributions to make to the common welfare? Distinguish, like the Greeks did, between sex for reproduction and sex for happiness, and I think you have the key. I, for my part, am a free woman and a priestess of the most ancient gods—that gives you the key to me."

"I can understand your studies changing your viewpoint," said Malcolm, "but what was it changed your appearance? Study doesn't do that; if anything, it makes you plainer than you naturally are because you don't get enough exercise."

"The thing that changed my appearance," said I, "was learning to know the Old Gods in the ancient Mystery teaching, for They give fullness of life, and I, who had been starved of life, suddenly began to feed upon Them. I changed, I grew young again, I grew vital; and men who had never looked twice at me, looked, and looked again, and I fed on their feeling for me. You may think me a vampire, but a vampire is one who takes too much or who takes all and gives nothing. I never did that. For remember, human beings feed each other magnetically and emotionally all the time—you have only to look into your own life to see that."

"And what happens to you if you go hungry?" asked Malcolm.

"Then you are restless, depressed or quarrelsome according to temperament."

"I'm all of them."

"But in my company you go to sleep like a baby that has had its bottle."

"You are a highly magnetic woman, Miss Le Fay, any one can see that a mile off; then why is it that instead of stimulating me, as one would expect, you calm me?"

"Because I know how to use my magnetism, how to turn it on and off at will. You will never find me guilty of the cruelty of increasing the pressure where there is no adequate outlet."

"I have discovered that, and I appreciate it. It means that I can be happy with you without having the life worried out of me, and I am deeply grateful to you. You have a terrific emotional effect on me, as I am afraid I have been unable to conceal, but you do not stimulate me sexually—no, not even when circumstances compel me to hold the end of your pigtail!"

I laughed, and Malcolm curled his lips in the grim smile that did duty with him for mirth.

Dusk had fallen and I was ready for work, for I do not work, if I can help it, during daylight.

I took Malcolm up to my robing-room.

"As soon as my hands are better," I said, "you shall have your robes."

"You make them?" said he.

"One can hardly expect to buy them ready-made," said I.

"Yes, I make them, and I make them entirely by hand, and I magnetise them as I make them."

"I should like to wear the robes you made me," said Malcolm.

"I can't make your sandals, though," said I. "You will have to get those yourself—ordinary bathing sandals, and I will gild them for you."

I left him there, and went on up to my temple to robe myself; I could hardly do so in front of Malcolm, for we strip when we robe. Nothing of mundane wear is worn in magic. He, for his part, would not get the full scope of the experience until he, too, was properly dressed; so perhaps it was just as well his robes could not be ready at once.

I stood before the altar, my hands upon it, and gathered myself together. There are times in magic, at the start of an operation, when cold fear takes me by the heart at the responsibility I am incurring. I am deliberately, guided by no other light than that of my human judgment, setting machinery in motion that will manipulate cosmic forces. I do not mind when I alone am concerned, but when another person comes into it, it is another matter. I spend long hours in meditation; I count time as nothing; I wait and watch for the signs to come along and will not move without them. Finally, feeling as if I were going to my own execution, I lay my hand on the invisible lever and engage the gears, and always, as I do so, I say the words of the Eastern pledge; I am thy sacrifice.

There are times in every magical operation when I ask myself if I am self-deluded—am I really what I think I am? This is due to the discrepancy between the two modes of consciousness—the normal brain consciousness, and the higher consciousness that includes subconsciousness and transcends it, for it contains not only the memories of this life, but of all past lives and all their knowledge. In trance work we disconnect the normal con-sciousness and use ultra-consciousness only; in magic we use both modes of consciousness simultaneously. We have to use the psychological analogue of double de-clutching, and inevitably there is a loss of power as the gears disengage and re-engage. It is at that moment that the horrible doubts and fears come in. They pass again as the power comes through and the magic picks up speed, but they are bad moments while they last. Usually we swing over them on the momentum of the ritual, but I had not yet come to the point when I could use ritual with Malcolm, and I had to make my transitions in cold blood. However, I survived—

The elements rage, the fiend voices that rave
    Shall dwindle, shall blend,
Shall cease. Shall become first a peace after pain, then a light—

It is claimed by initiates that Browning was one of us, and on the evidence of those lines I believe it, for I have passed through that gate so often.

I have passed out by the path of fear so often that I have almost ceased to fear it. I know it will be unpleasant, but I know it will be brief. The shadows began to close round me as I stood at the altar in my robes, but I set my teeth and went to fetch Malcolm. I do not mind when I am alone. It is when I am responsible for others that I get this fear. But I am the sacrifice!

It is to that thought I cling. If anything goes wrong, I am first in the line of fire.

Malcolm came eagerly in answer to my summons. He had passed through his gate of fear the previous day and the fascination of the Unseen was upon him. He followed me up the dark stair, and again I lifted the curtain for him, both literally and metaphorically, and we stood together upon the floor of Isis.

"Do I get on the couch?" he asked in a low voice.

"No, I replied. "You stand at the upright altar today."

I placed him facing the mirror at the side of Earth, and took my place opposite him with the mirror behind me. The hanging lamp shed a pyramid of shadow over us, and in the shadow the lamp upon the altar threw a cone of light upwards, bringing out in strong relief Malcolm's heavy jaw and beetling brows. His eyes were on my face, and I knew from the look in them that my features had changed even as his had in that revealing light. His was the face of the butchering priest; what mine was I could only guess from his startled, reverent eyes.

Malcolm's reaction helped to restore to me my sense of reality; the gears engaged and the magic began. I was not fully the priestess yet, however. I was still driving myself on willpower. I intended to work Malcolm up to the pitch of emotional intensity when he would touch those reserves of energy that give the maniac his strength and the artist his frenzy of creation. Then there would come off from him the magnetism that is used in magic and without which magic is not. It was not difficult to do, for I could take him along the line of his natural cleavage—his feeling for me and his memories of his past lives; but to hold him steady on the crest of the wave as it rose to breaking, and cross the bar between the planes on a great emotional crisis was entirely a matter of nerve and concentration, and if either failed, that was the end of Malcolm; it would not kill him, but if the fuse blows at that tension, the man is a burnt-out cinder thereafter. Then the work done, I had to bring him back to normal, stepping down the power and stepping it down; linking up the dissociated ends of consciousness so that there should be no gaps; easing him back into his body so quietly, so steadily, that no sign of the tension should show, and restoring him finally to perfect normality, ready to take up his day's work—*hic labor, hoc opus est*, and the more skillfully one does it, the less people realise what has been done.

I laid my hands on the altar and bid Malcolm copy me in all I did. The broad, perfectly proportioned hands with their slightly spatulate fingers, beautiful in their strength and sensitiveness, appeared in the circle of light. My hands are curious, they are not a pair; one is a man's hand, and one is a woman's, and on them I had the magnetised rings that give power. On the black velvet of the altar cloth, within the small circle of light thrown by the sacred lamp, lay the two pairs of hands—the virile, corded, muscular hands of Malcolm, and my smooth white woman's hands with their pink-stained nails. They were laid there in dedication and sacrifice; there is a peculiar sense of helplessness when the hands are laid on the altar; one is so completely at the mercy of the powers one invokes, so completely negative, opening one's soul to them; then, as the power comes in, one shares in it and becomes powerful once more. I felt the power beginning to rise, and called up my reserves from the earth centre and brought them to their focus in the third eye, the concealed astral eye, that is in the centre of the forehead, and felt the twisting sensation as it began to stir. I pinned Malcolm with my eyes as a snake pins a bird, for one has to be ruthless in magic, and then raised my hands and threw the power at him; threw it in hard, threw it in crushingly, because I had to break down his inhibitions and reach the deeper levels. I saw him quiver as he felt the force, but his eyes met mine unwaveringly and his hands came up opposite mine, palm parallel to palm, a foot apart. He could not bend back his wrists as I did, but the hands were absolutely steady and the arms behind them like bars of steel. Malcolm was a man of power, steady as a rock; single-pointed; unreservedly dedicated; I could not have asked for a better man to work with.

I had to magnetise Malcolm and make him see me as the priestess, so

I began the age-old chant that declared my power:

I am she who ere the earth was formed
Was Rhea, Binah, Ge.
I am that soundless, boundless, bitter sea
Out of whose deeps life wells eternally.
Astarte, Aphrodite, Ashtoreth -
Giver of life and bringer-in of death;
Hera in heaven, on earth Persephone;
Diana of the ways and Hecate -
All these am I and they are seen in me,
The hour of the high full moon draws near;
I hear the invoking words, hear and appear -
Shaddai el Chai and Rhea, Binah, Ge -
I come unto the priest who calleth me -

As I chanted and vibrated the words I moved my arms in the signs that correspond, and Malcolm, unable to follow these, dropped his hands to his sides and stood still. I made the signs of space and sea and inner earth; of hailing Aphrodite and chaste Diana of the moon, and finally the bat-wings of Hecate—for unless one can handle the dark aspect of a force, one cannot handle the bright—and in the end I gave Malcolm the full salute of a priest, and I think he knew it.

We faced each other, priest and priestess. Malcolm had to stand up to the forces as best he could; I might not temper them to him any longer. Then began the voice that is not my voice, the most tremendous form of mediumship there is—the cosmic mediumship that brings through the gods:

"I am the veiled Isis of the shadows of the sanctuary. I am she that moveth as a shadow behind the tides of death and birth. I am she that cometh forth by night and no man seeth my face. I am older than time and forgotten of the gods. No man may look upon my face and live, for in the hour he parteth my veil, he dieth."

Malcolm looked into the eyes of Isis.

"I am quite willing to die," he said.

"Kneel down."

"There are two deaths by which men die, the greater and the lesser. The death of the body and the death of initiation, and of these two, the death of the body is the lesser. The man who looks upon the face of Isis dies, for the Goddess takes him. They that die thus go by the path of the well-head that is beside the white cypress."

Unbidden, Malcolm folded his arms on the altar and laid his head on them.

"He that would die to the birth, let him look upon the face of the Goddess in this mystery. Be ye far from us, O ye profane, for one goes by the path that leads to the well-head that is beside the white cypress."

Malcolm seemed asleep, and the intoning voice went on:

O Isis veiled and Rhea, Binah, Ge,
Lead us to the well of memory;
The well-head where the pale white cypress grows,
By secret twilight paths that no man knows.

The shadowy path dividing into three -
Diana of the ways and Hecate
Selene of the moon, Persephone.

The high full moon in the mid-heavens shines clear;
O hear the invoking words, hear and appear!
Shaddai el Chai and Rhea, Binah, Ge -

The room had disappeared and I was standing in a vast underground cave with dark water at my feet. Before me, Malcolm knelt with bowed head and raised arms, but the altar no longer being there, the raised arms seemed to express supplication. I myself was no longer robed in the dull black of velvet that fits all the negative forces, but in soft, shimmering filmy indigo, blue and purple; upon my head was the horned moon, and about my hips the starry girdle of the constellations, and I knew that I was Isis in her underworld aspect whom the Greeks called Persephone, for all the goddesses are one goddess, personified under different modes.

There was nothing of the human left about me. I was vast as the universe; my head among the stars; my feet on the curve of the earth as it swung under me in its orbit. Around me, in translucent space, stood the stars, rank upon rank, and I was of their company. Beneath me, very far beneath me, all Nature lay spread like a green-patterned carpet. Alone on the globe that soared through space I stood, with the kneeling man before me, and there were none others in all creation save he and I—I, the ALL-WOMAN, and he, he Archetypal MAN, and the whole of the manifested universe was summed up in the relationship between us.

I was in my calm, negative, underworld aspect as Queen of the Dead, ruler of the Kingdoms of Sleep. In death men come to me across the dark river, and I am the keeper of their souls until the dawn. But there is also a death-in-life, and this likewise leadeth on to re-birth, for there is a turning-within of the soul whereby men come to Persephone.

I am also the Great Deep, whence life arose, to which all shall return at the end of an æon. Herein do we bathe in sleep, sinking back into the primordial deep, returning to things forgotten before time was, and the soul is renewed, touching the Great Mother. Whoso cannot return to the Primordial hath no roots in life—they are the living dead who are orphaned of the Great Mother.

I was that Great One in her most benign aspect, tranquil, brooding, as a woman broods over her unborn child. I was the Giver of Sleep, blessing the weary man before me with my great gift. He had come back to me to be a child again, as an over-wrought man always does, as he needs must do if he is to renew his strength to battle with life; for unless a woman can brood him as I brooded Malcolm that night, his nerves will wear bare of insulation as a frayed wire. It is only when for love's sake she can make him as the unborn that he renews his strength, for to him she is the soul of earth wherein are his deepest roots. The more dynamic the man, the more dependent is he upon his earth-contacts in his woman. These are not the contacts of passion; they are older, more primal than that; they go back to the days when humanity was as yet unborn from the earth-soul. I was his anima, his underworld contact, his link with most ancient earth and things primordial wherein are the roots of strength; through me he could touch them as he was powerless to do alone, for man is of the sun and stars and fire; but woman is of dark space and dark earth and dark, primordial water.

As that man who was all men knelt before me, I gazed upon him, and my own nature rose within me like a tide with the divine compassion of the All-Woman, and I stretched my arms with their wing-like draperies over him and blessed him, and the shimmering folds of blue and purple closed round him like a cloak and I drew him down to my kingdom.

Sink down, sink down, sink deeper and sink deep,
Into eternal and primordial sleep.
Sink down, forget, be still and draw apart
Into the inner earth's most secret heart.
Drink of the waters of Persephone,
The secret well beside the sacred tree.

As I sang I wove about him with my draperies, and all became dark and still and warm as the womb of Time, and he became as the unborn in their prenatal sleep. So was he rested. And as his rest deepened, he was vitalised.

Then at that deepest level, I fed his soul. Deliberately, knowing full well there must be repercussions in life and that I must pay, but knowing also that he would not have the strength to do that which I required of him if I did otherwise, I made the magnetic link between us by which power should flow—the power of woman; not the bright radiance of Aphrodite, but the dark, brooding warmth of the womb of Great Isis who is Nature. She is the giver of the strength of which in her Aphrodite aspect she is the caller-forth.

Malcolm would be dependent on me from henceforth, but then, if the truth were known, he was dependent on me already, for he had known me in my Persephone aspect in his sleep when he had dreamt that he lay with his head on a woman's shoulder.

And so, accepting the inevitable, I sang to him -

I am that secret queen, Persephone,
All tides are mine, and answer unto me,
Tides of the airs, tides of the inner earth,
The secret silent tides of death and birth -
Tides of men's souls, and dreams, and destiny -
Isis veiled and Rhea, Binah, Ge.

Then in my vision I drew him to me as he knelt so that his head rested against my breast, and gave him peace.

☾

The power began to ebb. The outlines of the room came up waveringly through the moon-mist as if through deep, dark water and I began to feel my human personality again. Malcolm still knelt before me at the altar and seemed to be asleep. I could see his greying red hair in the dim circle of light; I could see one broad hand lying flaccid on the black velvet; the other I could not see, for his cheek rested on it as he slept. I have never seen any being so utterly relaxed, and yet he knelt upright at the altar, held there by his own unconscious will. I had to bring that man back, and he had a long way to come.

Slowly, gently, for he must not come back too fast, I reversed the strokings with which I had soothed him to sleep—strokings that never touched him, and were all the more powerful on that account.

He raised his head and looked at me dazedly. Unsteadily he got to his feet, holding on by the altar.

"Where am I?" he said.

"You are back here with me," said I, "in my home, where you are happy."

"Yes, I am always happy there," he replied mechanically, for his mind was not yet fully back with him.

"Now I am going to cut the power and bring all back to normal. Hold out your hands—hold them thus."

I stretched forth mine, bent back at the wrists, and brought my flat palms against his, and as I did so the power broke. It snapped back like a piece of elastic, and we were back to normal, Malcolm and I, staring at each other.

"My God!" said Malcolm, and passed his hand over his forehead and shook the sweat off it in a shower of drops.

"How do you feel?" said I.

"Feel? I feel as if I'd had ten turkish baths one after the other. I'm one mass of sweat! What have you done to me? Let's sit down on something."

He reeled unsteadily to the couch and dropped down on it.

His hand went up to his collar.

"I'm going to take this off. I don't care what I look like."

Off came the sodden rag and was thrown on the floor. Even the ends of his tie were dark with moisture.

"My Lord!" said Malcolm, "Phew!"

He mopped his face and neck till the handkerchief joined his collar on the floor.

"I'm going to borrow a bath-towel off you when we get downstairs," he said.

"Now you see why we work in robes, and strip beneath the robe?" I said.

"My Lord, I should think I do! No suit would stand this sort of treatment very often. May I take my coat off?"

I handed him a small cloth I kept up there for cleaning the ritual instruments, and entirely unselfconscious and oblivious of me, for he was not yet fully back in his body, he sat there on the black altar of sacrifice mopping his broad chest, looking exactly as if he had been taking part in a fight.

I opened a cupboard in the wall, took out a bottle, and poured its contents into a long glass.

"Drink that." I said.

"What is it?" said he, eyeing it suspiciously, for he was a strict teetotaller.

"Apple-juice" said I, "unfermented." "Alcohol is best left alone on occasions like this."

"It's best left alone on most occasions, in my opinion," said Malcolm. "At any rate, it's best left alone by me."

The apple-juice, however, went down in one continuous stream.

"Replacements," said Malcolm. "My Lord, I needed that!"

The intake of fluid rapidly restored him to normal, and he began to be aware of the appearance he was presenting.

"My dear lady" he began, and catching sight of his bare chest, hastily buttoned his shirt. He recovered his collar from the floor, considered it, shook his head sadly, and thrust it into his trouser pocket.

"Can't tidy up. Can't apologise. Can't do anything. What actually happened? I went to sleep, didn't I?"

"You went sound asleep. Did you dream?"

"I think I must have. There seem to be vague shadows of dreams floating about still. I only hope I behaved with a reasonable amount of discretion."

"You never moved."

That's a comfort. I suppose you know what you're about. God help you if you don't. I'm no light-weight."

"If you sufficiently revived, shall we go downstairs?"

"Oh yes, I'm reviving nicely." He rose. "Lord, I'm unsteady on my feet! I don't seem to know where they are. By gum, now I know how the hysterical paralytics feel!" He dropped back on the couch and tested his own knee-jerks. "That's all right," he said with a sigh of relief.

He rose cautiously and made his way to the door.

"I'm going first down these stairs, if you don't mind. I'm not going to risk falling on top of you."

The enforced activity, however, rapidly re-coordinated him, and by the time he reached the bottom of the flight he was back to normal.

"My Lord, you do that to me often, and you'll have a corpse to bury!" he said.

"Not in the least," said I. "It will do you all the good in the world. Would you like to have a wash?"

"I'd like to have a bath," said he.

I dispatched him to the bathroom, armed with my largest bath-towel, and in due course he reappeared, pink as a cherub, clad in his own trousers as to his lower half, but having borrowed my bath-robe for his upper half.

"Next time I come to see you I shall bring a spare shirt," he said.

I knew he would be hungry, and had prepared a good meal, but I had not bargained for the wolf I found myself entertaining. Malcolm, behind his grim exterior, was simply a big schoolboy. What his learned colleagues made of him, I could not imagine, nor how even his brains had taken him to the position he held in a profession where social *savoir faire* counts for so much. It speaks volumes for the tremendous driving-force of the man that he had been able to overcome the innumerable obstacles of his own creating. But the more I saw of Malcolm, the more I liked him. There was that sterling sincerity about him, that utter good will and selflessness. I expect the first-class men in his profession appreciated him, but how the not-quite-first-class must have hated him!

At the conclusion of the meal he pushed back his chair from the table.

"I must be going. If I settle down in that big chair of yours, I shall go to sleep and be here for the night."

"It wouldn't matter if you did, so far as I am concerned."

"It wouldn't matter so far as I am concerned, either, feeling about you like I do at the moment. You've tamed me, Miss Le Fay."

"How are you feeling now?"

"Utterly amiable, my dear, utterly amiable. A child could play with me."

He retired to the bathroom to collect his sodden rags, and reappeared looking outwardly presentable.

He took my hand.

"I don't know what to say to you," he said. "I don't know what you've done to me, but you've helped me beyond anything I believed was humanly possible."

He looked at me for a moment, and then suddenly he dropped on his knees and put his head against me as he had done in my vision; and as I had done in my vision, I held him. Then he rose, and without a word, went out of the door. I watched him, striding away towards the river in the moonlight, looking like a giant refreshed.

"So much," thought I, "for Isis in her Persephone aspect."

CHAPTER
TWELVE

The next day being Monday, Malcolm had something to think about besides me and my magic, but in the quiet time between tea and the evening meal there came a knock at the door, and there he was. He stood before me and bared his head as if it were a ritual; I thought he was going down on his knees again, but he restrained himself, and followed me silently into my big room and sank into his usual chair beside the fire. He thrust his hand into his breast pocket and threw a bundle of papers into my lap.

"There's your record," he said, and lit a cigarette.

I gathered the papers together and read.

"When Miss L.F. proposed another experiment I felt no nervousness but sheer pleasure. When she told me she was going to make me a robe, I felt positively inebriated. Lost my head, in fact, for the moment. However, she left me alone to cool my heels and went to get dressed herself. By the time she was dressed, I had calmed down. "She made me stand at the altar and put my hands on it, and put hers there too. It affected me very much to see our two pairs of hands there, I don't know why. It seemed like a kind of union. I don't understand, but it meant a lot. Then she did plain, straightforward, common or garden hypnosis, and that was all there was to it.

"When I woke up, however, I was in a state in which I have never seen a subject come round from hypnosis. At a guess, my temperature was 103 or 104. I broke immediately into a profuse perspiration, which gave relief, though there was extreme exhaustion, almost amounting to syncope, and my mind was confused as if in slight delirium. I did not know what I was doing or where I was. I can only offer apologies for my subsequent unceremonious behaviour, but I really was not master of myself. "There was marked loss of sensory control of the lower limbs, the kinaesthetic sense being definitely aberrant. It threw much light on the hysterical paralyses and anaesthesias, and was of great interest to me. "I recovered rapidly, however, when I forced myself to move about, and food and drink restored me not only to normal, but to super-normal. I felt magnificent, and still do (3 a.m.). But under all the vitality there is

a profound peace and sense of relaxation, and so much happiness that if I had a voice, I
would sing.

"I am deeply grateful to Miss L.F. for her patience with me and her kindness to me.

R.A.M."

" 'R.A.M.?' " said I, "Aries, the Ram—of course you are! Did you get any sleep at all last night?"

"I got a bit. Two bits, in fact. One as soon as I went to bed, and the other just as it was getting light. But I haven't felt my broken night at all; I've felt fine all day, and still do. I have drunk of the secret well, Miss Le Fay—the water of life."

"Did you dream at all?" I asked, for I knew from his words that the subconscious content was working through to the surface.

"Yes, I did dream, and my dream, and the conclusions I draw from it, are in the rest of those papers you've got. Read them and be done with it, and then you can say whether you mean to throw me out or not. You won't like them, but you stipulated I should be frank, and I have been. Now it's up to you."

I turned over the papers and he lit another cigarette. I saw that his hand was not quite steady. Knowing what Malcolm's hands were like, I began to wonder what those papers contained.

"After leaving the house, I found myself in a very exhilarated condition, a bit above myself, in fact. An impulsive and ill-considered act on my part had met with a more tolerant reception than it deserved, and I was slightly inebriated in consequence. I walked home in this state, but as soon as I entered my own quarters my mood changed suddenly, and I realised I had done an exceedingly foolish thing, one that must never occur again. There was a sudden reaction, and I fell into a self-doubting mood, and became deeply unhappy.

"Knowing that I should not sleep, I acted on the advice of a colleague I had consulted, and took a sleeping tablet; this being ineffectual, I took another, and got into an unpleasant, nightmarish state between sleeping and waking which I very much dislike. The drug I had taken prevented me from rousing myself, but did not induce complete unconsciousness, and I became very disturbed and apprehensive.

"Something seemed to tell me insistently that if I would call upon Miss L.F. I would be all right, but this I was unwilling to do, thinking it wiser not.

"I struggled on in this state for some time, getting more and more desperate, but determined not to give in, when a man suddenly seemed to be standing beside my bed. I didn't see him, but I knew he was there, and I knew what he looked like. He was tall and thin, between fifty and sixty years of age, with a shaven, sunburned head, a hook nose, thin lips, grey eyes, and wore a long straight garment of white pleated cotton or linen with no sleeves. He had gold sandals on his feet, a gold collar round his neck, gold bracelets on his arms, and a gold band round his head. I knew at once that he was the chief priest whom I had worked under, and who had been the only man who had understood me or given me any sympathy. My confidence immediately returned, and I felt an enormous sense of relief. My sleep deepened, and I began to dream in good earnest.

"I dreamt that I talked over my difficulties with this man, and what he told me amounted to this: that provided I did not mind being sacrificed in the end, everything would be all right. He said I was always to keep the end-sacrifice in view, and I need not fear anything going wrong. He said I lacked faith, I said that I did not lack faith, nor did I fear any consequences to myself; but I did fear, and not without reason, in my opinion, the consequences to other people of the imperfections in myself. He seemed to think that it did not matter, but I was unable to take that view. I asked for some sort of guarantee or promise, but he wouldn't give it. All he would say was: "It doesn't matter."

"Then he said a thing which seemed to change my whole outlook, I cannot tell why; but as soon as he said it, apprehension gave place to confidence. He said—not in words, but in ideas that came into my mind—"You will remember what I told you—that next time you will be the priest."

"Then I seemed to have a dream within a dream, or rather a very vivid kind of memory picture of this man coming to me just before the torture started that was to put me to death, and saying those words.

"I woke up with a start, wide awake, no trace of the drug, though its action is normally prolonged. It seemed to me that I had just had a nightmare within my dream of being put to death by torture. I could see the torture chamber and all the rest of it, and yet I knew I hadn't had that nightmare, but only remembered having had it. It is very difficult to describe the impression I received of several different levels of consciousness overlapping each other.

"Everything seemed to have been cleared up. All my anxiety was gone. I felt quite sure of myself and not in the least apprehensive of any further loss of self-control, which is the thing that has been my great

155

dread, knowing that several times it has only been circumstances that have saved me from making a fool of myself. It seemed to me that as the priest—the genuine priest this time, not the pseudo one—I should have all the power I needed. That I was no longer working blindly in Miss L.F.'s hands, with all the responsibility on her, but that I had the necessary knowledge inside my head and that it would come back to me when occasion recalled it.

"In this optimistic mood I lay down again. I judged it unwise to take another sleeping tablet, but it did not seem to matter whether I slept or not, I was perfectly refreshed and very clear mentally. Feeling thus elated and self-confident, I determined to try an experiment on my own. I recalled in my imagination the scenes Miss L.F. had described when she made me imagine myself going with her into the Temple of Isis and actually seeing the goddess appear. I did this with extraordinary success; in fact it became so vivid that it all seemed real. I was tempted for a moment to imagine Miss L.F. beside me, as she had been on the previous occasion, but resisted the temptation and went on into the temple alone. When I got in there, however, I knew that she was behind the curtain in the Holy of Holies, but I had no right to go in there except at her invitation, and that I might never get that invitation. But on the other hand, I might. That was a point that was not settled yet. I knew this was so, but did not know what it meant, and don't know now.

"I went down some steep stone steps to a door below the level of the floor. I had the key, it appears, and let myself in. This was my own domain, where I was at home. It was a gloomy, sinister sort of place, but I felt more at home there than in the main part of the temple, just as today I am more at my ease in the path. lab. than in the wards, and get on better with the research men than with the ordinary students. I knew I was an outcast, but an important sort of outcast, and however much they disliked me, they could not get on without me. I am referring to the temple, not the hospital, but it applies equally to the hospital. History repeats itself, if these are really re-incarnation memories. But I am wondering whether they are, or whether they are simply a dramatisation of my inner state. In any case, they serve the same purpose as a psychoanalysis, so I will leave it at that.

"It is very difficult to describe the state I was in. It was more than a daydream and less than sleep. I could look on at it, and direct it, and yet I was in it and it was happening to me.

"I imagined myself going down a long underground passage, with water running in a channel at one side. It was monotonous, going down there in the dark, but I found I could speed up my pace till I flew rather than walked; all the same, I had to traverse that passage, I could not cut it short by any act of arbitrary will on my part. Finally I came out into a large cave with a very high roof; I could not see the top of it. I judged it to be a natural cave that had been improved upon. There was a main entrance at one side—it was roughly octagonal—and opposite that was a huge statue of a naked woman cut out of the living rock and not quite detached from it behind. The door by which I entered was alongside her right leg, and my head came about level with the lower edge of her patella, so that by raising my arms I could clasp her knees.

"The carving of this image was very rough and primitive, and she appeared to be much blackened and discoloured by smoke, as were, in fact, the upper part of the walls of the cave and its roof as far as I could see. The whole build of the woman represented was coarse and massive; she seemed to symbolise crude and brutal animal force. There flashed into my mind the memory of the various insect species, notably spiders, in which the females eat their mates after fertilisation has taken place. This was a destructive brute of a woman, I knew that; but I was her priest, and there it was—I couldn't do anything about it. There was another aspect, a beautiful aspect, of womanhood in the other temple, but I had nothing to do with that. It was with one of the priestesses of this other aspect that I had got infatuated, and this was what had got me into my trouble. The higher grade priests and priestesses used to come down to my cave temple periodically. I don't know why. I had to do some sort of ritual involving blood sacrifice for their benefit, I fancy. They got the benefit, and then cleared out and left the man who did the ritual.

"I remembered Miss L.F. telling me to pray to Isis, and the remarkable results I got from that prayer; so I prayed to this great image, whom I judged to be a primitive form of Isis. I remember I clasped her knees and got very worked up, pouring out my whole soul to her, ugly monstrosity though she was. Then suddenly she began to change, and instead of rough red sandstone blackened by smoke, she became shining like polished black marble, and I saw that she was Miss L.F., or rather a statue of her, being three or four times life-size. I thought of the words of Scripture—"I am black but comely." This statue was a most beautiful thing, though jet black. I had a kind of horrified admiration for it. I continued to clasp its knees, but as one would clasp a snake or a fish, I was afraid of it, yet fascinated by it. I knew inwardly that if I could break through my fear and sense of repulsion and throw myself wholeheartedly into the business, it would change into something beautiful, but I was unable to do this.

"Then the main door opened a few inches, and through the crack there slipped the priestess I was fond of. Naturally I was very pleased to see her, and came down from the platform and went over to her and embraced her. She reciprocated in a gentle kind of way. At any rate, she did not repulse me. I took her hand and led her up onto the platform, and we sat down at the goddess's feet and I embraced her again, with more warmth, and got from her the same kind of gentle response. All this was genuine dream, I was not directing it.

"Then there was a lot of singing in the distance, and I noticed for the first time that there was a pool of water in the middle of the floor and that it apparently fed the conduit that ran along the passage. Beside the pool was a big stalagmite which I knew was regarded as a sacred object.

"Then the dream suddenly changed back again, and I was still sitting at the feet of the goddess and caressing the priestess, who was taking everything quite quietly and as a matter of course. Then I woke up.

"I cannot describe the sense of buoyancy, self-confidence, and sheer happiness with which I awoke. Usually if I have a crude sort of dream I wake up loathing myself, and am despondent for the day; but the crude incidents in this dream I took in my stride in a perfectly matter of fact manner. I recalled the words of my male visitor: "It doesn't matter." These had evidently taken effect, and taken effect so effectually that it really didn't matter. I was simply frightfully pleased with myself at having had a chance to caress the priestess, and have been able to think of nothing else all day.

"I hope it will not be thought from this that I have any idea of translating my fantasies into action. I merely mention them, having been requested to do so, and for the psychological significance they possess. I had at first intended to keep them to myself, and prepared the earlier report; but then I saw that this would not work, and that I had got to be frank and abide by the consequences, otherwise I might vitiate the whole experiment and mislead Miss L.F. into a false sense of security."

No wonder, thought I, that Malcolm's hand had shaken as he gave this record to me. To a man of his temperament such a confession must have been like pulling teeth.

He was sitting smoking and staring at the fire, perfectly impassive and matter of fact, looking more like a granite colossus than ever. I wondered how best to handle him. He would not thank me for encouraging him, I knew that. It was not a simple problem to strike the right note, and neither make him feel snubbed nor embarrassed.

He evidently knew I had finished reading, although I had been careful not to lift my eyes from the page.

"Well?" he said. "Do I get my marching orders now you see what kind of man I am? I warned you I was not pure-minded."

"A man who is as honest as you have been, Dr. Malcolm, is a far more trustworthy friend than self-deluded people who think they have improved on Nature."

"You are, of course, perfectly right, only I wasn't sure whether you would know enough of human nature to take it that way. I was not safe to have as a friend when I was trying to pretend to you and myself that I was better than I am. I am in love with you, Miss Le Fay, it would be folly for me to deny it; but it does not follow from that that I am not going to run straight with you, because I am. I tried to get away from you, as you know, when I saw the way things were heading, and how frightfully fond I would get of you if I saw much of you. I was afraid of getting hurt—I have been hurt a good deal in my time. But after our first trip upstairs I was no longer afraid of that. It seems a queer thing to say, but I simply did not mind how much I was hurt. I was afraid of hurting you, however, especially after I had damaged your hands. I was also afraid that I might do or say something that would disgust you, or make me appear repulsive to you. But now all those fears have just vanished. As that old high priest said: it doesn't matter. I feel it doesn't matter—we take it in our stride. I talk to you as man to man, and you do the same with me. We're on to a big thing, and we aren't going to let any petty consideration upset us. I know you're out to avoid genuine evil just as much as I am. I wouldn't do anything to hurt my wife, and I wouldn't do anything to hurt you—I'd cut off my right hand—both hands—first, I know you wouldn't ask me to, and I don't suppose for a moment you'd let me, even if I wanted to— anyway, you'd be a fool if you did, for I'd walk out on you the moment after. So there we are; and if I explode, I explode at a safe distance, and that's my affair."

Not a muscle of Malcolm's face twitched, not a tone of his voice changed its timbre during all this recital. He might have been giving out notices to his students.

For a moment I could not speak.

"Why don't you answer? he asked.

"Because," I said, "I cannot. What you have said has moved me too much."

"Is it all right?"

159

"Quite all right."

"I don't appear repulsive to you?"

"Far from it. I honour you deeply, Dr. Malcolm. I don't know anything about your professional work, but I can understand why you are considered a great man, not just an eminent man, but a great man."

"My dear girl, don't talk nonsense. I simply do my job and fight like the devil with anyone who gets in my way. I only appear great in comparison with fools. It's not my greatness that's the marvel, it's their foolishness. They can't, or won't, see the thing that's poking them in the eye, that's all. Nothing in it, if you only knew. I draw attention to what ought ought to have been obvious."

"And how about all the years of observation and experimentation?"

"Oh, that's just routine. I told you I was tired of the central nervous system, didn't I? I am, too, dead sick of it. I'm not such a fool as to say there is nothing else to be learnt about it, but I've got stale at it. I'm going to give it a miss. I'm packing up my job at the hospital. I don't mind remaining on as consultant at some of the smaller places if I can be of use to them, and I'm sticking to the Maudsley. I'm sniffing noses with Malet Place, but they're shy of me. They'd take my name all right, but they're terrified of my iconoclastic views—afraid I'd kick their delicate psychological structures to pieces, and so I would, by God! They need a neurologist like me. I may be a physician by trade, but I'm a surgeon by temperament. Physicians are too damn ladylike for my taste. Give me a good old cut-and-come-again, hack you up, and sew you up, and finish the job and done with it!"

Then, in a milder voice, he enquired if I were going to give him any tea?

"Good gracious," I said, "haven't you had your tea?"

"I have not. I've been making a martyr of myself writing out your reports. I think I deserve some of your home-made scones, too, considering the way I've sacrificed myself on the altar of science. I haven't upset you, have I, Miss Le Fay, with my revelations?"

"Certainly not," said I. "I'm a much tougher-minded person than you are, for all your talk of surgical temperament."

Then I gave him a marvellous tea, and he ate every crumb of it. I don't suppose any woman before had ever made a pet of Malcolm, and he was correspondingly appreciative.

"I'm perfectly happy with you here," he said as he lay back in his chair replete. "I thought it would worry the life out of me, seeing much of you; but on the contrary, it calms me. Now look here, I've been absolutely frank with you, damnably frank, franker than I ought to be,

160

possibly. I wish you'd do the same by me, and tell me exactly how you feel about me."

"I'll do my best, but unless you understand me, you won't understand how I feel as I do."

"You told me you were just such another as She—something inhuman—but you're so damned human, and that's what I find so lovely about you. You don't mind my talking like this, do you? It's only talk."

"Talk is a valuable safety-valve. Talk away as much as you like."

"So I am discovering. I've always been silent as the grave over anything that really mattered, and I can see it was a mistake. I ought to have sworn like a trooper and kicked the furniture about. I do, as a matter of fact, over minor matters. I'm a damned irritable devil, you know, only I don't show it to you. But look here, we're talking about me, not about you. Come along, stick to the point, and tell me what I want to know."

"You want to know how I feel about you?"

"I do. I haven't a notion, except that you're frightfully good to me."

"I shall have to begin at the beginning, or you won't understand. I knew I had got to work with somebody. I knew that it did not matter at the start whether I liked him or not—I had not got to think of my own feelings, but only of the work. But I also knew that if the work went all right, I would get fond of the man I worked with; and yet again I had not to think of my own feelings, and I have been practising self-discipline so long that I genuinely do not think about my own feelings. I am becoming very attached to you, Dr. Malcolm, but I am not dependent on you for my happiness. You, on the contrary, I am afraid, are becoming very dependent on me."

"I am. Damnably so. Never mind. Go on."

"That, of course, is a weak link in the chain. But it is a phase that we shall work through and come out of; and I know that I have not got to check you back or repulse you, nor fear the consequences to either of us of your getting so attached to me."

"You mean you expect me to get over being fond of you?"

"No, not that; but I expect you to come in the end to the same place where I am, so that you can be fond of me, but not dependent on me, nor yet possessive."

"That, of course, is beyond my comprehension—as I am at present, at any rate. I may change, of course. I am quite prepared to allow for that. But until then I must just take your word for it."

"I want you to get to that point where you can love me freely and happily and unpossessively, and I am prepared to go through the difficult intermediate stages with you, till you get there."

"I think you are a bit out in your judgment of male human nature, personally; but as I say, I am willing to keep an open mind. So you want me to become a kind of he-She, do you?"

We both laughed. Malcolm's laugh was getting much less like a snarl, I noticed. His voice, too, was ceasing to rasp and becoming a nice baritone.

"Do you like me, Miss Le Fay? Tell me that."

"Yes, I like you enormously. I think you're a dear. In fact I've really got a very soft spot in my heart for you."

He was silent for a moment.

"Of course that wasn't what I really meant," he said at length.

"What do you mean, then?"

"Never mind. Doesn't matter. Best leave it alone, I expect."

"You mean, do you attract me as a man?"

"Yes, that's it. Do I?"

I thought for a moment, and he misunderstood my silence.

"No, of course I don't. How could I? I've had my answer and deserved it."

"No, you haven't had your answer," I replied. "I was trying to think it out so that it would sound comprehensible. To be attracted to you as a man is quite a different thing from being attached to you as a friend and having complete confidence in you as a fellow-worker, both of which things I feel. I understand your meaning, and I am trying to give you a true answer that shall not mislead you either way.

"I find the dynamic force in you very attractive because it is so interesting. You could give extraordinary experiences, and there is enough of the unregenerate Eve in me to be tempted to experiment with those experiences, though I know I must not, for the sake of the work on which I am engaged. Like you, I am afraid of leading myself into temptation, and that probably prevents me from getting a clear picture of my feelings towards you. I am, both by temperament and training, utterly self-contained and yet I have a need of you."

"I'm glad of that," said Malcolm in a low voice, "that means a lot to me."

"I am definitely not in love with you, and yet I like your being in love with me. I feed on your love for me, if you want to know. I draw power from it and it keeps me young. Some people would say I was a vampire, but I shall always be very careful not to take too much from you, for I wouldn't hurt you for the world and it delights me to see you come here and become relaxed and happy and at peace.

"But all that isn't personal feeling, which is what you really want to know. You spoke as if no woman could have any personal feeling for you, but that is not true. Shallow women couldn't; but for a woman who has eyes to see, you have a very curious kind of attraction. You have a curious kind of beauty, too, the beauty that goes with balanced strength and sheer fitness for function. You have not got a handsome face, but you have got a magnificent head, if you can understand the distinction, and I do not think any one, even a fool, could fail to be aware of the beauty of your hands. They are the most beautiful hands, literally beautiful, that I have ever seen on a man. I should imagine you would be a rather magnificent specimen when you were stripped, too. You are obviously very powerful about the shoulders.

"But that still does not answer your question. Yes, you do attract me, with a curious kind of attraction-repulsion that is much more powerful than pure attraction. At heart I have a certain amount of fear of you, though I do not like you any the less on that account—on the contrary, in fact. I suppose it is a relic of the days when I knew you as the sacrificial priest, I honestly do not think it is anything else."

"You do not think it is due to the way I followed you on the Embankment?"

"I do not, for that, strictly speaking, was a compliment."

"Well, we have certainly exchanged credentials," said Malcolm, leaning back in his chair with his hands behind his head and his feet on the hearth, almost horizontal. Though deplorable, his manners were utterly innocent of offense.

"Have I told you what you want to know?"

"Yes, I expect you have, though I have not got the wit to understand it."

"Have I hurt you, my friend?"

"A bit. But I asked for it. I don't mind. It's just as well I should know."

I got up and went behind his chair, and leaning over him, laid my hand against his cheek.

"Does that take the sting out of it?" I asked.

He put hand over mine and pressed it closer.

"It would take the sting out of anything," he said.

The minutes went by, and neither of us moved. At length Malcolm spoke:

"I expect I am damned ungrateful not to be pleased with what you said to me. Of course I wanted you to say that you felt towards me just as I felt towards you, though I knew perfectly well you didn't. It's just as well you don't, too. I'd obviously have to clear out if you did—the place would be too hot to hold me. As it is, I can just be happy with you in my own queer way. I promise I won't make myself a nuisance if you just don't mind having me around. That's all I need—the small amount of a vitamin that serves to maintain health. One needs very little, but one's in a bad way if one doesn't get that little. You're an extraordinarily understanding person. You seem to know how to give me just what I need. A woman like you is a godsend to any one placed as I am. God bless you for it. What are you standing there for, all this time? You'll get tired. Come and sit on the arm of my chair. Or don't you want to do that?"

I sat down as he bade me and he leant his head against me, even the eternal cigarette forgotten.

"I thought you wouldn't mind," he said.

We spent the evening like that, Malcolm and I. He never moved and never spoke.

When it struck eleven I rose. "You're going home to bed," I said. "You've got a day's work to do tomorrow."

He got up too. I think if the truth were known he had been asleep.

"I feel like a battery that's been put on charge. Just being like that with you has ironed all the creases out of my soul."

He came towards me, and I thought he was going to kiss me; but I didn't want that; nor, I was sure, would he in his cooler moments. We did not want to get on those terms if we were going to work together.

"Run along now, like a good child," I said, and touched his cheek lightly with my hand to take the sting out of my refusal.

"Bless you," I added.

"I am indeed blessed," he said, and swung on his heel and away he went.

Ten minutes later there was a ring on the phone.

"I say, I must tell you, they're making me an FRS! I found the letter here when I got back. It's the only thing I haven't got—I've got all the foreign distinctions, but I hadn't got that—done too much quarrelling, I expect."

"Oh, my dear, I'm, so glad!" I cried, and was, too; far more glad than if I had got the F.R.S. myself.

"Are you really as glad as all that?" came the voice on the phone. "I care about that much more than about getting the F.R.S. Lilith, I'm awfully fond of you!"

Click went the phone as he hung up on me.

CHAPTER
THIRTEEN

I t was some time before I saw Malcolm again. I heard his voice, however, although I did not see him—that brusque rasping voice that lost its harshness and became deep and vibrant when he was with me.

I was sitting by the fire; the tea-tray was beside me, and I was expecting Malcolm any minute—when the telephone rang. I answered it and heard his voice. It was very curt and formal, and the rasp was very pronounced.

"I have just rung to tell you I shall not be able to come round this evening. I've had a call to go down and see my wife. She's pretty bad, I believe."

"I'm so sorry," I said. What else could I say?

"Thanks. I thought you'd understand. I'll look you up when I get back."

"Do you expect to be away long?"

"I've no idea. Some days, I expect. I shall stay till things are finished—one way or the other."

"Is it as bad as all that?"

"She's had a stroke, so they tell me, but I don't know what she's doing with a stroke. I can't tell anything till I get down there. Goodbye, I've got a train to catch."

"Goodbye." This the same man who had said to me the previous evening: "Lilith, I'm awfully fond of you"? At one word from his wife he had swung right back. I felt just a little annoyed with him, and yet I could see the psychology of it—how, to a man of his temperament, loyalties came before feelings; he had laid the finger on the key to his own nature when he had said that he loved making a martyr of himself; the very fact that he felt strongly towards me made him swing further away from me when the claim on his loyalty came uppermost. All the same, I thought he would come back to me eventually; the soul can starve to death as surely as the body.

I sat and sewed at my iridescent garments, and waited. Then an idea struck me, and I began to sew at Malcolm's robes. It was witch-magic, of course, but I did not see any reason to be ashamed of it.

Five days went by, and I heard nothing from Malcolm, neither did he seem to be "on the line" psychically. He had gone from me completely.

I missed him. I missed him much more than I had realised I should. I also was troubled about him, for I knew he must be going through a very trying time, and there was that bond of sympathy between us that magical work always makes, and I felt for him. I could not be contented and indifferent while I knew Malcolm was suffering.

Then, late one evening, there came a knock at the door, and there was Malcolm, without hat or overcoat.

"Good gracious," I exclaimed, "where have you come from?"

"I've been back some days," he replied.

It was drizzling slightly, and his thick, rough hair was dewed with rain. As he passed his handkerchief over it, I saw that it was appreciably greyer, and his face was ashen.

"How are you," I asked.

"Rotten. Is it too late for a cup of tea and a bit of food? I've had practically nothing all day."

"Was it hunger for food that drove you to visit me?"

"I believe it was. I've been a fool not to come before and let you help me, as I knew you could. I felt better the minute I started down the stairs to come and see you."

I wondered whether his wife had died, but he was wearing a coloured tie, and I was certain he was a person who would be very punctilious on a point like that, so I concluded that she was still alive, and presumably out of danger, since he had been able to leave her. I asked no questions, but got him hot food and tea, and let him eat and smoke in silence.

At the end he said:

"You won't mind, will you, if I don't tell you about things tonight? It isn't that I don't want to tell you, but I'm not up to it at the moment. I've been through rather a bad time."

"My friend," I said, "you can tell me just as much or just as little as you want to, and I shall never question you, for that is my notion of friendship."

We sat in silence for a while. I had not put on the central lighting, and there were only the two reading-lamps and the fire to give light, and the corners of the room were invisible. I could not see Malcolm's face as he lay back in the deep chair; I could only see his sprawling feet in the circle of light thrown by the fire, but I knew by the way those feet lay on the hearth-rug that here was a man absolutely dead beat. I wondered what it was that had brought that man of iron and whipcord to this state of exhaustion.

"I wish you'd sing to me as you did the other night," he said. I rose from my chair and faced him across the width of the hearth, but he did not look up. Nevertheless I raised my arms in the ritual gestures as I began my song. Malcolm lay with his hand over his eyes, listening. I sang him first the song of the nostalgia of the soul for the values of Arcady.

> O great god Pan, return to earth again:
> O come at my call, and show thyself to men.
> Shepherd of goats, upon the wild hill's way,
> Lead thy lost flock from darkness unto day.
> Forgotten are the ways of sleep and night;
> Men seek for them whose eyes have lost the light.
> Open the door, the door that hath no key -
> The door of dreams whereby men come to thee.
> The shepherd of goats, oh answer unto me!

"The door of dreams -" said Malcolm without looking up.

"Yes, that's right. I know that way don't I, Lilith?"

"Yes,' said I, "you know it because you have never forgotten it. Some day I will read your past incarnations for you, and then much will become clear."

"Sing me some more. Sing me those songs about Isis and the moon."

So I sang to him the song that calls the goddess; and I sang the song that makes the priestess; and I sang of the way a man goes down by the secret twilight path to be sacrificed in order that the priestess may have power.

"I say, Lilith, you remember my dream of the pool in the cave and the stalagmite? Is that the same sort of thing as the secret well beside the sacred tree? Are the white cypress and the stalagmite the same thing?"

"Yes."

"And the waters of Persephone—are they the waters of life?"

"Yes."

"But why? I thought she was queen of the dead and the underworld."

"She is also the queen of the unborn."

"Was that her, that great image I saw?"

"No, that was Binah, the primordial form of Isis; the second image you saw, the black but comely one, was Persephone."

"I saw you as Peresephone."

"Yes, that was right; I had worked the Isis ritual with you as far as the Persephone point. I have been Persephone to you."

"What does Persephone do to me?"

"She is the queen of the unborn. I took you right back to childhood—and earlier. I made you as the unborn in order to rest you."

"That is the psychology of dementia praecox."

"And it is sound psychology, Rupert. If people would go back to Persephone when they needed to, they would not get dementia Praecox. That is the thing you get when life is too hard for you."

"I've been pretty near it, these last few days. In fact I believe I actually had it. Then the clouds lifted for a moment and I bolted round here. If they had found me in the morning as I was this evening, they'd have taken me off to the asylum."

"You remember the words in the ritual—"They are the living dead, who are orphaned of the Great Mother?" Isn't that dementia praecox? The living dead?"

"Yes, it felt like that."

"And now, in actual life, you have worked the Persephone ritual with me. You have taken refuge in the shelter of my aura. Presently when you are rested, I will give birth to you, and you will return to the world and take up your life again. But you have got to become as the unborn before I can do that."

"Yes, I know. Complete surrender. That is what I would
not face, and that was why I came so low."

He rolled over on his side in the big chair, drew his knees up to his chest, crossed his arms onto his shoulders and bent his head over them. I wondered what in the world was happening.

"Ever seen a foetus, Lilith? I've been lying curled up like that all day. Didn't want to move. Nothing seemed to matter. Then suddenly I felt a tremendous longing for you and I uncoiled and simply bolted, for it struck me that I had seen people in asylums lying like that, and I was scared."

Listen, Rupert !" and I began to sing with power:

I am the star that rises from the sea,
The twilight sea.
I bring men dreams that rule their destiny.
I bring the moon-tides to the souls of men,
The tides that flow and ebb and flow again;
That flow and ebb and flow alternately;
These are my secret, these belong to me.

I am the Eternal Woman, I am she -

The tides of all men's souls belong to me.
The tides that flow and ebb and flow again;
The secret, silent tides that govern men;
These are my secret, these belong to me.

Out of my hands he takes his destiny;
Touch of my hands bestows serenity -
These are the moon-tides, these belong to me.
Isis in Heaven, on earth Persephone,
Diana of the moon and Hecate,
Veiled Isis, Aphrodite from the sea,
All these am I and they are seen in me.

The high full-moon in the heavens shines clear,
I hear the invoking words. hear and appear -
Shaddai el Chai and Rhea, Binah, Ge,
I come unto the priest that calleth me.

"That's not the Persephone point," said Malcolm.
"No, it's not," said I.
He lay in silence for a while. At length he spoke.
"What you say is perfectly true, and I know it. My destiny is in your hands, but I'm not free to take it—I'm not free, Lilith!"
The last words were like a cry of pain.
"The soul is never bound, Rupert."
I spoke quietly, trying to steady him, for he was in no state to lose his head.
"You mean that if my soul were free, it would not matter about my legal and moral obligations?"
"The only bond on the inner planes is function. Are you in touch with your wife on the inner planes?"
No, I am not."
"Then you can fulfil all righteousness and yet keep your inner freedom."
"I am not sure that I understand you."
"Never mind about that now. Just take my word for it."
"All right." There was a pause. Then—"That's the first time I've accepted anyone's diagnosis without verifying it. Sing to me again, Lilith. That helps more than talking. I can't take in what you're telling me."
So I sang for him again the song of the sleep of Persephone, but I

sang it to the end, which he had not heard before.

Sink down, sink down, sink deeper and more deep
Into eternal and primordial sleep.
Sink down, be still, forget and draw apart
Sink into the inner earth's most secret heart.
Drink of the waters of Persephone,
The secret well beside the sacred tree.
Waters of life and strength and inner light -
Eternal joy drawn from the deeps of night.
Then rise, made strong, with life and hope renewed,
Reborn from darkness and from solitude.
Blessed with the blessing of Persephone,
And secret strength of Rhea, Binah, Ge.

Malcolm uncoiled himself from his huddled-up position.

"My condition has definitely improved," he said. "I've been lying like that all day and not bothered, and now I'm cramped already. That song has power in it, Lilith. I could see everything you sang about, and when you called me up, I had to come. I couldn't lie in a heap any longer. I *felt* that joy, Lilith. I never thought I should again, but I did. Listen, I'll tell you what happened down at Worthing during this past week. I want to tell you, I want you to know. Any one else would think me a monster, but you'll understand. You don't think a man's morally guilty because of his feelings, do you? It is what he does that counts, isn't it? He can't help what he feels. I can't anyway, and it's no use pretending I can. It comes up from deep down inside me and I have to cope with it as best I may.

"This is what happened—I got a trunk call, just as I was coming round to see you, to say that my wife had had a stroke and wasn't expected to live through the night. If that call had come five minutes later I should have been out of the house and round here and they wouldn't have known where to lay hands on me.

"Well, I went down straight away, and got there in time. I told you on the phone that I couldn't imagine what she was doing with a stroke, as low blood pressure was her problem, and I was right. It wasn't a stroke, it was an embolus. They were quite right about her not lasting the night, though, she was going fast. There was just one chance—operate. It was a poor chance, but she was dying anyway, and I decided to take it. Jenkins, that's her doctor, agreed with my diagnosis when I pointed it out to him, but he was all against an operation. However, I made him get hold of a surgeon; he had to get hold of a local man, there was no time to send to London."

"The surgeon was against the op.; firstly because he didn't think she'd stand it, and secondly because he'd had no experience of brain surgery, but he agreed to do it provided I'd take the responsibility and pilot him. I didn't mind that, that's one of my jobs, for I know brains in a way no surgeon does. We started in at nine o'clock that night. We were a scratch team. The surgeon was no brain surgeon; I'm no surgeon anyway; anaesthetics are a side line with Jenkins; the nurse had never seen an op. since she was a pro., and we were operating in a private house. However, it was a first-class job. She was out of the wood by next morning—I thought she was, anyway, but I stopped on another twenty-four hours to please Jenkins, and when I left she was sitting up in bed with budgerigars walking about all over her.

"Well, I got back to my rooms, meaning to leave my bag and have a wash and come round and see you, when all of a sudden the storm broke. I suppose it was the atmosphere of my rooms did it—I begin to realise what atmospheres mean now you've pointed it out to me. I went to those rooms when I had to break up my home, and I've been through a lot in them—depression, and all that; I suppose that they are as psychically septic as the surgical wards in the old infirmaries before the days of Lister. Anyway, I went down as if I'd been pole-axed. I can't tell you what I went through, Lilith. I had a most awful revulsion of feeling."

"You see, I'd only had to keep quiet for a few hours and all my problems would have solved themselves. Every one was against that op.; Jenkins didn't believe it possible; the surgeon didn't want to risk it; the nurse looked down her nose; the companion carried on like a maniac, calling me a brute and a butcher and the Lord knows what else. There would have been no odium attached to me if I'd kept quiet and let her die. In fact, Jenkins even said to me: "It won't be pleasant for you if she dies on the table." Yet what could I do? I knew she'd got a chance. Could I deny it her? Lilith, do you think me a fool?"

"No," I said. "Far from it. I have never known a bigger thing than that operation."

"I'm glad to hear you say that. I think I'd have turned my face to the wall for good if you'd said otherwise—I could feel the shadows closing in again for a moment. Yes, I suppose it was a big thing to do in the circumstances—it was too big for me, anyway. I'd bitten off more than I could chew. I didn't know it at the time, I was feeling rather pleased with myself, in fact. It was a jewel of an operation—a regular museum specimen—there was no holding the surgeon—I can't even remember the chap's name, but he was good, I'd never ask to work with a better— funny I can't remember his name. I felt quite satisfied about everything until I got back to my rooms, and then I had this awful revulsion of feeling. Lilith, I could have committed a murder when I realised what I'd done! I was past cursing, but if I'd had her there, I'd have killed her. If I'd had you there, my dear, I wouldn't answer for what would have happened to you, either. I wasn't human at that moment, I was a fiend. I haven't got over the horror of myself yet. Luckily it didn't last long. Something gave way inside me, and I became quite quiet and remote and everything seemed unreal and dream-like. I'd got no feelings at all. It seemed most merciful, but I can see now that it wasn't. The absence of pain was a danger signal, as it is in certain other conditions.

"Nothing happened. I got up and went to bed as usual. I even shaved. But I didn't eat my meals. I didn't feel the need of food. I was perfectly comfortable without it. And all the time I seemed to be getting further and further away, and to be caring less and less. I don't suppose I should have bothered to undress and get to bed much longer, but just lain in a heap in my chair—when suddenly I saw your face in front of me, and I had the first touch of feeling I'd had since I'd gone crack. And with the feeling came a sudden flash of realisation, and I knew I was in danger. I knew insanity was very near me. I didn't stop for hat or coat—I've left the lights on, too—I just shot out of my chair and down the stairs. I don't know if anybody saw me, but I hope for their sakes they didn't. You didn't see me at my worst. I was very different by the time I got round here. The worst is over now, but my goodness, Lilith, I feel a wreck! You've only just got me in time, my dear; if I'd gone through another night alone, there'd have been no mending me. Do you think you will be able to get me going again? I feel at the moment as if the only thing I were capable of is just to lie here, near you. If I left you, I'd go under again. What in the name of God are you going to do with me?"

"Keep you here, under my wing, till you're all right."

"But you can't. There'd be a scandal."

"Not unless you make it. I certainly shan't."

"What about Meatyard?"

"He's a walking scandal himself, he won't worry; and anyway, he's very attached to us both. He'll think the worst and be delighted."

"Lilith, I don't like to put you in such a position. It seems to me I spend my whole life trying to do the right thing and presenting all the appearance of the wrong one. Circumstantial evidence is always dead against me. You simply can't keep me here, Lilith."

"Oh, can't I? You wait and see."

"Where am I going to sleep?"

"In my temple."

"In your temple?"

"Yes, have you never heard of the temple sleep?"

"No, never. What is it?"

"I expect you will call it hypnotism, but it is different from that. I don't use my mind to dominate yours, I use it to lead it. I don't drive you, as English shepherds drive their sheep; I lead you, as Eastern shepherds do. I go out on to the inner planes myself, and make you follow me; and in the same way, I bring you back again."

"The same as before?"

"Yes, the same as before, only further this time—and your robes are ready." I lifted the mass of black velvet from where it lay on my workbox beside my knee. "They are just finished. I finished them this evening." I drew from its wrappings the glittering silver head-dress. "Take these," I said, "and go to the bathroom and robe. There are no sandals, so you will have to go barefoot. Nothing can be worn in the temple that belongs to everyday life—everything must be left behind—." "Sink down, forget, be still and draw apart."

Malcolm heaved himself out of the low chair and took his robes from my hands. He did not look at them, but just stood holding them and looking at me.

"You've made these for me yourself?"

"Yes."

He looked at the long seams.

"By hand?"

"Yes."

"Magnetised them?"

"They got magnetised in the making."

"I strip and wear these right next to my skin?"

"Yes."

"All right." He looped up the draperies over his arm and went off to the bathroom, moving very differently to the man who had stumbled across the floor an hour earlier.

I too went to my room and robed. I came back to the hall and stood by the hearth, waiting for Malcolm. In a moment or two I saw him coming through the low dark arch of the door beside the chancel, moving silently on bare feet till he stood before me.

I have never seen any human being change so completely. Malcolm was not a tall man, but he was very powerfully built, and his breadth of shoulder and depth of chest took off from his height and made him look shorter than he really was. In his robes he looked exactly twice his natural size. The long draperies lent him the height he lacked. The head-dress exaggerated it. His grim, hard face, tense with expectation, seen beneath the severe lines of the Egyptian nemyss, looked like the face of one of the nether gods. He was the archetypal primitive man. It was as if a gorilla were inside those robes. The only thing he lacked was the broad leather belt and bronze knife of the sacrificing priest. It took all my courage to face him, robed thus, in the half-light of the hall. He gazed at me. I too wore the black velvet and silver head-dress of the dark side of the cult.

"You look like the moon rising at midnight," he said.

I led the way up the steep stairs, Malcolm following silently in my wake. There was something grim and terrifying about the pad of his bare feet coming on behind me. I wondered how often I had gone down the long underground way from the white to the black temple with those softly padding feet following after. From the human point of view I was taking a long chance with Malcolm. On his own showing he had been well over the borderline of insanity. If I pushed him over that borderline again, murder would be merciful compared to what he would do to me. But I had no fear. Not the slightest quiver of uneasiness or even tension was in mind or body. I was the priestess of Isis tonight, and a mistress of all magic.

We came to the temple, and for the third time I lifted the curtain for him and he crossed the threshold. Unbidden, he went up to the cubical altar and laid his hands on it, staring down at the faintly flickering lamp. With the small silver ritual tongs I changed the wick and the light leaped up. From it, with a taper in a silver holder, I took the flame to the moon-lamp before the mirror. Then I got the incense going over the incense heater, transferred it to the censer and censed the temple. All this time Malcolm never stirred. Finally I came and stood at his elbow. He raised his eyes and saw me reflected in the mirror beside him.

It was a strange and dramatic picture that was reflected in the great mirror which took up the whole of one section of the wall. Framed between the pillars of polarity, the black and the silver pillars that flanked the couch altar, we stood side by side. Exactly matched as to height—for I am tall for a woman—but the one broad and powerful, the archetype of primitive strength, the other slender in the swathing draperies. Each one the exact opposite of the other in every aspect of being.

Malcolm stared at himself in the glass.

"Yes, that's me," he said. "I know it."

"The Goddess will come presently. When She comes, ask Her for strength."

"I don't need strength, Lilith, I've got plenty. What I need is understanding. May I ask Her for that?"

"Yes, if you feel you can stand it at the present moment." It was not for me to hold him back. "Come to the couch," I said, and he followed me.

I spread a fur rug over him, for although the temple was warm, he would be there for hours, and one gets cold, lying like that. He folded his hands on his breast and looked like a dead man on a bier. If anything happened to him there, I wondered how I should explain the stripped and robed Malcolm to the coroner, for there is always a chance of something happening on the further astral journeys. There are times when people go out and don't come back.

I did not fetch the stool this time to put behind his head, but carried across one of the thrones, for I too should be there for hours, and I wanted some support for my back.

Malcolm started when he saw me carrying it.

"Why didn't you let me fetch that for you?" he said.

But I had never thought of it. My strength was upon me for the rite, and I had picked up the great chair as if it had been a foot-stool.

The incense was smoking steadily. The newly-lit wicks had ceased flaring, and we settled down to our vigil. I put out my hand and struck softly nine times upon a rod-shaped gong that hung beside the altar. I heard the astral bells reply, and I knew from Malcolm's start that he had heard them too. Our eyes met in the mirror.

"You are the Goddess," he said. "Do I pray to you?"

I was startled. There had been no opening invocation, but Malcolm was through onto his contacts. The use of the actual woman as the goddess is high Tantric magic, and rare, but I could not deny it to him.

"Work in the mirror," was all I said. Our eyes met again.

"You are She, and I know it. Even if you deny it, I know it. You are not a woman to me at all, you are a goddess, and I worship you, I adore you, as I am free to do. I ask of you one thing—understanding. Give me that, and I will supply the strength."

He lay silent, staring into my eyes in the mirror.

Then he began again.

"I want to know how it all came about. I want to understand it. Why am I in bondage? Is it my fault?"

He lay watching me in the mirror, and I saw with utter insight right down into his soul.

"The priests are men set apart," I heard my own voice saying. "You had to be segregated or you could not function. This way of segregating you was as good as any other."

"Will I ever have paid my debt to my wife and be free?"

"Nothing is owing now. In these last days you have paid it."

"But that does not mean I am free to take the law into my own hands?"

"No, it does not mean that. Wait. You will see presently. But the priests are never free. You are in bondage to Isis. You will exchange one duty for another."

"I would ask nothing better!" I could hear the sudden leap-up of life in Malcolm's voice. I saw something moving in the mirror, and knew that the Goddess was formulating. A light haze began to spread over its surface. I have to conceive of the Goddess as behind me when She formulates, so I left my chair and went round and stood at Malcolm's feet with my back to the mirror.

"You are She," he said, staring into my eyes. "I am She," I replied, and lifting my hands, sent the power at him. He lifted his hands from his breast to receive it. We were like that for some time, palm opposite palm, six feet apart, with the power standing rigid between us like a solid rod. It was clearly visible, even to the physical eyes.

I spoke. "Is it your will to make the unreserved dedication?"

"It is," came the unhesitating reply.

"Will you let me take you and use you, asking nothing in return?"

"I will."

"It is well."

The power slowly began to work up for the greater magic. Hitherto I had used Malcolm as a source of energy, drawing magnetism from him in order that I myself might function with power; but now, this being accomplished, I began to give magnetism to the Goddess and Her form built up as I visualised it, and then power began to come through into it—power from that for which Isis stands; power from the moon and the moon-side of things, and the thing for which the moon stands. The image became alive in its own right. Then, strangest form of obsession, it slowly superimposed itself upon me, and, already fortified by the accession of Malcolm's magnetism, I received it, so that I became Isis for the time being (this is the old temple-working, not generally known), and Malcolm found him-self face to face with the Goddess who both was and was not me.

My consciousness seemed to be in abeyance in the background, somewhere behind the form of the Goddess, and yet I was She, and shared Her consciousness. All earth seemed mine, and all the starry heavens the sphere in which I moved.

I saw by the look on Malcolm's face that he had perceived the change. He slowly rose to a sitting position on the couch.

"You are She," he said in a low voice, "I have always known it."

"I am She!" replied a voice that was not mine. "Ask! I will answer."

Malcolm sat rigid, staring at the form before him. He had had no experience of such manifestations, and did not know how to deal with them, but the directness and integrity of his nature guided him.

"Who are you?" he asked.

"I am Isis the Moon," came the answer.

"What does that imply?" Malcolm was no longer awed into bewilderment; his mind was functioning, and he was pinning down Isis and vivisecting Her.

"I am the negative potency of the universe, represented thus to you by the work of magic."

"Are you real as I see you?"

"Is anything real as you see it?"

"No, of course it isn't. I understand. The psychology of sight is applicable to the vision—and then the psychology of dream, is that right?"

"It is."

"I understand."

"Then take me and use me. What is it you want?"

"I want understanding."

"That comes with the working. What else do you want?"

"I want—" Malcolm stirred uneasily and hesitated—"I want what every normal man wants. Do I ask You for that?"

"You do. It is I who bestow it, for I am All-Women ... Receive the blessing of Isis!" A blinding silver light filled the room and faded. When it had gone the Goddess was no longer there, but I was there—in power—as Her priestess. My human personality had utterly disappeared, and I was my higher self and a priestess—*the* priestess—the great high priestess, and as such I too blessed Malcolm.

"You have sacrificed, and you have served—the Goddess will not forget. She will repay."

"How will She repay? Lilith—how will She repay?" cried Malcolm the man suddenly.

"In Her own time. In Her own way. Through the channels She shall choose; but rest assured—She will repay." I held on to the magic with all my strength, refusing to allow it to slip to the personal level. Malcolm steadied and recovered his self-control. He bowed his head.

"I am in Her hands," he said. "Take what you want. I ask nothing."

Then, stepping down the power another grade, I stood before him in my own person, yet as all women, for by virtue of my womanhood I am a part of Isis, as are all women; and I blessed him as all women could bless their men if they only knew how, bringing through to them the moon-power by virtue of their womanhood.

I was the archetypal woman with my Goddess behind me; and before me was he, the archetypal man, who needed me, and I sang to him the Song of the Compassion of Isis. It is a strange song, begotten of magic; it is very old, and only priestesses can sing it.

Persephone, O Moon of men's desire,
Thy lambent light illumines with cold moon-fire!
Persephone, Persephone,
Moon of the night, we long for thee,
In outer space the springs of being rise;
With tidal sweep life streams across the skies,
And in men's hearts awake the slumbering fires -
Thou art the Queen of dreams and desires.
Persephone, Persephone,
Moon of the night, we come to thee!

The passion in the chant was working up, and I could feel Malcolm vibrating to it. Then the motif changed—the power was being brought through to earth now.

The moon is riding high and clear,
O lovely one, draw near, draw near;
To lonely men on lonely ways
Come down in dream of silver haze.
Persephone, Persephone,
All in the end shall come to thee.

I heard a sound like a sob from Malcolm and he held out his arms to me. I came to him, for something human had to be given that man if he were not to break. He took hold of me and crushed me to him in a kind of agony. It was terrible. I could feel every muscle in him rigid with strain. Presently he dropped back, exhausted, panting and sweating, and I took my soft chiffon handkerchief and wiped his face. He lay quietly with his eyes shut, and then a hand came out, feeling for me like a child's. I put mine in it, and sat down on the edge of the couch beside him.

And so the vigil of the temple sleep began. The great throne was no use to me, I had to endure it upright, unsupported, in a kind of crucifixion of muscular strain. It was the Asana* of vicarious sacrifice. After a time the muscles lock and become rigid and the worst is over—until one has to move at the conclusion. I have always found that these curious, locked positions are necessary to the bringing through of power, and that the power brought through is in proportion to the pain the postures cause. I am very supple, and very strong, and can endure more than most, being inured to such things, but they are real Calvaries.

At first I could not concentrate because I was trembling with the strain of the posture, but presently the muscles became locked and my mind was free.

Malcolm was sleeping peacefully as a child, his storms over for the time being. His face was lined and weary, but nevertheless it was at peace. I sat and looked at him.

I thought of the complete uselessness, and wastefulness, and folly of the sacrifice that had been demanded of him by conventional morality. It did no one any good that this man should sacrifice his manhood at an empty shrine, and the injury to him was cruel, for the love side of life is not an ideal, but a function. I thought of the castration of the priests of Attis; the foot-binding of the Chinese women; the head-boards of the Red Indian babies, and all the needless, purposeless, long drawn out torture inflicted by the superstitions and conventions of mankind, of which our orthodox morality is one of the worst, and with the power of the magic that was upon me at that moment I cursed our modern Moloch to its face and struck at its feet of clay; and what I did then because Malcolm's suffering had moved me, I did magically for all men placed as he, in their varying degrees of frustration and starvation, for thus is magic wrought. That which I did then, in those hours of intense power and emotion, up there in the darkness of the moon-temple with the river in flood outside, went into the group mind of the race to work like leaven, as I knew it would when I called Malcolm to the rite. There is freedom in the world today because

*Asana: meditation postures used in Yoga.

of what I did that night, for it opened the first tiny rift in the great barrier and the forces began to move channelling and eroding as they flowed, till presently the strength of waters came flooding through like the bursting of a dam and all resistance melted away.

So the night went by, and the Goddess visited me as She had visited him, and I once again renewed my vision of Her. When Malcolm said I was She, he was both right and wrong. All women are Isis, and Isis is all women in that Her power manifests through them according to their degree. Some bring through more, and some bring through less, but none, unless they deliberately inhibit, are without it. A trained priestess like myself brings it through in all its plenitude of power. Not all men can stand it; I need strong men about me, like Malcolm, to enable it to come through in its strength. It is a great and glorious thing, and brings health to the soul. The Greeks made a god of it and called it Dionysos; but after the ecstasy comes tranquillity, which is the blessing of Isis. I do not know how any can argue that that is wrong which brings so profound a peace.

CHAPTER
FOURTEEN

What Malcolm thought when he awoke in the morning to find himself in the temple with me beside him, I do not know, for I, too, was asleep, muscle-locked in my Asana, bolt upright and unsupported. The first thing I knew was that he was sitting up and staring at me.

It was practically impossible for me to move without assistance, and Malcolm had to support me and help me while I got my cramped limbs unlocked. His gentleness was a marvel to me, and his knowledge saved me the worst of the pain that comes from disentangling an Asana. Muscle by muscle, he rubbed and kneaded the stiffness out of my numbed limbs; finally, when I could once more move freely, I stood up and took him by the shoulders and said:

"Well, how are you? How did you fare?"

"My dear," he said, "I fared well. I have been blessed, and you know it, for you know who blessed me," and he lifted my hand from his shoulder and kissed it.

Malcolm, a middle-aged married man, with greying hair, thickset, stocky and rough-mannered, might not be considered a figure of romance by many, but to me, as he stood there before me and thanked me in his taciturn way, there was a beauty and nobility about him that shone like a great light in a dark place.

I led him over to the western wall and drew back a curtain revealing a shuttered window I had had made for ventilation. We threw back the shutters, and there before us shone the river in the morning light. Malcolm chuckled and pointed to the far façade across the water, where two lighted windows shone incongruously in the grey of the morning.

"I left my lights on," he said. "I shall get a scolding when I get back."

The sun was just coming up in a clear sky and the water began to glitter. It was ebb-tide now, but we saw by the state of the street that flood water had come to the very door during the night while we kept the temple vigil. There is a curious affinity between the moon-powers and water; I have never yet known moon-magic to be worked without water coming into it in some way or other.

Then we set out to go downstairs. Malcolm went first to give me a hand, for I was still very stiff; but soon wearying of this laborious progress, he picked me up without a by-your-leave and carried me the rest of the way. When he laid me down on the big sofa at the end of the fireplace he leant over me for so long that I thought he meant to kiss me, but instead he suddenly straightened his back and stood staring at the fire for several minutes. Then he walked off to the bathroom without a word reappearing presently, dressed and shaved and impassive to come face to face with Meatyard, who favoured him with a wink. Malcolm turned scarlet, and I thought for a moment he was going to strike him; but Meatyard, oblivious of his danger, was placidly laying the table for two. Malcolm pulled himself together and came over to me and looked at me with anguish in his eyes, only to find that I was smiling; then he smiled too, but wryly. Poor fellow, he was as innocent of all offense as an unborn child, but, as he had himself remarked, appearances always went against him.

I insisted that he should claim a holiday from the hospital; goodness knows, it owed him one; and for the next fortnight he spent his days with me, worked with me every evening, and slept on the big sofa in the hall. Meanwhile, also at my behest, his rooms were completely re-decorated and refurbished. All the dreadful old lumber with which they were garnished was disposed of, and new furniture, chosen by me, was sent in; needless to say, I never showed myself within range of vision of Malcolm's landlady, though I presume she suspected my presence. Men of Malcolm's type do not suddenly re-equip themselves along aesthetic lines without some kind of external influence being brought to bear on them. However, Malcolm was very much more comfortable, with a good bed and a modern grate, and properly shaded lights, and began to take quite a pleasure in his belongings.

Then, night after night, we worked together, and I taught him magic. Concentration presented no difficulty to Malcolm, for his was a trained mind; visualisation, too, was easy because of his habit of making diagrams for his students: neither had he any nervousness about giving himself up to the forces; but he could not, dared not, let himself go with me. It was the most difficult thing in the world to get him to separate the woman from the priestess. As the twig is bent, the tree will grow, and Malcolm had been bent with a vengeance. Again and again I tried to get him to see that he must deal with me as he would deal with a patient, and that I would do the same by him, but it was no use. Malcolm was afraid of emotion; he could not realise that one could keep the forces on the astral, and handle them there. He reminded me of a horse that fears to cross a creaking bridge lest it will not bear him. He could not realise the strength, certainty and accuracy of the astral workings in skilled hands. The terrible Puritan conscience, the most ignorant thing on God's earth, had made a deformity of his mind, and it was spiritual orthopedics to bring him back to naturalness.

Only after infinite patience and plain speaking did he come round to the view that sex and sin are not synonymous terms. It was, I think, only his scientific training that made him see that sex is a physiological function with psychological results. Then, and, then only, did he dare to turn a critical eye on the code to which he had been chained as a child. Once he got to the point of examining it, however, things moved rapidly, for Malcolm's mind was innately scientific and despite himself he could not help looking facts in the face.

"Do you think my loyalty has been a waste of time?" he said to me one day, for he was nothing if not whole-hearted.

"I think it has probably taught you a great deal," I replied.

"You would not be working with me today if you had not been through that hard discipline; but I do not think it has conferred the slightest benefit on your wife."

"No, I don't suppose it has. I could have had half a dozen mistresses, and she would have been none the wiser and none the worse off. Do you think me a fool, Lilith?"

"Do you remember the story of the Athenian who erected an altar to the Unknown God? You have worshiped the ideal; you have sacrificed to it and kept back no part of the price; that cannot go for nothing on the inner planes. It must have generated power. I think you have been blind, my friend, as you would not be blind in any other matter; blind because your mind was put in blinkers when you were a child. Now the blinkers are off and it will remain to be seen whether you have the courage to act."

"Lack of courage has never been one of the many weaknesses I am credited with."

"All the same, you lack courage in this matter, I fancy."

He thought for a minute. "Yes, I believe I do. It is the one thing in my life I have hesitated to grip. I ought to have faced up to it years ago and been fair to myself as well as Eva. If I had made a clean cut, it would have healed."

He thought for a while. At length he spoke, as if to himself. "Who is to be the judge in these matters? Is one ever justified in taking the law into one's own hands?"

"There lies the difficulty," said I. "It is easy enough to legislate for a perfect world, but we have to live in this imperfection. If we all took the law into our own hands whenever we felt like it, there would soon be no law left. While it is the law, we have got to keep it, and wait for other heights in other lives—that is where we who believe in reincarnation have the advantage. But though we may keep a foolish law, there is no reason why we should respect it; though we may bow the neck to *force majeure*, there is no reason why we should bow the mind. The Queen's writ does not run on the inner planes, we are free there."

"Free to do what we please?"

"No, never that. There is no such thing as absolute freedom, there is only the relative freedom of the right to choose the code one will observe. Free in mind, Rupert—free to know an idol from the true God. Free to recognise a social code as a social code, and not as the Word of the Lord. Free to find God in your own way, my friend, and not in somebody else's. Free to cut away the conventions and get down to fundamentals.

"You may not be able to do all that in this life—to be free as I am free, who have been upon the Path for many lives, but you can at least make a start. You can at least win to the intellectual freedom that admits of no authority that can override the truth. And remember, where you end in this incarnation, you can start in the next, and whatever ground you gain has broken trail for those who come after you."

" 'The blood of the martyrs is the seed of the Church,' " said Malcolm. "I would be quite willing to be a martyr, it is in my blood, my forbears were Covenanters; but is one ever justified in offering up another person? Would I be justified in sacrificing my wife, for instance?"

"There is such a thing as abstract justice, Rupert. One has an obligation to be just to oneself as well as generous to other people. Marriage is the only form of contract in which the law compels personal service, and in that I think it makes a mistake; unwilling service is never satisfactory service. Marriage is also the only form of contract in which the defection of one party does not automatically release the other. How can we expect what works badly in every other human relationship to work well in this particular one? Of course it doesn't. That is why there is so much low-grade happiness, apart from the actual wreckage with which the world is strewn."

"The churches wouldn't agree with you."

"The churches can please themselves. It is no business but their own what conditions they make for admission to their communion. The mistake comes when they use their influence to legislate for people outside their communion. History has never seen any good result come from religious meddling in politics. Do you realise that at one time, in Salt Lake City, it was compulsory to indulge in polygamy if you could afford it? That there were heavy penalties, both in this world and the next, for remaining faithful to one wife? The state has no right to deal with anything save the law of contract in legislation for marriage; there ought to be freedom of conscience in this as in other matters. How can the conscientious Catholic legislate for the conscientious Mormon, both deeply religious men according to their lights, and both quite sure that God is on their side? And who is to judge between them? The Church of England by law established? The assorted chapels that established themselves? Or the great bulk of the electorate who care for none of these things and have to cast a single vote on a mixed issue of social service, foreign policy, finance *and* divorce reform at one and the same election?"

"It's beyond me, Lilith, I don't know. I can't judge. I am too personally involved to be impartial. If you had been in my shoes, what would you have done?"

"If I were in your shoes I should have your temperament, and therefore would presumably do the same as you have done. If you ask me what you, with your temperament and your circumstances should do at the moment, I would say to you, do nothing on the physical plane; stand back from your own personality; withdraw into your own higher self that lives on eternally behind all your incarnations, and try and get down to fundamental principles and adjust yourself thereto; when you have made that adjustment, you will find things will work themselves out on the physical plane. That is the greater magic."

"And what is the lesser magic?"

"What we do with our minds in the light of the greater magic."

"What you have been showing me?"

"Yes."

"Won't the greater magic work without all that?"

"It will, but it works very slowly, and probably not in this life."

"Shall I injure my wife if I do as you suggest?"

"No, you will not touch your wife, for you will work on nobody but yourself. How the way will open up, no one can foresee; it may be through a change in your circumstances, or it may be through a change in your feelings, but changes there will be, for great forces are set in motion by these means, and they are forces of fundamental right—we do not take the law into our own hands or outline the results in any way

185

whatever. But I will tell you one thing for your information, Rupert, for this you need to know—whatever alteration might come about in your circumstances, it would make no difference in your relationship to me."

Malcolm's face underwent a curious change at these words. For a moment there was a flash of something savage, and then a look of relief.

"I am glad you told me that, Lilith," he said. "It has cleared up a lot."

"It has not cleared up anything, Rupert," I said, "I may be a free woman, but you, unless you change, will never be a free man."

He looked bewildered.

"I never have married," I said, "and I never shall marry. Why should I? It is not my work to bring souls into the world."

"I see," he said. "You are a priestess, set apart."

Yes," said I. "That is it. I am a priestess set apart."

Things went much better after that talk. Malcolm, though he would have denied it strenuously, was an innately religious man, and life had no meaning for him unless he could relate it to the fundamental verities. I understood him, because that too is my nature. Neither of us could have found any satisfaction in what we believed to be wrong or thought to be futile. The fact that my code was not the world's code did not affect the fact that it was my code, and who shall judge another man's servant? To his own master he standeth or falleth. The sin against the Holy Ghost is to break one's own code, or so I think, and I have myself seen the power of God come down as a flaming fire.

So I took Malcolm in hand, leaving him to work out his own problem in the light of the greater magic, for that is a thing in which no one may interfere, in which no one can assist—every soul treads that path alone—but teaching him the use of the lesser magic which gives effect to the greater, the lack of which explains why we so often have to wait till heaven for our prayers to be answered.

I must be pardoned if I speak in riddles on these matters, but not otherwise can they be spoken of. But what I cannot explain I can describe, and I will tell what I did with Malcolm.

Night after night, during that well-earned holiday from the hospital, I made Malcolm perform with me the simple ritual, so ancient and so effective, the ritual of the opening of the gates that enables one to pass out into another plane, or another state of consciousness, according as one uses the terms, for a plane is a state of consciousness and a state of consciousness is a plane.

I taught him the way of going out—the imaginary journey that ends

186

on the astral; and in my company I made him take it night after night, lying on the couch and looking in the mirror, till the way became familiar to him and he could pass down that path alone, and, what is more important, come back by the same route. The inner planes became real to him, and he became sure of their existence and learnt to gauge their conditions by his own reactions.

Once he turned on me and said "You are making me dream an artificial dream. This is not real."

"It is real for you, and it is true for you. What more do you want," I replied.

"But it is not real," he protested. "I am deluding myself."

"It is real on its own plane," said I, "and that is the plane of causation. We do not know how these things work, we only know that they do work. What you build in your imagination is a channel of force. The more real it is to you, the more powerfully it works, and all the things you call theatrical in my doings are simply designed to make it real to you."

So I talked to him, and taught him, and let him get used to things, and waited. We described our visions to each other—the visions I built and the visions he saw, going over the same ground again and again till they were utterly familiar to us both. This is the *mise-en-scene* of magical working that creates the astral temple. Our temple was now built, though Malcolm thought it was all imagination, and the next stage was ready to begin—the stage of making a priest of him. People try and make priests of themselves in order to be fit for the temple, but it should be the other way about—make the temple first, and then make the priest. There are good reasons for this.

I also taught Malcolm mystical alchemy, which is the yoga of the West. I taught him how to pick up the forces from the earth centre and draw them up the spine. These form the basis of all that follows. Only those who can do this can do magic. We in the West work with a tree; in the East they work with flowers, but it is the same thing.

Malcolm said to me once: "There is only one thing I don't like about you, Lilith, and that is the streak of ruthlessness in your nature."

"It goes with my tiger teeth," said I. "Would you care to be operated on by a soft-hearted surgeon with blunt instruments?"

"I would not," said he.

But still I had to bide my time and dared not show my hand to Malcolm, but had to wait upon his slow growth into realisation. "If you only knew," thought I, "how ruthless I really am, and the nature of the risks I am taking, I wonder what you would say!"

There is in me a tireless patience and tenacity; I can keep on keeping on, and it is the most powerful magic there is. I was in no hurry; there was plenty of work to be done on Malcolm before we were ready for the next stage.

I wanted to make him remember his past lives. That is important in magic, because a man who remembers his past lives has tremendous resources behind him. I also wanted to teach him the art of the Serpent Power—so little understood in the West—in which I was a specialist, when that befell which was due to befall, which I had known might befall any time when I told Malcolm that no change in his circumstances would make any change in our relations. He came to me one morning with a letter in his hand and bid me read it, walking about the room agitatedly while I did so. It bore the Worthing postmark and I gathered it was from his wife's companion. Mrs Malcolm, she said, had been going on very well indeed, but had been having a slight set-back in the shape of a return of her phlebitis. However, there was no cause for anxiety, it was a very slight attack, and Dr. Jenkins said there was no occasion for him to come down.

I handed the letter back to Malcolm. I could not see what there was in it to agitate the man.

"What ought I to do, Lilith?"

"Do as you are advised by the doctor on the spot," said I. "Or if you aren't satisfied, get a second opinion. Don't you take the responsibility again. It is too much to ask of any man."

He looked relieved. He, the most dogmatic, self-assertive, cocksure individual on earth in medical matters, was only too thankful to be told what to do by me in his private affairs.

"Get through on the phone if you're worried," I added.

He picked up the receiver and put through the call. In a few moments, by a miracle as marvellous as any of my magic, he was speaking to his wife's companion.

I could, of course, only hear one side of the conversation, but it was not difficult to perceive that Malcolm had got a fool to deal with, and a stubborn fool into the bargain. They had, apparently, dispensed with the nurse because Mrs Malcolm did not like strangers about her, and the maid and the companion considered themselves quite competent to do whatever nursing was necessary. Malcolm, however, did not consider them competent, and did not mince his words in saying so, without, however, making any impression on the foolish creature I could hear bleating away at the other end of the line.

Finally, he slammed down the receiver.

"Well," he said, "Jenkins is prepared to see her through without a trained nurse. What do I do about it?"

"Tackle Jenkins," said I.

Another call went through, but Jenkins was not available and a message had to be left. Malcolm paced the room like a caged tiger. I still could not see what all the fuss was about. Presently the bell rang for the return call, and he made a dive for the receiver. But again I heard the same twittering bleat from the other end, instead of a man's deep tones.

Malcolm put the receiver down, and came over to me by the fire.

"My wife says she has perfect confidence in Dr. Jenkins, and refuses a second opinion. What do I do now, Lilith? Go down and make a row?"

"No," said I. "Why should you? It is obvious they are quite happy in their own way and that you are not wanted. What is the point of forcing yourself on them?"

Malcolm rested both his hands on the high mantelpiece and stood staring into the fire.

"Why wouldn't that damn fool Jenkins speak to me himself." he demanded, but that was a question I could not answer.

"Lilith, I ought to go down—I'm going. Goodbye." Before I had time even to hold out my hand in farewell he had turned on his heel and left the room and I heard the front door slam behind him.

I felt exceedingly anxious about him. It seemed to me that another brainstorm like the last and there would not be very much left of Malcolm. However, there was nothing I could do but wait.

Next morning, before I was out of bed, the phone rang.

"Worthing wants you," I was told.

I waited, and a voice said:

"She's gone, Lilith."

I was so startled I could not speak for a moment, and Malcolm's voice came again, very agitated.

"Lilith, are you there?"

"Yes, I'm here. I was so startled by your news I did not know what to say. What happened?"

"Clot shifted, same as before. Struck the heart this time. Finished. Gone. All over."

"My friend," I said, "is there anything I can do for you? You know I'll do anything I can, don't you? You can rely on me."

"Yes, I know that, Lilith. It's you I am relying on. I don't know where

189

I'd be without you. It's the thought of you that's keeping me going. This has been a shock to me, you know. It's shaken me up more than I expected."

"It would."

"The funeral's Thursday morning at eleven. Think of me while it's going on, will you, Lilith? It won't be easy."

"I'll be with you," I said.

"I'll be returning by the afternoon train. May I come on and see you?"

"Of course you may. Would you like to sleep here that night?"

"I don't know. Not if I feel then as I do now. I'm a bit shaken up, you know. Feel I've been a brute, and all the rest of it."

"My friend, who could have done more than you did?"

"I don't know, I'm sure. I expect I'm being silly, but there it is. Goodbye, think of me on Thursday, won't you?"

And they say women are illogical! But that was Malcolm all over—he and his wretched conscience that did nobody any good and worried the life out of him.

CHAPTER
FIFTEEN

When Thursday came round I determined that Malcolm should not have the chance to go back to his rooms before he saw me, for I did not know what brainstorms might befall him if he got round there alone; so I took my black coupé and drove to the station in time to meet the first of the trains that could reasonably be considered an afternoon train, but Malcolm was not on it. I guessed that he had probably had lunch at the house on his return from the funeral, and would be on the next train, or even a later one, but he was not on either of these. I rang up my house to see if any telephone call from him had come through there, but Meatyard said that none had been received, so I settled down to my vigil, meeting train after train as the evening wore on, determined that Malcolm should find me there, even if he arrived on the milk train in the morning.

Then, finally, shortly before midnight, a slow train came in and I saw Malcolm get off it.

His hat was pulled over his eyes, his collar was up to his ears, he carried his own bag, and I thought I had never in my life seen any face with a grimmer or more forbidding expression; even I, who knew him so well, was almost afraid to approach him.

I went up to him and spoke his name. He did not hear me. Greatly venturing, I laid a hand on his arm. He swung round angrily but, seeing me, checked himself and a bewildered expression came into his eyes.

"Lilith, you here? What are you doing here?"

"I have brought the car to meet you. I didn't want you to go home alone. You are coming round to have a meal with me before you do anything else."

"But how did you know what train I was coming by?"

"You said an afternoon train—"

"But—Lilith, you haven't been here till now, have you?"

"I have."

"My dear—"

He put his hand through my arm and came along with me to the car, and I knew that whatever resistances his dreadful conscience had built up had broken down.

As I unlocked the car door he said:

"What can I say to you, Lilith? How can I thank you?"

Then we got into the car, and I drove him home.

Although it seemed natural to see him back once again in my big chair, there was a restraint between us, and he was abstracted. He was not even smoking. He wore a black tie, but a man is at such a disadvantage when it comes to mourning and showing his emotions. A woman knows how to make the best of such a situation but a man in a black tie is merely miserable.

So I let Malcolm sit, as his custom was, and brood his ideas till he should be delivered of them.

"I've got something for you," he said at length, and reaching over, he placed on my knee an old-fashioned jewel-case that I had noticed him nursing in the car. I shrank from it. I did not like the idea of his wife's jewels being handed over to me when she was hardly cold in her grave. He saw my movement, and replied to it.

"You needn't feel anything about them," he said. "She never liked them and never wore them. I simply kept them down at the house as being safer than my rooms. They belonged to my mother."

He took the case back from me again, and unlocked it, and I saw that it contained some very fine amethysts in heavy, old-fashioned settings, and cairngorms and agates, and suchlike. I could quite understand that the fluffy little woman Mrs Malcolm must have been could not have worn them, but they would suit me to perfection and go marvellously with my robes. I told Malcolm so, and let my pleasure appear in my voice, hoping it would distract him from his brooding.

It served its purpose, and his pleasure at my pleasure lit up his grim face and took some of the grimness out of it.

"I've had the devil of a time getting those things for you," he said. "That's what made me so late. I never dreamt you'd be waiting for me at the station; had made up my mind, in fact, that it was too late to come round to you tonight, and was dreading the prospect, if you want to know the truth. But I wasn't going to give up these things I wanted for you if I'd had to raid Hell to get 'em. I pretty nearly did, too. Do you know what that wretched creature, my wife's companion, had done? Got her to make a will in her favour! Poor Eva'd got nothing to leave but that didn't seem to worry either of them. She left Miss Nesbitt the house and the furniture, and all her clothes, and her income from me for life! Left her everything, in fact, save a few personal bequests to old friends, and instructed her to look after the maid, so the maid naturally stuck to her.

192

God, what a row there was! She'd got a solicitor of sorts, very much of sorts, if you ask me, to make the will, and he came to the funeral, and back to the house with us. I couldn't think who the dickens he was, I thought he was the undertaker's man. He looked that sort. And then we had lunch; and then we read this iniquitous will. I told the solicitor not to be silly. Miss Nesbitt was welcome to the clothes, they were no use to me, and could have the furniture if she liked, that was no use to me either, and I was willing to give her something in the way of a pension; but I wasn't going to keep on the house, I was going to sell that and be rid of it. Then the solicitor started bluffing. Asked me how I thought my professional position would be affected if the facts of my marriage came out! I took him by the scruff of his neck and the slack of his pants, and I booted him down the garden path, and over the gate, Lilith, not through it, and some way down the road. There may be a summons coming to me for assault, or there may not, I rather fancy not. He'd got plenty of grounds for it, but I'd got plenty of grounds for booting him, and he has to think of his professional position as well as me. It was the end of him for the moment, anyway.

"Then I came back to the house and told the companion to shut up and not be silly, if she wanted a pension; and she sniffled and snarled and sneered as much as she dared, but more or less shut up; anyway, she shut up as much as she was capable of. Then I went to get the jewels, but they weren't where I kept them, and the lock had been forced, and forced recently. I asked her where they were, and she said my wife had given them to her. I said they weren't Eva's to give and told her to produce them, and threatened her with the police if she refused. She stuck to her guns, and I phoned the police. The sergeant came round, and he and I went up to her room and got them out of her wardrobe from among her petticoats. He wanted to take her off then and there, but I said no, the woman was such a fool she might quite well have done what she did in good faith. In fact, I think she had. The solicitor was the real bottom of the trouble.

"Then Jenkins phoned me to come round and see him after his surgery. I didn't want to hang about any longer; I was tired out and sick to death of the whole business, and wanted to get back to you, but he insisted; said he wished to see me particularly, so I had to wait. I told the women to get me some supper, and they refused, and I lost my temper with them. I am afraid they heard some language. They got some food, but it was so foul it was uneatable, and I threw it on the floor. Then I went round to Jenkins and did his dispensing for him while he finished his surgery.

I haven't done any dispensing for years. I hope no one dies."

"Then, Lilith, there was a goal delivery! It seems he'd never had my message. They knew he would be calling at my house, so they phoned it on there, and Miss Nesbitt took it, and never said a word to anybody, but came straight through to me and told me that a second opinion was not wanted. It seems he'd protested all the time about sacking the nurse; he wasn't such a fool as to want to handle phlebitis with amateurs, but Nesbitt told him I grudged the expense and said she had got to manage as best she could. I rather fancy he'd been told a lot of tales about my brutality, and had believed them at the time, but in the light of subsequent events had begun to question them. He said what you did about the operation being a big thing.

Then he told me—my God, why had he never told me before?—"I thought you knew," he said. Just think of it, Lilith, it's been my speciality all my life to distinguish functional from organic nervous disorders, and I never spotted Eva! There was absolutely no physical reason why we should not have led a normal married life. I don't say it was altogether fake; there was a large element of genuine hysteria, if there is such a thing; but she made her health an excuse to get rid of me, and her companion, who had a kind of infatuation for her, liked making an invalid of her. She evidently thought I'd expect her to be a wife to me if she recovered her health, and she preferred to stop in bed. Think of it, Lilith, all these years—for both of us—what a damn fool arrangement! And they call that holy matrimony, and morality, and purity! I feel a fool, Lilith, that's what I feel."

He sat staring into the fire. I did not speak. I do not think he would have heard me if I had. I wondered what sort of a handful I should find Malcolm to handle, now that he had realised how his conscience had made a fool of him. He was quite likely to react to the other extreme.

At length, towards two o'clock in the morning, he spoke.

"You said that no change in my circumstances would made any difference in our relationship. Had you got something such as this in mind when you spoke?"

"I had. I felt certain your problem had been worked out. It had the feel of a finished thing to me. I did not know how the way would open before you, but I knew it would."

"You gave me that warning so that I shouldn't be—disappointed? For you must have known that if you hadn't I should have come straight to you and asked you to marry me. So I am still in bondage, Lilith, it seems. Free from the law of the land, but in bondage to your will."

"In bondage to nothing but yourself, Rupert. You haven't changed though your circumstances have."

"I suppose you mean I am like one of my wife's birds—been caged so long I don't know how to fly now I'm free. Lilith, I'm going to say a strange thing to you—I know you won't marry me, but do you mind my loving you?"

"Not in the least," said I.

"What do you feel about me? I wish you'd be perfectly frank with me, then I'll know better how to adjust my life."

"I have two sets of feelings for you, one as a woman and one as a priestess. As a woman I am very fond of you; there is a deep sympathy between us; but I think you'd make a dreadful husband, Rupert, and even if I were the marrying sort I wouldn't marry you. As a priestess— it is not easy to make you understand, I'll try to explain. As a priestess, I know that you are a priest, that I have to work opposite you, whether I like you or whether I don't, and I'd work opposite you if you were the Devil from Hell. You are a priest because you bring through the right kind of force and you have the stamina to handle the power. I work with the force, Rupert, not with you.

But there is also a bond between us because you were the sacrificing priest. Your will was magical, and you died a magical death, *willing* to possess me. That is what brought you to where you are. Strictly speaking, you have not got the grade to be where you are, and that is one of the things that is handicapping us. I have got to break you in, as it were; to train you and initiate you before I can use you."

"How did you come to take up with me at all, Lilith? That is what I have never been able to understand."

"I know my own. I know who belong and who do not; who are on my own Ray, and who are not. I know what is latent in your subconscious mind even if you don't."

"Tell me what is it you see in me?"

"I see two things. One is a capacity for selfless devotion, and the other is a tremendous surplus of vital force; a surplus that has been knocking you to pieces for want of an outlet; I can draw off that force from you magically and make use of it, and you will be all the happier for it."

"How do you propose to do that?"

"You—feel strongly towards me?"

"Yes."

"Well, the strength of your feeling projects it."

"Supposing I had not fallen in love with you of my own accord would you have deliberately drawn me to you?"

"I should. I have ends to serve that are not mine. I would have done even that for their sake."

"In cold blood?"

"There is no other way in which magic can be worked."

"Then—you have nothing but a cold-blooded policy towards me?"

"I have a cold-blooded policy towards you from which nothing will turn me, but there is something more than that, Rupert. Do you think I could work with you as I do if there were not sympathy between us? The magic breeds sympathy. How do you suppose the force could flow from you to me without a return flow from me to you?"

"Even so, it seems a cold-blooded proposition to me. I don't understand all this talk of forces. I love spontaneously, and I love you with everything that is in me. I can't help it. It wouldn't make any difference if you hated me and kicked me out. I couldn't stop loving you. You fascinate me. Everything you do fascinates me—every movement you make, every line of your body, the way your clothes hang on you, the flash of your jewels. And this house fascinates me—everything about you—even the river fascinates me because I associate it with you. It's not sensuality—that's never been a problem where you've been concerned, not so far anyway, we've both been too dashed careful. It's a kind of glamour and it feeds my soul, and my soul being fed, my body can manage. Besides—I don't know how to describe it, but you manage me so well. You've never once failed to send me away from here on a high tide of happiness. I don't know how you do it, but you do it."

"That," said I, "is my magic. Has it never occurred to you, Rupert, that other relationships are possible between a man and a woman besides what usually passes for sex?"

"I can't say that it has, but I know that there is a very curious relationship between you and me that both is, and is not, sexual. I know what I could feel for you if I let myself go; and normally I should expect to feel upheaved because I can't let myself go. But I don't. Why is it? Is that your magic art?"

"It is."

"Aren't we sailing uncommonly near the wind?"

"That is reckoned good sailing in a boat."

"Yes, of course it is. The sail should be just a-shiver. A fraction more helm, and over goes the boom and we're off on another tack. I get you. But you take chances, don't you, Lilith?"

"It is my business to take chances, the same as a surgeon. We've both got the surgeon's instinct, Rupert, that's why we pull together so well in magic."

"You think we do? I am afraid I don't understand things well enough to know whether we do or we don't. I only know I am happy with you. Lilith, I wish you would tell me, absolutely frankly, what you are trying to do, and what you are really aiming at with me. The time has come for plain speaking. I wasn't free either to ask or answer questions before. There were things that were better not spoken of, placed as I was. They were manageable as long as they were intangible, but if I had tried to define them, or lift the veil you kept in front of them, I felt we might have precipitated trouble and I did not dare risk it. Maybe I have known more than you think I have; maybe there is more to know than I realise; but anyway the time has come to go into the Holy of Holies, Lilith, to go behind that black curtain you talked of, and that you made me see. I'm not claiming it as a right; I'm not even asking it as a favour—I'm just telling you that it is so, and I think you know it."

"It is so if you feel that way about it, Rupert. If you know enough to ask a question of that nature, you are entitled to the answer. But tell me first, what do you conceive the Holy of Holies to be like?"

"I conceive it as an empty room. I think it has a domed ceiling, and I think there are concealed windows high up in the roof that can be uncovered to let in the moonlight. In shape I think it is oval."

"No, it is not oval, it is ovoid. Do you realise that the moon temple is the shape of the crux ansata—the Sign of Life? The Court of the Lotus pool is the shaft with the great pylon at its foot; the Hall of the Sphinxes is the cross-bar, and the Holy of Holies the loop. Now you know its geography you can move about there in the vision. But tell me further, what do you conceive to be the purpose of the windows up in the dome?"

"To let in the moonlight. I believe you work with moonlight in some way, and I have to help you."

"Yes, that is correct. And what do I do with the moonlight, and why?"

"Ah, there you have me, Lilith. I don't know what you do with the moonlight, nor how you do it, nor why you do it. I know you can't do it by yourself, though. You need me."

"You, or someone else."

"Yes, I suppose so. If it wasn't me it would be somebody else. I don't mean to you what you mean to me."

"Rupert, I am not being unkind to you deliberately, but I cannot, dare not, deny the law of my being. If I dared to become dependent on you I should lose you. As long as I can work with you impersonally, in cold blood, I can give you much, but if I once allowed myself to become personally involved with you, the magic would break and it would be the end of everything."

"Very good. I don't understand it but I accept it. If you say it is so, that is good enough for me. I have been given much, very much, far beyond my deserts. I don't want to spoil it by trying for too much. Forget my lapse and tell me about the moonlight."

"I cannot tell you much about the moonlight because not much is known. I can only tell you there are four things—space, the sun, the moon and the earth. Power arises in space, how, we do not know; it passes from space to the sun, and the sun transmits it to this universe. All the planets receive it, each after its kind, and relay it on—that is the basis of astrology. I am a moon priestess, however, and am only concerned with the moon-power. I receive power from the moon—I receive it from behind, at the nape of the neck mainly. You, on the other hand, receive power from the sun, and you meet the sun face to face. On the physical plane you, the male, are positive, and I, the woman, am negative, receptive; but on the inner planes, in magic, the polarity is reversed, and I am positive and you are negative, needing my influence to make you active and creative.

But remember, it is always the negative pole that does the work—the positive pole only gives the stimulus. On the physical plane you can only give life through me, and on the inner planes I can only give life through you. The position reverses. I shall never give life on the physical plane; all moon priestesses must be sterile, that is why I will not marry, there is no purpose in it. My work is on the inner planes and concerns the life of the race. I have certain things to do; I am a channel for their doing; it is in these that I want your help. They have to be done—once—in actuality, so as to bring the magic through on to the physical plane. The images are built, the forces are brought to a focus, on the inner planes, but to bring them through into manifestation on the physical plane they have to be done—once—in actuality."

"And what is my part in all this, Lilith?"

"First of all, I draw on your magnetism to supplement my own. I have been doing that for some time past, that is why you have felt so much more peaceful and contented, for you have more vitality than you know what to do with, and it knocks you to pieces. With what I draw from you I build up what is called my magical personality; I become as I imagine myself to be. I cannot do this with my own vitality alone, because one's own vitality only suffices for one's normal personality, and one has to borrow from someone else in order to build up a magical personality."

"How do you do it?"

"I will show you presently. You give to me when you feel strongly towards me; but there is a way of building, a magical way, that I will show you in due course."

"I am glad to know I do something. It is an awfully strong instinct with me to pour out my life for you. I don't know how to describe it. To give of myself, to make you take me. I had always thought a man wanted to possess a woman, but I don't; I want to be possessed by you."

"It was the last thing one would have thought, to look at that rugged, dynamic man; but I have noticed that it is always the weaklings who are most possessive; they are so habituated to being dominated that they want to compensate in favour of their self-esteem in the secret kingdom of love. A man like Malcolm, who dominates automatically by sheer weight of metal, likes being dominated by the woman he loves.

He spoke again. "I have been accustomed all my life to doing without what most men take as a matter of course. I don't fancy the physical abstinence has done me any particular harm—that takes care of itself more or less automatically. The thing I have felt most keenly is a kind of emptiness that is very hard to describe. It's not just loneliness. I can feel it with a crowd of students jostling round me and hanging on my words; I can feel it when I've been dealing with human beings all day till I'm sick of the sight of them and long to be alone. After all, human beings are my trade, and God knows I get my fill of them. It isn't lack of companionship—people are only too glad to listen to what I've got to say; I've only got to crook my finger and they sit up and beg. I could have a dinner invitation for every night of the week if I wanted it; you mightn't think it, to look at my ugly face and hear me bark, but I could—you take my word for it.'

I could quite believe him. He was a very dynamic personality, and such are always interesting. If he chose to make himself agreeable, he would have been very much in demand socially, for he was exceedingly eminent.

He went on. There have been times, when I was a younger man, when I have felt that emptiness so acutely that I have gone and sat in tea-shops and such places just to be with people. Now this is the funny thing, Lilith, you might think I'd gone there to make eyes at the women, but I hadn't. I'd gone there to watch the loving couples spooning; and out of that I got a very curious kind of satisfaction, as if a bit of their emotion were left over for me. I broke myself of it in the end because I felt it to be degrading, and I think I made a mistake. It didn't hurt anybody, that I can see, and it certainly helped me. Now would you say, in your terminology, that they were giving off magnetism when they were spooning, and that I was picking it up telepathically?"

"Not telepathically. That term is kept for astral communications. You were picking up the magnetism magnetically, sending out long processes from your aura and absorbing it."

"Then why isn't one doing that automatically, all the time, in buses and Tubes and such like?"

"Because one has to tune-in to a person's wave-length in order to do it. It isn't just automatic. Besides, there has to be a response. You get nothing from a person who is unaware and indifferent."

"Then how could I listen in to the loving couples? They were certainly unaware and indifferent to me, being wrapped up in each other."

"A person who is roused emotionally opens his aura and gives off emanations. I expect you, in your imagination, were identifying yourself with the girl's lover, and so, as it were, insinuating yourself into their atmosphere."

"Yes, I expect I was. But isn't that rather a dirty trick?"

"It isn't altogether desirable. There are better ways of getting the same results."

"Is it those better ways that you are concerned with?"

"It is."

"Do you want me to do with you what I used to do with those loving couples? Stand in an imaginative, not a physical, relation to you?"

"That is the precise experiment I want to make with you."

"But what is going to be the end of it all? For us, I mean, for you and me. I'm very fond of you, you know."

"We will face that when we meet it. I have already told you that there is always a safety valve in magic."

"I'm glad to hear it. I think we should be wanting a safety valve before very long if I began letting my imagination loose. There was a time when I was deadly scared of losing my head with you and putting my foot in it (to mix metaphors), and upsetting you so that you'd turn against me and have no more to do with me, and so I'd lose even the little I'd got. I was deadly scared of it, Lilith, and that was what made me so stand-offish and unresponsive with you. It wasn't that I did not feel like being responsive. It was that I wasn't sure that I'd know when to stop if I once started."

"It's the pressure behind you you're afraid of, isn't it, Rupert? The drive of all Nature behind you?"

"Yes, that's it. My intentions were of the best, but I wasn't sure of being able to carry them out. Nature might have got too strong for me. I warned you once that if you gave me an inch I would take an ell."

"If you and I got fooling about here on a sofa, yes. But in ritual it doesn't work like that. It is impersonal. It is just pure force, and it is not on the physical plane at all. The physical is simply the end result, and we never let it get there. When you and I work together in ritual, you are the archetypal man and I am the archetypal woman. Isis and Osiris, if you like. The force passes from the sun to you, and from you to me, and from me into the group soul of the race and back to the sun again. Or on the reverse flow, for it is an alternating current—from the moon to me, from me to you, and so to the group soul and back to the moon. What I do to you, I do to all men; and what you receive from me, you receive from Great Isis Herself, for I am Her priestess and you represent the people. Can you understand that?"

"Not altogether. It is a case of telepathy of some sort, I suppose."

"Telepathy is the active factor but it is more than that. We are telepathing the group mind of our race, but we are transmitting cosmic forces. Think of it this way, Rupert. I am what I am because I am a woman; and I am a woman by virtue of the feminine principle in life which formed me and expresses itself through what it forms. But there is more of that feminine principle than serves for the upkeep of the forms that express it, and we who are priestesses of the Moon know how to bring it through in its pure form, undiluted by matter, and we call it the moon-force. This was what was practiced in the temples of the Great Goddess in ancient times. It is practiced to this day in India, and they call it Tantra. Wherever a goddess is worshiped, it is the moon-forces that are worked with, and they are important. It is the lack of them that is throwing our modern civilisation so badly off its balance. The Catholics compensate in part with the adoration of the Virgin— Stella Maris, Star of the Sea—what is she but Venus Anadyomene— Venus born of the foam? And who is Regina Coeli if She is not the Moon? If you want to understand paganism, study Catholicism, its lineal descendant. "Plus ça change, plus c'est la meme chose." The Latin countries do not have the same sex problems that we do."

"Well, I don't know, my dear. It seems to me that we are playing with fire."

"Could not that be said of Watts when he stoked his steam-engine? It doesn't do to be afraid of these things."

"Now look here, Lilith, supposing we play with fire and things get out of hand, what is this safety valve you are always talking about?"

"We should earth the force and be finished with it, but it would be an end of the magic. Magic can only be generated under pressure, like steam power. That is why the priesthood has to learn to control its power."

"But supposing you hadn't been free, Lilith? I wasn't when we started this work. You couldn't count on my wife's dying."

"I have never been one of those who reckoned a woman's virtue of more value than a man's mental balance. I should still have blown the fuse if necessary."

He sat staring silently into the fire.

"I am sorry you told me that," he said at last.

"Why? Do you think the less of me?"

"No, not really. Of course it outrages my conventions, but I can see it is common sense. But—it throws such a big responsibility on to me. I might have come and pleaded with you if I hadn't known that—and if I'd managed to persuade you, reckoned it was all right. But now—no, I mustn't blow that fuse, it would be a coward's act. I must just go through with it."

"You realise that I am offering you up as a sacrifice, don't you?"

"Yes, and there's something inside me that likes it. It is bringing out the biggest thing in me; It's making me put out the whole of my strength, and I like that, Lilith."

He stood up and stretched himself, the big biceps muscles bunching under his sleeves. Then suddenly he turned on me and said again, vehemently, "I like it, my dear, I like it! And I'm not afraid of you any longer, either. Damn the consequences, we'll take our chances of them!" I saw that his eyes were blazing.

Then he suddenly stared across the room at the big window in which the stone arches no longer showed grey against the darkness, but dark against the grey.

"Dawn!" he said. "My God, it's dawn! We've talked all night, and I feel as fresh as if I'd just wakened. Let's go out and watch the dawn on the river."

I banked the fire against the dawn-chill that I knew we should feel on our return, wrapped my furs about me, and went out with Malcolm into the silent, grey-lit road. It was filled with river mist, but the freshness of the dawn was in it.

The sun was not yet above the horizon, but the western sky was pale. In the east a low star was still visible. We strolled slowly over the dew-drenched paving-stones till we came to the tumble-down wharf, and stood watching the river. The tide was coming in and the water swirled in great eddies about the piers. There was a profound silence in the fog-wrapped dawn—a silence unbelievable in a great city. The river alone was alive.

"Do you ever feel," said Malcolm, putting his hand through my arm, "as if the river were a bit of elemental nature in the midst of this big city?"

"Indeed I do," I replied, "that is why I came to live beside it. I must have nature contacts. The only times one gets them in London is when there is a great gale blowing; then they come in with the wind. Have you ever noticed," I added, "the difference between the atmosphere of Kensington Gardens and Hyde Park, divided by no more than a fence? The one is closed from dusk till dawn, and the earth magnetism gets a chance to well up during the hours of darkness; but Hyde Park is kept awake with lamps and never gets a chance to recuperate. It might as well be paved with asphalt for all the magnetism there is in the ground."

"No," said Malcolm, "I've never noticed it. I don't notice that sort of thing, I'm afraid. I never knew it existed. But I tell you what I do notice, I notice the atmosphere in your room. My God, that's powerful! Your place is like a lighthouse, Lilith. Long before I knew of your existence I used to watch it from across the river. It drew my attention. I can't tell you why. Of course it must have been there for me to see all the years I've lived in Grosvenor Road, but I never looked at it before."

"It will draw more than you, Rupert, as the power begins to come through."

"Yes, I suppose it will. I'll have to be prepared to take a back seat then. I can't expect to have you all to myself indefinitely. You're not that sort. Much too conspicuous. But I'm damn well going to make the most of you while I've got you."

He laughed and I turned and looked at him. I have never seen a human being change so completely. He was an utterly different man. His curious light eyes, that had always seemed like a snakes, had a sparkle in them. There was a healthy flush under his pallor; his red hair was ruffled. There was, in fact, something definitely Dionysian about him as he stood laughing in the growing light. Yet what had that man had except a change of attitude? Nothing from me, most definitely nothing from me.

I made him turn his back on the silver river and return with me to the house. I was cold even in my furs, and he, hatless and coatless, would soon be thoroughly chilled if left to play about as the spirit moved him, for there was no sense in him at the moment. He put his hand through my arm again, and back we went together, Malcolm in simply bursting high spirits. I thought of that glowering face I had seen between turned-up collar and turned-down hat a few hours ago at the station, and marvelled at the miracle.

The furnace was low, and there would be little heat in the radiators till Mr. Meatyard stoked up in an hour's time, so I brought the breakfast beside the hearth in the hall, and made it there. I made soda scones on a griddle on the embers, for there was a shortage of bread, and cooked bacon and eggs on an electric grill plugged into a standard lamp, and coffee in an electric percolator. Malcolm enjoyed it hugely, taking the greatest interest in the proceedings, and put his plate on his knees and tucked in like a schoolboy. The incongruity of the situation suddenly struck me and I asked him how many letters he had got after his name altogether? He said he didn't know, and demanded another egg.

Then he lay down on the sofa, and I tucked him up in a rug, and he went to sleep. I retired to my room to get some sleep too, but before I lay down on the bed I climbed up the long stairs to my temple to return thanks to Great Isis that the first phase of the experiment had passed off safely and the next stood ready prepared. I was very weary, for I had taken a big strain during the past hours, and magnetism had gone out of me and into Malcolm, but I felt that I had to make that pilgrimage.

It was dark and quiet and warm in the temple, and smelt of smouldering incense. It was alive with presences; one could almost see the shadowy forms with the physical eye, they were so tangible. They seemed to be going round and round in an endless procession, and as they passed the East a limb or a face or a bit of drapery would be semi-materialised. It was the dance of the Devas celebrating the dawn. Elemental power was here in full force now.

I laid my hands on the altar and thought of the horned moon, and Great Isis came to me. I felt Her presence, behind me, as always, for thus She comes to women. And I returned thanks, looking in the mirror and seeing there my own face, for I am She when I am Her priestess.

I returned thanks for the success that had so far crowned my work; I prayed for strength and insight to continue it; and I asked for a blessing on my priest. And as I thought of him as he lay sleeping in the room below with my cloak thrown over him, there came to me a wave of such intense tenderness that it alarmed me. I must not feel like this towards my priest, I thought, or I shall spoil the magic; and then it came to me that only thus could I do magic with him—the magic that was to be done through one man for all men in order to lift burdens grievous to be borne in a world that has forgotten the holiness of the Great Horned One.

PART III
THE DOOR
WITHOUT A KEY

Time arose and smote thee silent at his warning,
Change and darkness fell on men who fell from thee;
Dark thou satest, veiled with light, behind the morning,
Till the soul of man should lift up eyes and see,
Till the blind mute soul get speech again and eyesight,
Man may worship not the light of life within.

—Swinburne

CHAPTER
SIXTEEN

There was nothing save a carelessly knotted black tie to differentiate the man who came back from a month's holiday from the man who went away, yet everybody at the hospital knew there was a difference. His face was as mask-like as ever, his speech as curt, yet his students no longer backed away from him as if from the heels of a vicious horse.

He was demonstrating a case of glove and stocking anæsthesia, showing his students how to differentiate a hysterical paralysis and insensibility from one of organic origin; showing how in the one case the insensibility to pain ended in a straight line across the limb, bearing no relationship to any anatomical structure; and in the other it followed the distribution of a particular nerve.

"What is the cause of it, sir?" demanded a junior student, not realising that the simplest question is often the most difficult to answer. Malcolm looked at him, pushing his greying red hair back from his forehead with both hands in the characteristic gesture that had so often been mimicked at students' concerts.

"Ask them across the way," he said, jerking his head in the direction of the wing that housed the psychiatric clinic, a recent innovation with which he had a perpetual feud, and to which he was outrageously rude.

"Yes, sir, I know. But how does it work? Why doesn't she feel anything although there's no organic lesion?"

Malcolm looked at the crowding students, who hung waiting on his words. He looked back at the patient, who was watching him out of the corner of her eye with a smugly triumphant, faintly furtive air, and picking up the bandage that he had removed from her eyes, tied it round her head again as if she had been a wax dummy; then, with the mounted needle with which he had been testing the skin for insensitivity, he stabbed smartly six inches in the air from the anæsthetic hand—and was rewarded by a yell! He apologised to the indignant patient, who was now rubbing the hand that had been six inches away when the stab was given, and looked at the students, who looked back at him with their mouths open.

"Did you ever read Gurney and Podmore on "Phantasms of the

Living," sir?" came a voice from the back of the room, and Malcolm jumped as if he had been prodded by a needle himself.

"Yes," he said, "I have."

Students and teacher looked at each other again. Malcolm looked from face to face. Most of them were gaping, but a not inconsiderable minority were alertly interested.

"Yes," he said, slowly and thoughtfully untying the blindfold from the bit of pathological cannon-fodder beside him,

"Yes, I've read it. It's worth reading."

"So have I,"came a voice from under the muffling folds of the bandage that he had absent-mindedly allowed to slip down over the patient's nose.

"Oh, you have, have you?" said he, whisking off the bandage and looking at her for the first time as if she were a human being.

"Yes," said she proudly, "and I'm an example."

The students laughed, but the teacher did not. He stood looking at the woman, pulling the bandage slowly through his hands.

"What does it feel like?" he asked.

"It feels like going down in a lift."

The students laughed again.

Malcolm touched the paralysed arm lightly.

"I shouldn't do too much of it, if I were you," he said.

"You think that's what done it?" she asked.

"Yes, I do," was the reply.

The students gaped.

"Thank you, doctor, I'll bear in mind what you say," said the patient.

As the class dispersed, the student who had mentioned "Phantasms of the Living" came up to him. No student had ever done that before, and the older man felt a sudden, secret pleasure.

"Have you ever known a case of astral projection, sir?"

"Yes," said Malcolm, "I have. Have you?"

"Yes."

They looked at each other.

"What does it feel like?"said Malcolm.

"Just like she described."

They turned and walked slowly towards the door together, and Malcolm did a thing he had never done before—laid his hand on the lad's shoulder.

"I started it when my mother was in her last illness. I was abroad at the time, but I saw her as plainly as I see you, and then I followed her out."

His eyes turned to Malcolm's tie, but he did not like to ask the question.

"No, it wasn't that with me," said Malcolm.

He clapped the lad lightly on the shoulder in dismissal.

"Write me out your experiences," he said, "I'm interested in these things."

Crossing the wide quadrangle to the gate, he realised with another keen feeling of pleasure that there had been a curious sense of sympathy, almost intimacy, between himself and the student, himself and the patient. He had never experienced such a thing before, and he felt as if something hungry in him were being fed just as Lilith Le Fay fed it—after the same manner, though in a lesser degree, and it gave him a sense of well-being and satisfaction with life to which he had hitherto been a stranger, and his work suddenly seemed worth while to him in a way it had never done before.

He found himself halted by the traffic lights at the crossing to the Underground station. A sports car pulled up beside him. He glanced round and saw at the wheel the more irresponsible of his two clinical clerks, whose hide he removed piecemeal daily. The youth grinned.

"Give you a lift anywhere, sir?"

In all the annals of the hospital such a thing was unheard of. The youth himself marvelled that he was not struck dead as soon as the words had passed his lips, but the hospital terror was lowering himself comfortably into the bucket seat before he had time to take refuge in flight, and the drive home was enlivened by discussion of the relative merits of various very sporting makes of two-seaters which it appeared the senior physician was contemplating buying. The young man was, moreover, very intrigued when his passenger demanded to be dropped at Lambeth Bridge instead of being deposited at the famous rooms in Grosvenor Road. He watched him cross the bridge as if starting on the annual walk to Brighton, and being young and ribald, made a guess that was nearer the mark than he himself believed.

Malcolm walked fast, but in his eagerness he seemed to go on ahead of his body. He was like a starving man in sight of food. What he received from Lilith he did not know, but it was something that fed his whole nature. When he came away from her, he was contented, fulfiled, ready to turn to his work with interest; happy to think of her as forming the background of his life; but after a few hours he began to crave for her presence, and now, after twenty-four hours had elapsed, he felt as if he were being drawn to her by hooks fixed in his viscera. It was sheer joy, yet the pull was so strong it was painful.

211

woken up to the fact that eating was one of the arts, to be ranked with musical appreciation. His austere temperament had revolted at this at first; but once inured, had taken to it very kindly.

He knew that several hours of sheer happiness lay before him; but he also knew that some day, in some way it must all end, though he did not know how or when.

He cut across the corner of the road and found himself before the heavy, iron-studded door under its low arch. Lilith had never allowed the door to be cleaned, and it and all the façade were covered with a patina of London grime that seemed to protect the place from observation. Externally, it was part and parcel of the district and passed unnoticed. That door would open in a minute on another world. He raised the heavy ring-shaped knocker and gave the three beats with which he always announced his arrival. Then he turned and looked back down the road by which he had come, and saw across the water the shadowy outline of his own house all in darkness. He waited, wondering whether the door would be opened to him by Meatyard or Lilith, holding himself in till he knew.

The door opened more quickly than he expected, and the little gnome-like man with the bat-ears greeted him. He was disappointed. He liked Lilith to open the door to him; and yet, on the other hand, he liked to see her standing tall and straight and beautiful beside the hearth as he came to her across the wide expanse of the luxurious room. Perhaps, after all, it was worth while forgoing the welcome at the door in order to have the experience of drawing near to her as she stood awaiting him, and feeling the atmosphere of her presence grow stronger and stronger as he approached.

The little man left him to let himself in to the inner hall; and as he turned from closing the doors he saw, as he had known he would, the tall, graceful figure of the woman who awaited him; but, as did not happen in his day-dreams, he was seized, as always, by an agony of shyness. He strode hastily across the wide parquetry, his heavy tread disturbing the tranquil room like a stone thrown into a pool. He came up to the woman who awaited him, and stood helplessly. He wanted to take her hand, but could not bring himself to do it. He wanted to tell her how happy he was to be there, but the words would not come. He had had a sight of himself as he knotted his tie that morning; the tie was stringy, the collar frayed. His face was lined and ugly and ill-tempered; his manners, he was told on every hand, were disagreeable. How could he hope to please this beautiful woman and keep the friendship so

He went rapidly down the road that had now become so familiar, and turning the corner, saw the façade of the lit-up church as he had so often seen it from across the water; now he knew that he was welcome there, and for a moment it seemed as if such a dream could not possibly have come true.

He passed the prim little houses with their whitened steps and lace curtains. They seemed to belong to another world, another epoch. It was the world in which he had lived until he met his dream-woman; a world in which he had been a chained slave without hope or respite. And now it was all left behind; he did not belong to it any more; his bondage was broken. How, he did not know. Not by the death of his wife, that was quite certain. As Lilith had said, that did not change anything interiorly. A change had been coming in him before her death, which had simply forced into the open what had been going on under the surface. And there was more to come. He had got to change still further before he was where Lilith Le Fay wanted him to be, and he awaited that change with the eager certainty with which he knew the sun would rise in the morning.

Ahead of him, towering above the little stucco-fronted villas, was the Gothic façade of the church, its great west window dimly glowing with the shaded light within. He knew there would be a welcome awaiting him there in that warm, diffused light; and a bright fire; and a huge chair with soft cushions. And there would be talk of deep and strange things that stirred the imagination and quickened the blood and called up pictures before the eye of the mind. There would be a smell of incense, and rich colouring, and the gleam of silken hangings in the shadows; and under his feet thick soft carpets, and great expanses of dark parquetry that shone like water. Books there would be all round the walls; strange books, rare books; books that most folk did not know existed; and pictures that opened doorways into another world, the world of dream.

And she—she to whom he came, knew just what he needed. She never gave him food till he had rested, knowing he could not take it. There would be tea, hot and fragrant, and a cigarette, and pleasant, desultory talk in the warmth of her presence; the weariness would slip from him like a cloak, and his animation would return, and he would begin to be hungry and want his supper.

Then there would be a meal, all ready and no fuss; a meal with food that seemed simple, yet was a work of art. He, who had never in his life paid attention to food, living mainly on sandwiches, had suddenly

213

generously given him? Why had she given it? He did not know. It was beyond his comprehension. It was only the knowledge that she would put out a hand and draw him to her across the gulf that enabled him to face the agony he went through every time he came back to her after absence.

The firm white hand with the strange rings came out; he took it in his; they stood for a moment without speaking, but all the frozen, twisted emotion in him was easing, and unwinding and flowing out towards her.

"How are you?" she said in that deep, velvety contralto he loved so much, her eyes smiling at him.

"All the better for seeing you," he said, his hand tightening on hers. Then there was tea and cigarettes, and quiet fireside warmth and tranquillity. He lay back in the deep chair among the cushions and watched the fire, feeling her beside him. And presently animation returned, and he wanted to talk and tell her things; and his inferiority complex faded from him—such things as an international reputation and the F.R.S. and the F.R.C.P. never entered his head, he only thought of himself as an ugly, clumsy brute who was always doing the wrong thing—until things began to change, and he found his manhood and ease and breadth of vision, and such joy as had made the sons of the morning shout together. Then he left the world behind and entered into a new life and a new personality and felt within him the dawning of new powers—and all this was the magic of Lilith Le Fay, whom the world he had left would call wicked.

He looked at her as she sat tranquil in the firelight, her faintly Assyrian profile turned towards him, her long white hands with the great rings lying along the arms of her chair, her feet in silver mules resting on the edge of the wide hearth. She was the most beautiful thing he had ever seen in his life. Great pictures, great music could not compare with her. She had taught him the meaning and the value of beauty, and how it enriches the soul, and he had applied the lesson to their relationship.

He had given up his Saturday morning clinics and was free till Monday. She never told him in advance what she meant to do, but he had a feeling that this time it was important. He knew that the moon was full and the tide was high and the Vernal Equinox approaching, and he felt an anticipatory qualm. He was never really at his ease with Lilith Le Fay except when he was working at the strange rites at which he was fast becoming expert. His magic would soon match hers. He knew now how to send the power across, and how to receive it as she sent it back to him. If only—if only he could get over his shyness with her and be absolutely at his ease and sure of himself and of her—what possibilities opened up! And tonight, when he knew the big thing was coming, a bad attack of shyness attacked him.

The woman sitting quietly at the other side of the hearth was well aware of it. But she could look past it into the heart of the man, and was in no wise disturbed; she knew, however, only too well that his shyness and self-distrust made his working of the magic uncertain and prevented power coming through in the way it should. If he had been utterly ruthless, or utterly unscrupulous, or utterly sure of his technique and impersonal with her, it would have worked smoothly; it was his conscience that was making a coward of him, as she had always feared it would.

How was she to break through those inhibitions and set him free without letting loose an avalanche of emotion? If she once made Malcolm lose his head, life would be unlivable for him unless she gave herself to him, and that would spoil the magic, for magic is worked on tension. She could only do as she had done before—use him boldly and ruthlessly, though there was pity in her heart. It was the best thing, for marriage with Malcolm was out of the question and a liaison would not content him.

It would have been the easiest thing in the world to break through the barrier between them if she had chosen to use the direct route; she had only to put out her hand and caress him; but the reactions of that had to be considered, and they were not fair to the man. She must let him struggle on as best he might and trust to the inhibitions going down as the power came through in the ritual. It was, after all, the best way to work, the way they had always worked in the old temples, where the priestesses were brought from the House of the Virgins for the purposes of the ritual only. She could not make this man happy as a man and at the same time work magic with him.

They shared the light evening meal which was all that was permitted when work was afoot, and then returned to the fireside for coffee and cigarettes; and as they sat in the dim light of the reading lamps, the silences grew longer between them until both sat gazing at the fire, oblivious of each other.

CHAPTER
SEVENTEEN

At length the woman spoke.

"The tide will be rising by now," she said. "They are expecting a flood, I think. I saw the sandbags out all along the Grosvenor Road."

The man roused himself and looked at her.

"The moon is rising, too," she added. "It will soon clear the housetops and come shining into the room."

They waited in silence for another half-hour, and then a silver haze began to appear at the upper part of the great east window and a long ray of light stole in and lay like a pool on the dark shining floor.

"The power is beginning to gather," said Lilith Le Fay. "Shall we go and robe?"

Without a word the man went off to the spacious bathroom all black marble and shining silver that had so startled him the first time he had seen it. There, collar and tie, shoes and clothes soon lay in an untidy heap, and he stood forth mother-naked in front of the big mirror. He considered himself critically. He thought he looked considerably better without his clothes than with them. His experience of nudes had been gained in the dissecting room, and he appraised his body with the eye of an anatomist rather than of an artist, but what he saw gave him satisfaction. He was a good specimen of the human animal. His own strength appealed to him.

It crossed his mind that the woman upstairs might be making a similar survey before the other big mirror as she stripped preparatory to the rite, and he hastily pulled his mind back from any such thoughts. But the mind is an even more unruly member than the tongue, and although he might refine and intellectualise his ideas, they still played round the same subject.

"How extraordinarily opposite we are in every way," he thought as he girded his robe about him. "I'm fair and she's dark; I'm thickset and she's slender. I'm as rough as they make them, and she's everything that's sophisticated. I'm a bit of a gorilla, and she's—no, she's not any of the things with which women are usually compared. She's more like a hawk or a snake or a leopard."

He stared thoughtfully at his own face as he adjusted the folds of the head-dress about it.

"I'm the butchering priest all right," he thought. "How in the world do we manage to keep the peace, she and I? She's everything I'm not."

He stooped to strap the golden sandals on to his sinewy feet, then, straightening himself, looked in the glass again.

"Yes, by God, I *am* the priest!" he said to himself as he saw before him an image that looked like the embodiment of ruthless elemental power.

"I'm a primitive type," he thought. "I wonder if that's why she has a use for me? I believe it is."

Then he turned, and passed through the communicating door into the empty bedroom of the woman he loved.

He paused and looked around, noting all the silken luxury.

"The very essence of femininity," he thought, "and yet she is not wholly feminine by any manner of means. There is something curiously male about her."

He felt the thick white carpet soft about his feet round the sandal-straps as he crossed to the corner cupboard that concealed the entrance to the hidden part of the building.

"I wonder what I should have been like," he thought as he climbed the stairs, "if I had had a different upbringing? Supposing I hadn't had a conscience? and hadn't cared what I'd done to obtain the things I was after? Supposing in love affairs I'd had the same ruthless drive I've had in my work? Where would I have got to, I wonder? What sort of experiences would I have had? What sort of a man should I have become? Very different from what I am now, I suspect. Damn it all—I've had less than half a life!"

He was by nature a truculent individual who would tackle anybody and any difficulty that came in his way, but he was terrified of the hidden forces that he dared not risk unleashing. He knew that Lilith Le Fay feared neither man, god, nor devil, and would fearlessly cope with his demons, and, in fact, harness them to her service, but he shrank from letting them loose on her. Yet all the time he knew that it was with the elemental force in himself that she wanted to work, and that if he would not unleash it he was of no help to her.

He passed through the robing room and saw lying across a chair a shimmering pearl-grey robe, its folds partly concealing a pile of chiffon and lace. Now, for the first time, seeing that heap of clothing on the chair, he realised how completely she could divest herself of her human personality when she assumed the symbolic robes and stand forth simply as the impersonation of a force. As such, and as such only, she wished him to see her, yet how was he to separate the force from the woman? He did not know. He could not do it. She meant altogether too much to him.

He knocked softly on the door of the temple; it opened, and he saw Lilith Le Fay's arm hold back the curtain for his entry. He walked in, crossed to the altar, and stood with his back to her, resting his hands on the black velvet altar cloth in the little circle of light cast by the altar lamp.

"What a pair of stranglers hands!" he thought as he stood looking down at them. He noticed that the Pillars of Equilibrium had been shifted, and stood upon either side of him.

He heard a bell struck softly nine times, and the soft swish of draperies as the woman passed him, but he never raised his eyes. Then a pair of hands appeared in the circle of light before his own.

They were by no means delicate hands, though long-fingered and supple. The bizarre rings that usually decorated them had been removed, and so had the nail lacquer. They were just a pair of woman's hands, firm-muscled and white-skinned.

Then the hands were lifted as the woman stepped back a pace from the altar, and he too stepped back a pace and lifted his own as the ritual required; and as the ritual also required, he raised his eyes and looked into hers.

They were calmly expressionless and intent. There was nothing of the human woman about her, she was simply the priestess, she cared for one thing and one thing only, the strange force she served, and at the realisation there rose in him a sudden wave of intense bitterness. Why should he be thus frustrated and life denied him? He, a man, had a right to a man's life simply because he was a man. Life owed him that much, and he claimed it. He had had enough of the denials and frustrations of the social code; he wanted a woman—this woman, and he would get her if he could. Something that was elementally savage rose up in him, something that he had always known was there and that he knew to be dangerous—dangerous to him as well as to her. He had used it before now in scientific fights, but never in personal ones, and never on a woman. But it was breaking loose now, and he was encouraging it, for he was sick of frustrations and denials, and repudiated the code that imposed them.

He had forgotten all about the ritual. It was not a ritual, it was a reality. The woman facing him across the altar stood for everything that had been lacking in his life. She was no longer Miss Le Fay whom he

219

respected, nor Lilith whom he loved; she was simply a woman who represented all women; she had in her hands all that women give or withhold from men, and he represented all men who had ever been thwarted and frustrated and wronged by the selfishness and ignorance and cowardice of women, and she should pay him not only for her own wrongs, but for the wrongs of all men thus frustrated.

There was in him a fierceness of rebellion that was ready to fight, and go on fighting, against what he felt to be a falsity and an injustice. What was natural in him had its rights as against society, and society had defrauded it and misled him, and he had at long last, risen in rebellion.

The primitive, archetypal, subliminal levels of consciousness had come to the surface and made common cause with his rational mind, and his intelligence was at the service of his subconscious urges. He was a powerful, elemental being; primeval man at one with Nature, with the drive of all life behind him. Looked at from one point of view he was completely letting himself go, and was as dangerous a brute as any woman could be called upon to face, alone in an empty house; looked at from another, he was bringing down fire from heaven, and, as always, it was stolen fire.

His curious pale eyes were glittering like ice in his mask-like face whose pallid skin was beginning already to glisten with sweat. They were the eyes of a madman, or of a Viking gone baresark. The woman watching him from the other side of the altar saw his hand drop to his hip, and knew that he was after the leaf-shaped bronze knife that should have depended from a broad leather belt girdling his loins, and knew, too, that the levels of consciousness were coalescing—the subliminal and the superliminal. Malcolm at the moment might be a dangerous brute, but he was also a powerful magician. She knew also that the line was a very narrow one between a very nasty experience at Malcolm's hands and a very potent piece of magic, and deliberately she took her risk.

Malcolm and she were watching each other like two duellists. The power was through to the personal level now, and on the personal level it had to be handled, picked up, steadied, and swung up the planes again. She saw him inch by inch sidling towards the left, and knew that in a minute there would be a dash round the altar. If she spoke, she could break the spell, the spell of the up-welling primitive, and bring the man back to normality, but she did not wish to break the spell, and did not speak. Instead, she herself began slowly to edge round the altar so that it remained between them, its flickering light and rising spire of incense an effectual barrier against the tide of elemental force that was coming up from the depths through the channels opened by the unleashing of Malcolm's passions.

They had exchanged places now, and she was in the west and he in the east with the mirror behind him. As he came into the east, the place of the priest, a change came over him; it seemed as if the different levels of his consciousness all came into focus together, and were united, so that the past lived again in his soul and the future came into view; he was the sacerdotal outcast he had been, and the great adept he would be, and the adept was built upon the outcast.

As once before, the woman he loved was alone with him in the Holy of Holies, hidden from the eyes of the profane by the veil that Isis always draws across Her doings; but this time he had not come as a thief in the night, but was there by the summons of the Goddess; there by right, in his appointed place, doing the work for which he had been sent. It was terrible work, sacrificial work, but he would do it aseptically, with clean hands.

He had, he knew, to descend into hell and let loose the elemental forces that should provide the motive power for the magic; he had to do it as a man, and as a priest, for the two are inseparable in magic, trusting to the woman who faced him across the altar, the high priestess, to handle the unleashed forces and by her knowledge and her power transmute them into magic on a higher arc.

He looked into her eyes through the smoke of the incense that rose from the altar, and saw that they were steady and serene: she seemed to stand in a core of calm in the heart of the cyclone he had let loose about himself and her. She stood upright upon her feet between the pillars of equilibrium, poised and at ease, her hands resting lightly upon the altar, palms downwards, whereas his were gripping it as if he were about to spring. She was giving him no help with the magic of the elements, that was his task as the sacrificial priest; she was waiting as high priestess for him to do his part and hand over to her the forces he had called up from the depths.

The room had faded from his sight and he was in the cave of Black Isis doing the great rite that was only done once in four years. People might call it black magic, but he knew that it was not evil although a man lay dead on the altar, but was simply crude elemental power. If they had left it at that level it would have been evil, but they would not leave it there; the high priestess would take over from him, and transmute the power, and take it through with her to the temple of Great Isis, where it would flow out through the curtain of the holy of holies like a beam of moonlight, and vivify the mummified form of the Goddess that lay between the sphinxes, for thus is the magic done; and therefore is the Holy of Holies left empty.

The woman who was watching him saw the change come in him and braced herself to meet it. Her mind, too, went back to the dark cave-temple and the grim, outcast priest who had desired her and who had destroyed himself to get her. There were the makings of greatness in him, as both she and the great high priest had recognised, though the time had not been ripe.

Then her mind opened upon another scene she had never known before—the scene of the torture, when, by magical means, her spirit had been called back to confront the man who had caused her death, and force a confession. But in the high priest there had been more insight than in the judges, and he and she, facing each other across the body of the strapped-down man on the torture-table had agreed that the appointed time would come. And to her mind there came another and strangely contrasted scene—the consulting-room in Wimpole Street, where Malcolm had broken down, as he had finally broken in that other life after the long hours of torture, and it seemed to her that the recapitulation had been done and from that moment the magic had begun.

She knew that Malcolm had shifted the level of consciousness, and was no longer aware of the room, but in a hypnoidal state; it was her part, controlling the rite, to remain steady on the physical plane, handling the forces. She gazed into the eyes that stared into hers with hypnotic intensity. The man's face did not seem like flesh and blood, but like an alabaster mask with the glittering eyes set in it; he was very much the priest and not in the least a man who has lost his head. He was not simply himself, getting what he wanted; he was a ritualist in a rite, representing something that was greater than he, representing all men whom life had wronged as it had wronged him, and in his own person magically breaking their bondage. That which he was experiencing, had, by the knowledge of this woman who was using him, been linked up with cosmic forces and thus made magical. What was happening was primitive, archaic, terrible, and yet it was holy, and as spiritual in its way as any of the theological virtues; it was the elemental foundation on which the structure of life was built, without which life could not exist, ignore it how we will; and she, a woman, had to acknowledge its validity.

She placed her hands on either side of the altar lamp, and he reached across and took her by the wrists, and she found herself gazing into those glittering, pale, expressionless eyes at close range. There was no escape now, Malcolm had got her, to do with her what he would, but between them was the sacred point of flame and the rising spire of incense smoke, and the rite was holy.

She had no fear, only a feeling of tremendous tension, and Malcolm, she could see, had neither doubts nor inhibitions. She knew, however, with her greater experience, that the magic had to be worked out on the astral, and that if it came through to the physical plane it would, as magic, be short-circuited and spoilt. She wondered if Malcolm knew this, and realised that it was impossible he should know it with his conscious mind, but that, along with the memory of past incarnations, the knowledge might linger in his subconsciousness and give him guidance. And as the minutes went by and he made no move, she felt more and more certain that it was from the archaic levels he was working, and that archaic memories would guide the elemental energies that were rising within him.

And even as she watched, the mirror seemed to open and another world appeared. She and the priest working opposite her were vast forms of light, their feet in the dark chaotic deeps, their heads in starry space, between them the earth as an altar and their hands linked across it. Malcolm held her by the wrists, but not tightly, and she twisted her hands round inside his and grasped him by the wrists also, and so they stood while forces whirled about them. She was conscious of a rhythmical pulsation in space, and with one side of her mind she knew it was Malcolm's pulse-beats she was feeling, and with the other side she knew it to be the throb of the cosmic rhythm; also she knew that these things were not two things but one thing, and that the pulse of the man's blood was made one with primordial force.

Then it seemed to her that they rose in space till the altar of the earth no longer intervened between them; there was about them a haze of silver light, like a moonrise, and she knew that it was magnetism given off by Malcolm.

Then, on the plane of earth, she saw the etheric double of the man project from his physical form and stand before her, face to face; it drew nearer, she felt its silvery coldness, it began to coalesce with her. It was made one with her, absorbed. In the vision which they shared they hung in high space among the stars. It was as if she had mounted up on powerful wings, drawing the man with her like the nuptial flight of bees.

Then the tension relaxed, the power dropped, and they came swiftly back to earth again. She saw Malcolm holding on by the altar with both hands, the sweat dripping off his chin. Slowly his strength failed him, and he sank to his knees, holding on by one hand and covering his face with the other. She came round the altar, and took hold of him by the shoulders and supported him as he sank to the floor. For some minutes he rested in the attitude of the Dying Gladiator, and then his elbow gave way under him and he lay flat on the ground. She knew well enough that he was not dead, but any other person would have questioned whether life still remained in him.

Calmly she composed his limbs as if for burial, crossing his hands on his breast, and sat down beside his head and took it in her lap. She placed the flat of her palms on either side of his face, and sat as sit the Indian gods, and waited. The man hardly seemed to breathe. The woman seemed stabilised in strength. There was absolute silence in that secret room.

Slowly, gradually, she felt life flowing back into the body that rested against her knees. She knew that now Malcolm was sleeping and that with the dawn he would awake.

The hours went by, and there was no sound, no stir in the silent room. The incense had burnt itself out and the lamps were burning low. Then, at last, the faint sound of tugs hooting on the river outside penetrated the silence, and the man stirred slightly; but the woman still waited.

Malcolm sighed and shifted his position; then lay quiet again, but she knew that he was awake and aware of what had happened. She wondered whether or not he knew that his head rested on her knee. Then a pair of hands came up and covered hers that had held his head all night.

"You have shown me the way to the Door without a Key," he said.

She did not reply, but answered him with a slight pressure of her fingers on his cheek. Stillness returned to the room, but it was a living stillness.

Finally the man spoke, but to earth once more.

"I can't stay like this indefinitely, can I, Lilith? I've got to bestir myself sometime. But it's a great effort. I've been out, I think, a very long way. And you, my dear? How is it with you?"

"It is well with me," she replied, "for I have accomplished what was planned."

"I felt you had," he said, "and I'm not worrying about it."

Slowly, reluctantly, he lifted himself to a sitting position and half turned and looked at the woman behind him, who, still seated like an Indian goddess, had not stirred.

"How is it with you?" he asked.

"It is well with me," she replied again.

"It may be, but you've paid for it. You've paid the price of this night's work, Lilith."

"So have you."

"Oh yes, we've both paid. These things are bought with a price, I take it. I don't grudge it, and I don't suppose you do, either. You look as if you'd had a bad haemorrhage, Lilith; I've seen people after a major operation in better shape than you are. Let me look after you. I'm beginning to get my strength back to me with every minute that passes.

He rose, and coming round behind her where she sat, as she had sat all night, erect and unsupported, he put his arms round her.

"Lean back against me," he said. She did as he bid her, smiling up at him. He looked down at her.

"My God, how you're changing," he exclaimed. "You look so serene and lovely."

"Life is coming back to me, too," said she.

"I see it is. I have never seen anyone change so rapidly. You looked like your own mummy, Lilith, when I first woke up. Now you look like a young girl. I know you aren't, but that is how you look. A freshness, a kind of dewy freshness, like a flower."

Presently she lifted her weight from his knee.

"I too must wake up," she said. Reluctantly he released her and helped her to rise.

"I have had an experience," said the man, "which I don't suppose can ever be repeated."

"No, it can never be repeated," replied the woman. "We have done the first part of that which we set out to do, and it is finished."

"*Consummatum est*—turn down the empty glass," said the man. "I know, I quite realise it. I am very glad you have succeeded, my dear, and I am very glad that I was able to help you."

"God bless you, it has been a great experience. I wouldn't have missed it."

Lilith looked steadily into his eyes without speaking for a moment. Then she spoke:

"I have to thank you. We have done what we set out to do. Something is present in the world that was not there before, and it will work itself out in its own way."

"It is time I went, is it?"

Lilith hesitated, and turning away, stood watching the great mirror as if it opened on to another world and she were communing with that which moved therein. Malcolm had a momentary vision of stars moving through indigo deeps and rays of light that passed between. At length she turned and faced him, as if that with which she communed had given her counsel.

"I don't want you to be unhappy," she said. The man did not reply, but stood silently gazing at her. In some indefinable way he seemed to have drawn apart and become remote, as if he had already severed his spirit from hers.

She turned away from him and gazed into the great mirror again, as if far vistas opened in the shadows, and as the man watched her she seemed to become vast, formless, primordial, like the rock-hewn woman of his dream. For a moment he thought she had vanished, dissolved into that cloudy shape. Then his eyes adjusted their focus and he recovered the hard outlines of reality. Yet it seemed different. The outlines were sharper, the colouring brighter than reality. It was as if Lilith were edged with light; her loose flowing draperies fell into the straight lines of sacerdotal robes and her head rose above them with a majesty that needed no crowned head-dress to make it royal and priestly.

"I have never belonged to any man, and never shall," she said quietly, "though many men have known me. I have been called the Cosmic Harlot and the Ever-Virgin. Both are true of me, but you cannot be expected to understand that—to you I am the woman you love. And I love you, too, after my manner, but I am a priestess set apart, not altogether mortal. There are two sides of me—the one that sits and sews and talks to you by the fireside, and the other that comes up here and works the rituals.

"I can give your manhood fulfilment—more than you can dream or believe, even though you cannot possess me. I'd like to show you what a woman can be to a man. You deserve it. You've been starved so long." An extraordinary animation came into her face and a wave of magnetism radiated from her. "I'd like to show you, Rupert, for I know—I know so much!"

The man stood silent.

"Do you remember the story of Eros and Psyche? That is a true story, Rupert, an exceedingly true story. Do you remember the conditions that Eros laid down? He would come to her by night, in the dark, and she must never see his face. She could hold Love in her arms, but she must not try to possess him. And that is how it is with us who are initiates. It is different with us from what it is with the once-born, for we belong in Another Place. We live in the Higher Self. To me, the person you know as Lilith Le Fay is only a little bit of myself. It is my *persona*, my mask, that I wear as the Greek actors wore theirs for the part they had to play in the sacred dramas. My personality is the mask I have made for myself for the part I have to play in this drama, which is also sacred. But you do not understand that, Rupert, because you live in your lower self; you do not know "the far voyaging soul."

"You must take me on trust. We must each obey the laws of our own nature, you and I. No one can do otherwise and be true to themselves. You have got to live in this world, and I have got to live in two worlds, and this is the best I can offer you—I will mate with you after another manner—coming and going in my own way. I, who am all women, can minister to the manhood in you, and satisfy it, and more than satisfy it—take it up to the Godhead. Will that content you, Rupert?"

"I don't know, Lilith, I don't know—I don't pretend to be an initiate. I simply love you and want to be happy with you, that's all."

"I will make you happy, but you mustn't try to possess me."

"Possession is a strong instinct with some men. It's their notion of love."

"It's a false notion. No one can possess another without destroying them. That is why marriages are such makeshifts. The one is only partly satisfied, and the other is half destroyed. The far-voyaging soul must be free, coming and going in its own sphere. Let us learn to love as those love who are free from the Wheel of Birth and Death."

She caught hold of him by both shoulders, her eyes shining.

"Rupert, do this with me! It is the next phase of the magical working—the next thing that is to be brought through into manifestation. Work this with me, and we need not part yet."

He looked at her wearily. "I doubt if I've got the strength for any more, Lilith," he said.

"You have—you have!" cried the woman, her cheeks flushed, her eyes shining. "This will give you strength as the other gave you peace. Do this with me, it will be all right. Trust me, for I know!"

The man hesitated a moment. Then:

"My dear," he said, "I'll do anything you say, you know I will," and he put his head down on her shoulder and she held him.

CHAPTER
EIGHTEEN

Malcolm went through his work at the hospital in a kind of daze. If the earth had opened under his feet he could not have been more bewildered. He had never, in his heart, believed that the woman he loved would make him that strange proposal. He ought, he supposed, to be thankful for that, and in one way he was, but in another it scared him.

Lilith Le Fay was a very beautiful, very sophisticated, very vital woman; entirely emancipated and with an experience of life concerning which he had deemed it better not to enquire. Would he, Malcolm asked himself, be able, to put it bluntly, to fill the bill, or was he in for another shattering disillusionment, from exactly the opposite cause to the original one?"

He recognised the inevitableness of an animal factor in his own nature. Once he had regarded it as a thing to be overcome; certainly as a thing that should be under the full control of the will. His failure to overcome it he regarded as being due to a divided will—it was only by a narrow majority, not by a unanimous vote, that he trod the narrow way. An ideal love, he believed, would be one that transcended the senses, and though he frankly recognised that he was incapable of attaining such heights, he nevertheless believed that in the legalised license of a marriage it was a decent man's duty to keep his animal propensities within bounds. Though he himself did not remember the days before anæsthetics, he had worked as a student under men who did, and who used to regale the students with tales of the good old days when hospital porters were picked for their strength and surgeons kept their oldest frock-coats for operating. It had seemed to him, in the light of subsequent experience, that this state of affairs was by no means extinct, and that analgesia for conception was as urgently needed as for delivery. If marriage had been a shock to his bride, it had been a disillusion to him, and he carried the scar as well as she. It was an accepted fact that the developing brain of civilised man had expanded his head till its entry into the world was a nice problem in mechanics; it seemed to him that, in a similar way, woman had risen superior to Nature, while, most regrettably, man had failed to evolve. Consequently either he had to drag her down, or she had to drag him up; and as far as he could see, the victim had to make the best of it.

He had a shrewd suspicion that Lilith Le Fay had not the slightest intention of taking him by the scruff of his unregenerate neck and raising him heavenwards; that she considered all such attempts to be misdirected energy and herself proposed to meet him on the level. This worried him greatly, for he feared she did not realise on what level she would have to meet him. He had fondly hoped that with the coming of an angel into his house the wild beasts with which he had wrestled so manfully would quit Ephesus for ever and curl up on the hearthrug; but Lilith proposed to set them free. So far from taking advantage of their new-found liberty, however, they all seemed to be lying dead from shock at the bottoms of their cages. Malcolm was sorely tempted to turn in for a drink at the first tavern he passed on his walk home from the hospital.

For once again he was walking along the Embankment in the dusk, following the path that had led him so far from the beaten track of normal life that he felt sure there could be no returning, and, he might just as well go on and see it through. This thought nerved him somewhat, and when he came to Lambeth Bridge, he crossed it.

In answer to his knock the door swung open, and framed in its arch stood Lilith Le Fay. Her hair, which she had hitherto worn wound in a coronet round her magnificently-carried head, was in a Grecian knot on the nape of her neck; nor were her robes of the rich velvets and brocades in which he was accustomed to see her, but of shimmering folds of chiffon, like clouds across the moon, and through their veiling mist he could see her underdress of silver. She was indeed a moon-priestess tonight. He felt like Actæon with the dogs waiting around him.

As he bared his head the lamplight fell on his face. Lilith looked at him with her penetrating eyes; then took him by the shoulders and made him face her.

"Well?" she said.

"I'm all right" he replied, forcing himself to meet her eyes. "I had a busy day at the hospital, you know."

She did not answer, but let go his shoulders and turned and went ahead of him into the great hall, leaving him to follow at his leisure. The only thing that rendered the situation in any way bearable was his inner certainty that in some way Lilith Le Fay would pull him through.

Halting on the hearthrug, he gazed dumbly at her as she turned to look at him.

She laid a hand on his shoulder again. "What is it, Rupert?" she asked.

He smiled wryly.

"I suppose I'm a fool," he said.

"I suppose you are," said she, and laughed softly. She shook him gently by the shoulder she held. "Sit down," she said, "and I'll make you some tea."

He dropped into a chair, almost disappearing among the cushions in its roomy depths; then out came the inevitable packet of Players, and she left him quietly smoking as she went to make the tea.

There was an amused smile on her lips as she manipulated the kettle. Rupert really was the most amazing person. She had seen Hamlet in Modern Dress, with no one looking the part, and Rupert Malcolm, whether as great scientist or great lover, was invariably equally incongruous. Wherever he was, whatever he did, he was always utterly himself, for it never occurred to him to be anything else, and he considered himself a very ordinary man, save when in a rage, and then he suddenly turned into a crusading baresarker.

Watching him as he drank his tea in what might have passed for a bad-tempered silence, but which she knew was worried brooding, she realised once again how completely he acquiesced in the code that held him bound; and more clearly than ever she saw how mankind makes its own cages out of an inner bondage. Malcolm was legally free, and could hardly feel any moral obligation to a woman who had malingered for twenty years at his expense, yet here he was, the conventional widower, mourning the dear departed, who had not been in the least dear to him and for all practical purposes had departed twenty years ago. Lilith Le Fay gazed at the man and marvelled.

As if reading her thoughts, he said "Do you realise it's less than a week since my wife died?"

"Yes," said Lilith. She did not add any comment, for she did not choose to show her hand. She had a feeling that Malcolm was using the recently dead woman as a kind of chaperone.

Lilith sat, chin in hand, staring into the fire while Malcolm slowly sipped his third cup of tea. She was divided between the desire to give him a good shaking and the knowledge that not yet was her work finished with him; not yet could she lay down her weapons and enter the sabbath peace. If she abandoned Malcolm to his own devices now, he would slip back into the old, miserable, treadmill existence, and it hurt her to think of him doing that.

Never, it seemed to Lilith, had they been so far apart since he had stood glaring angrily at her from behind his desk in Wimpole Street and she had used her knowledge to dominate him—for his own sake and for the sake of Great Isis, who needed him. He had been used, and now he must be paid. In spite of himself she had made him serve; in spite of himself she must bring him into harbour.

She gazed at the rugged head seen in profile. Malcolm looked more than forbidding, he looked morose. She asked herself what purpose it could serve to adventure with him again? Yet somehow she could not leave the thing unfinished. Ends had to be tucked in, or they would give trouble.

Then, a sudden resolution taken, she said: "Come, let us go to the worship."

Malcolm looked up sharply, coming back from a long way off like a diver coming to the surface, the bad-tempered look vanishing as animation returned to his face, he merely looked worried and unsure of himself now.

"What do you want to do?" he said. "I thought all that was over."

He looked suspicious and a little scared.

She did not choose to explain, but rose, and he had no choice but to follow her. With a gesture she directed him to the bathroom, where he should robe.

Reluctantly, sullenly, like a boy going to have a beating, he took off his clothes and threw them on to a chair, shivered, and put on the robes. Without glancing at himself in the mirror he pulled the silver head-dress down over his brow and climbed stolidly up the long stairs, looking neither to the right nor the left.

There was no Lilith Le Fay to lift the curtain for him this time when he came to the entrance to the temple; he had to push aside its folds for himself. He entered, and saw her lying motionless on the altar of sacrifice, thus forcing him to take up his position in the place of the priest.

He stood looking at her, sullen and lowering; she gazed back at him impassive as a sphinx.

He saw that she was not looking at him, but over his shoulder into the mirror that was behind him. He saw by her eyes that she was seeing something therein that was not of this world, and that she was watching its actions, for it was moving. Secure from her observation, he watched her face.

For a moment he hated her. The magnolia skin, the beauty of the dark eyes and hair, tantalised him. He longed for them, but felt they would crumble at a touch. He was, in fact, as deeply divided in his self-imposed asceticism as he had been in his lusts. But the woman was not

232

watching him; she was watching something else with which she was communing mentally.

Gradually it became borne in upon the man, standing thus tormented and frustrated, that he had simply to keep quiet and let things happen. It was not in his power to do anything; he was as frustrated by his own inhibitions as he had been by his circumstances, and with a sudden flash of realisation he saw the truth of Lilith's words: "It would make no difference even if you were free."

This had been abominably true, and bitterly he knew it. His release had not altered her attitude towards him; she could have done just as she was doing now whether he were free to offer her marriage or not. He felt resentful. His wife's death ought to have altered everything; whereas it had altered nothing. He set his jaw and stared sullenly at Lilith Le Fay.

But presently his sullenness changed to misery, and it seemed to him as if he were holding on to her with his eyes like a drowning man clinging to a rock; and again came to him the feeling that she was communing with something, and that with this something he would be expected to cooperate. In a flash he realised that the work of the new phase had already begun, and for a second he backed away like a startled horse. Then he steadied. Let come what would come—he didn't know how the thing worked, or what was right or wrong when looked at from this point of view. Of one thing he was certain—Lilith Le Fay was not out for evil. He had seen her do things strange beyond all imagining, bold beyond all daring, but they had all worked out for good. He trusted her. She had never let him down yet, and he did not think she would now.

He could feel the beginnings of the gathering of power. The magic was starting to work. He was in the place of the priest, and whatever this unknown force might be, it meant to work through him. He steadied himself and waited. Let it work! It was the only way. He needn't do anything. It was a natural force, and it would use him, its natural channel; all he need do was to let it use him.

He concentrated on the idea of passivity, of presenting an open channel to that which would come to him from behind, and through him to her. Great Nature was drawing near; the tide was rising along the appointed channel.

Then, for the first time, he knew himself as part of Nature. Such a thing had never entered his head before, for all his study of comparative anatomy. He knew that, deep in him, was a level that had never been separated from the earth soul, just as the image of the primordial woman in the Black Temple had never been cut away from the living rock but was united to it along her back-bone, and he knew that he too, at the spinal level, belonged to Nature, and that through the channel of that hollow rod Nature would use him, and gave himself up to Her power.

Then in a flash he felt the levels coalesce; that which he had previously known as purely physical he felt to be spiritual as well. The force was rising from the spinal to the cerebral level and passing out of the province of physiology. Then he felt it lift level again, and pass out of the province of psychology into that which lies beyond. A vision of starry spheres seemed around him. The room had faded. Lilith had changed into Isis and he himself was the Nature-force rising up from primordial deeps to fertilise her! He was not a man, he was a force. He was part of the earth-life, and Nature was manifesting through him; and she, Lilith, was not a person either; she was the goal of the force—that was all. It was quite simple. The force had taken charge. There was no thought, no feeling, save the terrific pressure of force that used his organism as a channel of manifestation. The less of personality there was in this the better—let the force do its own work!

It was like being struck by lightning. The power came, and passed, and as its reverberations went rolling away into space, he saw as the clouds parted before his eyes the face of Lilith Le Fay, but made young and lovely, and he gazed at her as Adam must have gazed at the newly-created Eve when he awoke from his deep sleep and found her beside him.

The straight run-through of power had blown clear all the obstructions and blockings and tangles in his nature just as a choked channel is cleared by a force-pump. From level to level the power had risen, and cleared the channel as it went. He was a man utterly re-made. How, and by what, he could not say. He only knew that, exhausted and at peace, he was ready to sing with the morning stars as soon as his strength came back to him, and that his mind had the crystal lucidity of sunlit space.

He stared at Lilith, and wondered what she had made of it all. He had never seen her look so lovely. The remoteness that usually veiled her had vanished, melted away, and he felt that her nature was open to him, that there was no dividing-line between them. Their souls were no longer two circles, bounded by their peripheries, but two centres of radiation whose rays met and mingled. It was the sense of the breaking down of barriers that struck him most profoundly. There was, at that moment, no line of demarcation between him and her; the straight run-through of force had swept it away. From him to her it had passed, been raised by them to human level, and so back again whence it came.

He saw how the sense of sin, for which marriage is advised as a remedy, prevented the straight run-through of power, and by confining the force to its lower levels, stopped it from ever reaching its divine aspects, but by turning it back too soon, short-circuited it so that it never passed in its fullness from the man to the woman, and there was no breaking down of barriers—"Bitterly we re-embrace—single still."

In one flash there came knowledge. Later on, he would think it out as ideas, but now he just knew, though he had no words for what he knew.

Lilith came and stood beside him, and took his hand and they looked in the mirror. There was nothing to be seen now in the crystalline darkness of its depths, stretching away into far space in another dimension; nevertheless it seemed to the man that they opened upon an inner world, and that again and again, by the same magic, they could be opened and re-opened. The world of dreams and the wake-world met on that threshold, and he knew now the secret of passing over.

For in the great moments of life we cross the threshold in a kind of trance that has been described by those who have known it as a lesser death—when St. Theresa swooned in the Divine Union, when Keats first looked into Chapman's Homer, when the Vikings leapt baresark into battle, they knew that lesser death and its illuminations. Whoso has never experienced this flux of the soul in some transcendent experience lacks the key to Life.